# A CHILD TO HEAL THEIR HEARTS

BY
DIANNE DRAKE

# SAFE IN HIS HANDS

BY
AMY RUTTAN

Now that her children have left home, **Dianne Drake** is finally finding the time to do some of the things she adores—gardening, cooking, reading, shopping for antiques. Her absolute passion in life, however, is adopting abandoned and abused animals. Right now Dianne and her husband Joel have a little menagerie of three dogs and two cats, but that's always subject to change. A former symphony orchestra member, Dianne now attends the symphony as a spectator several times a month and, when time permits, takes in an occasional football, basketball or hockey game.

Born and raised on the outskirts of Toronto, Ontario, **Amy Ruttan** fled the big city to settle down with the country boy of her dreams. When she's not furiously typing away at her computer she's mom to three wonderful children, who have given her another job as a taxi driver.

A voracious reader, she was given her first romance novel by her grandmother, who shared her penchant for a hot romance. From that moment Amy was hooked by the magical worlds, handsome heroes and sigh-worthy romances contained in the pages, and she knew what she wanted to be when she grew up.

Life got in the way, but after the birth of her second child she decided to pursue her dream of becoming a romance author.

Amy loves to hear from readers. It makes her day, in fact. You can find out more about Amy at her website www.amyruttan.com

# A CHILD TO HEAL THEIR HEARTS

BY
DIANNE DRAKE

First published in Great Britain 2013
by Mills & Boon, an imprint of Harlequin (UK) Limited.
Harlequin (UK) Limited, Eton House, 18-24 Paradise Road,
Richmond, Surrey TW9 1SR

© Dianne Despain 2013

ISBN: 978 0 263 89915 3

Harlequin (UK) policy is to use papers that are natural, renewable and recyclable products and made from wood grown in sustainable forests. The logging and manufacturing process conform to the legal environmental regulations of the country of origin.

Printed and bound in Spain
by Blackprint CPI, Barcelona

**Dear Reader**

Years ago, my husband and I met a wonderful little boy named Ryan. Ryan was an amazing kid—smart, full of life, optimistic. But Ryan had muscular dystrophy, and the degenerative process was so advanced in him that he never walked, never played ball, never did so many of the things his friends did.

He wanted to, though, because he never saw himself in terms of being different or disabled. Which was why the summer camps he attended were so important to him. All the kids there had pretty much the same abilities he had, and the fact that swimming or horseback-riding was a little different for them did not make a difference. For the time Ryan and his friends were at camp they got to be kids, doing kid things like all their other friends did.

Ryan wasn't given a lot of time on this earth, but he exceeded all expectations—went to college, became a high school teacher, travelled the world. Much of this independence he gained through his camp experiences, and because of what I saw resulting from those summer weeks, where his differences didn't matter, I decided to write about a camp much the same as Ryan attended—where kids, no matter what their condition, are allowed to be kids.

Did you go to camp when you were a kid? What kinds of memories do you have? I went to camp every summer and loved it. I didn't fall in love there, the way Keera and Reid do in my story. But I remember some pretty good summer crushes, some mighty cute boys, and a lot of great fun. *Definitely* some great fun (and my first kiss!).

Wishing you health, happiness and great summer camp memories!

*Dianne*

PS I'd love to hear about your summer camp memories.
Please feel free to check out my website at
www.Dianne-Drake.com and contact me through that.
Or e-mail me at DianneDrake@earthlink.net/
I'm on Facebook too, at Facebook.com/DianneDrakeAuthor

**Recent titles by the same author:**

P.S. YOU'RE A DADDY
REVEALING THE REAL DR ROBINSON
THE DOCTOR'S LOST-AND-FOUND HEART
NO. 1 DAD IN TEXAS
THE RUNAWAY NURSE
FIREFIGHTER WITH A FROZEN HEART
THE DOCTOR'S REASON TO STAY**
FROM BROODING BOSS TO ADORING DAD
THE BABY WHO STOLE THE DOCTOR'S HEART*

\**New York Hospital Heartthrobs*
\*Mountain Village Hospital*

**These books are also available in eBook format
from www.millsandboon.co.uk**

**DEDICATION**

Dedicated to Ryan McDonald,
who squeezed every last drop out of his young life.

# CHAPTER ONE

"COMING!" KEERA'S sleep-scratchy voice barely cleared the bedroom door and there was no way the person outside on her front porch could hear her. But she didn't really care. This was *her* time. Off work.

She wasn't on call, and after tomorrow she had no hospital obligations for the next week. A few days off after an entire year on. Blessed vacation time for eating, sleeping, reading. Most of all, quiet time to herself. No one to intrude, no one to disturb her. Time alone was all she had on the schedule and she adamantly didn't want to be disturbed before her holiday started. But as chief of cardiac surgery, she didn't always get what she wanted. Case in point, someone was knocking right now, and rather vigorously at that.

"OK, OK. Give me a minute," she grumbled on a weary sigh, the sentiment directed more to the neon green clock light blinking acrimoniously at her from the nightstand than to anything or anyone else.

She blinked back at it, wanted to throw a shoe at it when she saw it was telling her the time was ten after two. And she'd only been in bed since twenty after one. Meaning she'd had fifty full minutes of sleep.

"Figures," she grunted as another knock jolted her out of her blearies. Then another knock, louder this time. Last time this had happened to her, it had been the National Guard come to fetch her in the middle of a torrential storm. *"Hospital's on emergency alert, Dr. Murphy. Don't want you driving in this because of the conditions, so we've come to take you in."* Yep, that had been quite a night, being hefted up into the back of a military helicopter and jostled around fallen trees and power lines.

But tonight there was no rain. No storm or adverse condition of any kind going on. And as Keera's mind started to clear, she began ticking off the various reasons someone might be doing exactly what they were doing. Worst-case scenario—full-out disaster that wasn't weather-related. Best-case scenario—emergency surgery waiting. But why not simply call her, like they always did?

Maybe they had. Maybe she'd slept through it. "I *said* I'm coming," she shouted, cinching her robe as she plodded out to the entry hall. "Identify yourself, please," she shouted, even though a glimpse through the peephole revealed the uniform of a police officer. "And show me some identification."

"Will do, Miss Murphy," the man out there shouted.

*Miss* Murphy. After fast-tracking her way through medical school and all the other stages that had preceded cardiac surgeon, that's what it all boiled down to, wasn't it? Unmarried doctor, unmarried *miss*... Successful at career, unsuccessful at life. It was pretty much everything that defined her.

Keera pushed her long red hair back from her face, and looked out again. Saw what she required from the first officer.

"Officer Carla James," she said, obliging Keera with a sight of her ID. Short woman, slightly rounded, definitely hiding behind the taller officer.

"And Officer Brian Hutchinson," the taller one added,

bending down to Keera's peephole so she'd get a good wide-angle view of his face then his badge. "Would you please open the door?"

"Is it medical business?" she shouted at them, as she unlatched the first of three safety chains then finally pulled back the dead bolt. A little extra precaution as a result of living alone.

"No, ma'am, it's not," Officer Hutchinson said, stepping forward as soon as the door opened to him. He held out his leather wallet for her to match his photo with his face. Then tucked it away when she'd nodded her satisfaction. "I'm sorry to say it's personal."

That's when the first grain of relief shot through her. Keera Murphy didn't have a personal life. Everything about her was medicine. "How? I mean, what?"

Officer James chose that moment to step out from behind Hutchinson, and the only thing Keera saw was the bundle in her arms. "I'm sorry. I don't understand." Were they bringing her a patient? A child? No. This was a mistake. Didn't make sense. They were at the wrong house, or had the wrong person. That had to be it. They wanted the Keera Murphy who was a pediatrician, if there was such a person, and she was the Keera Murphy who did cardiac surgery.

"I'm sorry to say, there's no easy way to do this," Officer Hutchinson continued. "But earlier this evening your husband and a yet unidentified passenger were killed in a single vehicle crash off Mountain Canyon Road. Your daughter was thrown free, and escaped without injury. We did have her checked at a clinic near there, and except for some scrapes and bruises she's fine. In shock, I think, because she's not talking, maybe a little lethargic due to the trauma. But the doc who looked at her said she was basically good."

"I'm glad, but this is a mistake because I'm not married." Keera took a step backwards, braced herself against the wall. "Divorced. No children."

"Kevin Murphy," Hutchinson continued. "Kevin Joseph Murphy, ma'am. Your husband, according to some legal papers we found at the scene. House deed, this address."

"But we're not… Haven't been…" She shut her eyes, trying to focus. Kevin was dead? Their marriage had been a real stinker and their divorce nasty in epic proportions, but she wouldn't have wished this on him. "You're sure?" she finally managed.

"Yes, ma'am. We have a full identification on your husband but not his passenger. We were hoping…"

Keera glanced at the officer holding the child, wondering why they'd brought her here. Wondering if this was the child who… It had to be. Who else could she be but the child he'd fathered while they had still been married? "Maybe the passenger is his *second* wife. Melanie, Melodie, something like that." Or the one after her, if there'd already been another as Kevin seemed to have his women in fast succession. "Melania, that's her name. Melania." Keera's head was spinning now the information was finally beginning to sink in. Kevin was dead, most likely along with his second wife. And their child… "She's not mine," she said.

"But you were listed as Mr. Murphy's wife and next of kin, so we assumed—"

"Wrong assumption," she said, cutting him off. "Old information. My husband and I divorced a few months ago, the papers you found were probably from part of the agreement." Or, in their case, disagreement. "He called several days ago, said he had some final papers for me to sign, and that child…" She shook her head. "Part of his second marriage." Kevin's secret to keep, along with his mistress.

"Then we have a problem," Carla James said, "because we have nowhere to take the child for the night."

A little girl, she'd been told. Keera had never actually seen her. Hadn't ever wanted to see her. Didn't want to see her now, even though that was about to change. "Surely, there's a foster-home with an opening. Or some kind of contingency in place for situations like this one?"

Both police officers shook their heads.

"Social services?" Hopeful question with an answer she'd already guessed.

"That would be me," a perky young woman said from behind Officer James. "My name is Consuela Martinez, and I'm the temporary case manager assigned to Megan. And right now I don't have a contingency plan that would be in the child's best interests. We were hoping her family—"

"But I'm not her family," Keera interrupted.

Consuela stepped out in plain sight, the yellow of the porch light giving her more of a jaundiced look than it should. And just like that Keera switched to doctor mode, her mind ticking off various conditions that came with a yellow tinge...one of the reasons Kevin had strayed, *he claimed.* Too much doctor too much of the time. Sadly, she hadn't had an argument to counter his because, in the end, she *had* loved her medicine more than she'd loved her husband or their marriage.

"Look, I know there's a contingency plan," Keera said. "When a child is involved there's always a contingency plan." It was said without conviction because she really didn't know that to be the case. But she hoped it was, or else...

"You're right. Usually there is. Except right now. Every spot we have for someone Megan's age and developmental stage is filled," the case worker continued. "But I can have a callout to other agencies in other areas by morning, or we might be able to shift a few children to other situations, and after that—"

"Are you taking flucloxacillin, by any chance, Consuela?" Keera interrupted, so totally *not* wanting to hear that Megan had no place to go tonight.

Consuela looked confused. For that matter, so did both police officers. "Um, yes. I am. For an outer ear infection. Why?"

"You might want to call your doctor first thing in the morning and mention that you're having an adverse reaction to the drug. Nothing serious, so don't be alarmed. But it's worth noting." And that didn't change the problem at hand, as there was still a child bundled in Officer James's arms who needed a place to stay. "Sorry," she said. "Force of habit. Part of my job is paying attention to the details, and I've been told I can go overboard about it."

"It's good to know you're conscientious, Doctor," Officer Hutchinson said, "but it's two-thirty, and we're not getting any closer to figuring out what to do with—"

"With my ex-husband's child." It was an irony coming back to slap her hard. This was his secret child, the one he'd told her he'd fathered but had only told her on the child's first birthday. His first devastating confession, followed by how much he loved the baby's mother, how he wanted a divorce, wanted to keep their house for his new family... But none of that was Megan's fault, was it? "You're sure there's really no place for her to go tonight?"

"The county home," Consuela said, "which I try to avoid when I can, especially for children so young. It's a large facility, too many children. The younger ones get... overlooked."

"It's an—"

"An institution, ma'am," Officer James volunteered. "In

the traditional sense. But if you're rejecting the child, it's our only recourse, because I can't stand on your doorstep all night, holding her."

"No, of course you can't," Keera said, taking a step backwards as she felt her resolve start to melt. Another step, pause…taking a moment to gird her resolve. Then another backwards step, and finally the gesture to enter her home. And as Officer James passed her, Keera took her first good look at Megan, and if it weren't for the fact that the room was filled with people…strangers, she would have fallen to her knees. Would have cried. The lump in her throat started to choke her, and the light feeling in her head caused the room to spin. "Please, lay her on the sofa. I can sit up in here with her, she shouldn't be alone." *Shouldn't be in an institution!* No child should ever be in an institution.

Keera glanced at Consuela, who'd stopped at the mirror in the entry hall and was staring at her yellow-tinted complexion. "But this is only until morning," she warned the social worker. "If you don't have a placement for her before I leave for the hospital, in exactly three hours, you'll find her in the daycare center.

"Oh, and, Consuela, I can't look after her longer than what I've said. I'm not good with children. They don't respond to me, and outside normal medical situations I wouldn't know how to respond if they did. So, come morning, do you understand me? My early surgery will be over by ten, followed by routine rounds, and I don't want to go into my rounds knowing I still have a child to worry about."

It made her sound unpleasant, like a bully or, worse… heartless. Which wasn't at all what she'd intended. But how did a person go about dealing with a situation like this? She'd just taken in the child who had caused the final curtain to drop on her marriage, and she wasn't sure there was a proper way to deal with that.

"So, before you go, do we know if she has any allergies?" Kevin had been allergic to shellfish. "Or medical conditions that require attention...or medication?"

Consuela, who'd finally torn herself away from the mirror, shook her head. "Her doctor is Reid Adams, and his practice is in a little town called Sugar Creek, Tennessee. About an hour or so west of here. But we haven't been able to get in touch with him yet. He's at camp."

"Camp?" Keera asked.

"Youth camp, for kids recovering from leukemia and all the associated conditions. He's the camp physician, I've been told. And I do have a call in for him." Consuela stepped around Keera, who made no move to help Officer James settle Megan on the sofa. "And, Dr. Murphy...she's a good child. Very quiet. She won't cause you any problems."

No, the child wouldn't. Not now, anyway, because Keera's problems were in the past. And while little Megan hadn't caused them, she was a result of them. "Noon at the very latest. Please find your contingency plan by noon."

Ten minutes later, when the house was quiet again, Keera settled into the chair across from the sofa and simply stared at the child. Lovely little girl. Blonde hair, like Kevin's. Probably blue eyes like his, too. Sadly, there was so much turmoil for one little life. Poor thing. Her heart did go out to Megan for so many reasons.

"It's good that you don't have to understand any of this," Keera whispered to the child, while she pulled her feet up under herself, preparing to spend the rest of her night right there, looking after the girl. "But you're going to be fine. You're a beautiful little girl, and everything's going to be fine."

* * *

"I'm sorry, Doctor, but I really don't have anything to tell you." Reid Adams tossed the ball into the grass then stood back to watch the stampede of children go after it. No matter what else was going on in his life, coming to camp was always a highlight. "I'd have to look at her records before I could say anything, but I'm not in my office this week and—"

"Then find someone who can do it for you," Keera snapped, then hastily added, "Look, I'm sorry I sound so grumpy, but…"

"Normally, if someone sounds grumpy, they're grumpy," Reid said, stepping behind the large oak tree as two little girls came running in his direction. Black hair, dark eyes, dark skin. Hispanic beauties, and the lights of his life. His reason for existing wrapped up in a couple of very energetic little girls, aged five and seven. "And I think your situation with Megan would make a lot of people grumpy if it happened to them. No relatives turn up yet?"

"An elderly aunt who refused the child, as well as some male cousins the social worker thought weren't suitable. Apparently there are other family members being contacted, but I may have the child through the afternoon, and I'd feel better knowing about her health situation."

He liked her voice. A little husky, but not so much she sounded like a three-packs-a-day smoker. More like bedroom-sultry husky…an image that caused him to blink hard, clear his throat and, more than anything else, remind him that this was a kids' camp and he was surrounded by a bunch of kids who didn't need a distracted counselor.

"Daddy," five-year-old Allie squealed, as Reid sidled around the tree, only to be waylaid by seven-year-old Emmie, coming at him from the other side.

"I found him first," Emmie shouted.

"Did not," Allie argued, latching onto Reid's leg. "I got him first."

"You both got me first," he declared.

"Excuse me," Keera said. "Dr. Adams?"

"Sorry about that," he said, chuckling. "But my daughters are persistent, and they won't take no for an answer when we're playing. Not that I'd ever want them to. So, getting back to Megan Murphy. I've seen her once, I think, and nothing stands out. But it's a new practice, I'm barely settled in, and I don't know enough about any of my patients yet to even recognize them, or their parents, on the street. Sorry about that, because I'd like to be more help. But let me call either Beau Alexander or his wife, Deanna. They're covering my practice this week and they might know something. Or be able to see what's in the records." Pause.

"Girls, girls! Stay away from that fence! That's the rule. You've been told if you go near the fence, you'll get a time out with your first warning, and broccoli with your dinner with your second warning."

"You punish the children by threatening them with broccoli?" Keera asked. "I'd think that would be a healthy choice. Something you'd encourage them to eat."

"It is, but most kids come naturally equipped hating broccoli, so I use that to my advantage. Then, by the end of the camp session, we'll have introduced them to a couple of ways broccoli can taste really yummy... Excuse me, I have the younger group here this week. When I mention broccoli to older kids, I usually use the term delicious. And the thing is, the majority of these children will leave here and ask their parents for broccoli. Just an FYI—raw with dip works great!"

"Raw or cooked, you're a magician, Dr. Adams, if you get them liking broccoli."

"Nope, just a single dad who's figured it out. If it works with my two, it'll work with anybody's kid. Anyway... Angelica, Rodney! Take off your shoes *and* your socks before you go wading in the creek! Both socks, Rodney."

"Look, I appreciate your time, Dr. Adams, but—"

"Reid. Call me Reid."

"Reid. I'm sorry for sounding so grumpy, or frazzled, or whatever you want to call it, but I'm not good with children, don't know if I even like them so much, and I really don't want to be responsible for one, even if it's only for a few more hours. I was hoping...actually, I don't know what I was hoping for. But you clearly have your hands full with your camp kids, so I'm going let you go. But before I do, could you answer one more question for me?"

"Got time for two, if they're quick." Truth was, he wasn't sure he wanted to hang up. Keera Murphy sounded nice, except for the part where she wasn't fond of children. In his life that was definitely a problem. But she wasn't in his life, so it didn't matter. "So go ahead."

"Megan's two, and she's not... She's still in diapers. I had her in hospital daycare all morning and the ladies working there said she made no attempt to go to the bathroom or even ask someone to take her."

"Does she speak?"

"No, but that could be the trauma."

"She's had a full battery of tests?"

"Everything we could think of."

"Then she's probably just reacting to her circumstances. Once things are normal around her again I'm sure the diapers can come off. And if she's not totally trained, it's perfectly natural for children that age to be a little resistant. But if you have other concerns, please feel free..." He spun around in time to catch Emmie ready to lob him with a big red water balloon. He was fast enough to dodge it, but in trying for the evasive maneuver he dropped his phone. By the time he'd manage to pick it back up, Keera Murphy had hung up.

"Who was that, Daddy?" Allie asked him. Now she was sneaking up, hiding what he guessed was also a filled water balloon behind her back. So, he could take it like a man or, actually, like a daddy, and let his youngest have her turn at dousing Daddy, or he could spin and run like crazy. After all, he was well over six feet tall, considered well muscled by some. Legs that had helped him finish in the pack at a few marathons. So if he couldn't outrun a little girl... "She was a doctor."

"Who takes care of little kids, like you do?" Allie asked. The expression on her face was so determined, he knew what he had to do.

"No, not that kind of doctor, sweetheart." He braced himself for the hit. "Remember when we talked about what having surgery means?" OK, so most parents weren't quite as forthright as he was in his child-rearing ideas, but he didn't believe in lying, not even when it was about something Allie probably wouldn't even understand and definitely didn't need to know.

"Where they have to make a zipper so they can see your insides?"

He chuckled. "Actually, yes." Which meant she did listen to him. Music to the ears of a long-suffering parent. "She's the kind of doctor who makes the zipper."

He thought back to the conversation with Keera. Strained, at best. Maybe more like totally stressed out. Someone he pictured as nervous. Someone he also pictured as... One momentary distraction was all it took, and Reid Adams fell victim to his daughter, who landed the perfectly placed water balloon center chest. "Got me," he shouted, dropping to the ground, where five or six other children converged on him and bombarded him with water balloons the way his own daughters had done.

"No fair," he shouted while laughs and squeals muffled any protest he wanted to make. Not that he really wanted to protest. This was part of his fun. What meant the most to him now was thinking about how his daughters would be exhilarated, and knowing that his two little conspirators had led a group of normally sedentary kids into an adventure was, probably, the most fun of all.

Then he wondered about Dr. Keera Murphy. Would she have seen any of this as fun? Or worthless, as she wasn't a big one for children? More than that, why did it even matter to him? And why did he make a mental note to do a little Internet surfing on her when he had time?

"No more water balloons," he shouted, trying to stand up. But to no avail. As he rose to his knees, a whole new group of water ballooners swarmed him, loaded down with filled balloons of every size, color and shape imaginable. He barely had enough time to cover his face before the fun began.

"I know what I said, Dr. Murphy, and I've got a line on someone who might take her later tonight or some time tomorrow, if there's nobody else available. But Mrs. Blanchard prefers her wards to be toilet trained, and as Megan isn't, I'm not sure she'll get all the attention she needs."

They were sitting in the parents' waiting room across from the hospital daycare center. A very cheerful place. Lots of bright yellows and oranges, like they were tying the conventional child stimuli colors into their parents. This was only the second time Keera had ever been there. The first had been that morning, when she'd left Megan in the able care of Dolores Anderson, the director. "She could be traumatized."

"Maybe, and if that's the case, I'm wondering if a pediatric hospital ward might be the best place for her temporarily."

"Seriously, you want to stick her in a hospital?"

No, that was not acceptable. While she didn't have any strong urges toward the child, she wasn't some cold-hearted dungeon master who wanted to lock all the un-trained kiddies away until they potty trained themselves. This was a child who needed attention, not isolation, and so far all of Consuela's ideas seemed more like isolation.

"Look, just keep trying with Mrs. Blanchard, OK? If she won't take Megan, maybe she'll have a suggestion about who can."

"We'll work it out, Doctor. I promise, that's all I've been doing today."

Consuela was deliberately not making eye contact with Keera, trying to keep her gaze focused on anything else, and Keera accepted that. She'd probably do the same thing if she found herself in that same spot. But what Consuela didn't understand was that so far today childcare had been a breeze because she'd had the help of the whole hospital daycare staff there to get her through it.

Tomorrow was another story. It was her day off—the start of her week off, in fact. And that's when the reading commenced with a whole stack of medical journals she'd had for a year or more. Nowhere in those plans was there room for a toddler.

"I'm not criticizing you, and I hope you don't think that I was. But I grew up in the foster-care system. A lot of it in institutions, and it's horrible. Being passed off from one place to another, never knowing where you might end up next. I never got adopted because I was older when I went into the system, so I was in a grand total of nine different homes and three different institutions, all before the age of eighteen. And, no, I wasn't a good child because of that." She closed her eyes, fighting back those memories.

"This child doesn't need that kind of trauma in her life." As much as she'd disliked Kevin by the end of their marriage, Keera knew he would have been a very good father. A doting daddy. Megan didn't deserve to go from that to cold indifference, which was what would happen if she was sent to an institution. Or even the wrong foster-family.

"It's not always a traumatic situation, Doctor. We have very good caregivers."

"Yes, I'm sure you do, and I admire people who would take on the responsibility. Right now, though, Megan needs more that what you're able to find her, and I know that's not your fault. But it's not her fault either. Yet she's the one who's going to be bounced around or institutionalized."

And she was waging the battle with the wrong person. She knew that. But the right person—the one who should have made arrangements for Megan in the event something like this happened—was dead. True to Kevin's form, he hadn't thought about the practical things. Hadn't when they'd been married, hadn't after they were divorced, and now his daughter was paying the price.

"I'm sorry about your childhood, Doctor, and I understand your frustration but, like I said, I'm doing my best. There aren't any distant relatives suited to take her, or who even want her, for that matter, so I have to come up with another plan. But you've got to understand that in the short term Megan might have to go to a hospital pediatric ward, a group home or even the county home. It's not what I want to do but what I may have to do if you can't or won't keep her for a little while longer."

"In the meantime…" Resignation crept in a little too

quickly, but maybe she saw something of herself in Megan. Abandoned child. It was hard to get past that. "If I keep her a day or two, that doesn't mean I want to be a temporary guardian or any other kind of custodial figure. It simply means I'll feed and clothe her while you continue looking for a better situation."

"Which I'll do," Consuela promised.

"Good. So now I've got to go to the grocery and buy a few things a toddler would eat. Maybe pick up some clothes, toys..." OK, so she was relating to the situation but not to Megan herself. It was the best she could do. Better than most people would do, she thought as she bundled up the child and took her to the car. This was an honest effort, and it kept the child out of all those awful places Keera knew so intimately. Shuddered even thinking about them. Dark places, bad for children...

While having children had never been part of her plan—past, present or future—there'd been a time when she'd needed what Megan needed now, and no one had reached out to her. So how could she refuse?

"Megan, did you have a good day today?" she asked as they wended their way through the hospital corridors on her way to her car. "Play with lots of nice toys? Meet new people? Conquer any toddler nations?"

In response, Megan laid her head against Keera's shoulder and sighed.

"You're congested," Keera said, listening to the slight rattling she could hear coming from the girl's lungs. Immediately in doctor mode, she veered off into one of the pediatric exam cubicles, pulled her stethoscope from her pocket and listened. Nothing sounded serious, but the fact remained that the child had something going on that needed to be attended to...sooner, not later. And every thought in her went to Reid Adams.

# CHAPTER TWO

"IT'S OK, MEGAN," she said, barely creeping along the mountain highway. "We'll be there soon, and Dr. Adams will take good care of you." She hoped so, even though she wasn't sure the message had gotten through because he hadn't called her back. Something about mountains and cellphone interference.

"You've seen him before, and he's very good." Not that the sleeping child cared. But Keera did. She wanted some familiarity for Megan, and Reid Adams was the closest thing she could think of. And maybe, just maybe, he'd have a solution for the child's situation. "We're not far away now, so you just sleep there, and when you wake up things will be better. I promise."

What was she promising, though? What, really, could a trip to an isolated camp in the mountains in the middle of the night do for Megan? Nothing. That's what! But it made Keera feel better. Feel like she was doing something rather than simply sitting around waiting for something to happen or, worse, doing the wrong thing. Reid Adams was all about children, he had children. And for some strange reason, he seemed like her best port in the storm. A beacon of light.

"He'll know what to do," she reassured the sleeping child. "Yes, I'm sure of it." Because if he didn't…well,

Keera didn't want to think about the alternative, since it wasn't acceptable. That was something she knew in profound ways no child should ever have to know. Confusion, fear and long, empty days and nights when the futility threatened to eat you alive. "He'll fix you up, and he'll help me help you, too."

Those were mighty big expectations for one pediatrician to fulfill, but it's all Keera had to cling to. Reid Adams had to come through for both their sakes. He just had to!

He wasn't sure who she was, but for some reason he thought he could wager a pretty good guess. Carrying a child in her arms, she was trying to make her way up the dirt path without stumbling, and she was quite obviously not a woman of the woods. Determined, though. With the scowl of a mighty huntress set across one of the softest, prettiest faces he'd ever seen in his life.

Which was what had brought Keera Murphy to mind. She'd tracked him down and she was bringing him the child. He wasn't sure why, wasn't even sure that he liked the idea that the huntress had set her sights on him. But something about a woman who would trudge all the way out here in the middle of the night just to find him did fascinate him.

"You would be Dr. Murphy?" he asked, as she approached the porch of his cabin.

"I would be. And this is Megan Murphy. She's sick. Since nobody knows her, nobody knows a thing about her, well, with you being her physician and all, I thought you'd be the best one to take a look."

"You couldn't find another physician closer to you? Or even track down one of my colleagues?"

"You didn't get my phone call?"

"Mountains and cellphones aren't always a good combination, even in this day and age. Reception out here is spotty, which is why we still rely on the landline."

"Well, I called because I hoped she'd remember you. With everything she's gone through, I thought that would be good. Maybe it doesn't matter, but…" Keera started up the wooden steps and Reid took the child from her arms, immediately seeing how sick she was.

"How long has she been this way?" he asked, turning and nearly running into his cabin.

"Just the last few hours. She'd been getting progressively sicker and I wasn't too worried about it at first, but when I listened to her chest a little while ago, the congestion had more than doubled from earlier and her temperature had elevated two degrees."

He laid Megan carefully on the sofa then dashed into the next room after his medical bag.

"Well, I hope I didn't do the wrong thing bringing her here." She shrugged. "And I'm sorry for the intrusion. Maybe I panicked a little." Panicked because she'd known what would happen if she'd taken Megan to the hospital. The system would have gotten her. As much as she didn't want the child, she also didn't want the child to end up in the system, which was what would have happened because a trip to Emergency tonight would have started that process. "I didn't know what else to do."

"You followed your instinct. Did what you believed was best. It's not a bad thing, Keera." He took a quick blood-pressure reading, followed by the rest of Megan's vitals, then pulled off his stethoscope and laid it aside.

It was a simple action yet so sexy. And she wanted to kick herself for noticing. "I may have overreacted, but—"

"Look, I don't know the dynamics here. Don't know why social services left the child with you when, clearly, she's not your responsibility. Don't know why you avoided a quick trip to an emergency room rather than driving all the way out here. But I'm not going to ask. We all have our reasons for the crazy things we do, and I don't mean crazy in a literal sense but more from a point of observation. Seems crazy to me because I don't know what makes you tick, but obviously it doesn't seem crazy to you because you understand the situation. So as far as I'm concerned, it's all good."

"I appreciate that," she said sincerely. "Thank you."

"Don't thank me yet. I want to keep Megan for a day or so. It's probably a slight upper respiratory infection, although I want to make sure before I let her go as I don't think she's up to another trip back with you so soon. So I'd like to keep her in the infirmary here for a little while, if you don't mind. It's empty and I can quarantine her there just to make sure the other kids don't come in contact with her. Then I'll get her hydrated and start her on some medication to make her feel better." He frowned. "Unless you'd rather admit her to a local hospital because she is a little dehydrated. Your choice."

No choice. This was where Megan had to be, at least for the night. "And the infirmary is…?"

He pointed to a door at the rear of the living room. "Through the kitchen, out the door, first building you see beyond my cabin. The clinic is on the other side of the compound."

"Why do you keep them separated?"

"These kids are very susceptible to illness. Don't want sickness anywhere near regular medical duties."

"Makes sense."

"Also, I bought the camp as is. Didn't have one place large enough to house both the clinic and infirmary. Anyway, there's always someone on duty. Usually me, sometimes Betsy, the camp nurse, who stays in the cabin adjacent to this one. We alternate nights taking call.

"As far as the infirmary, I think you may have to help a bit there because Betsy's pregnant and I don't let her near the sick kids. Which means it's basically you and me, and I do have a volunteer who isn't medical but who had leukemia when she was a kid and enjoys helping out where she can."

"You need to know I'm not good at pediatrics."

"Maybe not, but I don't have a lot of options if we're going to keep Megan here. Like I said, there's always the hospital…"

An unacceptable choice. That was her first thought. Her second was that she could leave Megan here, go home and let Consuela, the social worker, deal with the rest of it. This was certainly her chance to step aside and know Megan was in good hands, but something inside her was stopping her from taking it. "So you want me basically quarantined with her?"

"Not quarantined as in locked up. We have a guest cabin. Nothing fancy, but a place to sleep for the rest of the night, if you want it, while I watch Megan. Then in the morning we can work out the schedule."

"Maybe she'll be ready to travel in the morning." And maybe in the morning Consuela would call her and tell her she'd found a perfect placement. Maybe even a good family who would eventually adopt Megan. One who'd been on the waiting list, praying for a beautiful two-year-old girl. Sure, it was a long shot, she knew that. But it was also a very nice dream—a dream she'd never had for her own.

"That's possible," he said. "But unlikely. In the meantime, you look like you're due for a few hours of sleep."

Yes, she did want that sleep. More now that he'd mentioned it. Hypnotic effect—her eyelids were getting heavy.

"Definitely no hospital, so I guess it looks like I'm staying. I think I'll talk to Megan for a minute then I'll take you up on that cabin. Oh, and, Reid, I really am sorry to put you through this. If there's anything I can do…"

"How about I carry her to the infirmary then you can tuck her in while I run over to the girls' dorm and check on my daughters?" He smiled. "They may think they're getting away from Dad, but it's not happening. Anyway, one last kiss goodnight while you settle Megan in, then I'll point you in the direction of the guest cabin and you're on your own. Oh, and breakfast is at eight. Big white building in the middle of the complex. Meals are prompt, but if you sleep in, I always have cereal and milk in my own kitchen."

He was tall, a bit lanky. Wore wire-rimmed glasses, needed a haircut. She liked his scraggly look, though. Light brown hair, slightly curly, slightly over his collar. Slight dimple in his chin. And, oh, those blue eyes. Wow, they were perceptive. So much so they almost scared her. "I don't sleep much so I'll be good to grab something with everybody else."

"I'm just saying…" he said, scooping Megan into his arms and heading out to the infirmary.

Keera opened the door to the infirmary, saw exactly four beds. It was a tidy space, not large, not lush. Just basic. "Do many of your kids get sick?"

"Not really. By the point in their recovery that they're allowed to come to camp, they're usually pretty far along in the whole process, with all kinds of specialists making the determination whether or not they're ready for the whole camping experience. In other words, barring normal things like colds and flu, they're usually doing pretty well."

"Well, it sounds like you're doing important work. So don't you think the owners would put a little more effort into the medical facility that might have to treat those kids? I mean, this place will suffice, but it could certainly stand some updates and expansion." After Reid laid Megan in the bed, Keera pulled up the blanket to cover her. "Closer to the clinic would be nice, too, to save you some steps."

"Are you always like this?"

"What?"

"Outspoken. Opinionated. Whatever you want to call it." Grabbing a fresh digital thermometer from the drawer in the stand next to the bed, he pulled it from its wrapper, punched the button and waited for it to calibrate. "Something to say pretty much on every subject." The thermometer end went under Megan's tongue the same time his eyes went to Keera's. "I'm right about that, aren't I?"

"It's been said." Amongst a lot worse things. "I'm a cardiac surgeon in a large hospital, and—"

"I know who you are."

"How?"

"Internet search."

"When?"

"Earlier. After you called. You sounded like someone who might come back to haunt me later on, so I decided to read up. Good thing I did, because…"

She smiled, almost apologetically but not quite. "Because I came back to haunt you."

The thermometer beeped and Reid pulled it out and read it. Then shook his head. "One hundred three and a couple of decimal points." Immediately, he pulled up Megan's eyelids, took a look. She responded by whimpering and trying to jerk away from him.

"I talked to Beau a couple hours ago. He'd looked at the records we have for her, saw nothing significant. In fact, the only time she's been to the office was when her parents first moved to Sugar Creek, and they were establishing me as their pediatrician. I gave her a preliminary exam, sort of as a baseline, and there was nothing remarkable. She's developed properly for a child her age, and according to her parents there's no history of any chronic illness or condition.

"But that's me taking their word for it because they never had her medical records transferred to us, and there's no mention of a former pediatrician, so right now we really know very little. Which means we're coming into her care pretty much blind."

"Trust me, blind is bad."

"I get the feeling that has nothing to do with Megan."

"Actually, it has everything to do with her. But not in the medical sense."

Pulling out his stethoscope, Reid listened to the child's chest, her heart, her tummy then pulled out his earpieces. "Didn't hear anything more remarkable than what you probably heard. Bilateral congestion, wheezing." He shrugged. "Indicative of any number of things. Which means I'm going to need lab work that I'm not equipped to do here."

"Did it before I came here. Results should be in by morning. And I have her X-ray in the car."

"You come prepared. Too bad all my patients don't come in with all their tests already done."

"Like I told you, I don't know a thing about children. Don't treat them, don't operate on them, don't want to. But getting everything done beforehand seemed logical."

"Well, even though you've complicated my life by bringing her here, you've made my complication easier."

"You're not supposed to treat anybody who's not at camp? Is that the problem? Because I can talk to the owner or director. Apologize. Make the appropriate donation for her care, if that's what's needed to make this better."

"Actually, I own the camp so I can do what I want. And donations are always welcome. But just so you'll know, she's got the start of a rash on her stomach, so I think she's probably coming down with measles, most likely in the early part of its three or four days of infectivity. Meaning while she's in here I can't have other children anywhere near her. So if somebody else needs the facility…" He shrugged. "I'll treat her here for now, certainly for the night, and we'll do the best we can with what we have. But I can't make any promises beyond that. Fair enough?"

"More than fair," she said, grateful for what he was offering.

"Have you had measles, by the way?"

"Not that I remember. But I don't remember a lot of my childhood, so I don't really know."

"Vaccinated?"

"That, I was. Required in school." When she had gone, which hadn't been too often. "Could this be something else, though? An allergic reaction of some sort?" Reid Adams was an acclaimed pediatrician—she'd done her Internet surfing as well. So it was highly unlikely he'd make a mistake of a pretty basic diagnosis. Still, an allergic reaction resulting in a rash beat measles any day, so she was keeping her fingers crossed.

"If I were a betting man, I'd bet she's going to have a full-blown rash by this time tomorrow."

"And you still want to keep her? Especially with all the other children being so susceptible? I mean, I could take her to a hotel someplace close, so she wouldn't have to suffer that long drive back tonight."

"She's too congested to move her any place, if we don't have to. It would risk complications. And she has to be sick somewhere, doesn't she? Seeing that you're not in favor of taking her to the hospital, which would really be the only place I'd approve sending her..."

"If she absolutely needs to be in a hospital, that's what I'll do. I just have personal preferences about not leaving an already abandoned child in an institution." Keera looked down at the girl, and her heart clutched. Poor thing, she didn't deserve cold detachment, but that's all Keera was capable of giving. She knew her limitations.

"She's not my child, but I want what's best for her, and while I know you're a pediatrician and you'll disagree with me, I don't happen to think it would be in a hospital. And I don't say that lightly as I work in a hospital."

"Couldn't agree with you more about hospitals." He pushed a strand of hair away from Megan's face then stood. "Don't like them myself if they're not necessary. Look, I really do need to go say goodnight to my girls, then I'll be back to put an IV in her and give her some fluids to keep her hydrated. I think that will be easier than trying to get her to drink anything right now. It'll only take me a couple of minutes..."

"I'm really sorry about this," Keera said, feeling the need to apologize over and over because of what she was doing to Reid and his camp. It was an inconvenience at very best and a danger at worst.

"She's sick. Bringing her all the way out here might not have been my first choice, but it's a difficult situation. Can't say I understand your decisions, but I'm not going to argue about them. So why the worried look?"

"I'm still concerned about exposing the other kids. I didn't think about that before I came here, and I feel terrible."

"See, the thing about being a pediatrician is you're always in contact with something that's highly contagious. In my office, I actually have separate waiting areas for

kids with something *catchy*, as I like to call it. They never
go to the general waiting room, never come near one of
the other kids. Bottom line, I'm cautious and it works. So
does the fact that we're surrounded by the great outdoors
so there aren't any environmental factors that would help
promote exposure."

"You sure?"

He nodded, smiled. "Sure."

"Do you have a solution for my fear of children as
well?"

"Afraid of children, yet you're a good doctor."

"Definitely afraid of children. Don't know what to do
for them, or with them. I was a nervous wreck every time
I had to rotate through Pediatrics when I was a resident."

"Somehow I don't picture you being a nervous wreck
about anything."

"I appreciate the compliment, but I'm serious about children. They're not my strength. Speaking of which, there's
something you should know about Megan. And it's not really her so much as the whole situation. But only because
you're her doctor."

He motioned Keera to the door. "Tell me as you walk
me out."

She did, then stopped at the door as he stepped out into
the night. "Without dragging out all the dirty laundry, what
you need to know is that Keera is the child my husband
conceived with another woman while he and I were still
married, still going through the motions that made it look
like a good marriage. We had our share of problems, like
all couples do, but I didn't know he was cheating on me.
Didn't even know his affair produced a child until she was
a year old, and he was wanting out of our marriage so he
could invest himself fully in his other family. That was a

year ago. Haven't seen him since except across the table at the lawyer's office. And I'd never seen the child until…"

"Yet here you are with her, going above and beyond the call of duty to get her what you think is the care she needs." Reid whistled quietly. "I'd say that's pretty admirable in an uncomfortable situation."

"It is uncomfortable. The authorities brought her to me…well, I'm not really sure how that worked out because once I realized they intended to leave her with me the rest of it turned into a blur. But there were some papers in the car—it was a car crash that killed them—and my name was on the papers. Papers from before we were divorced, I think.

"Anyway, the child was fine, so they brought her to me because they believed she was mine. Then they more or less coerced me into keeping her because they didn't have a place to put her for various reasons, she got sick, here I am…"

Reid laid a steadying hand on her arm. "And here you are, frantic."

"I'm sorry. In surgery I'm in control. But with Megan?" She shrugged. "It's hard, Reid. And I really don't have the right to be burdening you with all this. I wouldn't have, except she got sick and…"

"And you fixated on me as your solution."

"Not my solution. Megan's solution. You're her doctor. Which is a lame reason for me showing up here the way I did, but I panicked because my alternative was to take her to the hospital, and as a place to work it's fine, but for a child…" She stopped explaining. "So, how are we going to deal with all these problems I've created for you?"

He chuckled. "Minor glitches."

"I wouldn't call them minor as it involves more than I

ever expected. I mean, tying up your infirmary, keeping you away from your daughters. And your...wife?"

"No wife. Never married. Adopted daughters. Long story."

"Well, whatever the case, I haven't made things easy for you here, so..."

"So, that donation you mentioned?"

She nodded. "Happy to do it."

"Money's always great, but I'm thinking about some clinic time while you're here. That way I can sneak off and see my girls."

"I'm all for you getting to spend time with your daughters, and I'll do anything I can to help make that happen. But seriously? You want me working with your kids after what I just told you?" It was probably the most uninspired thing he could have suggested.

"Think of them as future adults and you'll be just fine."

"Wouldn't it be better if I simply hired a temp to come help you? Two temps, three. However many you need?"

"But you're going to have to stay here with Megan anyway. Or were you thinking about leaving her here with me and vanishing into thin air?"

She smiled an especially guilty smile, because that thought *had* crossed her mind a time or two. "Not thin air. I'm too easy to track down."

"But she's a ward of the state, and you, apparently, have been given some sort of temporary custody. Which means you can't just walk away from her. At least, I wouldn't think so. And I don't think you'd do that anyway, otherwise you'd have taken her to the hospital in the first place and just left her there." He grinned. "Or left her on my doorstep when you had the chance."

"OK, I'll admit it. Leaving her here might have crossed my mind..."

He chuckled. "You're too transparent, Keera."

"And you're too perceptive, Reid. But I meant what I said about children. So if you still want me to work with your kids here, knowing what you know about me, I'll give you a couple of days as I'm the one who messed you up. You'll have the right to terminate my services, with no notice, though. Just thought I'd throw that in there for your protection."

"What happens if you discover you don't mind working with children? Or, better yet, even like it?"

"I'll return to my blessedly all-adult practice with the memories. But you're not converting me, Doctor. If that happens, I'll concede a slight change of heart after the ordeal is over, if I have to—which I don't expect I will have to do. But that's all you'll get from me."

"OK, then. Now that the ground rules are established…"

"What ground rules?"

"The ones where I'm going to work super-hard to change your mind and you're going to fight me off every step of the way." He smiled, mimicking a gauntlet sliding over his right arm. "You threw down the darned gauntlet, so don't blame me for picking it up and seeing what I can do with it."

She couldn't help it. She liked this pediatrician, in spite of his choice of medical specialties. Liked his humor, liked his rather frazzled look. In fact, while the prospect of children underfoot didn't exactly appeal to her, spending a few days with Reid underfoot suddenly seemed like a nice way to pass time that would have been time lost in books and sleep. He was cute.

"Fine, I'll do what I need to do. But I wouldn't be putting on that other gauntlet just yet." To honor the deal, she extended a hand to him then had to bite her lower lip to keep from gasping when he took it, as the smooth feel of his skin on hers ignited a spark that arced all the way up her arm.

"So, about that IV..." he said, rather reluctantly. "Let me run over to the dorm for a minute then I'll be right back. In the meantime, maybe you could check over supplies. I'll start the IV as you don't do kids and you could get everything ready."

Backing his way down the steps, he only turned round when he'd reached ground. Or maybe he lingered. In her mind, the uncertainty she saw there most certainly had to be over his routine gone horribly wrong, but she wished it could have been more. And while she wasn't open to a relationship of any lasting sort, a nice flirtation from time to time wasn't off her list. Except this man ran a camp for kids, and he had kids of his own—a reality that slammed her back to earth in a fraction of a breath as she went looking for IV supplies.

But a little while later, after his round of goodnights had been said to his daughters, and as she watched him skillfully master the insertion of an IV catheter into such a tiny vein, she was almost changing her mind again. No flirting allowed! Admire the man, admire his skill. Every bit of this was trouble and if she was smart, she'd turn round, go home and hire him some temps.

But she wasn't smart. Not about the kinds of things going through her mind, anyway.

"You don't spend much time away from them, do you?" Keera asked, catching Reid staring out the door at the cabin where the girls were sleeping. Megan was tucked in for the night, resting as comfortably as she could under the circumstances.

"Try not to. I mean, I work, have to take call when it's my turn. But I have fantastic friends who look after them at home, which makes life easier for me. And now, even when they're here at camp, in the dorm, I can visit them when I want."

"If you want to be free to go over there whenever, I can spend the night with Megan."

"That's not it. I know they're safe, and just a few hundred yards away. But I'm over-protective. Can't help it. Emmie had leukemia when I adopted them. She was a little over two and Allie was still a baby. Their mother…" He shrugged.

"I never really knew what happened. Apparently, she brought Allie into the world so her umbilical cord stem cells could be used in treating Emmie. They're only half-sisters, but the match was perfect. Their mother—her name was Maria—stayed around long enough to see that Emmie was responding to treatment, and then one day she didn't come to the hospital. I'd heard she'd come here seeking medical care for Emmie, and once she'd found it she'd gone home to Mexico, but I really don't know.

"Anyway, after that…" He shrugged. "Emmie improved, Allie was placed in foster-care for a while, but there was always a thought that if the stem-cell therapy failed, there was still potential for a bone-marrow transplant, with a sibling donor. So, Allie was brought back to the hospital to stay, and that's where I met the girls, actually. Allie wasn't sick but she was put on my service to care for."

"And you adopted them?"

"It became legal six months ago. But I've had them for nearly four years. Because they had to stay together, and because of Emmie's leukemia, they weren't considered highly adoptable. Then the restrictions for adopting parents were huge because of the medical considerations. One thing led to another and I took them. I don't regret it."

"And Emmie, is she in remission?"

"I like to think of it as full recovery because she's so healthy now. But, yes, she's in remission. We've got one more year left before we can celebrate her *recovery*."

"Lucky girls," Keera commented.

"Lucky me. They slowed me down, forced me to look at life differently. I was on a pretty self-destructive path, indulging in just about every unhealthy kind of lifestyle habit there was. Smoking, fast foods three times a day, little to no sleep, amphetamines when needed. But when you have kids, you have to be...better." He smiled. "Or else they'll beat you down to a bloody pulp and walk all over you.

"Anyway, we have some choices here. The camp doesn't wake up for several more hours so, like I said earlier, you can go find the guest cabin and take advantage of the time while I stay here. Or you can stay with Megan while I take advantage of the next few hours. Your choice."

"My choice would have to be the noble thing, wouldn't it?" she said as she headed back into the clinic. "So save whatever's left of the night, and I'll be fine in one of the infirmary beds. Besides, I think it would be better if I stay closer to her because if she wakes up there's a chance she'll remember me."

"No arguments here. So, there are clean scrubs in the supply closet. Feel free to use the kitchen in the back of the infirmary and help yourself to tea, coffee, anything you want. And if you need me..." He held up his cellphone. "Or lean out the window and shout. I sleep with my windows open, and I'm a light sleeper."

"Literally?" she said, grabbing a pair of scrubs from the closet then pulling the curtain around the bed next to Megan's to afford herself a little privacy while she changed.

"Dad training is good for a lot of things," he said.

Megan's response was to whimper then turn on her side.

Keera's response to that was to sit down on the edge of the bed next to Megan, lay her hand gently to her cheek to feel for a temperature then go immediately for a cold compress.

Reid, on the other hand, stood back and watched. Then decided that for someone who didn't like children, and who claimed she didn't have a way with them, Keera had a way with them. A very nice way, when her guard wasn't up.

One o'clock, two o'clock, and now it was going on three and he hadn't gone to sleep yet. In fact, he wasn't even sleepy. Which was highly unusual, because most of the time he was worn out by the time his head hit the pillow. His head had hit the pillow at least twenty times in the past three hours, but hadn't stayed there. All because Dr. Keera Murphy, the avowed child-hater, was next door, and she was all he could think about. Pretty, with her coppery long hair and her green eyes. Feisty with her opinions. But compassionate, in spite of her blustery no-kids-allowed attitude.

He'd seen the way she'd held Megan, and protected her. He'd heard the way she comforted her. Nothing about that showed any kind of dislike for the little girl, so he wondered why the attempt at an outward persuasion against children when he didn't believe that was her inner feeling.

*We all have our fears,* he reminded himself, returning to the bedroom window for at least the tenth time to look over at the infirmary, to the single light shining inside it. *Fear.* Such an immense word. His biggest fears were for his daughters. Always. And specifically for Emmie's health. What were Keera's fears?

He wondered about that as he thought back over the years, back to a time when his own life had been fearless. Or, as some might describe it, stupid. Actually, as he might describe it now that he'd grown up. He'd been typically bachelor-selfish, making his various conquests along the way. Doing nothing so different from the majority of hotshot interns and residents. Bad life, bad attitude, all changed for the love of two little girls.

And out of that love had grown his fears. But he wouldn't trade what he had now for anything from his old life because even now, thinking about the way he'd been made him shudder.

Or was he shuddering because he could see the silhouette of Keera in the infirmary? She was awake, like he was, and standing at the window, too. Looking over at him perhaps?

# CHAPTER THREE

"I'VE GOT YOU set up in the guest cottage," Reid said, giving Keera a gentle nudge.

Keera opened her eyes, looked up and there he was, looking down at her, almost as disheveled as she felt. "What time is it?" she mumbled, rubbing her eyes, trying to focus, and hating the fact that the sun was already up to remind her she'd only gone to sleep a little while ago.

"Going on to eight. Did you sleep well?"

"Like a baby. For three hours. Megan had a restless night. She kept waking up, calling for her mommy." She glanced over at the child, who'd finally gone to sleep after several fussy intervals. "And she was spiking a pretty high fever for a while, which finally broke around four. Poor thing was miserable."

"Well, there's a nice shower waiting for you in the guest cabin, if that'll make you feel any better."

"If there's a bed in the shower, that'll be perfect."

"I don't know about you, but I used to have nights when three hours of sleep were a blessing."

"Back in my residency," she said, sitting up and stretching. "Which, thankfully, has been over with for a while. And my hospital had a very strict policy with its surgical residents about taking care of ourselves. If we came in and looked the least bit tired or sluggish, we'd get bumped out of the OR and they'd put us on chart duty and paper-work for the entire shift. Once or twice doing that and you learned to get your sleep."

"You were lucky, then. Where I did my Pediatrics res-idency, they were so short-staffed we were always tired and sluggish." He smiled. "Makes for a better story than well rested and perky, doesn't it?"

Keera laughed. "Want to hear about all the paper cuts I got the first time I had to spend a day on chart duty?"

"Good try," he said, holding out his hand to pull her out of bed. "But I can top that with the time I worked thirty-six hours straight in the middle of a blizzard, and I was the only pediatrician in the hospital. Didn't even get a nap in."

She swung her legs over the edge of the bed, then stood, and immediately brushed her hair back from her face. "Yes, but did you get physically wounded, the way I did? Paper cuts can get infected, you know."

"Do leg cramps, aching feet and a sore back count?"

"*Six* paper cuts, Reid."

"And the only food available the whole time was from a vending machine." He smiled. "Can't top that, can you?"

"Yuck. Vending machines? Seriously?"

"Nothing but snack cakes and candy bars and potato chips for thirty-six hours."

"Enough!" she said, holding out her hand to stop him. "You win. I can't top that because we had a catering ser-vice…even though I was barely able to hold a fork to eat my shrimp Louie salad."

"You just don't give up, do you?" he asked, leading her to the tiny kitchen in the rear where a fresh pot of coffee was awaiting her.

"Where I come from, giving up came with serious side effects," she said, pouring a cup for Reid first then one for herself.

"And where would that be?" he asked lightly.

"The streets," she said, quite surprised how that had slipped out so easily. Normally that was a piece of her life she didn't put out there for other people to know about. Too often they judged or pitied her. Gave her funny looks or were wary. None of which she wanted. "Growing up was rough. My mother and I had a hard time sometimes," she said, then took a sip. "I made it through, though, probably because I'm too stubborn to give up."

"Then I'd say stubborn suits you."

"Most of the time," she conceded. "Look, I need that shower you mentioned."

"Take all the time you need, as long as it's not longer than an hour. I've got clinic this morning after breakfast, and the kids will start lining up in about an hour. So I can watch Megan only until then."

"Clinic?"

"We do basic checks, vital signs, that sort of thing, just to make sure we're not wearing them out. Most of the kids are in early remission or recovery, and they're not always the best judges of how they feel, so we keep a pretty close eye on that."

"I could do that if you want to stay here for a while and rest, because you look about as strung out as I feel. And as that's my fault, the least I could do is some of your work."

"Sounds like an offer I shouldn't refuse," he said. "You take the clinic, and I'll stay here with Megan, get some paperwork done, do a supplies inventory, answer some long-overdue e-mails from parents interested in sending their kids to camp here."

"Do you have more than one session a year?"

"Actually, we run eight, various ages and stages of recovery."

"And you personally oversee them all?"

He shook his head. "I oversee the one Emmie attends. Which will probably change in another year or two when she'll be old enough she doesn't want Dad hanging around her all the time. For the other sessions I have some of the best medical help in the country come in." He smiled with pride. "People are generous."

"I'm impressed."

He shrugged off the compliment. "Kids need to be kids, no matter what their medical condition. Camp Hope simply facilitates that."

"And you're too modest."

"Not modest. Just grateful something like this worked out in my life. Like I told you, I was a real screw-up before the girls."

"Then good for the girls for bringing out all the potential in you. Anyway, let me go grab a quick shower then... what, exactly, will I do in clinic?"

"Vitals, a few meds."

"Anybody on chemo?"

"No, we don't do chemo here. Our kids have, for the most part, already gone through that stage a time or two. Although giving chemo's an option for the future because even kids who are that sick need a diversion, which Camp Hope would give them. Right now we just don't have the facilities for it. Someday, though...maybe a chemotherapy facility. Who knows, maybe even an entire hospital devoted to leukemia.

"Anyway, right now we do follow-up therapy with drugs for nausea, and a couple of our kids are getting prednisone and methotrexate. It's all basic stuff, pretty much. Each kid has a chart. Medicines are stored away according to the child." He handed her the key to the medicine storage. "So check their ID with the chart and, well...you'll figure it out.

"Betsy can come in later and help after her morning

sickness has ended for the day. Just let me know if you need her, and I'll give her a shout."

"Basic stuff," she repeated. "I guess I find it difficult to believe you'd leave me alone with your kids. You don't even know me."

"The Internet's an amazing tool. I know what I need to know. As in do you want me to tell you what color dress you wore when you received your Surgeon of Distinction award last year?"

"I don't like awards and accolades."

"So you said in your acceptance speech. Oh, and it was black—with sequins. Nice look."

"Yeah, well, I prefer scrubs." With that, she turned away and headed for the door. Keera stopped by Megan's bed on the way out though and straightened her blanket. "I'll be back in a little while," she whispered. But the child didn't so much as stir, so Keera tiptoed away.

"Good morning, Doc Keera," the first boy said, as he held up his banded arm for her to read his name.

"Good morning." She looked at the band and smiled. "Gregory Carson. So, you get…" She glanced through his chart to see what was ordered for him.

He gave her a quizzical look. "Weight, temperature, blood pressure, pulse," he said. "And a pill for my nausea. It's what we all get, except the pill. I still need it. Some of the other kids don't."

"Really?" Gregory was astute. Very much on top of his condition. Which impressed her more than she'd been expected to be impressed.

He nodded. "Every day while we're here. Then I go to the doctor once a week when I'm home. Sometimes twice, if I'm not feeling well. I'm in early recovery, so they need to make sure nothing is changing."

The child was so matter-of-fact about his condition and, more than that, his whole life situation, that she wasn't even sure how to respond. "How old are you?" she asked him.

"Seven and a half, but you can consider me eight, if you want to." His broad grin revealed a missing tooth.

"Well, since you're *eight*, I think you're old enough to take some responsibility for yourself, like recording your own pulse, maybe taking your own temperature, and weighing yourself. The more control you take over your physical condition, the better off you'll be." Her check of him revealed his blood pressure, temperature and pulse to be normal. Weight consistent with the past several days. A little under his normal but not losing.

"Does that make sense to you?" she asked, as she recorded the numbers in his chart.

"I—I don't know. Isn't that what a doctor's supposed to do?"

"Or a nurse. Or your parents." She looked up from the chart and smiled at him. "Or, you, if you think you're old enough. I mean, almost eight…that's getting pretty old, you know."

OK, so maybe her doctoring approach was a little beyond his years, but it made sense that gaining more confidence in dealing with his condition would serve him well in the long run. Living with the idea that his cancer might recur had to be frightening, but spending every moment of his life depending on someone else to tell him he was doing fine had to be difficult.

Of course, she'd never had leukemia, never been chronically ill, but she'd spent too many years being dependent on someone else's conclusions about her, and it was such a helpless feeling.

"So, here's what we're going to do as soon as I can get

it squared away on the schedule—and only if you think you're old enough to take on some responsibility. I want you to come back over here to the clinic, and we're going to talk about making your own choices. Then, if we have time, maybe I can show you how to do some medical procedures. But only if you want to."

He frowned, not sure what to say.

"Do you want to do that?" she asked him.

"Yes, I think so," he said, sounding nearly as tentative as she felt taking the initiative. But it was a good idea. She knew it! Would have loved someone teaching her the right initiatives to take when she had been as young as Gregory.

"Good. So, do you have a computer with you?"

He nodded. "It's mostly for games."

"Games, and in a little while we're going to start using it to track what doctors call your vital statistics. Do you know what those are?"

This time Gregory shrugged.

"Don't worry," Keera said, patting him on the shoulder. "It's easy stuff. But it's also very important. So, about your pill…"

After she shooed Gregory out the door, she went through much the same process with the next child, Charlie. Aged seven. And Heather, aged eight.

"So what are you teaching these kids?" she asked Reid an hour later, after all the kids, including Emmie, had gone through their routine morning check-up, and those who needed medication were medicated.

"Yesterday we went over some of the physiology of leukemia. Talked about white blood cells and how they—"

"They're not much more than babies, Reid. They don't need the physiology lectures. What they need are the practical, day-to-day aspects of coping with their condition. They're all in some form of remission or recovery or whatever you want to call it, but they need to know what's normal for where they are in their recovery, and how to take care of some of their basic medical needs. Which I told a few of the older kids I'd teach them, if that's OK with you?

"And while I know you're so close to it, with your daughter in recovery, I think your tendency may be to baby them or protect them more than they should be protected."

"So you're here for one day and you know what's best for them?" It was said not so much in anger as in practiced reserve against the way he might really feel.

"That's not fair. I'm responding to a medical condition, and—"

"And you don't have a clue, Keera. Not a damn clue." Now the anger was peeking through, but only a little. "Last night you were pretty clear about how you don't like kids and now you're changing my program?"

"Not changing it. Just giving some of the kids a different option. You know, more control."

Reid took a deep breath to steady himself, then physically squared his shoulders. "OK, I know you want to help and I appreciate that, but these kids…they put all their trust in us, rely on us, and if you get yourself involved more than I asked you to, somewhere down the line one of these kids is going to put trust in you that won't be fulfilled.

"You can't do that to them, Keera. Medical procedures are one thing, but what you want to do is embark on a course that will change their lives in some way, and while I'm all for that, and would do it myself if I had time, the program this camp follows isn't about giving a few minutes of commitment then moving on. These kids depend on us, and you're about to step into the position of having them depend on you. Which isn't what you want, is it?"

He was right. She'd overstepped without thinking it through. She saw that now, and felt bad, especially as she was the intruder here. But her approach to medicine had never been laid-back. In fact, her approach to life had never been laid-back, and that's all Reid seemed to be—laid-back. Truthfully, her preference in men had always been for someone who was forceful. Of course, look what that had gotten her. Married to a man who had forced himself right out of their marriage and away with his mistress. Still...

"I didn't mean to do something I wasn't supposed to," she said. "And you're right. I don't want these kids relying on me then maybe getting hurt in the process. That's not what I meant to do."

"I know it's not. And to be honest, I'd love to expand my program here. But I don't have the means or the volunteers. Until we're larger, and can support larger programs, we're minimalists, and that's the best we can do."

"Then say the word and I'll tell the kids there's been a change of plans." She drew in a stiff breath as the sinking feeling set in that she was about to bite off way more than she'd ever expected to chew. "But I'd still like to do this, if that's OK with you. Because it is the right thing. Also because I promised and I don't want to let these kids down. So to prove how strongly I believe that empowering them over their conditions is the right thing to do, I'll..." Keera swallowed hard. "I'll stay for the week to follow through with teaching them. Only if you want me to, though."

"*Seriously?* You'd really stay and help?"

"Seriously," she said. Then instantly felt queasy.

"When I called you outspoken and opinionated, I guess I didn't know how much. But go ahead. You promised, and if the kids are expecting it, then we should give them what they're expecting." He grinned. Extended a hand to her. "Welcome to the staff of Camp Hope."

Or, in her case, Camp Hopeless, she thought as she

shook his hand. "So, this is how I'm going to spend my summer vacation." Keera watched Reid's face, couldn't determine what he was feeling. He had an odd expression, and she didn't know him well enough to read it, but she could only guess that he was wishing she'd never come here. "It's the right thing, Reid. I promise, they're old enough."

"As interpreted by the doctor who doesn't like children?" he asked.

"As interpreted by the doctor who was forced to grow up too young and take on responsibilities no child should ever have to face. But it got me through. My independence is what saved my life many times over. And while you might not agree with me, I sincerely believe that giving these kids a bit of independence over their situations will save their lives, too.

"Maybe not in dramatic ways. Or maybe it will be in a dramatic way for one of them. Who knows? But, whatever the case, it's going to count for something. And, yes, it's also being interpreted by the doctor who warned you she wasn't good with children. I am good with my patients, though. Damned good, Reid, because I learned my childhood lessons well."

"And never had time to be a child?" he asked, his voice now sympathetic.

"I didn't need to be a child." With that, she moved past him into the infirmary to spend the next shift sitting with Megan and planning her first lesson—*"Taking your temperature."*

Poor Megan looked miserable, lying there in bed, with a rash finally popping out on her. She was awake, though. Looking around. Alert. "Remember me?" Keera asked, keeping a sideways glance on Reid, who was trying very hard to seem busy with a supply inventory when she knew he was really trying to keep an eye on her. She didn't blame him. All things considered, she'd be doing the same if the situation were reversed.

Megan shook her head. "Want my mommy," she whimpered.

Keera didn't know how to respond to that so, instead, she said, "You came to visit me yesterday. Then I took you to play at the hospital, and we came here last night when you weren't feeling so well. My name is Keera. I was a friend of your daddy's."

"She was in a hospital daycare center?" Reid asked from across the room. "Exposing all the other children? Have you notified them yet?"

"You really want to be critical of me, don't you?" she said, smiling for Megan's sake, even though she was gritting her teeth underneath.

"You get high praise for surgery, but this isn't surgery, and I haven't seen enough of your style to know whether or not I'm a fan. But I'm giving you the benefit of the doubt here. You're out of your element, so that does start you off with a few extra points in your favor, since you're trying."

"Well, in or out of my element, I did call the hospital first thing this morning. Talked to the daycare director, let her know. Offered all the apologies I could muster. Unlike you, she wasn't grumpy about it. She said contagion happens all the time with kids and they simply look at it as a way to bolster young immune systems."

"You say that with a lot of indifference."

"No. I said it with a sigh of relief because I really don't like going around spreading infectious conditions everywhere I go. Especially here, where these kids have compromised immunity. But as far as the center goes, I got lucky because the director told me the children are all vaccinated before they're allowed in, that they sanitize the entire area several times a day, so not to worry."

She frowned. "Are you OK, Reid? Yesterday you weren't this...testy. In fact, you weren't even this testy earlier this morning. Is it because I suggested a program?"

"No. I'm just not a big fan of change."

"But I thought that's what you wanted for Camp Hope. Growth. Change."

"It is, but I don't have to adjust to it easily. That's just me. Kicking at progression when I'm the one egging it on."

"We do get used to our ruts, don't we?"

"Sometimes a rut isn't such a bad place to be. When Emmie was sick, she'd have these periods where she wasn't as bad, maybe not even sick at all, and I found myself praying to stay there. I didn't want to move forward, or sideways or backwards, for that matter. That one spot was..."

"Safe?" she asked.

He nodded. "Even though there was always the possibility that tomorrow might be even better, if today wasn't so bad, I didn't want to move away from it."

"Uncertainty can be paralyzing. When I was a child, nothing ever stayed the same in my life, and I think I was like you. If it worked, I didn't want it to change. But life changes every time we blink our eyes, doesn't it? And for Camp Hope, I was that blink."

"You're welcome here, Keera. I'm sorry your little girl is sick, but we'll manage it. It all just disrupted my routine, which..."

"Makes you grumpy."

He smiled. "Welcome to my world."

"We all have our quirks. You're likely to see my grumpiest come out if my surgical instruments aren't lined up a certain way on the tray. Or the wrong music gets played. I have a sequence I follow, never vary it, and if someone changes that, for any reason…" She shrugged. "Let's just say it can get ugly. I'm not mean, mind you, but I'm very demanding."

"I can't picture you any other way. Look, I'm sorry, Keera. Sorry I came at you so abruptly this morning, and I'm mostly sorry about my reaction to what's really a good idea. Because you're right, these kids do have to take responsibility for themselves, but sometimes when I look at them, all I see is…"

"Emmie. Who's spent most of her life being dependent on her daddy. I do understand that, Reid. For me it's a practical matter, and for you it's personal."

"What's personal is she doesn't need me so much any more. Which scares me, because at the end of the day I'm a father before I'm anything else. And it has nothing to do with her leukemia and everything to do with it. Maybe it's also because I don't know what normal's supposed to be. The three of us really don't have that in our family."

"Is being a single dad that difficult?"

"Yes and no. Because there's never been a mommy in the picture, we make it work the way it needs to. As they say, it is what it is. But I'd be lying if I told you that doing this alone is easy, because it's not. When the adoption became final, the judge congratulated me and told me single parenting is the new normal. Not sure what that's supposed to be, though."

"One person's lack of normality is another person's normality." Keera smiled sympathetically at Reid. "And as far as Emmie goes, she's seven. Trust me, what she's going to need from you has only just begun. And that has nothing to do with her medical condition." She turned her attention back to Megan, who'd dozed off again. "But what she's going to need…"

Her voice trailed off because Keera knew. Dear God,

she knew in all the ways no child should ever have to know. Love was the start of it, which Reid had in abundance. And protection. And guidance. None of which she'd ever had given to her.

But Emmie, Allie and Megan would all need room to grow and develop as well, and that was something she'd created for herself because no one else had ever been there to help her. It was something Reid would eventually have to create for his daughters, like it or not, in spite of Emmie's physical condition. And something someone would have to create for Megan.

"Do you suppose if I wandered over to the dining hall, I might be able to beg a scrap of toast or a sandwich? Seems I haven't eaten since…" She thought for a moment. "Lunch yesterday. Except for an apple on my way here last night."

"That's an option. Or there's my kitchen. I wield a pretty mean toaster. And I have jam…"

"Please say strawberry!"

"Allie's favorite. Can't be without it."

"Then, by all means, lead me to Allie's favorite. I need a little fortifying before my first group of kids expect me to teach them the intricacies of taking a temperature. And maybe a couple of scrambled eggs, if you've got them."

"With green peppers and onions?"

"In my fondest dreams!" She smiled. "Oh, and, Reid? Don't worry. As fussy as you are over your daughters, I'm sure your girls will keep you in first place until they meet the boys who will steal their hearts away from you."

"Like I really wanted to hear that," he said, on his way out the door to go and fix Keera's meal.

Fifteen minutes later he returned with a tray complete with eggs, toast, and orange juice. Keera couldn't remember when something had smelled so good. Something about being at camp made her ravenous, and this was a perfect brunch. "You hungry?" she asked Megan, wondering if the child might eat a piece of toast.

Megan shook her head.

"Would you eat a small piece with strawberry jam on it?"

Apparently the bribe of strawberry jam caught her attention, because Megan nodded tentatively, then proceeded to eat an entire half a slice of toast and drink a small glass of apple juice before she slid back down into bed and rolled over on her side.

"You're persuasive," Reid commented.

"Strawberry jam is persuasive. I'm merely the means to that jam." She pulled the blanket back up over Megan and returned to finish her own food.

"So, how did your father manage it when you started to not need him as much?"

"He didn't," she said without a hint of emotion. "In fact, I was the daughter of a single mother. No daddy in my life. Not even in absentia. My mother…she wasn't interested in lasting relationships, I suppose you could say. Men came and went, none ever stayed."

She glanced at her watch. "I promised to squeeze my class in between agility training and lunch, if you could stay here with Megan for about thirty minutes. Or maybe one of the volunteers…"

"Sally Newton said she'd be glad to sit with Megan when we need her. She's a retired schoolteacher, loves the kids with a passion. Had leukemia herself when she was a child. So let me give her a call as I need to go and oversee agility."

"Am I making you late?"

"That's fine. It takes about ten minutes to get the kids settled down anyway, so I'll be just on time." He was finally feeling less stressed than he had all morning. Basically, he liked Keera. Liked her strength. Or, as some might call it, her brute force. And she was a force to be reckoned with, make no mistake about it.

He did have to admit, though, that he wasn't sure about her ideas about the children. On the surface it sounded good, and what she wanted to do with the children seemed reasonable, because he was all for these kids taking responsibility for various aspects of their health, even at their young ages. Keera seemed to have an agenda, though. She'd alluded to a rough childhood and needing her independence to get through it.

Still, there was something bigger. Something deeper. Maybe something to prove? And that's what worried him a little because the only agenda here was giving these kids everything they needed to be a kid in recovery. Simple plan with a single purpose.

He wasn't going to stop her, though, because he did see the value in it. And maybe when he got to know her better, he'd be a little more trusting. *Provided* he got to know her better. Which he hoped he would.

"Well, Dr. Reid, for a pediatrician you're a pretty darned good cook. My full stomach thanks you for the wonderful breakfast, or lunch, or whatever it was."

"My culinary skills thank you for the compliment. And just so you'll know, I can make a pretty good grilled cheese sandwich, if you're hungry later on."

"Good to know, just in case. Anyway, let me go sit with Megan for another ten minutes, then if you could ask Sally to come round?"

He nodded on his way out the door, stopping first at the sink to scrub his hands.

"And, Reid, the class is the right thing. I'm glad you're going to let me try it. I know you're worried, but I really believe these kids should take part in their care, and I want to get started because there's so much to teach them and I've only got a few days."

"I'd be lying if I didn't say I was concerned, because I am. Yes, it's important to empower them, but it could also be said that because their lives are so overwhelmed with their conditions they don't need to do anything more than they already do. You know, give them time to be children."

"How about giving them time to be responsible children? Because they do have to go about their lives differently, and you can't deny that. That's not robbing them of their childhood, though. It's only adding another layer to it."

"You don't ever give in, do you?"

She smiled. "Not unless I'm backed into a corner."

"No corner here. Although I'm going to warn you that for a woman who doesn't like kids, you're waging a mighty tough battle on behalf of these kids. Could it be the facade is cracking a little?"

"I don't have to like kids to want to do the right thing by them."

"You're right, you don't. But battles are waged because of passions, and you're waging a battle for them, Keera. Seems like someone's trying to fool someone, doesn't it?" He gave her a wink then grabbed a paper towel to dry his hands. "Now, let me go find Sally."

"Is her little girl sick like Emmie used to be?" Allie asked. She was sitting on the step outside when Reid left the infirmary.

"Aren't you supposed to be in arts and crafts?"

Allie rolled big, sad eyes up at him. A gesture that always melted him right down to nothing. Even at five, she knew that. "I missed you."

"And I missed you too, Miss Allejandra Lourdes Reid.

But you need to go back to arts and crafts." He scooped the child up into his arms and walked across the compound with her, heading to the building where Allie should be occupied with finger-painting and sculpting with modeling clay, while the older children were involved in basic agility exercises on the obstacle course. "And, no, Dr. Murphy's little girl isn't sick the way Emmie was. Do you remember what I told you about something being contagious? How when some people get sick, other people can get sick from being too close to them? What Emmie had wouldn't make anybody else sick, but what Megan has can make people get sick if they get too close to her, which is why you can't go inside the infirmary. I don't want you getting sick."

"Will you get sick, Daddy?"

"No." And this was where he didn't want to launch into the explanation of vaccinations and how some illnesses, like measles, you'd only catch once. Which he'd had. "Doctors have special ways to protect themselves."

"Good," she said earnestly. "Because I don't know how to take care of you yet."

"Yes, you do," he whispered, as he headed down the back steps and handed the child over to Ciera, the arts and crafts volunteer. Hated like hell watching Ciera take Allie away.

Turning away to head off to agility training, he saw Keera watching him from the infirmary window, and wondered why someone like her didn't like children. What had she missed out on in her life that had scared her off so badly from what he believed to be one of the fundamental joys of life?

"You just don't know you like them," he said to himself. "But you will. Another few days here, and you will."

# CHAPTER FOUR

"HOW DID IT GO?" Reid asked, catching up to Keera, who was crossing the compound, her arms loaded with supplies, on her way back to the infirmary.

"Pretty good. We learned all about thermometers, what a body's temperature indicates, and how to take and read temperatures. I had them taking each other's temps, and I think there may be a few budding doctors in the group. Including Emmie. She's quite a little leader."

"As in bossy?" he asked.

"As in taking charge and being helpful. She's a sweet little girl, Reid. You're doing a good job with her. Oh, and she and Allie and I have a date for lunch in a little while. They want to show me something. Sally said she'd sit with Megan, so I hope that's OK? Because I asked the cook to pack us a little picnic. You're invited too. Something about the wading place."

He smiled. "The water's nice there. Not very deep. And so clear you can see the bottom."

"Well, apparently I need to go wading, and as I've never been, I've got able volunteers who want to teach me. All with your permission, of course."

"Something about being around a strong woman seems to be bringing out the best in my girls."

"I'm not overstepping the mark, am I?"

He shook his head. "They asked me first. I said yes."

"And you're coming?"

"I'll try. I need to do a physical on one of the kids, but that shouldn't take too long."

"Something wrong?" she asked.

He shook his head. "Physician request. It happens all the time."

"Good, then I'll see you at the wading place. But be warned, we might be talking *girl* things most of the time."

"See, that's the part of single parenting that's tough. They need a woman's touch, and it's just not there. I don't have a sister near by, and my mother and dad are in South America right now, running a medical clinic in Ecuador. No aunts or female cousins either."

"No girlfriend?"

"Had a fiancée for a while, but she didn't like the idea that I adopted a sick child. She thought it would take too much time away from her. And she was correct about that. It did. So she was right to dump me. Haven't really had time for a social life since then."

"Which leaves two little girls without a female influence in their lives."

"Right. It's amazing what you can pick up in the parenting magazines, though," he said, grinning. "I've got a whole stack of them, if you'd ever care to…"

She shook her head. "I was talking to social services a while ago, and they're going to place Megan with a nice foster-family as soon as she's medically able. And don't even begin to think I can be as generous as you and take her in, because I can't.

"She's the…well, she's not the reason my marriage ended, but she was one of the factors. My husband's secret baby. So while I know it's not her fault what her daddy did, and I totally understand that she's the only true innocent in a very ugly situation, I can't spend the rest of my life looking at her, knowing that…"

"That you failed?"

"Yes, I failed. But that's not even it. I didn't even know how to try. And Megan's that reminder."

"So you'll let her go to some stranger because of something you perceive as a lack in yourself."

"Fostering that little girl has never been an option for me. My lifestyle won't allow it."

"Yet you'll go on a lunch date with my little girls. That seems to conflict with your *no-kids-allowed* rule."

Stepping into the infirmary, Keera dropped her armload of supplies on the nearest desk, then spun to face Reid. "You did a good thing adopting your girls. You're a good man. A generous man. A very caring man. And that's all you.

"But I don't want the responsibility, OK? I feel sorry for Megan. My heart is breaking for her and I want to make sure she gets into a good situation. But that's not me. I work. I sleep. Then I work some more. Nothing there's going to change because I don't want it to change.

"So don't think that because I've agreed to give you one week of service here, and go on a picnic with your girls, that I'm going to come out of it with some big change of heart. My life is fine the way it is. It's not empty. I'm happy."

"And pretty damn defensive about it, too," he added.

"And pretty damn honest about it, Reid. I know what I can and can't have, and what you have…" She shook her head. "I can't have that."

"But can you have dinner? Tonight, after the kiddies are asleep? I've got enough people on call to cover us, I'm sure Sally will be fine spending an extra couple of hours looking after Megan, and there's an amazingly elegant little café about ten miles down the road. It sits on top of a mountain, and they say the sunset is breathtaking."

"In scrubs?" she asked. "Because that's all I have to wear."

"There's a little mercantile on the way. We could stop and do some shopping. Maybe for Megan as well, because she'll be up and out of bed by tomorrow or the day after."

An evening out with a man sounded surprisingly good. So did shopping for Megan. And while she and Reid didn't see eye to eye on a lot of things, she really liked him. Was curious to see him away from his element. "This isn't you asking me out on a date so you can get some personal satisfaction that you broke down my code a little, is it?"

He laughed. "Are you always so ungracious about what's just a simple gesture of friendship?"

"Not ungracious." She tilted her head up to look him straight in the eyes. "Just cautious."

"I don't want anything from you, Keera, except the days you promised me. Because, believe it or not, I'm as *cautious* as you are. Maybe even more, since I've got my daughters to consider."

"Then I suppose it's a date." She smiled. "Cautiously speaking."

"Eat one more bite," Keera encouraged Megan. Who would have guessed one bowl of soup could have taken so long? But Megan was being stubborn, and Sally was standing ready to swoop in and take over as soon as Keera admitted defeat.

"Maybe she's not hungry," the older woman said. "It doesn't always do to force children to eat if they don't want to."

"She's going to get too weak," Keera protested. "And

it's just soup." She felt totally defeated, failing at such a simple task.

"But does she like the soup?" Sally asked.

It had never occurred to her that Megan would have food preferences. Which just went to prove, even more, that she wasn't the one to take care of this child. "Do you like the soup?" she asked Megan.

Megan shook her head, indicating an adamant no.

"Then is there anything you would like to eat?"

"Strawberries," she said. "Want strawberries."

"Which would be toast with strawberry jam." She looked at Sally. "It's what she had for breakfast."

"And it's what she'll have for lunch. Let me run over to the kitchen, and I'll fix some."

"Is that all you want?" Keera asked Megan.

This time Megan nodded in the affirmative.

"They do have their opinions, even at that age," Reid said on his way in, as Sally flew out the door. He pulled out a stethoscope and listened to Megan's chest. "Bet you like peanut butter, too, don't you?" he asked the child, once he pulled the earpieces from his ears.

"Yes," she said. "And bananas."

"Then we'll see if we can find you some peanut butter and bananas for dinner. OK?"

Megan nodded.

"See, it comes naturally to you," Keera said. "And I don't have a clue."

"Well, I have an advantage. Not only am I a father, I work with children every day of my life. Before I went to med school I didn't have a clue, but I've learned. And that's what it's about, Keera. Learning. Trial and error, in my opinion, is the best way to figure it out. Oh, and she's not as congested as she was last night. I think the medicine is working. And as she's eating, it's time to yank the

IV. You want me to get rid of that nasty old tube in your arm, Megan?"

"It itches," she said, nodding.

"Well, we don't want you itching."

Keera stood back and watched the natural interplay between Reid and Megan, and admired the way he was so at ease with the child. It was like he knew exactly what she wanted. In a way, she envied that as it was a rapport she didn't have with her own patients. If ever there was someone who'd been put on this earth to work with children...

"Try," he prompted Keera.

"Try what?"

"To find your way in. One little thing—that's all it will take."

"Except I don't have a clue what that one little thing is."

"There's no specific one little thing. Like I said, trial and error. Think about something children love. Something you loved when you were a child."

She thought for a moment then smiled. "Megan, after you eat your toast and strawberries, would you like..." she glanced over at Reid, then back at Megan "...ice cream?"

Megan's eyes lit up. "Yes," she squealed.

"Then ice cream it is," Keera confirmed, feeling the same sense of accomplishment she usually felt after a long, grueling surgery.

"And you think you don't have a way with kids," Reid said. "One bowl of ice cream is going to go a lot further than you thought. Just wait and see."

"One bowl of ice cream doesn't make me parenting material. And even with that, you had to prompt me."

He laughed. "When Emmie was younger, and on chemo, getting her to eat was maybe the hardest thing I had to do, other than standing around and feeling so helpless. Bribes were good, though. What worked as often as not was a good honest talk with her about the importance of taking a bite or two. Kids her age…even kids Megan's age…do understand, and sometimes we forget that because we're so busy trying to convince them in a child's logic. But they live in an adult world as well, and you have to keep that in mind."

The adult world she'd known as a child had been harsh, cruel. Unfair. "I think it's better to let them live in their childhood world as long as they can, because when the adult world takes over…" She shrugged, then turned to Megan. "I'm going to get your ice cream now. Vanilla or chocolate?"

"'Nilla," she said, then smiled for the first time since Keera had known her.

Beautiful little girl, beautiful smile. She did look like her daddy, though. Especially the depth she saw in Megan's eyes. Kevin had always had that depth, had always seen things so deeply. She thought about their marriage as she dashed to the kitchen to scoop up the ice cream. It had started so well, all the regular hopes and dreams and plans. Then had ended so badly she'd blotted out most of everything past the midway point.

How did something like that happen to two people? It scared her because while on one level she understood how they'd grown apart, on a much deeper level she didn't understand it at all. Which meant she was doomed to repeat her mistakes—the reason why she wasn't going to do that ever again.

"Where'd you go?" Reid asked her, when she returned with the ice cream, only to find Megan munching away quite happily on a piece of toast.

"What do you mean? I'm right here."

"I don't mean in the literal sense," he said. "There was this look in your eyes when you came back in."

"Ex-husband stuff. Megan looks like him."

"And that bothers you?"

"Not really. But I was wondering how a marriage could go as wrong as ours did. There was a time when we were good, but it didn't last very long. And from the point we started losing, there was no way to get any of it back."

"But did you try?"

"Honestly, I don't know. Wouldn't have mattered, because he was already so invested in his other life."

"But you still loved him?"

"I'd like to say yes, or even no. But I don't know if I ever did, at least in the way you're supposed to when you commit your life to someone." She glanced down at the ice cream, and smiled. "But now I have his little girl, and I'm sure she'd prefer her ice cream not melted. So..." She stepped around Reid but stopped. "I'm not an indecisive person, Reid. Most of the time I'm probably more forceful than most people you know. Which is what made the end of my marriage so bitter, because it turned out that's the trait he hated most in me."

"As they say, 'One man's mistake is another man's opportunity,' or something like that."

"Only if she wants to be another man's opportunity. But I don't." And she meant it. Some people were meant to be alone, and she was one of those people. Although there were times she wished that weren't the case. "See you in a little while at the wading place."

The wading place turned out to be a wide spot in the pristine stream that ran serenely through the property. Surrounded by trees and rhododendron bushes, it was very isolated, and so clear and perfect that the pebbles on the bottom glistened like diamonds in the sun. Before they were even settled into a picnic spot, the girls had their shoes off and were wading across the shining pebbles, the water only coming barely above their ankles.

"I think I was just an excuse to come here," Keera said to Reid, who meandered in a few minutes after she was settled on the blanket. "This is…beautiful. It's a shame Megan couldn't have come along, too."

"Another day," Reid said, dropping down beside her. "To be honest, this spot is one of the reasons I bought the whole camp. I was looking at three different places for sale—two were former camps that had closed, and one was an undeveloped piece of property. I'd known for a while this was something I had to do." He smiled as he began to remove his shoes. "It came to me in a dream one night. Inspired, I think, by a picnic I'd taken the girls on earlier that day. Emmie was pretty sick, but she'd really enjoyed her time outside, and I thought about all the other kids with leukemia who barely ever get to see the light of day.

"Then I remembered all the fun times I had as a kid when I'd gone to camp…one thing led to another and I literally had a dream about being a camp leader.

"It stayed with me, so after a while I started looking into what it would take to set up a camp. The answer was, pretty much everything I had. But money's replaceable, you know. Children aren't. So I started looking, took the girls along with me. And when we were walking over this property and stumbled on this spot…well, you see how the girls reacted. What could I do?"

"Other than buy it for them and go broke."

Reid smiled. "So I'm flat broke for a while. No big deal. I have a good medical practice, and I'll earn it all back, and then some, over time. The thing about the camp is this is where I really learned to not think in terms of material possessions so much as value or worth. It changed my whole outlook on life. Allowed me to give something to the girls that goes beyond what money can buy."

"Allows you to give that to other people's girls and boys as well. I like the way you're putting your medical skills to other less traditional applications. I'm basically a traditionalist. I need four walls and surgical instruments, and anything else throws me for a loop. But this is…well, in a sense I suppose you could call it a hospital, because it does tend to the needs of children who need tending."

"A hospital without walls," he said. "I like that. So, are you coming wading, too?"

"Are there things in the stream that can bite me?"

Rather than answering, Reid nearly doubled over laughing. "Maybe tadpoles," he finally managed, "but I don't know if they even have teeth."

"I'm serious. I've never really been a nature girl, and sometimes I'm not so brave in the unknown."

He pointed to his daughters, who were busy splashing each other.

"OK, I get it. If they aren't afraid, I shouldn't be afraid."

"And I won't desert you, Keera. If I see a menacing tadpole swimming in your direction, I'll shoo it away."

"My knight in shining armor," she said, as she slid out of her sandals and rolled up the bottoms of her scrub pants.

"It's hard to believe you've never been wading," he said, extending a hand to help her up off the ground. "Makes me wonder what other kinds of things you've never done that I might be able to show you."

She took his hand and let herself be pulled to her feet. But once she was up he didn't let go of her hand. Instead, he held it as they walked towards the stream. Like lovers, they strolled along the path, hand in hand, shoulder to shoulder, as if they'd done it before. Or should have done it before. "I've lived a sheltered life," she admitted at the stream's edge. "You know, die-hard city girl."

"Well, welcome to the country, city girl." He led her into the water. She clung to him even harder.

"It's not like a wading pool," she said as she relaxed.

"No, it's better."

"Yes," she almost purred. "It's much, much better." But she wasn't sure what, exactly, was better. Was it the water or the fact that she liked holding Reid's hand? Or the fact that he still wasn't letting go? That was the part she liked best, she decided. Definitely the part she liked best.

"It's only for a week," Reid said, laughing as Keera picked out the tenth outfit for Megan. Clothes, plus dolls, accessories, all kinds of little-girl things.

After a little wading and a quick picnic, they'd returned to camp and she'd spent the rest of the afternoon with Megan, reading to her, playing games, even watching her sleep. Something about the child pulled her in. Maybe it was the fear she saw in her eyes, or that look of being a little girl lost. A look she was sure she herself had had most of her childhood.

Her heart did go out to Megan, more and more with every passing minute, because each minute brought the poor child closer to the reality that awaited her. A reality Keera couldn't change. So even after an afternoon spent renouncing the material things in life, Keera was having a good time trying to compensate for Megan's terrible losses by piling new material things on it. And, admittedly, she loved little-girl shopping, and wished desperately Megan could have come along to be part of it.

"I want her to have nice things wherever she goes to. Wherever social services puts her."

"I imagine they'll gather up some of the things she already owns," he said.

"Which will only remind her of what she's lost. No, I'll buy her everything she needs for her new life."

"But what if she has a favorite doll or book? Doesn't she deserve to have those with her?" He liked this fierce attitude she was taking up on Megan's behalf. Whether or not she wanted to admit it, Keera was investing a little of herself in that child, and that was a good thing. Although Reid wasn't about to fool himself into believing that she would keep the child, as she'd been brutally honest about that more than once.

"What she deserves is to move into her new life without sadness left over from the old one," Keera said as she grabbed the cutest little pink, fuzzy pajamas off the shelf, looked them over, then went back for an additional pair in yellow.

"So, what about you? We've been here an hour, our reservations are in twenty minutes, and you're still in your scrubs. Remember how we came here to buy you something respectable to wear to dinner tonight?"

"Twenty minutes?" Keera rolled the shopping cart at Reid, then spun away. "Go ahead and start checking out," she called back to him as she literally ran to the ladies' department. "By the time they get most of it rung up…" The rest of her words were lost as she rounded a corner, while he stood in the middle of the aisle, simply smiling. Losing her had definitely been her ex-husband's mistake. Huge mistake!

It was a thought still on Reid's mind a few minutes later when Keera skidded into the checkout line behind him, her arms loaded with…well, he wasn't sure. Dresses, underwear, shoes? No way she could have done all that shopping in such a short time. But, as it turned out, she had, because as the last of Megan's items were scanned, Keera added her armload to the end of it. After she'd paid, she grabbed one of the bags and headed straight for the ladies' room, from which, a minute or two later, she emerged looking remarkably put together in her little black dress, matching shoes, and...make-up.

"How did you do all of that in...?" He glanced at his watch, exaggerating a shrug.

Laughing, Keera brushed her fingers through her hair. She'd pulled it out of its no-nonsense ponytail a minute earlier, but hadn't had time to run a brush through it, and it looked like the mane of a wild horse. Untamed, a bit flyaway. But she was dressed otherwise, and actually felt pretty good about the way she looked. "Years of practice, street clothes to scrubs in a minute flat. My best record." She grinned. "This took a little longer."

"Longer? I think if you could patent the formula, husbands all over the world would buy it. I know my dad and my brothers-in-law would."

"Just a matter of practice," she said, taking several of the bags from Reid then following him out to the car. "My mother and I had to...let's say we had to be on the move at any given second, so I learned early on that I either had to be fast or things got left behind." Including her, several times.

"Well, you look amazing," he said, eyeing her from head to toe. "Can't imagine how you'd improve on it if you'd had, say, half an hour."

"Primping for half an hour's a waste. In that same thirty minutes I could have a patient totally prepped for an incision. Or have that incision made, and be well on my way to exploring an occluded artery."

"Nice dinner conversation," he said, holding open the car door for her.

"Except we're not at dinner yet." Stepping in, she smoothed her dress and tried to pull it down a little over her legs, but it was a bit short, riding halfway between her knee and thigh when she stood and scooting up even shorter than that when she was seated. A fact she caught Reid checking out. Surprisingly, she liked seeing that he liked what he saw. "And I promise to be on my best behavior as soon as we arrive at the restaurant."

"Coming from you, that almost sounds boring."

"Maybe it will be," she said, as he climbed in next to her. "So, you're sure it's OK, both of us being away for the evening? And your girls?"

"Tonight I'm running second place to cook's basset hound, who's the dorm guest for the evening. Besides, I promised the girls I'd tuck them in later."

"Do you read them bedtime stories?"

"Sometimes. Or we just talk. They tell me about their day, I modify my day for them. We talk about their plans for the future. Those kinds of things."

"Sounds nice."

"Didn't you ever do that with your mother?"

"My mother was…she was usually working when I went to sleep. We didn't have a lot of time for the traditional mother-child kind of thing. Or, in your case, the daddy-daughter thing."

"Too bad, because I enjoy it. Probably more than my girls do. For them it's a bedtime ritual, but for me it's about staying in touch and keeping myself involved in their lives."

"Lucky little girls," she commented, settling in to watch the view.

All those years ago, when she'd moved to Tennessee, it had been to get away from the harsh realities her life had slammed her with. Being the daughter of a prostitute hadn't been easy. Neither was big city life when you were a little girl alone. So she'd promised herself someplace nice when she got away, and that was the first thing she'd done.

She'd loved Tennessee, loved the mountains, the blue skies. Even loved the occasional bear that had come raiding her trash cans at night. For Megan's sake, she hoped the child would have an adoptive family who stayed in Tennessee. A family like Reid's.

Or...would he adopt her? Would he want one more daughter to tuck in at night? Traditional families were good and social services usually held out for those, but untraditional or single-parent families were good, too. Just look at Reid's family. As a child, she'd have loved having a parent like him instead of what she'd had.

So, maybe seeing if Reid would adopt Megan would be worth pursuing. Just not now, though. She'd have to wait until he knew her better and got attached to her. She'd also have to wait until she knew if Reid even wanted more children. Although he certainly seemed like the type who would.

"But overall a situation like yours wouldn't do for me. Like I said, I'm not cut out for it. Half the time I'm not even home at bedtime, and if someone expected me to tuck them in or read to them, they'd be out of luck."

"You really don't want children, do you? I've known a lot of women who say they don't but they eventually change their minds. Especially when their biological clock..." He stopped, exchanged a quick glance with her. "None of my business, right?"

"I don't hide the fact, Reid. Never have. So it doesn't matter whose business it is, because it's simply a statement of fact. And even when my so-called biological clock starts ticking, nothing's going to change."

"Even if you meet the man of your dreams who wants children?"

"*Especially* if I meet the man of my dreams, because he's not going to want children. That's part of my dream."

"You're a hard case, Dr. Murphy. And you'll be quite a challenge for some man someday."

"I take that as a compliment, Dr. Adams." So maybe the harder she pushed the child away, the more he might be inclined to keep her. Because she truly wanted Megan to have a daddy like Reid. All children deserved to have a daddy like Reid.

"The mountain trout is wonderful," she said, taking the last bite of her food. "Everything about this restaurant is wonderful. Do you bring the girls here?"

"No, they prefer pizza. But every now and then I need some adult food, and an evening without the girls, so The Trout is usually my destination. An hour from Sugar Creek gives me a nice drive, time to relax. Nice scenery along the way. Then all the ambiance here."

"I guess I'm surprised you'd leave them."

"Sometimes you have to." He grinned. "Parents have lives too, you know. And Brax—my partner's father— loves taking the girls for pizza, along with his grandkids. They have a pizza night once a week."

"So, how does parenting work with your medical practice?"

"My partners, Deanna and Beau, have a couple of children, and Brax is always ready to babysit. So they were more than happy to throw my girls into the mix when I moved there. Like I said, there's pizza night, and Brax is always willing to stand in if I'm called out."

"Sounds like you got lucky."

"I did. We originally lived in Memphis—it's where I

did my residency, then I stayed. But that's where Emmie was so sick for so long, and I didn't want her to always have the reminders around her. So, when her medical care scaled back to where it is now, we started over. Little town, big life. It's perfect for us. And with the camp being so close…" He shrugged. "It works."

"So, have you ever considered adding a Mrs. Adams to your family? I know you said you're not dating right now, but what about the future?"

"She'd have to be awfully special. Like I said, I'm pretty protective of my girls, and I don't want to upset the balance only to find it doesn't work."

"Like my marriage. Definitely a balance out of whack there."

"But you got out before there were kids." He swallowed hard, looked embarrassed. "Well, except the one."

"Except the one," she repeated.

Keera was so easy to talk to. In fact, Reid had never known someone he'd wanted to open up to the way he did with her. Maybe it was because she was safe. Because she wasn't out to snag a doctor the way so many women in his past had been.

With his past couple of dates, the subject of marriage had come up almost immediately. Marriage, the future as a couple, building a house together…first-date nonsense in which he didn't want to indulge. Besides, if they'd known what they were trying to snag—a doctor whose every last cent went to his camp or to his daughter's medical care, who worked more hours than any one should ever have to, who lived in a rented, cramped cottage rather than owning a sprawling mansion—there wasn't much there to snag.

He chuckled to himself. It wasn't the lifestyle he'd thought he'd have when he'd committed to being a doctor. No, it was a much better one. He wouldn't trade a second of it, hard knocks and all.

"So, have you given any thought about what you're going to do with Megan once she's better? Keep her until social services place her, give her up right away?"

"Hope that social services can find her a good situation as soon as possible. Or maybe that's something I could do. She deserves someone who wants children. Someone who wants to be a mommy or a daddy, together or separately."

"Which is still not you?"

Keera laughed. "Which is *still* not me. Good try, though."

"She's an amazing little girl. Smart. Very pretty."

"And very much the product of an affair that was, in part, responsible for the demise of my marriage."

"Ah, yes. The illegitimate child."

Infuriated, Keera spun to face him. "Don't you dare call her that! Whatever her parents did isn't her fault and she shouldn't have to…" Stopping, she saw the amused look on his face. "OK, I get it. You're testing me. Trying to see if I might have feelings for her. Or if I would come to her defense. Well, yes and yes. I'm not heartless, Reid. I just know who I am."

"You're sure about that?"

She hunkered down into her chair and folded her arms stubbornly across her chest. "Absolutely. I've had a lot of years coming to terms with me, and I know exactly who I am and what I'm about."

Sometimes, though, she did wonder how much she really knew, or didn't know. After all, she was spending a week at a camp for kids, even enjoying it, and nowhere in her knowledge of herself would she have ever thought something like that could happen.

"Look, it wasn't my intention to turn this evening into

a battle. How about we get off the subject and talk about something else? Because the cherry cheesecake here is the best in the whole state, and I don't want you missing out because I've said something to get your gut roiling. So…" He tried coaxing her with a smile, and only succeeded in getting the scowl off her face.

"Maybe the weather? Or the fact that I'm backpedaling on my opinion of what kinds of responsibility I think the children at Camp Hope can handle?"

No luck moving back to neutral territory yet. He tried again. "Medical school? We could talk about that. Like what made you decide you wanted to be a doctor?" He watched, saw her face soften a bit. Let out a sigh of relief. "I'll start off by telling you mine then you can tell me yours."

"Mine isn't much to tell," she said, relaxing a little.

"Neither is mine. I came from a large family, three sisters, two brothers. I was the oldest, always in charge of looking after the younger ones. My parents are both doctors, by the way. Dad's a surgeon, Mom's an anesthesiologist. So I grew up in the life. As it turned out, they produced a family of doctors. I have a brother and two sisters still in med school, one brother in his surgical residency, and a sister who's a full-fledged obstetrician."

"Which means your parents were good role models," Keera commented.

"They were. Still are. But it was a hectic life growing up, never being able to plan anything when they were on call. Never being able to count on them coming to school events."

"Don't tell me. You played clarinet in the band."

"Almost. I was the quarterback on the high-school football team. It got me a scholarship to college, so I played in college, too."

"Sounds like a charmed life," she said.

Her face was so impassive he didn't know what to make of it. "Not charmed. We were like any other family, with our ups and downs."

"Which is why you know how to be a good father now. Because you understand all that."

"Some of it. Although I'll admit my girls present me with challenges I could never anticipate. The thing is, when I ask my mom for advice, she usually smiles and tells me to go with my instincts. Like that helps."

"But she's right. At the end of the day, all the parenting books in the world are only words when you have two little flesh-and-blood human beings to deal with. Children, I might add, who haven't read the parenting books and don't know the proper way you're supposed to be parenting them."

"Good insight for a non-parenting type."

Finally, she smiled. "I grew up poor. Good insight was about all I had to get me through."

"You mentioned that your mother worked a lot?"

"Sometimes days in a row."

"And no father, so what about brothers and sisters?"

She shook her head. "It was only the two of us."

"But you got to medical school. How did that happen?"

"Getting an education wasn't easy because we moved around a lot for my mother's work. Anyway, I liked knowledge, so when I wasn't able to go to school I'd find a library and read. Anything, everything.

"I really liked the sciences and found out, early on, that I loved biological sciences. From there it was reading about human anatomy, and the next logical jump was medical articles and textbooks. I practically memorized *Gray's Anatomy*, and by the time I was fourteen or fifteen there probably wasn't an advanced physiology book

I hadn't devoured. Knowledge was my…everything. And all that reading got me a college scholarship."

"I'll bet you passed your med-school exams without batting an eyelid."

"I did," she admitted. "I was told I was one of the top scorers in the country. And the rest, as they say, is history. I made it through, found my job, secured my future."

"And your mother. Is she proud?"

Keera shrugged as she picked up her coffee cup. "I haven't seen her since I was thirteen. The state took me away from her, put me in foster-care, except I was too old for most foster-homes. I went to a few, but they didn't work out so I spent the remainder of my formative years in the guardian home as a ward of the state."

This wasn't what he'd expected. Not at all. "I…I don't know what to say."

"There really is nothing to say. My mother was a prostitute, and by the time I was thirteen she was expecting the same from me. We lived in cardboard boxes in alleys and in the backseats of abandoned cars. Sometimes we'd find a vacant house, or rent a room where the roaches and bed bugs were thicker than the nicotine stains on the ceilings. Sometimes she'd be gone for days, and I'd have to scrounge for food in garbage cans.

"That was my life, Reid, until the authorities caught up to us and took me away. Something I don't talk about because it's in the past."

"I'm so, so sorry." Now he understood her need for independence. "But you've done an amazing thing. Most people—"

"Most people would have let it beat them down, but I didn't. It's no big deal. In fact, the only big deal I want to talk about now is that cheesecake. And if it's as good as you say, I want two pieces. One for now, one to share with Megan tomorrow."

For once he didn't know what to say, didn't know how to respond to her indifference. But maybe he didn't have to. Keera had given him insight into the strongest woman…no, make that the strongest person…he'd ever known. But she wanted to take cheesecake back to Megan, which meant that maybe he'd be able to help her find an even deeper insight into that same person—the softer side of her. Because whether or not she wanted to admit it, it was there.

And whether or not he wanted to admit this to himself, he thought he might be a little in love. Or at the very least head-over-heels infatuated. "Waiter, seven pieces of cherry cheesecake, please. Two for here, five to go." He glanced over at Keera, who once again wore her typical impassive expression. "One for you and me tomorrow when we give the girls their cheesecake."

"Cheesecake two days in a row. Sounds decadent."

"Decadent but good." He reached across the table and took her hand. "And for what it's worth, I like your strength. But you do have a gentler side, Keera. You just don't let it out."

"Because I don't want it to get out. Softer sides are what get you hurt."

"Or what make you human."

She shrugged. "Softer sides aren't all what they're cracked up to be. Personally, I like being tough around the edges and all the way through."

"But I see you, Keera Murphy. And I know better."

"Then quit looking so close, Reid, because if you think there's anything more there, you're only seeing what you want to see."

"Or what you want to project."

She pulled her hand from his. "What I want to project is who I am. You know, what you see is what you get."

"And what I see is someone who isn't comfortable with her softer, gentler side."

"What you're seeing is someone who doesn't have a softer, gentler side."

"Is that a challenge?" he asked, smiling

"It's a fact."

"We'll see," Reid warned, as the waiter placed the cheesecake on the table. "We'll just see." Truly, he was looking forward to what he would see.

# CHAPTER FIVE

"Ok, you're looking at it upside down," Keera said. "Turn it over, take a look at the numbers, then tell me what you're seeing."

Gregory studied the digital thermometer for a moment, frowning at first as he pondered it, then finally smiled and pronounced, "Ninety-eight point six."

"Good! Now, tell me what that means." Megan was inside asleep, within earshot, and Keera was teaching today's class outside, on the infirmary's front steps. Her hospital without walls. Or, in this case, her classroom without walls. When she'd been homeless as a child, she'd loathed being outside. Now she couldn't get enough of it.

"It means perfect," Gregory said, smiling. "I don't have a fever."

"Excellent! So, what do you do next?"

"I write it down in my journal?"

"That's right. But how?" she asked him.

"I write the date first, then the time, then the temperature."

"Very good!" she exclaimed, actually feeling pride in his accomplishment. "I'm proud of you for learning so quickly. So now I think that tomorrow you'll be ready to move on to taking your pulse. Remember what I said about that? That it's the number of times your heart beats per minute."

"And normal is from sixty to one hundred. I read that on the Internet last night." Gregory beamed from ear to ear. "I texted my mom, told her I want to be a doctor like you and Doc Reid. Do you think I can do that, Doc Keera? Do you think I can be a doctor when I grow up?"

"I think you can be anything you want to be, Gregory. And if that's a doctor, you'll be a very good one."

He stood up from the chair he'd brought outside and crossed over to Keera, who was sitting on a step, and gave her a great big hug. "That's from my mom," he said when he backed away. "When she texted me back she said she was happy, and to give you a hug for her."

Surprisingly, Keera was touched by the simple gesture. She'd taught a little boy to take his temperature and it was like she'd taught him a valuable life skill that opened up a whole new world of possibilities for him. Who knew? Maybe it had.

Simple accomplishments and small steps to a child were life-changers, she suddenly realized. Too bad she hadn't had an adult in her life to show her how that was...*how anything* was when she'd been Gregory's age.

Somehow, fighting to survive took precedence over just about everything else because, back in the day, her small step had been a full belly and her simple accomplishment a place where she could take an honest-to-goodness bath. Of course, those life skills had taught her how to survive, hadn't they? And they'd made her as tough as nails. All in all, not bad skills to have in the life she lived now. At least, that's how she chose to look at it. But she was still very proud of Gregory.

"His mom called me a little while ago," she told Reid a couple of hours later. "She was actually crying, she was

so elated over a silly little thing like taking a temperature. It was…"

"Gratifying?" Reid asked her.

"I was going more for embarrassing. But I suppose it
was gratifying." She was sitting at the front work station
in the infirmary. Reid had made coffee and he'd poured
two cups for them. Megan was awake, sitting on the side of
the bed, playing dolls with Sally and intermittently watching a video cartoon.

"When you wake up in the morning and don't know if
your child will survive the day, even the silly little things,
like taking a temperature, can make you grateful." Sitting
down across from her, he took a sip of his coffee. "I had
some pretty rough days one time when Emmie was having
a particularly bad crisis. She'd been on chemo for a while,
it was her second time, and she'd lost her hair. That, plus
she didn't have enough weight on her body to sustain her.
She was always so cold. Nothing made her warm up, and
she'd lie in bed, under the covers, and shiver so hard…"

He paused and swallowed hard, and Keera reached
across to lay a comforting hand on his arm. But said nothing, because her words would only intrude on a moment
that required nothing more from her than compassionate
support.

Their eyes met for a moment, stayed locked on each
other until Reid finally broke the silence. "Do you know
how beautiful your eyes are?" he asked, totally out of the
blue.

"My eyes?" she asked, keeping her hand in place.

"Beautiful eyes. Like Emmie's are. But when she was
sick…the only way I can describe them is hollow," he continued after a moment. "They were hollow and so distant. It
was like my little girl was slipping away from me, Keera.
She was getting further and further away every time I

looked into her eyes, and there was nothing I could do to get her back. I think that was the first time I really, truly thought I m-might lose her." He pulled his arm away from her hand, and reached up and stroked her cheek.

"But I remember sitting there at her bedside one afternoon, watching her look out the window at a little bluebird that had landed on the ledge. It was looking in at her, and she laughed. Her eyes were bright again, so full of life just for that single moment—a moment that froze in time for me. And her laugh—I hadn't heard it in months, but when she laughed, well, I can't begin to describe how grateful I was to hear it. It gave me hope.

"For the first time in I don't know how long I finally let myself think about a future, about how things were going to get better for her. A simple laugh from Emmie or making plans to be a doctor from Gregory, it's the same thing. It's about hope.

"And for a kid like Gregory it's everything because he's never made plans for the future, like most kids do. You know, things like when I grow up I want to be a firefighter or an astronaut. This was the first time his mother has ever heard that from him, and it's because you gave him a different kind of hope for his life. With that one simple accomplishment. You showed him he can have a life."

"I don't know what to say," she murmured, quite touched. "In surgery I know I make a difference, like save a life, but it's never quite so…I guess the word is *profound*. They thank me, I wish them well, and it's all well and good. It's what I'm supposed to do because I'm good at what I do. But it doesn't affect me one way or the other."

"Because you won't let it affect you."

"Because I don't want it to affect me. If I were to get involved on the kind of personal level you seem to be involved with your kids on, I would lose objectivity. Become too vulnerable to things that could, ultimately, diminish my work as a surgeon. And I can't afford to lose that objectivity because, for me, that's what saves the lives of my patients."

"It's not your objectivity that saves lives, Keera. It's you. Who you are."

"Who I am is what I do, and I'm fine with where I am in that equation. You know, one equals the other. It's good. I'm used to it, and it works for me like your life works for you." She smiled as she gripped her cup. It was a sad, reflective smile, though. "But you really don't like the way I live my life, do you?"

"I'm not judging you, Keera. Please don't think I am. But I think the bigger question is: do you like the way you live your life? Because I'm not sure you do."

"What I like is the result I get at the end of the day when my surgeries are over with and my patients are stable."

"But isn't there some loneliness in that result? Because without my girls, no matter what I've done for my patients, that's all I'd have if Emmie and Allie weren't there to remind me that I have a purpose outside being a doctor."

"Being a doctor is my purpose, though. The only one I want. And the result I get doesn't come with loneliness. More like…well, to use your word, I experience gratification because I enjoy my work, and I also enjoy the ability to make things turn out the way they should."

"You're talking about results, though, not people. Do you ever see your work in terms of the people involved? Or having something more than work-related gratification? Maybe being happy? See, for me, being a pediatrician makes me happy. Sure, it's gratifying, but I want more than that. And being a pediatrician, working with kids the way I do, I find it."

"Isn't enjoyment the same as being happy, though?"

He shook his head. "I enjoy a good ice-cream cone, and maybe for the moment or two I'm eating it I feel a certain sense of happiness. But that's not the deep, abiding kind of happiness I want, or need, in my life."

She paused, thought about his question for a moment, then shook her head. "Then if I don't have the same kind of happiness in my life that you have in yours, does that make me shallow? Because in terms of my patients, good results do make me happy. I want all my patients to have a good result.

"But as personal involvements outside my professional life…if I did get involved personally then my objectivity would fly out the window, and I can't afford that in order to go after that elusive happiness you're talking about. People trust me for a certain outcome and it gets right back to how I'm gratified I can make that happen. Like it or not, that's who I am."

Reid reached across the table and laced his fingers through hers. "That's who you *think* you are. But there's more to you, Keera. There's a genuine quality I don't think you recognize, but I can see it and when you're ready to see it, you will."

"Or maybe I won't. You're the real deal, not me, and we can't all be you, Reid." She wanted to be offended by his comments and presumptions and especially by his intrusion, but there was nothing about Reid she could be offended by because she was right. He was the real deal. Genuine, caring. And she liked his touch, liked the way his friendly gestures toward her seemed so natural.

In fact, they seemed so natural she feared they could be become habit-forming. But she wasn't reading anything into them other than friendship because that's the kind of man he was—the kind who made friendly gestures, squeezed an arm, held a hand, without pretense or thought.

"You have a good life. Probably a great life. One most people would want. But that's not me, Reid. If anything, I'm probably the most self-aware person you've ever met, and the one thing I'm most aware of is me. I am who I am, and I accept that, even for the things you see as limitations. Or character flaws."

"Yet you must have had a romantic notion once, because you got married. And marriage is all about seeking happiness. You know, happily-ever-after."

As reality sank in and she realized how much she enjoyed his lingering touch, she unlaced her fingers from his and gripped her coffee cup with both hands.

"Happily-ever-after is a myth, and when I got married I was in love with the idea of being in love. It's everywhere you look, everywhere you go. You know, you have to be in love, or be nothing or no one. Television and movies revolve around it; the advertising world makes billions selling it. Mothers teach their daughters that to be fulfilled you have to grow up and marry a Prince Charming, and the bestselling books on the market are all about finding that one true love.

"So, yes, I bought into it for a little while, but I don't think I ever really loved him. Not in the traditional sense. If I had, I would have been more involved in our marriage, and fought harder to keep it." She shrugged. "But I wasn't involved, although he really should have divorced me rather than cheating. Because I believe in absolutes, and in a marriage that's one of them. If you do the deed, you do it the right way or you don't do it at all."

She pushed back from the table. "Look, I promised Megan we'd play some games, and right now Sally's having all the fun with her. It's my turn. And I was also thinking that now, as she's feeling better, maybe we could expand our horizons a little since she's not too happy about being confined. So, you're the pediatrician. How long before she can go outside?"

"Today, if she's up to it. But as the contagion period is four days before the rash and up to four days after, I still don't want her around the children. So if you could take her out somewhere east of the hospital—we don't have activities out there today, and it's a pretty area. I think she should enjoy it."

"Yes, if she's up to it. Or maybe we could sit out on the porch for a while. Whatever works best for her. And you? What's on your agenda for the rest of the day?"

"Nature hike down to the river, a picnic lunch, then some well-managed, very tame river-rafting. I have a company coming in this afternoon that specializes in river adventures, and the kids are going to have their first outing in a rubber raft. The gentle kind, not the white-water kind that goes over rocks and waterfalls."

"Sounds like fun. They're going to enjoy it. I know I would have when I was their age." She smiled. "You take very good care of these children, Reid. They're fortunate to have you."

He certainly knew how to make a difficult childhood bearable, and while her childhood couldn't compare to what all these kids had gone through, she wondered how she might have benefited from having someone like him in her life when she had been a child. Yes, these children, and especially his daughters, were very, very lucky.

"It's not just me. A lot of people are generous with the kids. Tomorrow we're going on a zip line. You know, when you harness up and zip across a wire from tree to tree?"

"The kids are all up to it?" she asked, genuinely surprised.

"It's the training facility. Very tame, very safe. And like the rafting, I think they'll love it because it's something they haven't been able to do before. Then in a couple of days my medical partner's coming in, bringing in a few of his horses for the kids to ride. Horseback riding is always a highlight around here and we try to get it in once with every camp session."

She laughed. "I'm wondering if you're wasting your time being a doctor when camp counselor is so definitely your calling."

"The way it is now, I've got the best of both worlds," he said, grinning.

"Yes, I think you do."

And he seemed so happy whichever world he was in. That was remarkable, and she wondered how he did it because all his worlds were so vastly different. It spoke of the quality of the man, she supposed. And Reid Adams was quality through and through.

Yes, Reid Adams was definitely the daddy she wanted for Megan. She knew that for certain and now all she had to do was find a way to convince him of it. After all, for a man who loved being in a family, like Reid did, one more child shouldn't matter to him. In fact, he should welcome the opportunity…she hoped.

"He's really a very nice man," Keera explained to Megan as she settled the child into the porch swing. The compound was empty this afternoon, except for a couple of volunteers puttering around in the gardens, and it surprised Keera how much she missed the activity that had surrounded her these past few days, even though she really hadn't been out into it very much. And the children. Yes, she actually did miss them as well.

"And a very good doctor. What I'm hoping is that I can convince him to take you in, then you could come here whenever he does, and you'd also have two sisters."

Of course, at her age Megan didn't understand all this. In fact, she was dozing off, her head resting on Keera's lap, so not only did she not understand, she also wasn't listening.

But for Keera, hearing her plan expressed aloud made it all the more real to her. While she couldn't keep this child, and social services didn't seem to be making any headway in placing her in a suitable situation, Megan was a sweet little girl who deserved better than this limbo she was in right now. Keera wanted the best for her, and every time she thought about that, the only thing that popped into her head was Reid. He *was* the best. But the arrangement had to be by his choice and not her persuasion. That much she was adamant about. Reid had to do the choosing.

Of course, that didn't preclude her from making the right choices for Megan that would help her get chosen for ever.

"So, what I have in mind is that tomorrow I'm going to go into town and ask him to watch you for a little while, so he can get to know you better now that you're not feeling so bad. Then the day after that I'll figure out a way to have him spend even more time with you. I think that, given the way he feels about children, once he gets to know you, he won't want you going into the foster-care system, the way I don't want you there either.

"So when that happens, I'm going to have to rely on you to turn on your girlish charms to help woo him into daddyhood thinking. Think that's a good plan?"

Of course, Megan didn't respond. She was now sound asleep, well past the dozing stage and into a deep slumber, with her breathing heavy and even. Smiling, Keera pushed back the blonde hair from Megan's forehead and lightly stroked her cheek. So much innocence, she thought. At that age, her own innocence had already been taken from her, by the way she'd lived, by the things she'd seen. She didn't remember being two, but life around her must have made its impression on her. Even on someone so young. Even on Megan.

"It's not going to be easy for you," she whispered, "but I'm going to make sure you get what you need. I promise, Megan. I may not be the one to take care of you, but I know who is. And you'll never, ever have to go into the foster-care system." Easy words, tough challenge. But as a child of the system herself, she knew the life she didn't want Megan to have. "I promise," she said again, as Megan curled up in a precious little ball, hugging a teddy bear. It was such a cozy sight, it almost made Keera wish she could be a part of something like it.

A flash of the two of them together crossed her mind... mother and daughter. Nice thought, but not practical for either of them. Especially not for Megan. And Keera knew better, knew and fully realized her potential as well as her limits, and understood that all this domesticity wasn't in her. Maybe in fantasy it might be there, but not in reality.

In some ways, she was her mother's daughter. At least in those aspects. Megan deserved so much better than that. So much better...

"You up to a short walk?" she asked Megan later, after she'd rocked her in the swing for an hour and had caught herself enjoying the relaxation. It wasn't something she did too often—simply sit and do nothing. Admittedly, it had been nice, just existing without an agenda or a to-do list. No patients to take care of, no worries. Just listening to the birds, taking in the magnificent scenery.

"Mommy," Megan whimpered in response. "Want Mommy."

"I know you do, sweetheart. I know you do. But right now you have to stay with me for a little while longer." She didn't know how to tell the child her parents were dead.

Telling anyone a loved one had died was the worst, but in her world she dealt with adults. How to do it with a child, especially one so young, she didn't have a clue. "Let's walk over to the woods…" Instinctively, she felt the girl's forehead, not like a doctor but more like a mom, to see if she had a fever. Which she didn't. "Or we can go back inside. Whichever you want to do."

Megan didn't respond so Keera took her by the hand and led her off the porch and in the direction of the woods. She didn't expect to go very far, and was surprised how Megan resisted when she'd decided it was time to turn back. So they trudged on, only now Keera was carrying the child, pointing out the very few things she knew about nature…birds, flowers, trees, none identified by their proper name. But Megan was two, so Keera wasn't too concerned about that.

"Look at that tree," she said, putting Megan down and pointing to a giant pine. "It grows needles, not leaves. And pine cones." She bent to pick up a fallen pine cone then placed it in Megan's hands. "See how pretty that is? You can keep it if you want to."

Megan did look at the pine cone, clenching it tight in her little hands.

"That's the seed, Megan," she explained. "A whole tree can grow from that." She felt a little silly explaining that to a child too young to understand, but it seemed like the right thing to do. "You plant seeds in the ground, and they grow trees and bushes, even grass and flowers. But this one will grow a tree just like that one." She pointed to the pine. "Isn't it beautiful?"

"I'm surprised she's up to it," Reid called from the trail behind them.

Keera spun, surprised to see him there. "I thought you were rafting with the kids."

"They're rafting, I'm not. Sometimes I can be…over-protective, let's call it. The kids don't need a doctor hovering over them all the time, and that's really who I am to them. So I stayed through the picnic lunch and made sure they all understood what they were supposed to do. Then let some of the camp volunteers take charge. After that I left." He grinned. "And nobody noticed I was gone, they were so excited to get on the water."

"Poor Dr. Adams, feeling so under-appreciated," Keera teased. She glanced down at Megan, who was beginning to look weary, leaning hard against her leg and clinging. "I think you're going to be needed here shortly to carry her back, if that makes you feel any better."

"Needed maybe. But only for my brawn."

And a very nice brawn it was. "I'm surprised she's held up this long. But it's been fun, hasn't it, Megan?"

In response, Megan shrugged, then hugged her teddy bear and her pine cone even tighter. "She's missing…you-know-who."

"I expect she would be. So, what have you told her?"

"Me?" Keera exclaimed. "I can't tell her. I don't know how. I mean, she's too young to really understand, and I expect you've got to use the right words so you don't cause some sort of trauma that would pop up later in her life. So maybe her social worker will have a better idea of how to do it." *Or you,* she wanted to say. But she wouldn't be so presumptuous. Still, if he volunteered, she wouldn't turn him down.

"But she's been asking so she's going to have to know."

"That's one of the reasons I'm not suited to the job. I don't know what to do."

"Child experts say be honest and simple in your explanation."

Keera shook her head. "Not now. Maybe I'm not a child

expert, but I don't think telling her…well, you-know-what is a good idea when she's still not feeling well. There has to be a right time for it, and I suppose you play that by instinct."

"Which in you seems pretty good."

"Or resistant. Because I don't want to." She lowered her voice and whispered, "I don't want to break a little girl's heart."

"Maybe you're right."

"I know I'm right, Reid. Now's not the time."

"Then I bow to your instinct, because it's better than you think. Look, I'm going to run down to the river, it's only a few hundred yards, and wave to the kids as they float by, then we'll go back to the infirmary."

He scooped Megan into his arms, and urged Keera to follow him. "Just because they don't need me hovering doesn't mean I can't hover a little bit. Right, Megan?" he asked the child.

She responded by pressing her head to his chest, and it looked right. Like they were meant to be together. In fact, it looked so right it gave Keera some hope that her plan might just work.

Reid knew exactly what Keera was up to. She wanted him to fall in love with Megan then keep her. It was a good plan, and so far Keera wasn't pursuing it too aggressively, for which he was grateful because while the idea of adopting other children had crossed his mind more than once, he wasn't sure if he was ready for it. But he knew that's what Keera wanted, even though she was about as subtle in her pursuits as anyone he'd ever seen. It was there, though, in her eyes, in the way she looked at him, the way she looked at Megan. Good heart in the right place, but a heart that was a little trussed up.

Whatever the case, he had faith in her maternal instincts—more than she did, apparently. So he'd go along with her plan for a while, let her continue to think she was pursuing him, but take every opportunity that presented itself to turn that around on her without her knowing he was doing it, and pursue her into mommyhood.

Now, that was the perfect plan.

Could he take in Megan, though, if his plan failed? Adopt her, make her his third child? Maybe that was something to consider, a second-best plan. God knew, he knew how to raise a two-year-old. That, and his girls were secure, so in his future he could see fitting one or two, maybe three more children into his family.

In fact, he'd already approached his daughters with the idea, and they'd put in their order for all girls. Dr. Reid Adams and his half-dozen or so daughters. It brought a smile to his face. And since he wasn't rushing toward the altar any time soon, adoption seemed the best way to make that large-family dream happen. Then if, somewhere down the line, some woman wanted him, and his daughters...

But that wouldn't be Keera, by her own admission, so he was steering clear of her in that regard, as much as he didn't want to. Steering clear and hoping to hell he could keep his head, his wits, and even his sanity, because Keera was... He thought about all the things he wanted and she was all of them except for the one thing. *And that one thing was huge*. She didn't want to be a mother. For him a family with lots of kids wasn't negotiable, especially as he had already started on the course and was loving it.

"Here they come," he said to Megan, as three big, yellow rubber rafts came floating gently around the bend in the river. "Can you wave to them, Megan?" To help her, he raised her right hand and waved it for her.

"Looking good!" he shouted, as the first raft of children waved and yelled at him. They were all animated, yelling, clapping, wearing orange life-vests and black helmets, having the time of their lives. Briefly, Reid glanced over at Keera, who stood there unaffected, her arms folded across her chest. Staring at the…well, not at the children. And not at Megan. "Bet I can beat you to the next turn in the river," he shouted.

"Can't," one of the boys shouted back.

"Can too," he shouted in return, then passed Megan back to Keera. "Looks like I've got to take up the challenge. Sorry, but I think you're going to have to carry her back to the clinic. She looks like she could stand a good nap, probably sooner rather than later."

With that, he sprinted off into the trees, leaving Keera standing in the woods holding Megan in her arms. He didn't go too far, though. Just far enough that she couldn't see him duck behind a large tree and watch her turn and hike back to her cabin, toting one very heavy little deadweight.

*"I'm on to you, Keera Murphy. And I know I'm right about you. Deny it all you want, but by the end of this week you're going to be that child's mother through and through."*

OK, so maybe his talk was more confident than the way he actually felt, but in his heart he knew that if she only let herself go…

The shouts of the kids coming from downriver prised him away from watching her, and Reid turned and ran to his next rendezvous point. *"Yes, Keera,"* he said, as the kids floated into view, *"you're going to discover—"*

"Dr Adams!" came the unanimous shouts from the lead raft. "How'd you get here so fast?"

"Because I know how," he said, but not to the kids, as

his mind was still on Keera. Sure, he might know how with the kids, but did he know how with her?

Hell, he didn't even know why he wanted to know how. But he did. In a big way.

# CHAPTER SIX

"I'LL BET YOU'LL be glad when life gets back to normal,"
Keera said, settling onto the porch swing outside the infirmary door, while Reid was seated in the chair across
from it. "I really am sorry I'm disrupting you so much. I
mean, you're not even getting to see your girls as much as
you probably want to."

"Emmie and Allie are having the time of their lives
without me hovering over them, which is what I usually
do when I have the chance. And it's not like they were
staying here with me in the first place."

"Yes, but you snuck in visits in your free time, and now
you're barely getting any free time."

"Well, Emmie, I think, is particularly glad to get away
from all that togetherness for a while. She's growing up,
needs her space, even though I'm not ready to give it to
her yet. Here, or back home in Sugar Creek. So you being
here is a blessing in disguise for them."

"Knowing when to let go—one of the challenges of
being a parent, I suppose."

"One of the many. Lately, though, the big thing has to
do with fashion. I'm not good at it, don't have a clue. I remember the way my mom used to dress my sisters, but…"

"Old school," Keera chimed in. "I'll bet she dressed
them old school. I mean, we come from a day when col-

ors coordinated and matching patterns with similar patterns made sense. Now anything goes as long as it's fun. Nothing has to coordinate, nothing has to match if you feel good wearing it and it expresses...you."

"Don't I know. And what I'm finding out is that my daughter is hiding her clothes. *'Oh, Daddy, that's so gross,'* she always tells me. Then I never see the outfit again. Did you do that when you were a kid?"

"I never had enough clothes that I could hide something. But I definitely had my preferences." She smiled, remembering how she used to love window shopping.

She and her mom had never gone in to buy, and most of what she'd worn back then had been shoplifted from various thrift stores. It had always been her job to distract the store clerk while her mom had stuffed her coat with whatever she had been able to lift in mere seconds.

Usually it hadn't been pretty. Usually it hadn't even come close to fitting. Sometimes it had been in good shape, though, and she'd pretended it was brand-new. "Want me to take your girls shopping? Let them express themselves to me rather than having Daddy foist his taste on them?"

"I thought you'd never ask. How about after the zip line tomorrow afternoon? I'll sit with Megan then that will free you up to take the clothing nightmare away from me."

If ever a plan had played directly into her hands, this was it. How perfect was that? Leave him alone here, let him bond a little more with Megan...yes, perfect. "Well, I've never been shopping for kids' clothing, except that once for Megan, but it can't be that bad, can it?" she said, laughing.

"Just wait until tomorrow. Then you'll see."

"Well, call me crazy, but I think I might be looking forward to it."

"I know I am," he said, smiling. "And the girls will be excited to have some female input rather than letting dear old Dad horn in on their fashion creativity."

"This is where someone might normally make a profound parenting comment, offer condolences, or say something to the effect that you're better at it than you think, but as I don't have any experience in childhood situations or parenting, I don't think I'm qualified."

"Sounds like a cop-out to me. Especially when I'm clearly drowning and need a lifeline." He faked a pained expression. "Or sympathy."

"How about dinner? I'll cook. Not sure how, or where…"

"How about we spend our separate time with our respective girls then meet up later when they're all tucked in, and have our own meal?" Pausing, he smiled. "I don't know how my parents did it, taking care of so many kids going in so many directions and still finding time for themselves. But they did, and I guess I never even gave it any thought until now. Because the thing I'd like to do most is go for a walk, take you down to the river, have a late-night picnic and spend some time relaxing under the stars. But you have your responsibilities, I have mine, and those responsibilities come first."

"Would have been a nice evening, though," she said, trying not to sound too dreamy, or too disappointed. Because she could picture the evening playing out, and it was so real she almost felt immersed in it. But being immersed in an evening with Reid was a dangerous thing, because she was beginning to like him too much, and like was tantamount to love or other places she couldn't go. "But you're right, work and children come first," she said, shaking herself back into the true Keera Murphy mode.

"Maybe we could have sandwiches on the porch?"

"Or skip the sandwiches, and just spend some quiet time," she suggested.

"Quiet time is good, too. But what just happened here?"

he asked. "How did we go from planning a meal together later on to whatever you just said?"

She laughed. "I was thinking in practical terms."

"And what about eating a meal together isn't practical, as we've already done it before?"

"The timing. After you do this, after I do that. Get the kids settled down, finish the day's worth of charting, plan tomorrow's class. Relaxing without a purpose after all that just seems nice. At home I'd just go straight to bed, but here relaxing seems almost required, doesn't it? You know, sit back, watch the stars, listen to the bullfrogs court their lady loves. Just breathe."

He pushed his glasses back up on his face and grinned. "Then it's a date to relax and breathe."

"You are different, Dr. Adams. Like nobody I've ever met before."

"Because men always want something else from you?"

Most of her life they had. Until she'd perfected her demeanor and polished her defenses. Which had started at a very young age, and had only gotten better over time. "Yes, to a point. I grew up in a situation where there were always men coming and going. So I got my fair share of looks, and I knew what they'd want, given the opportunity."

"Which makes you cautious."

"I try to be."

"Do you assume every man is giving you one of those looks?"

"Not every man. But I don't need to waste my time distinguishing between them because I'm not interested. Been there, failed miserably at it, saw every one of my character flaws exposed, and realized I can't go near it again."

"Said adamantly."

"Adamantly," she agreed. "But breathing is a practical matter and I'm looking forward to breathing with you later on." To show him her practicality in the matter, she leaned forward and extended her hand to shake his. But when his smooth palm glided across hers, it wasn't only his palm she felt. It was also the thousand impractical goose-bumps that were suddenly marching up and down her arms, up her neck, down her back.

His response was simply to arch his eyebrows at her then stand up and walk away.

And her response to that? More goose-bumps.

"She's what?" Keera asked, totally composed.

"Chest pains. Shortness of breath. Rapid pulse, elevated blood pressure. She's in her cabin, sitting on the couch, refusing to budge, and seeing as you're a cardiac specialist…"

"Surgeon," she corrected. "And I can't come because I'm the only one here to sit with Megan."

"And I can't leave Clara alone to trade places with you." So they were in a spot. He in one spot, she in another, and never the twain shall meet. Which also described their lives, it seemed. "Let me call Sally and send her over there."

Keera glanced over at Megan, almost hating to leave her. They'd been reading stories, having a nice evening together. "Then I'll get some supplies ready. You keep her head elevated, give her an aspirin."

"No aspirin. She's allergic."

"Fine, just try and keep her calm. Keep checking her vitals. Are either of your girls with you, by chance?"

"Emmie is. Why?"

"Send Emmie over here, and I'll give her an IV set-up, plus whatever drugs I can scrounge for a cardiac episode. Is Clara coherent?" Clara, the camp cook.

"Very."

"That's good. So hang up. Call Sally and I'll—"

"Daddy sent me," Emmie said. She was standing in the doorway, a little out of breath from the hard run across the compound.

"So fast."

Emmie nodded. "Miss Clara is having a heart attack," she said so matter-of-factly it rattled Keera. It also reminded Keera a little of herself at that age—all seriousness, no innocence or typical childishness.

"Look, you go back out on the porch and wait. OK? We don't want to expose you to Megan's measles."

"Measles are a normal childhood disease," Emmie explained, without budging from the infirmary doorway, "but my daddy doesn't want me exposed to anything that will make me sick."

She raised a finger to Emmie to indicate she'd get back to her in a moment, then returned to Reid on the phone. "Look, Emmie's here, so I've got to go. I'll be there as fast as I can."

"Clara's not going to die, is she?" Emmie asked.

"We're going to do everything we can for her. Beginning with this." She grabbed a box of IV tubing and catheter, and a bag of normal saline from the supply closet. "Take this to your daddy."

"Could you talk to him, tell him I'm all better now? That he doesn't have to take care of me so much any more? Or keep worrying. That he needs to have some fun, because he doesn't. Not ever."

"He's asked me to take you and Allie shopping tomorrow. We'll talk about it then, OK?"

Emmie nodded on her way out the door, her arms full of medical supplies, and Keera stood there and watched her run across the compound to the cook's cabin. Only when she was inside did Keera leave the door and return to the locked drug supply to find whatever medication might be necessary to see Clara through her heart attack.

By the time Sally arrived, Keera had a fairly substantial bag packed, but before she left the cabin she took a moment to go over to Megan. "Look, I've got to go away for a little while. Sally's going to stay and read more stories to you, and I'll be back as soon as I can. I promise, Megan. I'll hurry back here as soon as I can."

"No," Megan said very quietly.

"I'm sorry, but I have to."

Big tears welled in Megan's eyes. Tears that surprisingly tore at Keera.

"She's going to be fine, Doctor," Sally said. "I'll get her settled down, and she'll be fine in no time."

"I hope so," Keera said, bending down to give the girl a kiss on the forehead. "But that doesn't make me feel any better."

"They're resilient at this age. Bounce back from disappointment very quickly."

Maybe they bounced back, but did they get over it? That's what worried Keera about Megan, because she had so much to get over in her young life. More than any child her age should have to worry about.

"Oh, and if you don't mind, as soon as Megan dozes off, I'm going to do the same in the bed next to hers. So take the night off if you'd like, because I don't intend to budge from this place until morning."

"Are you sure?"

"It's hard to keep up with these kids. I love them to death, but they're wearing me out. That bed there is looking pretty inviting."

"Call me if you change your mind."

"Not going to happen," she said, sitting down on the

edge of the bed with Megan. "Trust me, five minutes after Megan's having pleasant dreams, I will be too."

Keera gave the older woman a hug then headed to the door. But she took one look back before she left, saw Megan watching her. And she felt...just like a mother for an instant. A mother torn between her child and her duty. Which was why she couldn't be a mother for real, because duty would always have to win.

Sighing, Keera stepped out into the night then flew across the compound and entered Clara's cabin, to be greeted by Reid, who was wearing a troubled expression.

"She's not...?" Keera asked, stepping into the tiny entry hall.

He shook his head. "We've got it sorted out and I'm pretty sure it's indigestion. But I'm going to send her to the hospital to be looked at anyway."

"Then why the grim face?"

"Emmie told me she came into the infirmary and saw Megan."

"Just in the doorway. Which is probably not close enough to have been exposed, especially as she's up to date on her vaccinations."

"How could you have let that happen, Keera? You know I don't want these kids exposed—"

"I didn't *let* it happen," she interrupted, whispering because she could see Emmie and Allie peeking out of the next room at them. "She came in, I gave her the supplies and she left. It took place over the course of about a minute."

"She shouldn't have been in there for a full minute. Don't you understand? She's vulnerable. All the kids are vulnerable, with compromised immune systems in many cases, and I shouldn't have—"

"What? Let me stay? You shouldn't have let me stay?

Because you're right. You shouldn't have, and I shouldn't have accepted when you offered. But you did, and I did, and as a result Emmie was exposed to measles. She's healthy now, though. You're the one who said it."

"Healthy now doesn't mean she still doesn't have immunity problems. She does, and she's very susceptible to colds and flu and...measles."

"And her daddy's phobias. She wants to talk to me about it, Reid. She's pretty upset that you want to keep her so isolated. And I must say I'm impressed at the level on which she communicates. It's very adult. Maybe too adult." She looked past him, saw the girls still peeking out. "Like this. Suppose Clara *was* having a heart attack. They're in there, watching it. Did you know that? Talk about your daughters being exposed to something they shouldn't be."

He spun round in time to see his daughters scamper off into the kitchen. Then he went after them, took them to the rear bedroom in Clara's cottage and shut the door. "So you're giving me parenting advice now?" he said, once he'd returned to the front room.

"Not parenting advice. Just telling you that you can't always predict parenting the way you can't predict life. And also telling you what I think she's afraid to say to you. Emmie wants you to have your own life, Reid. She's worried that you don't because you're so fixated on her. I used to worry about my mother—all the bad things she did, all the bad situations she ended up in.

"I was too young to worry like that and Emmie's too young to worry about you the way she does. But it's up to you, as the parent, to change that for her."

"Easier said than done."

"Maybe so, but I'm right. And this is something I understand better than most. Look, you go wait with your daughters and reassure them about Clara's condition, and

I'll give you a second opinion about her heartburn. Then you can take the girls back to their dorm for the evening, and as Sally's settling in with Megan for the night, I'll fix us a late dinner. If you haven't eaten?"

He smiled. "You're back to cooking for me?"

"You've had a rough evening. It's the least I can do." With that, she pushed past him into the living room, where Clara was sitting up on the couch with her feet propped up and an ice pack on her head. "Dr. Adams said he believes you're suffering from indigestion. Mind if I take a look?"

Clara motioned her over to the couch. "I cook healthy for the kids, but I don't always eat my own cooking. Looks like those burritos got me this time."

Keera sat down next to Clara, took her pulse, blood pressure, listened to her heart. Blood pressure high, heart sounded fine. "The thing about burritos is they're good in moderation. But when your indigestion gets so bad it can be confused with a heart attack, that's when you have to reconsider your eating choices. Otherwise next time it could be a heart attack, which you might ignore because you think it's only indigestion again.

"And I don't want you ending up on my operating table, Clara. The kids here need you, need the way you cook for them and take such good care of them. So you owe it to yourself to take as good of care of yourself as you do them."

"I've never been a skinny person, Doctor," she said, sniffling. "I come from large stock."

"You can be large and still be healthy." She patted the woman's hand. "And I don't think you'd look right being skinny. Look, I don't know if Dr. Adams mentioned this, but we want to admit you to the hospital for the night for some tests. Just to make sure it's not cardiac related. If it is, they'll get you taken care of. If it isn't, and you're up to it, you can come back to camp tomorrow."

"What about breakfast and lunch? Somebody's got to do the cooking."

"Don't worry about the cooking. I know my way around a kitchen, if that's what I have to do."

"But we have different diets for different kids."

"If it's written down, I can read. All I want you to do is rest and let the doctors at the hospital take care of you. We'll figure out everything else tomorrow. OK?"

"You're not cold, like they're saying you are," Clara said, as the ambulance pulled up to the front of the cabin.

"Who says I'm cold?"

"Allie, but it came from Doc Reid. Only Allie interpreted it as meaning you needed a blanket."

"He thinks I'm cold?"

"That's what you want him to think, isn't it? You do kind of put it on, you know."

Maybe it *was* what she wanted him to think. Maybe it was the way she wanted the entire world to see her. Because there was safety in that frostiness. But it hurt, hearing someone say it out loud, because she wasn't cold deep down. She knew that. If only Reid knew that as well.

"So, what's the plan?" Reid asked. She was puttering around Reid's cabin kitchen. Looking pretty good at it. But she looked pretty good at everything she did.

"Looks like I'm going to be the camp cook until Clara gets back," she said, trying to sound as cold as he thought she was. "So I'm going to go over there right now and familiarize myself with the kitchen. Oh, and about that dinner I promised you." She pointed to a sandwich on a plate, sitting there alongside a glass of milk.

"That's it?"

"That's it," she confirmed in her best, and iciest, voice.

"You're angry because you've got to cook?"

"No, I'm angry because you decided it was necessary to discuss my cold demeanor with your daughter, who discussed it with the camp cook." Facing him, she leaned back against the counter and folded her arms across her chest. "Cold! Really? Is that what you think of me?"

"How about cold by design?"

"I'm not a cold person, Reid. Maybe reserved but not—"

"I didn't mean to offend you."

"Because you didn't think it would get back to me."

"There's that. But it was something mentioned the first night you were here."

"So this is where you're going to tell me you've changed your mind?" she asked.

If anything, she was blazing hot tonight, and sexy as hell. "Look, you're not an ice maiden but you do put on this air of chilliness. Which, by the way, I don't think is the real you."

"But why mention it to your daughter?"

"I was irritated that you'd barged in and disrupted my entire life, not to mention my camp. So I may have spoken in haste, called you a cold…"

"A cold what?" she asked.

"It wasn't meant for little ears. She accidentally overhead."

"A cold what?" Keera persisted.

"And I corrected myself, and left her with the impression you were cold, as in temperature-wise."

"A cold what?" she asked again. "Let me hear you say the word."

"OK. I called you a cold bitch, because I knew your intention was to leave Megan here and walk away. And I meant it. For a few minutes. Now I apologize, because I was wrong."

"Because you got caught?" she questioned, fighting

back a smile. He was kind of cute, trying to worm his way out of this one. He definitely looked like the little boy who'd got caught doing something he wasn't supposed to, and she couldn't help but be more endeared than enraged.

"Clara's fine," he said, trying to change the subject.

"She doesn't think I'm cold."

"We're back to that?"

"We never got off it." Walking to the fridge to put away the milk, she brushed past him and paid particular attention to their proximity because she didn't want to touch him, didn't want another epidemic of goose-bumps. But the intensity between them was suddenly making her nervous. She could feel the heat of his stare on the back of her neck, which was where her goose-bumps began again. Oh, to be cold at this precise moment, because she was feeling anything but.

How could any man make her so acutely aware of herself? Make her feel so self-conscious? Make her feel so vulnerable to thoughts she didn't even know he was having? But that she herself definitely was having?

In truth, he was awakening something in her that was a complete and messy surprise. Did she want this man? In the physical sense she was almost willing to admit she might. She was only human and, God knew, she did come with those needs like everybody did. Only she fought harder to keep them under control. So the really messy part here was how he'd got through the barriers.

Thankfully, she still had her controls in place so he'd only get so far. Which was as far as goose-bumps and a few straying thoughts.

"What I think is that you show me exactly what you want me to see, and believe. What I also think is that maybe you kid yourself about what you feel, even about who you are. Don't know why, not going to guess." He grabbed her arm and pulled her back to him. "But I have a confession of my own to make. I'm attracted to you. And when you talked about men looking at you...I looked."

She looked up into his eyes. Swallowed hard. "But we can control the urges, Reid."

"Because we want to or because we have to?"

Nothing in her wanted to because she liked the way he held her—his grip not rough yet not gentle. And she liked his dominance. It was firm but not unrelenting. "Because it's the only practical thing to do."

"Depends on your definition of practical," he said, pulling her up roughly against his chest.

Keera looked up, put her hands on the sides of his face to hold him where she wanted him, which was no place but here, in this moment. Then she wound her fingers up through his hair, tugged it slightly and smiled when he started to breathe faster. Breaths to match hers. The edges of their bodies melted into each other.

Keera's body ached from a terrible emptiness, one never before filled, and she was so acutely aware of Reid, more than she had ever been of anything or anyone else in her life. The way he looked down over the tops of his glasses at her—glasses that she removed and laid on the kitchen countertop. How his light evening stubble felt under her fingertips. But what made her quiver, as she explored his face, was the slight dent in the center of his bottom lip. And that discovery about him, and about herself was where the exploration stopped and the kiss began.

In that instant their mouths pressed together hot and tight as his free hand entwined through her hair. Gasping when he eased her head back and kissed down her chin, down her throat, she responded by putting her palms flat to his chest, as if to push him away. Only she gripped the fabric of his shirt, two hands clinging tight to him, feeling the muscles underneath. Hard, smooth... "We shouldn't," she gasped.

"And we won't," he agreed, without retreating a step. "In a minute."

The growl of his sex-charged voice was heavy and hypnotic to her ears and just the sound of it caused her whole body to ache like she'd never known it could. A betrayal of sense and soul, and she fought to get it back, but as his kisses returned to her mouth, all she could do was kiss him back. And hang on for fear she might drown if she didn't.

But all too soon reality overtook the moment, in the form of a jingling cellphone, the jingle being the specific one he'd assigned Emmie, and Reid stepped back, cleared his throat, and assumed the role of daddy.

"What do you want, sweetheart?" He listened for a moment. "No, like I told you a little while ago, it wasn't a heart attack. She'll be fine. I just talked to them at the hospital and she'll be back tomorrow afternoon. And, yes, I did feed her dog. He's outside right now, and I'll bring him in when I go to bed." Another moment of listening, then, "I love you too, sweetheart. Tell Allie I love her, too. Then turn off the cellphone and go to sleep."

Once he'd clicked off, Reid grinned sheepishly. "So, is this where we ignore what happened and go on like we were?"

"It was a kiss," she said, her voice sounding wobbly. "Just a kiss."

"Just a kiss," he said, picking up his peanut-butter sandwich. "Between colleagues."

Keera nodded, trying to appear practical about the matter. "A kiss between colleagues." And one that had shaken her to the very core. Which meant what?

That was the question she didn't want to answer.

# CHAPTER SEVEN

"I DON'T WANT to do this," Keera said, as the instructor secured her into the zip-line harness. "I'm fine keeping my feet on the ground. Never did have a need to simply go flying through the air without an airplane around me. And I don't like all this protective gear…" Harness, pads, goggles. "It pinches, and I especially don't like helmets."

"Necessary for safety and insurance. And it sets a good example for the kids. Especially when you're not fussing and fretting about it," Reid said, then took a picture of her with all her gear.

"But I am fussing and fretting," she said, looking over at Megan, who was sitting under a tree with Sally a good distance away from the rest of the children. "And complaining outright, as it wasn't my idea to do this."

Reid laughed out loud. "Like I said, you have to set a *good* example for the kids. They're watching you, you know."

Yes, they were all watching her, so she pasted a smile on her face and gave them a thumbs-up sign. "It's all a lie," she said under her breath. "I don't like this, don't want to do it."

"Role model," he reminded her, nodding sideways in a gesture toward to the kids. "They have high expectations of you. Even Megan does."

"Megan's too young to understand most of this, and why would the others expect anything from me?" she asked, as the instructor cinched the harness tighter.

"Because they like you, and trust you."

"Then they don't know me," she said, scooting her elbow pads into place then pulling her goggles down over her eyes. "And the last thing I want to be is a role model. Too much responsibility, especially when children are involved. They need someone like you, not like me." And she'd survived perfectly well without a role model in her own life. Or with the worst role model a child could have, depending on how you looked at it.

"Too late for that. You've been thrust into greatness, Keera, as far as these kids are concerned, and there's no turning back. They trust you, respect you and even look up to you. And your confidence in them learning to take responsibility for themselves has made you more of a role model than you can know, because these kids have never had someone who trusts them that much. Not even me."

"It wasn't trust. It was practicality. And you know how that governs my life. It should govern theirs as well, as far as their health issues are concerned."

"But they don't see it that way. To them, it's a very personal thing, making you their—"

"Role model," she said, tightening the chin strap of her helmet then bending over to adjust her knee pads. Taking a quick look at the kids out of the corner of her eye, she saw the way they were watching her, and realized every last word Reid had said was true. Which made her feel uncomfortable for sure, yet strangely moved. "Fine, I'll do this, and I won't make a scene. But I may have to scream, and there's nothing you can do about that."

"I'll bet the kids will love that."

"Yeah, right," she said, turning to the group of kids now

that she was all garbed up and taking a proper bow. Only to be met by applause and shouts of excitement. "And if I die…"

"You're not going to die," he said, walking her over to the platform.

"But if I do…"

"Then I'll be properly put in my place, and you can come back and haunt me, and tell me *you told me so.*"

"And I will," she said, as she began her climb up the wooden ladder nailed onto the post holding up the zip-line platform. "I promise you, Reid Adams, I will haunt you until your dying day."

He'd tossed and turned a bit last night, thanks to the kiss. But somehow he'd finally settled down into a sound sleep and had slept like a cozy baby. In two-hour stretches, as he was up and down, gazing across the compound at Keera's light, wondering if she was sleeping or if the kiss had her tossing and turning as well.

So far that morning they'd been only colleagues and sparring partners. She'd cooked breakfast for the kids while he'd done morning rounds. He'd cleaned up the kitchen while she'd taught her class on taking vital statistics. Then they'd met to collaborate on preparing lunch, and now this. So far there was nothing personal between them. In fact, it was almost like last night hadn't happened. But it had, and there was no denying it. Short, intense and unforgettable. The best kiss he'd ever had.

Looking up, he watched her finally make it to the platform and wave over to Megan, then he pointed his camera up and snapped another picture, and turned it on to video record.

"Seriously, Reid? Do you have to record every aspect of my total, abject humiliation?" she yelled down to him.

Laughing, he stepped back to get a better, wider shot

of the whole event about to take place. "Total and abject is when you get halfway across the line and can't go on, and someone has to come and rescue you."

"You did that?"

"No. But I'm just saying…"

"You're just saying it to put the onus on me."

"But I'll have a video."

She glanced down at all the kids, who were much more eager to do the zip line than she was. "One time, then I'm taking Megan back to camp."

"What if you enjoy it?"

"I won't!"

"That sure of yourself?" he yelled.

"That sure of myself. I *will not* enjoy this."

"Then shall we make a wager? If I win, you take me out to dinner. You win and…well, name your prize. Within reason."

"If I win? I'll have to think about it."

"Don't bother. I'm going to win this bet."

"That sure of yourself, are you?"

He shook his head. "No, but I'm that sure of you."

He watched Keera position herself on the platform and take last-minute instructions. Then he saw her hesitation as the instructor hooked her to the line and she inched towards the edge of the platform. It wasn't such a high wire. In fact, he'd gone zipping on higher, much more extensive wires. Zipped over canopies of trees, skimmed along mountains. Taken an all-day outing once, combining zipping and hiking. All that had been back before he'd become a dad, and had had dad responsibilities.

Sometimes he did miss that freedom. Wondered what it would be like to share his parental responsibility with someone so he could afford a little time away. Mostly, though, he loved the responsibility, loved everything that came with it.

Although, after last night, some of the longing had returned—longing he'd put on hold the day he'd made his decision to adopt the girls. Well, it was good to know it was still there. Unfortunately, it was now dusted off and raring to go, and as long as Keera was here, it wasn't going to go back into storage. The fifty or so photos of her he'd taken already, and now the video, were proof enough of that.

"Do you seriously think I'm going to step off this platform?" she called down to him.

"Want me to come up there and give you a push?"

"What I want is an activity where I can keep both feet planted firmly on the ground. Something sane, like taking a hike. Or jogging."

"One step, Keera. That's the way everything starts in life. With one step." And she needed that step because she did keep everything so locked up.

She looked down at him again then looked over at the kids, and shrugged. Then took that step, to the shouts and screams of the children, who were jumping up and down, applauding her. In a few seconds she was on the opposite platform, raising her arms in the air in victory. Waving at the kids. Shouting her own glee at the task completed.

"I didn't hear you scream," he said, showing her the playback of the video.

"Because it happened so fast. One moment my feet were on solid ground then the next I was flying."

"See, I told you." he said, helping her off with her helmet. "Want to do it again?"

"Think I could?"

"We have two hours here. I'll bet you can do it several more times."

"That was…" She smiled. "Pick your restaurant, Reid.

You win. You were right. So revel in it now, because that's all you're getting from me. One admission and one only. It was fun. I loved it."

"One admission leading to one dinner but an admission with so much significance. Because victory is sweet. Trust me, one is all I need from you." And maybe another kiss at the end of the evening. But he wasn't going to hope too hard for that. Once was pushing it, twice would be... well, very nice, but also a very long long-shot. Still, long-shots were good to bet on because when they won, they paid off big.

"I'll talk to him, but I can't promise he'll like anything we've bought today." They'd been shopping for two hours, and the clothes were cute. Not traditional, not frilly. More like bright, and fun, lots of colors, lots of layers. And accessories. Oh, my heavens, his daughters were starved for accessories. Apparently their daddy was quite practical in some aspects of his personality, and allowing his daughters to express their true creativity was one of those aspects.

When they'd hit the accessories aisle of the little girls' section in the boutique where she'd shopped for Megan, it had been like a whole new world had opened up for Emmie and Allie. Bows and matching socks, purses, belts. And shoes to match specific outfits. These girls lived in basic colors and basic sneakers. Red and pink shoes were entirely new to them, and she couldn't quit buying.

In a way, a whole new world was opening to her, too. Partly because of Megan, and partly because of Emmie and Allie. It was so much unexpected fun, like the zip line. It was also all the things of which she'd been deprived when she'd been a girl that were coming back to remind her now, and she was regaining, vicariously, some of what she'd never had. Even now, her own shopping was practical, quick, and of necessity. And always, always basic.

But this...instead of regretting her past and even parts of her present life, she was enjoying every minute of the outing with Reid's daughters, and being ever mindful that Megan could be part of this in the near future, if all went well.

Also wishing Megan could be part of it now. She truly would have liked to include her.

"Was your daddy like that?" Emmie asked innocently, as she plowed through the section of hair accessories, looking for individual pieces to match each of the six outfits she'd picked out so far. "Like my daddy is?"

"I never got to know my daddy," Keera said. "He went away before I was born."

"He's lost?" Allie asked.

"I suppose you could say he is. But I don't think he wanted any little girls the way your daddy does."

"Would he want you if you were a boy?" Allie asked.

Keera laughed. "No, honey. I don't think he would. Some people don't want to be mommies or daddies."

"Like you?" Emmie asked, picking out a green and yellow hair bow. "I heard you and daddy talking and you said you didn't want children."

"You don't want Megan?" Allie asked.

This really wasn't the conversation she wanted to be having with the girls but apparently it was the conversation they wanted with her. "I like children. I like both of you a lot. Megan, too. But I work almost every day, all day, and I wouldn't have time to be a good mommy, and Megan needs a good..." Well, she was hoping for a daddy, but how could she say that to these two?

"She needs a good home where someone's there to take care of her more than I could. Look, would either of you like ice cream?" That was the way to do it. When the situation got tough, cure it with ice cream. Yet another reason she wasn't cut out for motherhood. Simply put, she was stuck for what to do.

How in the world did Reid do this day in, day out? It was beyond her, and she realized she admired him not only for wanting to do this but for being good at it. And as she ordered two chocolate cones and a dish of strawberry, she realized even more that this was where Megan needed to be.

"They had a great time," Reid said. "I'm not sure about their—or your—fashion choices. But I suppose I'll get used to that, won't I? And I really insist on paying you back for everything you bought."

"Donate the money to the camp. I want this to be my treat."

"Because you're a surgeon who earns more than a county pediatrician?"

"Actually, I'm sure I do. Which isn't the point. We had a nice time and I thoroughly enjoyed the afternoon. So, please, don't spoil it by being…"

"Practical?" he asked, smiling.

"You're using my own life to prove me wrong?"

"You're the one who insists on being practical. So what can I say?"

"I can say that you've done a good job with the girls. I'm impressed you manage it all so well. Your life, your work, your parental responsibilities…"

"I manage it because I want to. It's all about priorities, I suppose. You know, the overall priorities, then the moment-to-moment priorities."

"And I manage my surgical practice the way I want to,

so I guess that pretty much tells you everything there is to know about my priorities."

"Which will never change?" he asked.

"Which I don't anticipate will change. Don't want to change."

"Even if your life situation changes?"

"Another thing I don't anticipate or want." Pulling into the parking spot of The Overlook, she looked at the building and almost wished she'd chosen the restaurant. This place was so romantic. Too romantic maybe? Rustic, and with a view the literature said couldn't be topped anywhere in the vicinity. And in the aftermath of that kiss. What was she thinking?

That she was flirting with things best left alone. That's what she was thinking. But this time she was better prepared. She knew she succumbed too easily to, well, it was either his charm or the clean mountain air, or the moment, or any number of the other reasons two people found that fleeting mutual attraction. And it was only fleeting. Had to be! She was going to make sure of that or she wasn't Keera Murphy, the cold bitch. Make that the *stone*-cold bitch.

But darn it. Once she stepped inside the restaurant, saw the dimmed lights, heard the violin music, her knees nearly buckled. And they really did buckle when she and Reid were shown to the table with the best view in the restaurant, and she had to hold on to that table for support. It was stunning at twilight, with the pinks and grays of the evening sky peeking over the distant mountains. "How did you manage this?" she asked Reid.

"Owners' names are Gwen and Henry Carson."

"As in Gregory Carson?"

He nodded. "They've struggled to hang onto the place, with all their medical expenses. Amazing people, though. They do it all, and take care of a recovering kid, too."

"So this is going to be another exercise in how I could or should be a parent, even with my circumstances, and the Carsons are going to show me the way? Is that why we're here? It's an object lesson?"

"No, but they are going to serve you one of the most amazing meals you've probably ever had."

"Which is meant to prove that I, too, can be a super-mom, like you're a super-dad, and they're super-parents?"

Suddenly, she had no desire to be here, no desire to spend the evening with her face being rubbed in her inadequacies. Sure, she felt guilty about Megan. Her feelings for the little girl were growing. She liked taking care of her, reading her stories, taking walks with her, playing games. But that was largely due to the circumstances—she was out of her element, living a life that wasn't hers. And now, with so many people trying to prove the point, she wasn't comfortable any more. Didn't want to be here, being forced to face the obvious.

So she wasn't going to stay and subject herself to that, no matter how the evening was *intended*. It was as simple as that. Reid could stay, and she'd leave the money to pay for it because nowhere in that bet had there been a mention of dinner for two. Or an object lesson on essential parenting guidelines, which this was all about.

Was she angry? Maybe a little. Or feeling guilty? Probably some of that thrown in there as well. Because she couldn't do it all and she knew it. Knew her inadequacies and didn't have to be reminded of them over the soufflé. But she also knew her strengths, one of which wasn't going to be the commendable kind of parent Reid, or even the Carsons, were. So she pulled her credit card from her purse, slapped it down on the table, and said, "Enjoy yourself. Don't hold back and, please, just slip the card under my cabin door when you return to camp." With that, Keera spun around and marched straight out of the restaurant, quite sure she could hear Reid following her. But she wouldn't turn around to look, not even when she got to the car and had to pause a moment to find the key fob in her purse.

"It was supposed to be a simple dinner," he said. "I'm not sure what you read into it that turned it into something else, but I'm sorry if I said the wrong thing."

"There's not one wrong thing," she said. "Everything's wrong. A week ago I didn't know this camp or you existed, and Megan was only a name and not a child with real-life needs. And this time next week I'll have my real life back and this whole mountain fantasy where I end up being mom of the year will be over and I'll have my elbows up in somebody's rib cage, repairing their heart. It's all I can do, Reid." She looked up at him.

"All I'm supposed to do. It's the reality where I control my life and everything in it. And it's where I don't feel guilty because I can't do the noble thing, the way you can."

"Control is that important you?"

"It has to be. Or else I end up…like this." She spread her arms to take in the whole expanse of town that could be viewed from their vantage point.

"What's so bad about this?"

"For you, nothing. For me, everything. Absolutely everything." She drew in a steadying breath and leaned back against the car. "You were right, you know. I am cold. Because I want to be cold. It keeps the world from intruding, and it keeps me in the place I need to be. Where I belong."

"Which is alone."

"Which is unaffected. I know you want me to be that little girl's mother, or at least her guardian until a permanent home can be found for her."

"That's true."

She laughed, but it was a bitter laugh. Or one filled with regret. "You sound like your daughters. The subject came up when we were shopping and I think they were amazed that I couldn't step in and rescue Megan the way you stepped in and rescued them. But being the good role model that I am, I distracted them with ice cream because I didn't know what to say. So tell me, does the person who takes the low road really sound like the best candidate for motherhood?"

"She sounds like me when I struggle to find the right way to go. There's no book with all the answers you'll ever need to know, Keera. Not about parenting, not about life in general. But it works out, one way or another."

"For me, it works out when I'm scrubbed and ready to step into the OR."

"Having a child doesn't mean you can't do that."

"You don't know me, then. In my life all I can do is one thing. Look, dinner here was a bad idea because this place...you...Gregory's parents...suffocate me with my inadequacies. And I'm really not hungry. So, please, go back, have a nice evening on me. I'm sure you can catch a taxi back to the cabin. Or I can catch a taxi and leave you the car. However you want to work it out."

"Why do I scare you so much?" he asked.

There were so many reasons on so many levels, but most of all he reminded her of the things she'd never be able to have. Reid was everything, he had everything. And she was a shell. She knew that, and was OK with it. "You don't. I'm the one who scares me."

"Because of this?" he asked, tilting her face up to his. "Because you don't want to want it?"

With that, he lowered his lips to hers, but it was not a kiss filled with fire and raw need. It was tender, and gentle. Filled with hope she so desperately wanted to feel. Wanted to hold on to. "We shouldn't do this," she said, hating that she had to pull away from him. But she had to, because she so feared getting lost in the very thing she knew she couldn't have yet was only now beginning to realize she desperately wanted.

"You're right," he said, smiling. "We shouldn't. But once wasn't enough."

"Why do you even want to…well, do anything with me? Nothing can come of it."

"Or everything, depending on your perspective."

She shook her head. "There's only one perspective, and I think maybe the mountain air's gone to your head, Reid. Or perhaps you need more adult companionship. I don't know which. But have you thought this through? If nothing else, think of our proximity. We live more than an hour away from each other."

"Half an hour if we meet in the middle."

"And neither of us have that hour or half-hour to spare. And in the end we're too different."

"And opposites never attract."

"Not in reality," she said.

"So then why do I want to kiss you so badly, and why do you want me to?" he asked, clearly on the verge of their next kiss. "And we're pretty much opposite in everything?"

"Too many children around, and I'm back to believing you're craving some adult companionship."

"So, any adult will do, right? Any set of lips? Any curvy, sexy-as-hell hips…"

"Hmm," she murmured, as his lips met hers, but this time with a hunger that no romantic meal was going to satisfy.

"Wow," she said groggily, rolling over and looking at the naked body stretched out next to her. She certainly hadn't expected what was lurking beneath his clothing. Reid had a magnificent body, lean and well muscled. As a doctor, she knew physical perfection. As a woman, she'd never known she could enjoy it so much. Every inch of it. "Time to get up, leave this hotel and get back to camp, before anybody notices that we're missing."

"What time is it?"

"A little after one. And even though Sally is always happy to watch Megan, I want to spend the rest of the night with her. Which means we've got to go back to camp before it gets any later and people start wondering if we're doing what we just did." She smiled. "And I mean it, Dr. Adams. Appearances are important."

He reached over and twined his fingers through her hair. "I never knew how much I liked red hair before last night. But I definitely like red hair."

"I know," she said, not sure whether to be bold or opt for being demure.

"Nice red hair."

She sighed. "Seriously. We've got to go, Reid. Somebody's going to find out." She sat up and pulled the sheet up to cover her breasts, but he immediately reached over and tugged the sheet back down.

"I like your breasts as much as I like your hair. If you're going to kick me out of your bed, the least you could do is give me one last look."

She liked being admired, liked that it was Reid doing the admiring. "Technically, I'm not kicking. Just urging." And, oh, how she didn't want to. But getting here had been such a fluke, and then discovering how good they were together? Suffice it to say he'd melted the stone-cold bitch into a puddle, and she wasn't ready to have that end. But, practically speaking, it had to. Because they weren't practical together. Neither was this relationship. A few hours together were good, but anything beyond that... "And if you're not going to avail yourself of the shower, I will."

"Please, avail away. But leave the sheet here, because as much as I like your red hair and your breasts, well, all I can say is that watching you walk away from me, naked, is my fondest fantasy. Well, one of them."

His grin was wicked, his demeanor sexy and funny—everything she'd always wanted and had never had. Still couldn't have, and that's the only thing she could think of as she gave him his show on her way into the shower. She couldn't have any of this.

In another few minutes it would be over, and it all would be relegated to the past tense and dreams to be put away on the shelf. But no regrets. She was a modern woman, and modern women had flings. It was accepted. Something totally different from her mother's life and lifestyle. Although this was the first time she'd ever slept with a man outside marriage, which meant...

Actually, she wasn't going to ponder that one. No, she was going to take a shower and go about her plans for the rest of the night, and let Reid worry about what to tell his children, or anybody else for that matter, if he lollygagged too much and they didn't get back to camp at a respectable time.

But a little while longer in bed with him would have been nice. Sighing, Keera turned on the shower full blast and stepped in, and let the water pellets ping her skin a little harder than she usually did because she'd felt alive in his arms these last hours, and now she wanted something else to make her feel alive. Only a few minutes away from Reid and she needed a physical reminder...

*"What have I done?"* she whispered as she sank back against the shower wall and let the water beat hard against her.

"Room for one more?" he asked, snapping her out of her reverie.

"We shouldn't," she said, desperately wanting to anyway. "Because after tonight..." Keera shrugged.

"What? We're done?"

"We should be."

Reid turned on the grin. "Because we're not practical?"

"Something like that," she said, as he pushed back the shower curtain and entered. "I don't do this. Tonight, you and me. It's not me."

Picking up the bottle of body wash, he raised it and squeezed so that the pink soap inside slithered down between her breasts, all the way to her belly, and below. Then he began to spread the soap, the palms of both his hands making a circular motion on her flesh that left her gasping for breath. "Oh, this is definitely you," he said, taking particular care to tweak her nipples to erection then linger there, stroking, pinching lightly, then returning to his circular motion as his hands continued on their journey, down her belly, and even further down, until one hand forged ahead and the other hand reached around to grab her bottom.

"Reid, no." She gasped, "We shouldn't."

"Go on," he urged. "We shouldn't what?"

"Stop," she choked out, as the paroxysms of his efforts began to overtake her.

"Now? You want me to stop now?"

"No!" she practically screamed. "We shouldn't stop. Not now! Please, don't."

"As if I could," he growled, as she quivered beneath his fingertips. "Or would."

But they would have to at some point. That's what she was thinking when their shower was over, and an hour later when, car lights off, they drove into the camp and parked behind her cabin. Then Reid left her with a quick kiss to her cheek, while she went to the infirmary, tiptoed past a sleeping Sally, and slid into the bed on the other side of the aisle. Still feeling the lingering of that kiss, and everything that had come before it, as she pulled the sheet up over her.

It was dark, and the camp was quiet and asleep. And somewhere out there Reid was sneaking away like a thief in the night. In a sense, though, that's what he was, because he had stolen something from her. Not her virginity, not even her sense of moral purpose. More like her certainty.

With Kevin, there had never been doubts or questions or a roller-coaster of emotion. Their meeting, their dating, their marriage had always been the practical matters she'd wanted them to be.

With Reid there was nothing practical about it. Not one little aspect. That's where her certainty wavered because, for the first time in her life, she wasn't sure she wanted to be all that certain. Wasn't sure she could be any more. And that's what scared her. What truly, honestly scared her.

Raising herself up to peek out the window, Keera saw Reid heading round to the rear side of his cabin and imagined him going in through his kitchen door. An affair with Reid Adams—and, yes, this was an affair of some sort—was like zip lining, where she was flying through the air, tethered to a very small cable. The zip-line cable she trusted because it was proven. Her own private cable wasn't proven, however, which meant disaster could surely be sneaking around in the dark, the way Reid was.

Only this time she wasn't wearing a safety helmet or any of the other protective gear. And she feared that she needed all she could get—to protect her heart.

# CHAPTER EIGHT

"IT'S WHERE?" KEERA asked, clearly alarmed by the forest fire that was now engulfing one of the surrounding ridges. She and Reid hadn't had contact for an entire day. In fact, she'd refused to even look at him. But the memories had lingered, made her mellow, caused her to sigh wistfully more times than she wanted to. Nice aftermath with too many warm, leftover sensations. Then this. Life changing too fast, too unpredictably.

"About four miles east of here. I talked to one of the rangers a little while ago, and he wants us to get ready to evacuate. They're hoping that if weather holds, and everything works in their favor, they'll get it contained before it makes it all the way down to this valley. But he also advised that we need to get the kids out of here pretty soon."

"Then that's what we do," she said, seeing the worried look on Reid's face. He had a lot at risk here. Everything he owned, a life's investment in jeopardy. "So, in spite of trying to look calm, I know you're not," she said. "And I think I need to know the worst-case scenario."

"Other than the obvious problems that I may lose my camp, or the smoke that's going to make some of these kids sick, I just went down to the highway, and the roads are already congested. People driving crazy, trying to get out of the valley. I don't want the kids caught up in all that mess."

"Do you have a back-up plan?"

He nodded. "Already implemented. But I'm worried about the time crunch."

However it worked out, it was time to disband camp and in doing that leave all kinds of unresolved feelings behind. Couldn't be helped, though, couldn't be prevented, couldn't even be postponed. Because once she walked away from this place, that's exactly what would happen. Nothing would be resolved, not about her growing feelings for Reid and especially not about what to do with Megan. "How much time do we have?" she asked.

"Not a lot. Maybe an hour, an hour and a half before it starts getting critical. So let me call a staff meeting, get everybody in on this, because we're going to have some disappointed kids. Today was the day we were going to go horseback riding."

"Have you called your partner and told him not to come?"

Reid nodded. "He's my back-up plan. He's up in the sky right now, looking at the fire, assessing our best options. We do mountain search and rescue, so he's authorized to be overhead. And he's ready to come and grab us, depending on the roads."

"Helicopter?" she asked.

Reid nodded.

"Seriously?" The more she heard about Reid's medical practice, the more impressed she was.

Reid grinned. "Which was why I got my pilot's license recently. The chopper is what we make house calls and hospital runs in. Oh, and we go out on horseback for some of the closer house calls. Personally, I prefer my motorcycle over the horse."

"You're a pilot *and* you have a motorcycle? Let me just say *wow* to your diversity." Keera laughed. "I wouldn't have taken you for a cowboy doctor. But a pilot? I can see that. And I can definitely picture you in leathers. I hope you wear leathers on the motorcycle."

"That would make me some kind of a bad boy, wouldn't it?"

"I saw the bad boy in you last night, Reid. Trust me, the leathers would only enhance what's already there."

Blushing slightly, Reid cleared his throat. "That's me, pilot-cowboy-bad-boy-doctor. But today I'm all camp counselor, who's trying to figure out the most efficient way to get these kids out of here. Which I think will be by air. Also, by taking the kids out in the chopper we can keep them together better until we can make arrangements for their parents to come get them."

"And they'll have a blast doing this, as long as we don't let them know why we're evacuating. You know, turn it into an adventure rather than an emergency." She regarded his brooding expression and her heart went out to him. Sure, she'd spent the night with him. And, sure, she admired him for what he did here. But he was struggling, and so distressed, yet he was trying to hold it all together for everyone else. Who held it together for Reid, though? As far as she knew, nobody.

"The kids are going to be fine, Reid. Trust me, everything's going to turn out OK. They'll be safe, and that's all that matters."

"You're right. That's all that matters." That's what he said, but it's not how he'd sounded when he'd said it.

Keera stepped forward and wrapped her arms around him. "Your camp's going to be safe, isn't it? I mean, it's not in any real danger of…"

She couldn't bring herself to say the words, because she knew how much of Reid's life was tied up in these few wooded acres, and to even think it was at risk made her gut knot.

"The big danger here is the smoke, right? If the wind shifts?" She was saying that to reassure herself, although nothing on Reid's face was reassuring about anything, and she knew what he was thinking, what he was dreading.

"Let's hope so," he said, responding to her embrace by wrapping his arms around her. "But if it burns...well, what I can say?"

"You can say that you took care of the kids first."

"That's right. You're always practical, aren't you?"

"Yep. Always practical." She forced herself out if the embrace. "So now what?"

"Now we get everybody the hell out of Camp Hope."

"Then I'll get the staff together while you figure out what we need to do to get this camp shut down."

"About last night," he started, then stopped when Emmie came running up to him and latched onto his hand.

"When do we get to go riding?" she asked. "Because I told Molly and Nathan I'd show them how because they've never been on a horse before, and I have!"

"Sorry, sweetheart," Reid said. "But we're going to have to save that for another day. Beau can't bring the horses right now."

"But he promised," she whined.

"And we'll do it another time." He looked over at Keera, who was already running in the direction of the dorm. "Today, instead of horseback riding, it's helicopter rides for everyone. So go tell your friends to get ready, that Doc Beau is going to be here with his chopper in a few minutes."

"Really?" Emmie cried. "We're going to fly? You're not going to say *no* when it's my turn? Because you always say *no* when we're home."

"I'm not going to say *no*. Before long you're going to be going up and over that mountain," he said, pointing to a ridge in the opposite direction from the fire.

"Promise?"

"Cross my heart," he said, crossing his heart as she shooed Emmie back to the other children.

"Everybody's alerted, and getting ready to get out," Keera shouted, running up to him minutes later. "And I was thinking, maybe the kids can all come back later this summer and make up their last couple of days. I know if I can get the time off I'd come back and help you."

He glanced up in the sky, looking for Beau, saw the helicopter off in the distance. "Did you say what I thought you said? That you'd come back?"

"If you needed me to. I mean, I did volunteer for a week, and I'm still good for it."

"I appreciate that, Keera. You don't know how much. And I appreciate everything you've done here so far, even if I've given you a hard time about certain things."

"They're your kids, you have the responsibility."

"And I'm stubborn."

"As stubborn as I am?" she teased.

"Is anybody as stubborn as you are?" When he saw Beau's helicopter making its final approach the somberness slid back down over him. "Guess it's time to get this thing started."

"You don't like the idea of these kids flying, do you?"

"I don't like the idea that this might overstress some of the kids, and I won't be on the other end to take care of them. Because they will hear about the fire. Might even see it from the air."

"I called the sheriff in Marston Springs, Reid. He's going to be contacting Beau about where to land then he's going to get the doctor over there ready to look at the kids once they set down."

"That's a good instinct," Reid said appreciatively, as the camp staff began to gather around him. "Remind me to invite you back to camp some time."

A minute later all but a couple of people who were busy attending to the kids were huddled around Reid, who was on the phone to the ranger. "Looks like the wind is shifting, and it's coming this way. Not fast, but we're going to start airlifting out of here immediately." He drew in a deep breath.

"You all know the emergency plan. Beau will take charge of getting you on the chopper, Betsy is gathering up the medicines we need to take with us, and Keera has arranged to have the local doc meet us over in Marston Springs. Other than that..." he shrugged "...have a safe trip, and I'll see you on the other side of the mountain.

"Oh, and anybody who wants to drive out is welcome to try. The highway is congested, but if you know your way through Moores Valley, he suggests using the Moores Valley road and taking the turnoff to Marston Springs from that."

As it turned out, only Clara opted to drive, and that was because of her basset hound. The other six volunteers agreed to go by chopper and take care of the kids when they arrived at the other end.

"And Megan?" Keera asked Reid.

"We'll fly her out with the rest of the kids, put her in a chopper with the volunteers to keep them separated. Or you can drive her out. It's up to you."

"What about you?"

"Hanging in to the bitter end. I can't leave until I know everything here is as protected as it can be. And I'm hoping to rescue all the computers. I've got the data backed up to the cloud, but the equipment is expensive and I'd like to save it."

"But you can't stay here by yourself," Keera protested. "It's not safe. What if something happens to you, and you're the only one here? Who's going to help you?"

"Nothing's going to happen to me," he said, taking hold of Keera's hand and heading towards the clinic. "I'll get everybody out, load up what I can, and hang around a day or two to shut the place down if the fire doesn't get it, maybe let parents back in to pick up their kids' things, and hope nothing happens."

"What about your girls?"

"Beau's going to take them back to Sugar Creek with him, and he and Deanna will look after them."

"Will they look after one more?" she asked.

"What do you mean?"

"Megan. Will they look after Megan while I stay here with you?"

"You can't stay! It's not…"

"Safe?"

"It might not be safe. And you're not experienced."

"Does that mean you're experienced with forest fires?" she asked.

"No. Until a few months ago I was a city boy. Only came to the country to be closer to my camp."

"Then shut up and quit arguing with me. If it's safe enough for you to stay behind, it's safe enough for me. I'm not leaving you here alone, and I'm not going to fight you about it."

"But Megan needs a familiar face. She's already gone through enough, and to be put in the arms of strangers again…."

"And she'll have a familiar face in a day or so. Look, Reid. I've already made up my mind, and there's not a darned thing you can do to stop me, short of tying me up and throwing me on the helicopter." She smiled. "And I'd like to see you try."

"Are you sure about this, Keera? Because if the fire accelerates…"

"Then we'll be in it together." She shrugged. "No big deal. We'll take that back road you suggested."

"It's a very big deal," he said, tilting his head down to give her a gentle but oh-so-brief kiss on the lips. "And I appreciate it. Oh, and so you'll know, you're not the woman I thought you were."

"In a good way or a bad way?"

"Tell you later," he said looking towards the east, as the normal smoke in the mountains, which was actually mist and humidity that lurked just above the treetops, was being engulfed by real and very ominous black smoke. "Because right now I've got to go get the kids ready to ride."

Keera's first instinct was to run to get Megan ready, and when she got to the infirmary Megan was wide awake, looking much better than she had in days. "I don't know what's going to happen after today," she said to Megan as she relieved Sally of duty and helped dress the little girl in street clothes, "but it's not going to be an institution. I can promise you that. Even if you have to come and stay with me for a little while until arrangements can be made."

She glanced wistfully out the window and saw Reid lead a parade of kiddies across the compound. "I'm still not giving up on him, though. I'm just not as optimistic that I have time to convince him to be my solution."

Once Megan was dressed, Keera did a quick exam to make sure she wasn't running a temperature or had some other problem going on, then she bundled her into her arms, carried her outside and fell in line with the rest of the people awaiting their turn for a helicopter ride. The adults were waiting with a sense of trepidation while the kids were anxious and excited. But Reid looked more worried than he had earlier. He kept glancing up at the ridge in the distance, watching the smoke get thicker. And closer.

"Maybe we ought to go, too," she said, sidling up next to him. "Get everybody out of here first then drive out together."

He took Megan from her arms. "It's all I have. All I own. This camp. I've put everything I have into it. And I have to be here, no matter what happens to it."

"But you have your girls, Reid, which makes you a lucky man. The rest..." She looked around, saw the man she assumed to be Beau waving her over. "I think it's time for Megan to fly."

"She'll be fine. Sally's going to hold her, and I'll let Beau know she's to go home with them for the time being."

"By chopper?"

"No. Deanna's driving over to get the girls because Beau's going to hang around and join in rescue efforts."

"But that will expose Emmie to measles."

"Desperate times, desperate measures. If she gets measles, I'll get her through it."

Something about Beau's courage brought tears to her eyes. Or maybe it was the smoke beginning to waft in. She didn't know which it was but she nodded numbly as she watched Reid walk forward to place Megan in Sally's arms. Suddenly a lump the size of her fist formed in her throat and that, added to her already spilling tears, caused her to run forward and take the child from his arms. "I need to do this," she said, sniffling as she carried Megan the rest of the way over. "Look, sweetheart, I'll see you in a little while. I promise. These nice people are going to take you on a ride, and you're going to go stay at a very nice place where they have horses."

"Mommy," she whimpered.

"I know you want her, but Mommy can't be here, sweetheart." Megan hadn't said very much over the past few days—Megan had assumed because of the trauma from her accident combined with being sick—and it was so good to hear her voice. In fact, it caused the lump in her throat to swell a little more. "And we'll talk about that next time I see you. But right now, promise me you'll be good. Can you do that for me?"

Megan nodded, and Keera kissed her on the forehead. Then reluctantly handed her over to Sally, who took her immediately to the helicopter. In another minute they were lifted off the ground and turning away from Camp Hope. And Keera felt so hopeless. Maybe as hopeless as she'd felt all those times when, as a child, her mother had abandoned her. The same way she was sure Megan was feeling right now—abandoned and cast off to strangers.

"They'll be fine," Reid said, as he slipped his arm around her waist. "Deanna's great with kids. So are Brax and Joey...he runs the ranch. They'll take good care of her. And just so you know, I think she was calling *you* Mommy. She's growing attached to you, Keera."

She swiped at her tears. "I hope not, because life's about to jump out and bite her in the ugliest possible way, and..."

"You want to keep her, don't you?"

She shook her head. "I want you to keep her because I can't. She needs a good family now, and you and the girls are the best one I know. You can give her a life that I can't, and she deserves that."

"But it's still not for you—the whole family thing."

"You're right. It's still not for me." For the first time in her life she actually regretted the words. "There are things inside people they can't change, and for me, that's one of them."

"Do you think I ever anticipated being the single father of two little girls?"

"Maybe it's something you didn't anticipate, but you come from a background that doesn't limit you in the capacity it takes to be a father. And not just a father but a good father. I'm limited, Reid. More than you can know. More than I want to know."

"And limits can't be overcome?"

She laughed. "You're always the optimist, aren't you?"

"When it comes to you, yes, I am. Maybe that's because I don't see limits, maybe it's because I see someone fighting hard against so much potential. I still think it's in you, Keera. I'm not sure how to convince you it's there, though."

He couldn't, because it wasn't. But it was so nice to hear him tell her she had potential. No one ever had, not for any reason, and not in any endeavor. Too bad she was hearing about a flat-lined potential that couldn't be shocked back with a defibrillator.

Less than an hour later, after the chopper lifted off for the last time, the camp felt utterly desolate. Reid wasn't sure where Keera was and, right now, standing out here in the compound alone, watching the tail of the helicopter disappear over the ridge, he was spooked. Had to admit it. He was spooked, and it wasn't about being here so much as it was about what he stood to lose if the camp got caught in the fire.

"It's getting closer," Keera called from the porch of the infirmary. She'd been gathering up all the new clothes and toys she'd bought for Megan and packing them into a box to take away with her when she left. "I was looking out the back way, and it's moved down quite a lot. So, what can we do? Should we be hosing down the buildings or something?"

He could feel the grit of the smoke in his lungs now. Or maybe it was his imagination because that's what he expected to feel. Either way, she was right. The fire was marching down the side of the mountain like an invading army, and there wasn't much he could do except put as much gear into the camp van as he could, and keep his fingers crossed.

"If it comes any closer, yes." Who was he kidding? If the fire came any closer it would take the camp with it no matter what they did.

"Is there anything to pack up and take with us?"

"Don't know," he said on a discouraged sigh. "I don't really have much here that's of any value. I've packed all the girls' things, and gone through and gathered everything of value the kids left behind. As far as medical equipment…" He shrugged. "It's insured, and none of it was new to begin with."

"So why stay?"

"Because I'm the captain of this ship. It's all I own. When I decided to do this, I invested everything I had in it. Guess it goes to show you how fragile life is, doesn't it?" He looked up at the fire, which was now visible from their vantage point. A while ago it had only been the smoke threatening Camp Hope, now it was the fire itself.

"But the kids are safe. I talked to Betsy, and they're having fun on their adventure. The Marston Springs sheriff let the kids all ride in his police car, sirens blaring, and now he's treating them to ice cream. The doctor there said every last one of them is fine, and the parents have all been notified and are on their way. Deanna Alexander's already on the way back to Sugar Creek with the girls, so it's a good outcome, Reid. Maybe not the one you wanted, but everybody is safe. So it's time to go."

He looked up into the sky. "Maybe you're right. But damn it all! Why did this have to happen?"

She took hold of Reid's hand and walked with him over to where her car was parked next to the camp van. "Life dealt me a pretty bad hand once so I know what bitterness feels like, and it's not a good feeling because it consumes you, and sucks in everything around you. I understand your bitterness, Reid. But I also understand your strengths, and those strengths will get you through this."

"My girls," he said. "They're my strength."

"The camp is important for them—for Emmie because she's a survivor, and even for Allie because she has a connection to leukemia as a donor that few people ever have. So, if it burns down, you'll build it up again and your girls will be there to help you. It's as simple as that."

"Would that be two or three girls?"

"I shouldn't have said anything. But I thought…"

"You thought one more wouldn't matter."

"That's bad of me, isn't it?"

"Not bad so much as…unfortunate. Because you've got all the qualities. You just don't want to see them."

"My qualities." She laughed bitterly. "Like I told you, my mother was a prostitute, Reid. A prostitute! We lived on the street, half my meals came from whatever I could scrounge from garbage cans, and we were homeless half the time. Or when she did manage a room, she'd put me in the closet while she…she did her thing with the men. Sometimes I lived in cardboard boxes or under bridges, and I hardly ever got to go to school because we never stayed one place long enough.

"Then when I was thirteen, social services finally took me from her, but only because I went to the library every

chance I could to read, and confided to my favorite librarian that my mother wanted me to do...do what she did. You
know, turn tricks for money because I was developed, and
pretty. And young. So I talked to the librarian, who was
nice to me, and she helped. If she hadn't, I don't even want
to think how it might have turned out.

"But after that, after I was in the system, I was wild,
couldn't be controlled, couldn't be kept in a home because I did everything I could to act up. Kind of like my
mother was, come to think of it. But I was smart, which is
the only saving grace I had in this life because I whizzed
through school once I was allowed to go, and even managed to graduate early. Got scholarships, and the rest..."
She shrugged.

"The rest isn't fit to be called mother because I'm not
going to let anything stand in my way of achieving what I
need to achieve. That was the only promise I made to myself through everything, and I've never broken it. I won't
let *anything* stand in my way.

"But I know my limitations, and I'm more than ready to
admit what I'm not capable of doing. I've been a wife once
and failed miserably at that, but Kevin moved on to a life
he wanted. A child doesn't have that same option when a
parent is bad. I didn't, and I don't want to put another child
in the same position I was in. Which is why I'd hoped..."

"Hoped I'd keep Megan."

"So sue me for trying. I don't want bad things for her.
In fact, I want only the best."

"Which isn't you?"

"Which isn't me. But I'm good with it."

"I saw how reluctant you were to let Megan go a while
ago. That's not being good with it, Keera. If anything, I
think you're kidding yourself. And I'm sorry about your
childhood. I can't even begin to imagine what it must have

been like for you, but you persevered. You got through it and look at you now—what you do, who you are. You're not the little girl who lived in cardboard boxes, and you're not your mother."

"Maybe I'm not but..." Pausing, she smiled. "But I'm me, the person I designed me to be. And I didn't design children into that."

"Then update the design."

"What if I did? What if I *updated* and tried, then somewhere along the way realized that I had been right about it all along? That I wasn't cut out to be a mother? Or, God forbid, that I was like my mother? What would happen to Megan then? I mean, living in a situation where you're not wanted. I don't think you can understand that. It's desolate. There's no hope. And I don't want to do that to her."

"But what if you discovered that you *are* cut out to be a mother? Keera, you're so strong that if you turned out to be like your mother, it would only be by choice. You are who you want to be, and you're completely in control of that, no matter what you might think."

"No matter what I might think? What I think, Reid, is that rolling the dice on who I am is taking a big risk. That's what it would be."

"But if you're capable of designing yourself into the person you want to be, and you want to be a mother, doesn't it stand to reason you can design that into yourself?"

"You've got an argument for everything, don't you?"

"Not everything. But I know I'm right about this. And I do understand how you're afraid you'll turn out to be just like your mother. But, Keera, I can promise you that's never going to happen. You just have to trust yourself more to believe it."

"Most of my life I've tried so hard not to be like her because..."

He took her hand and held it. "Your mother's life was a choice, Keera. Just like your life is a choice. You get to control what you do, what you want, what you want to include. And your mother has no influence in that because you've become your own person.

"I think, though, that you use her as your excuse—to succeed, to excel. You know, be the success you are to prove yourself to the mother who never loved you. The thing is, you can't change what she was. That part of your life is over with, and whatever bad things you were taken away from are in your past.

"Now you don't need to have an excuse to succeed, because all the qualities you'll ever need are in you, totally independent of anything your mother did or was. It's you, Keera. Not her. You can't go back and make her love you, and you're never going to turn into her. So I only hope you'll find a way to trust that and move on. Because until you do, you're depriving yourself of happiness and all the good things you deserve."

"Look, I appreciate what you're trying to do but I really was on the verge of abandoning Megan here a few nights ago and that, if nothing else, should tell you who I am. I didn't want her, and I was angry I had to deal with her. You were her doctor, you ran a camp for kids. I saw you as my solution. And I still do, but differently. And that *is* what my mother would do."

"But it's not what *you* did. That's the difference. She would have, and you didn't. That's all that matters, Keera. You didn't do it."

"That tendency is in me, Reid. Can't you see that? I would have left her here that first night if I'd had the opportunity."

"That tendency is there because you won't let your mother go and, subconsciously, you're sabotaging yourself into thinking you'd be just like her given the opportunity. It's time to quit trying to prove you're not her and start trying to prove you're you. But I can't be the one to convince you of that. It has to be you."

"I appreciate your faith in me, as misplaced as it is."

He'd give her credit for one thing. She was as stubborn as hell, and he didn't know what it was going to take to crack that shell of hers so she could see what was inside. Truth was, she was afraid to look, afraid of what she might find. Even though he understood why, he still couldn't understand why she refused to take that hard, objective look and see all the things he saw. Especially when, just a little while ago, she'd actually gone teary over putting Megan on the helicopter.

Well, at least he saw the conflicts for what they were. What he couldn't see, though, was the reason for his own emotional entanglement. He knew who Keera was and what she resisted, which was essentially everything he wanted in life. Yet he was fascinated. More than fascinated, actually. He was downright captivated, and he didn't know how to undo that. But he had to. That's all there was to it. He had to.

# CHAPTER NINE

IT WAS TIME to get out, but Reid was still working methodically, trying to pack away as much as he could in the camp van. Just working. Not talking. And not looking at the fire creeping its way across the valley the way she was drawn to looking. Because he didn't want to see his future. Much the way she didn't want to see various aspects of her own life. Some things were too painful to face—for both of them.

"Anything else I should get?" she asked him. "I've got a little more room for a few small things." Her eyes stung, her throat ached. Her lungs were fighting for every breath now. But she wasn't going to leave him here alone.

Pausing in his frantic efforts, he wiped the sweat from his face with the back of his hand, then shook his head. "I've done all I can. It's time to go. You lead, I'll follow. We'll stick to the highway unless it's too congested, then I'll call you."

"When it's over, Reid, no matter how it goes, maybe I can help you get the camp up and running again. Not so much in the physical sense but I've got some contacts, people who might be able to take on some of the responsibility." She smiled. "I've operated on some people in mighty high places, so all I have to do is call."

"You'd do that?" he asked, walking her to her car. "Stay

involved here past, well…past all this?" For the first time
since the kids had all gone he looked across the valley at
the fire, saw how close it was to the east end of his acreage.

"I would," she said.

"Why? Why would you be willing to help me when…?"

"When I don't like kids?"

"That's not what I was going to say, but it is a good
question as you're not fond of them."

"See, that's the thing. I'm not *not* fond of children. In
fact, I've enjoyed my association with Megan, and even
with your girls. But I lack that elusive thing some people
call the parenting gene, so I'm not a nurturer by nature.
Which doesn't mean I'm a kid-hater. More like an avoider.

"But this camp, Reid, it's so important. I know what we
did, what we had was only a one-night thing, and I'm not
kidding myself about that. It was good. Fantastic. But it
was last night, and today I'm extending my hand in friendship because you're going to need help with something
that's worthy. Whether or not you accept it is entirely up
to you, but the offer stands.

"I'll help do whatever needs to be done when the time
comes, if you want me to. Or stay away, if that's what you
want. But right now let's just get out of here."

"Agreed," he said, as he opened her door for her. "And
I'll see you on the other side of the mountain. Oh, and…"
He bent down, gave her a quick kiss on the lips. "Thank
you," he whispered. "For everything."

"Be safe, Reid," she said, as she moved her car forward.
"Please be safe," she whispered to herself as she looked in
her rear-view mirror and saw him climb into his van. "So
we can meet on the other side of the mountain."

She wouldn't see what he'd done. And by the time she'd
figured out that he'd turned off onto an access road at the

edge of the property, she'd be safe in Marston Springs. And he'd be attempting one last-ditch effort, by moving all the volunteers' cars as far away from the camp enclosure as possible then hosing down the buildings. It wouldn't be easy, probably wouldn't even be successful, but he couldn't go down without this fight. And he couldn't have fought knowing someone he loved was in the path of danger.

She wasn't, though. Not now. So parking his van a good distance from the compound, he got out and went, on foot, back to the area, where he started, one by one, to move the cars away. Potential gasoline explosions and all. Although there weren't any good places to stash them, he did take them to a cleared area on the west side of the property— a baseball field. The first car, then second one. Driving frantically, wishing he didn't have to waste the time, wishing he could have had his volunteers do this, but knowing they'd had to take care of the children instead.

Still, getting rid of the explosion hazard made him feel like he was doing something, even if it was futile, and as he ran back that nearly quarter-mile to get the next car, he saw a vehicle approaching him. "What the…?"

"I saw the keys in the cars," she shouted out the window at him. "Figured out you'd want these cars moved at some point if you were going to fight it. Then when I saw you turn off on the access road…"

"You saw that?"

"I'm a surgeon. I observe everything."

"You can't do this. Can't be here."

"But you are."

"Seriously? You're going to get stubborn with me now?"

Rather than answering, she rolled up her car window and continued down the road, while he was left to run back and bring yet another car up. Which was when he met her on the road and stopped. "I'll be fine here. You don't need to do this because…"

"Because I want to? Look, Reid. My life doesn't count for much outside the operating room, but this camp, it adds something and, like you, I'm not going to let it go up in flames without a fight. So…" She gave a shooing gesture then spun away and continued her run down the road to fetch the next car. And so it went until all the cars were cleared away.

"Bet we're not leaving yet, are we?" she asked him when they were both finally back at the compound, running hand in hand.

What they found was not promising. The fire had encroached by jumping the dirt road on the east, and was spreading quickly along the fire trail all the way up to the compound itself—in patchy splotches, though. Thankfully not one great consuming wall of fire. Right now advance small fires were burring rather lazily, like they were waiting for the rest to catch up to them. But they were shooting off blazing embers, one after another. Little bursts of fireworks that would have been lovely in a holiday celebration but so deadly here, and now.

"I'll get the hose," Keera said, as Reid went in the opposite direction to grab a shovel.

When she returned with the hose, she saw him smashing the little blazers down as they hit the dirt, ignited the flower garden and a couple of wooden chair sitting on the edge of the compound. Then the tool shed. That's where Keera went into action, turning on the water and dousing the little wooden structure as best she could.

She had success, initially. The roof suffered damage, but the fire went out without much of a protest and it was a good thing because one of the outlying, unused cabins took an ember to the roof, which quickly had the whole roof flaming, taunting her to come get it, too. Which she did, or tried to. But by the time she dragged the hose over the ground and got it aimed, the roof was already half-gone, which meant the cabin itself wouldn't be long in following.

"Reid," she shouted, looking overhead as another burning ember floated merrily on its way, headed towards her cabin! "I can't contain it here."

"Get back!" he shouted, as his attention caught on the same ember that had caught hers. "Let it burn, and stay away."

Not to be deterred by the embers, she did let that cabin go and immediately ran to her own cabin and started to douse at almost the same time as the roof started to blaze. But her position wasn't good enough and the pine tree that loomed above it caught fire, too, and exploded into flames quicker than anything she'd ever seen burn. Another loss, only this one she fought valiantly, alternately spraying the walls and roof of the cabin as best she could.

The problem was the fiery tree above it had spread the flames to the next tree over, then the one after that, and that's when Keera realized that every last one of the guest cabins in that row would fall victim.

After that she looked around, saw Reid still beating out the small ground fires, which were overtaking him now. Saw that the next structure to go, after the guest cabins, would be the dorm, where the children stayed. And the one after that the dining hall.

"We can't save it," she said, wiping sooty sweat from her brow. It was a realization she hated with everything in her. But it was a fact. The fire had encroached enough that everything on the outer sides of the compound would go up. The dorms, Reid's cabin. Maybe not the clinic, though, which sat in the open and isolated from everything else.

"Reid," she yelled. "All of this." She shook her head. "We can't save it. But your clinic..."

"No! This time we've got to get out of here for real," he shouted back. "It doesn't make a difference now."

"But it does, if we can save that one thing."

"We've got to leave," he said, running up to her. "Before we get trapped."

"But the clinic!"

"Keera, it's only a building. A stupid, damned building." He grabbed the hose away from her, turned off the nozzle, and dropped it to the ground. "It doesn't matter any more. It's all...done."

"But the clinic, that's where you can start over, if we save it. And I want to try, Reid. Please, let me try."

He grabbed hold of her to tug her away from the compound but she resisted and pulled back. "You don't understand," she cried. "You have to fight for the things you love, the things you want in your life. If you don't..."

"I'm fighting for you, Keera, not for the clinic. It's time to go."

She shook her head. Bent down and picked up the hose. "No," she choked, as sooty tears rolled down her cheeks. "We have to try."

"Is this because if I lose everything I won't adopt Megan as I'll be too involved in trying to start over?"

"Wh-what? How could you even think that?"

"What am I supposed to think? That you've had a change of heart, fallen in love with me, even though I have kids? That you want to do this because you want to build a life around me, my children, and even this?"

"Reid, that's not fair!"

"Isn't it? I'm about to lose a large part of my dream, and here you are, fighting harder than I am to hang onto it. Which doesn't make any sense. So why wouldn't I think you're doing this because it's about you? You've never shown me anything that would make me think otherwise!"

This couldn't be happening. He couldn't be saying these things to her. "You don't mean it," she said. "You're talking crazy because the camp is burning down."

"It's not crazy talk, Keera. It's what I think."

"Then you think wrong." She turned and started to walk away. Then spun back to face him. "To hell with you, Reid Adams. To hell with this camp, to hell with your life." They were words that broke her heart because all she'd wanted to do was save a little piece of his dream for him—his starting point for rebuilding that dream.

"Oh, and if you're afraid that now's when I walk away and abandon Megan with you, to hell with you on that one, too."

Keera didn't turn round again. Not to see the expression on his face, not to watch him follow her. No, she went straight to her car, got in and didn't look back. Not when she fetched Megan in Marston Springs and dropped off the camp belongings with Betsy, not when she headed for the highway that took her home. And not even when she had to pull off the highway and have the hardest cry of her life.

"What have I done?" she asked herself in the mirror as muddy tears streaked down her cheek.

The toddler sleeping in her car seat didn't answer. Neither did the reflection in the mirror. Only her heart did, and it wasn't telling her what she wanted to hear.

"OK, let's get you ready to go to daycare," Keera said, as she looked at the mess of toys spread from one wall to the other. Her guest room, now a temporary nursery, looked like a tornado had hit it. So maybe she wasn't the tidiest temporary mom. Her once-weekly housekeeper picked up every Friday, which gave Keera and Megan a fresh start on a new week of messiness. Four weeks in a row now had turned it into a workable routine. Scatter for six days, pick up on the seventh.

And thank heavens for the hospital daycare center. That alleviated her problems in ways she'd never anticipated. They were open seven days, twenty-four hours, and the care was excellent. She knew, because that's where she took her breaks now, instead of hiding away in her office to review a patient history or grab a thirty-minute nap. Now her breaks were spent coloring or finger-painting or sharing graham crackers and milk with Megan. Something she actually enjoyed.

What she didn't enjoy, though, was being alone, having no one there to tell her if she was doing the mothering thing the right or wrong way. She had no instinct for it, but common sense seemed to be working out pretty well. And social services were still looking for an adoptive family. Although Keera wasn't pressing them now.

In fact, she'd told the social worker she'd like to keep Megan for a while longer, and she'd even gone to the effort of starting to legalize her guardianship. Why? For Megan's security, above all. Megan needed this time to adjust. She knew her real mommy and daddy weren't coming back, and she'd become so clingy with Keera that Keera didn't have the heart to send her away until she was more ready than she was now.

But also Reid had been right. She'd thought about his words, over and over, and had eventually come to realize how she'd spent a lifetime trying to prove she wasn't her mother, trying to do exactly the opposite of what her mother had done. Yet in her own heart she'd never truly discovered what she would do without that motivation.

What she would do, though, was love taking care of Megan. Which she did. And which was why, while she still wanted the best adoptive situation for her, there wasn't such an urgency about it now. At some point the time would come to give her up. Keera knew that, rationalized it every single day. Even dreaded it. And when that time came Keera knew her heart would break.

But this was all about Megan now, and what was best for her. Still, for now, every day was a new and better step. And who knew what would happen in the future? For sure, she didn't.

So even though everything was up in the air, Keera was happier than she could remember being. But she missed Reid. Missed him desperately. Unfortunately, that was a bridge that had burned down with his camp.

The newspaper and Internet had carried accounts of the camp's destruction. Nothing specific, only that it was closed down now and that the owner was making no comment about its future. No injuries had been reported from the camp, none from the forest fire either. It had started with a campfire in an unauthorized area. One single, lousy campfire and she'd lost countless hours sleep because she missed Reid, missed the camp, missed his daughters, missed all the things she hadn't known she'd wanted until it was too late.

"After work, we're going to go do some shopping, maybe buy a pizza for dinner," she told Megan. She was surprised a child so young would love pizza the way Megan did, but the child begged for it practically every day. "And tomorrow, when I'm not working—" and blessedly not on call "—we'll go to the zoo. You'll get to see lions and elephants and zebras. Do you know what a zebra is, Megan?"

"No," the girl said.

"Then after you're dressed, how about we find a picture on the Internet?"

"Is it purple?" she asked. Like she'd discovered Megan's

favorite food was pizza, she'd also discovered her favorite color, and had even had a decorator come in and redo the guest room in little-girl decor, predominantly purple.

"No, sweetie. It's black and white, with crazy stripes."

"Crazy stripes," Megan parroted.

"A whole bunch of them." She helped Megan put on her own socks then put on her shoes and tied them. Purple shoes, pink socks. Pink was a definite concession in a purple girl's life. The thing was it was amazing to see how many opinions Megan had. Until she'd brought her home, Keera had had no clue a child so young had preferences and opinions, and, boy, had she been wrong about that.

Little Miss Megan, once she became comfortable in her new surroundings, was all opinion and preference. So much so that in an adult it might have been annoying. But in a two-year-old it was as cute as could be. Which officially put her in the category of moms prejudiced by the cuteness of their children—to the point of near-blindness.

But that was OK. This new life was agreeing with her.

What wasn't agreeing with her, though, were her feelings for Reid. They hadn't talked since that day, which was kind of surprising. In fact, for the first week she'd answered her phone with lightning speed, expecting him to call. The second week—not so much. And now, unless it was work related she didn't bother picking up because another call that wasn't him only punctuated how much she missed him. "I'd have thought he would have called to see if we made it home safely."

The timeline for that call was well past now. And she knew it, felt it in her heart and in the pit of her stomach. She'd made her impression, the one she'd intended to make, and was now suffering the consequences. Her fault entirely, and she didn't blame him for that. Only she wished she'd had time to change his mind.

Now he was back in his practice and picking up what was left over from his dream, and she wasn't part of that. And she couldn't be because he didn't want her. Had declined her phone calls the first few days after their break-up.

Break-up? From what? One night together and a whole bunch of conflicting feelings? How could they have broken up when they'd had nothing to break up from?

"Then after the zoo, maybe we'll go to the bookstore as you don't have enough books, and all little girls need lots and lots of books and bedtime stories." To tell the truth, Keera was looking forward to the bedtime stories maybe even more than Megan was. That's what surprised her. As she settled in with the child, it was like she was experiencing childhood again, a better childhood. The childhood she would have liked for herself.

And somewhere, an hour away, Reid was doing the same with his daughters. In a way it was comforting, knowing they were sharing the same experience under the same sky. But in an even bigger way it was heartbreaking because she'd gone and done the one thing she'd vowed never to do. She'd fallen in love. Only not the way she'd fallen in love the first time. This time it was different. Real. Everything. And everything she couldn't have.

"These are the clothes you're going to have to wear. I'm sorry you lost everything you bought with Keera, but I left them behind and saved the computers instead." He knew, for sure, that he couldn't duplicate Keera's effort, not in clothes, not in the girls' sentiments, and he felt bad about that.

Felt bad about a lot of things, like how Emmie and Allie had begged for weeks to have her take them shopping again. Once he'd almost given in and called her. But one call and he'd lose his resolve. And Keera Murphy wasn't the kind of woman he wanted around his daughters because they got attached, and Keera was incapable of attaching back.

Sadly, he'd gotten himself pretty attached as well. And while there was a part of him that wanted to believe her efforts to save his camp had been genuine, how could he truly believe that when she'd expressed her sentiment clearly, over and over? She didn't want children, and she did want him to adopt the one she had.

"But for now you're going to have to make do."

"But, Daddy," Emmie whined.

He shook his head. "You know what I told you. That for a little while we've got to watch our money. I've got a lot of expenses ahead, and I can't afford..."

Who was he kidding? What he couldn't afford was to have his heart ripped all the way through. It was hanging in tatters as it was. Seeing Keera again would only finish the job. "Work with me here, OK? As soon as I get some of the mess at Camp Hope sorted out, we'll have a shopping day and you can buy whatever you want. But that's going to have to wait for a few weeks." Until he had more time, more energy, more hope.

It was hard hanging on, not just for him but for the girls. Especially when all he owned was some charred acreage and a few remains of buildings. And who would have known there was so much to do in the aftermath of a disaster? Insurance claims, getting the unsafe structures leveled, permits for the work, planners and architects for the camp's future.

During the day, when he was busy, he was optimistic. But the nights were what got to him, when memories of that one perfect night with Keera crept back in spite of his best efforts to keep them out. Then from there, the losses.

Too much, too many. He couldn't sleep. Couldn't let the girls see how much he was struggling because they depended on him to be strong. To be Daddy.

"How about a date tomorrow? We'll have ice cream, maybe go to the park or see a movie? How does that sound?"

"OK," Emmie said, her voice definitely lacking enthusiasm.

"OK," Allie mimicked, in the same voice.

One thing was sure, next time a woman walked into his life he wasn't going to bring her around the girls for any reason until everything in the relationship was sorted out and there was a future involved. Because the girls missed Keera, talked about her every day, begged him to get her back.

Something he couldn't do. But something he would if he could. And wanted to so badly.

# CHAPTER TEN

"LAST NIGHT, DADDY," Allie said, her eyes filling with tears. "She didn't want me to tell you. Made me promise, cross my heart."

Reid placed his hand on Emmie's forehead. She was burning up. Practically incoherent. Pale. Sweating. He'd seen this before, last time... Except she was having associated abdominal pain now. So maybe it wasn't another flare-up of leukemia. "That's OK, sweetheart. You're not in trouble."

"Is Emmie sick again?" Allie's bottom lip trembled. "Like last time?"

"She's sick, but not like last time," he said, trying to sound upbeat for both his girls' sakes. Truth was, he didn't know. He hoped, and his objectivity as a doctor told him the symptoms didn't quite match. But as a father, all his worst fears were pummeling him.

"Is it back, Daddy?" Emmie managed to ask. "Did my leukemia come back again?"

"It might be something you ate, as your belly hurts." Or appendicitis. Yes, that's what it was. Appendicitis, which opened up a whole new set of worries, because a quick appendectomy was complicated in the aftermath of leukemia. "I think, though, we're going to have to take you to the hospital and have some tests run to see what it is."

He turned to Beau Alexander, who was already on the phone to the hospital. "If you don't mind, I'd like Joey to fly me. Don't want to waste time in the car."

"He's already fueling up the chopper," Beau said, squeezing his partner on the shoulder.

"Oh, and I have a surgeon on standby, just in case. She's not a general surgeon, but she's agreed to step in and offer an opinion, and she's getting the best general surgeon she knows rounded up, in case we need to go that route."

"Which hospital?"

"Not Mercy. And before you argue with me that you'd feel more comfortable taking Emmie where she's gone before, let me say that you've been moping around here for the past month, and all I've heard is how great Keera is, what a good doctor, good surgeon she is. So I called her, and she's taking care of getting everything ready to receive Emmie at Central Valley. By air, it's only fifteen minutes longer, and I think that right now you're going to need her support."

"And we'll watch Allie, of course. For as long as this takes," Deanna, his wife volunteered.

"I'll step up, too," Brax Alexander, the patriarch of the Alexander family, said. "Can't claim to be a pediatrician but I have my way with the kiddies, so I'll take on your cases until you're ready to get back to work. So there's nothing to worry about here, son. We've got you covered."

Reid let out a huge sigh of relief. He hadn't only become part of a medical practice here in Sugar Creek. He'd become part of a family. "I really appreciate everything."

"You just get that little girl all better and get her back to us as fast as you can," Brax said.

"And patch it up with Keera," Beau said, sliding his arm around his wife's waist. "It's time for you to be happy."

But with Keera? "We'll see," he said as he gave Allie

a kiss, then scooped Emmie into his arms and headed to the front door. Truth was, there wasn't much to be happy about and he wasn't sure he could even fake it, not now that Emmie was sick. If it was leukemia again he'd have to find a way to be strong. If it was appendicitis then maybe having Keera there, making the arrangements, would help. He didn't know. Just didn't know.

The trip was far faster than he'd expected, and he never set Emmie down the whole way. No, he held on to her for dear life, and when Joey landed the helicopter on the hospital's helipad, and when an army of medics rushed and took Emmie away from him, he couldn't think of a time when he'd felt more desolate.

"They'll take good care of her," Keera said, stepping up behind him as the chopper lifted skywards and headed back to Sugar Creek. "I got Wade Andrews, head of oncology and our leukemia specialist, to take charge of her team, and lined up Annabelle Gentry, the best general surgeon I know, in case it's her appendix. Oh, and Brett Hollingsworth, head of Pediatrics, is on his way in to oversee her general care while she's here. I've got her set up in a private room in Pediatrics, and had a bed brought in for you so you can stay."

"I don't know what to say, Keera."

"You don't have to say anything. This is about Emmie, and you know how I feel about her and Allie."

"They've missed you," he said, as she slipped her hand into his and pulled him towards the hospital door.

"I've missed them. You don't know how much I enjoyed our girls' day out. It was a first for me, and it made me realize how much I missed when I was that age. Also how much I like…" she smiled "…being around children."

"See, I told you so."

"Yes, you did, and we'll talk about that later on. Right now, though, tell me about Emmie."

"I didn't know she was sick. Apparently she hasn't felt well for a couple of days—general malaise, vomiting, which she never told me about, achiness, tender belly, feverish. Allie knew, but the girls conspired to keep it a secret because they were afraid if they told me, that would make it be leukemia again."

"We all have ways of deluding ourselves, don't we? Even when we're young, I suppose. Oh, and Allie called me a little while ago."

"Allie?"

"Yep, Allie. She didn't want to talk to you because she was afraid it would make you sad, so she called me. Had Brax dial for her."

"He's a pushover when it comes to kids. Can't ever say no to them."

"Well, he didn't say no to Allie and, Reid, what she said was so sweet. She told me if Emmie is sick like she was before, she wants to be the donor. Actually, she called it a door—near, but I knew what she meant."

"I—I… Twice in a row, I don't know what to say."

"You don't have to. I'll say it for you. You're an amazing father, and you've taught your daughters to be generous." As they stepped into the hospital, they headed straight to Pediatrics, where the team Keera had assembled was fast-working on Emmie. Blood was being drawn, X-rays being taken. Pokes, prods, IV, oxygen, all the usual.

"We're going to get her through this. Whatever it is, I promise, we're going to get her, get both of you, through this."

Reid swallowed hard, looking through the window of the procedure room. "The camp burned to the ground," he said.

"I know. I read the accounts. I'm so sorry."

"Emmie's been helping me with the plans to rebuild. I think I may have a budding architect, because the architect I've hired is actually going to incorporate some of her ideas. He said a kids' camp from a kid's perspective is what I need, and he told her that when she grows up to keep him in mind when she's looking for a…" He slapped a tear from his cheek. "I feel so damned helpless. Done this twice before, I don't know if I can do it again."

Keera stepped up behind him and slid her arm around his waist. "We may not have worked out as a couple, Reid, but I'm your friend, and I'm not going to let you go through this alone. Whatever you and Emmie need, whenever you need it, you don't even have to ask."

"I know," he said. "And I'm sorry. You don't know how much I wanted to answer your calls or call you. Or just come here and see you. Every day, Keera. Every single day of every single week since that day when you walked away from me."

"You were right, though. I didn't give you anything to trust. I was adamant about who I was and what I wanted, and there was no room inside that for us. But it did hurt, Reid, hearing how you believed that my wanting to help you with the camp was me trying to manipulate you. You had a right to that opinion, and everything I'd said or done was responsible for that opinion, and I wasn't even angry at you. It hurt, but I understood."

"Dr. Adams," Dr. Hollingsworth said, stepping out into the hall. "Emmie's pretty sick, but we're not sure yet what's causing it. We've got the first round of tests started, and what I'm proposing, because of her past history, is that we put her in the ICU for close observation until we start getting things sorted out. Might be for a few hours, might be for a few days, until we have everything worked up."

"You don't think she needs her appendix out?"

"There's a possibility but, given her history, we're reluctant to look at that as our first course of action as she's got several swollen lymph glands."

Reid nodded. "I did notice that when I examined her, which is why my first thought was…"

"A recurrence of her leukemia," Dr. Hollingsworth said. "And if Emmie was mine, I'd be thinking the same thing. But Keera said she's been active, not feeling bad."

"I asked Beau when he called me earlier," Keera explained.

"That's right. She was fine. A little tired the past couple of days but before that she was energetic as all get-out."

"In my experience, leukemia doesn't just take you down from being healthy and active one minute to where she is now. So, while we're not going to rule it out, we are looking for other causes. And make no mistake, she's a very sick little girl. But we're optimistic. In the meantime, it's going to take us about an hour to get her transferred to her ICU bed, so the doctors' lounge is available if you'd like to go and wait. And our cafeteria is open around the clock in case you want to grab something to eat. I'll page Keera as soon as we get Emmie situated, then you can come and see her."

"I appreciate it," Reid said, extending his hand to the man.

"Oh, and that camp of yours. I've heard good things. Hope you can get it up and running again because I have a couple of patients who could benefit, and I could be up for a little volunteering myself."

"Working on it," Reid said numbly, because numb was all he felt. Numb, but not alone.

"Are you sure I can't get you something?" Keera asked as they shut the door to the private room that would be Emmie's once she was out of Intensive Care. "Coffee, tea, a soft drink?"

She felt totally helpless because there truly was nothing she could do to help him except stay with him. And that wasn't helping, at least not in the way he needed.

"Thanks, but I'm good."

"You're going to have to keep yourself going for Emmie's sake. You know that, don't you?"

"Is this my pep talk?" he snapped.

"No, it's your reality check. I know you're scared, and I wish I knew what to do to make that better for you but other than being here, trying to take care of you, I can't."

"That's right. Keera the nurturer."

"That's not fair, Reid. And I know you're snapping at me because of Emmie. But I always knew my limitations, and was honest about them. So, please, don't take it out on me now, because I do want to help you."

"I know," he said, sitting down on the side of the guest bed. "And I'm sorry. It's been a horrible few weeks, thinking about everything I did wrong. Then with all the arrangements concerning the camp...now this." He looked up at her. "You didn't deserve what I said about you that day, and you don't deserve it now. I am sorry, Keera. Truly, sorry. Please, believe that."

"I do," she said gently. Then chuckled. "Oil and water. That's us, isn't it?"

He patted the bed, inviting her to sit down next to him. When she did, he pulled her into his arms and simply held her. "Not really. I seem to recall a pretty good mixing."

"We were good, weren't we? And in more ways than *that*."

"In more ways than *that*. But *that* was pretty spectacular."

"Look, Reid. When this is over, when Emmie's back on

her feet and all cured of whatever it is she's caught, and
I'm going to believe she caught a bug of some kind until
someone tells me otherwise, well, anyway, when it's over,
I really do want to help get the camp going again. I've
been thinking about it for weeks, wondering what I could
do that wouldn't pit us against each other, for starters. So
I've decided to rebuild the clinic for you, if you'll let me.
Make it a real clinic, though. Not just a make-do cabin.
Furnish it with everything you need rather than all the odds
and ends, like you had. Will you let me do that for you?"

"Insurance money isn't stretching far enough to get me
everything I need. I was on the verge of committing to
another make-do clinic simply to get it up and running."

"But I want to do better for the kids." She pulled away
from him and looked straight into his eyes. "And I'd like
to help with the actual building, as in setting up the inte-
rior, if you'll let me. But if you don't think we can work together again, I'll write you a check for whatever you need."

"That's generous. For the third time tonight I don't
know what to say."

"Say yes. It's a simple word, and the beginning of something that will be so good."

"The thing is, if Emmie's leukemia has come back, I
don't know if I can go through with plans to rebuild. Not
now, anyway. Maybe not for a long time to come."

"Then let me take over. You take care of Emmie, and
I'll make sure your camp plans go forward."

"Why do you want to do this?" he asked. "Especially
after the way I treated you last time you made the offer
to help."

"Because I believe now. Believe better, believe differently. And it's also because—" Her cellphone interrupted her, and five seconds later she jumped up from

the side of the bed. "Got to leave for a couple of minutes. Be right back."

It was time to visit Megan. She was going through one of her sullen periods, which happened when she missed Keera. And only Keera could take care of fixing it.

"I'm here, sweetheart," she said, picking up the girl, who instantly clung to Keera for dear life.

"She has a real attachment thing going," Dolores, the daycare worker, said. "Kept telling me she wanted her mommy."

"I know she does." But there was no mommy to be had.

"That's you, Doctor. You're mommy to her, no matter what the circumstances. You're the one she wants now."

Keera smiled, not sure what to do. Her initial fears of not being able to manage this were gone. So were her fears about her lack of natural instinct, because she did have her common sense intact. And as far as Megan being Kevin's child, it didn't matter any more. He'd done a good thing bringing this child into the world, and she wasn't a reminder of anything except she was a little girl who needed a real mommy or daddy. "Look, I'm going to keep her with me for a little while. When she gets over this, I may bring her back."

Or she might just beg off the surgical rotation for the morning—she only had one minor procedure scheduled—and ask one of her associates to take it. Then she could stay with Reid and keep Megan comforted as well. For someone who wasn't a nurturer, she seemed to being doing an awful lot of that lately. "I'll call you or whoever's on duty later on and let you know what we're going to do. And in the meantime, I think Miss Megan and I might go down to the cafeteria and find us a banana and yogurt for breakfast. Does that sound yummy to you, Megan?"

With her head tucked as tight as it could be into Keera's

chest, Megan gave her a nod. "Then afterwards we're going to go visit Doc Reid. Do you remember him? He's the nice man who took care of you when you had measles."

She nodded again.

"Oh, by the way," Dolores said as Keera left. "Social services called here yesterday, looking for you. I didn't take the call but I saw the note and wasn't sure if the message got to you or not."

"It didn't," she said, as a lump formed in her stomach, realizing the very best news for Megan could be the very worst news for her.

"Well, you're supposed to call your caseworker as soon as you can. She said it's important but not urgent."

Keera nodded reluctantly, now facing a reality she wasn't sure she wanted to face. "Later. If she calls back, tell her I've got a crisis here at the hospital but I'll get back to her later."

After a quick trip to the cafeteria, then with yogurt, milk, a banana, and a couple of coffees in hand, not to mention a toddler, Keera hurried back up to Reid's room, stopped in her progress by Brett Hollingsworth, who asked her to tell Reid that Emmie was being moved to the ICU right then.

"You've sure turned...well, I guess the only way to describe it is domestic. Just look at you, here in Pediatrics with your child, comforting a worried father, taking on the role of camp counselor."

"Wrong on all counts but one. I am comforting a worried father, because he's my friend. There's nothing domestic involved in that."

"I've heard rumors coming from daycare that you try to get down there to group-sing every day." He grinned. "You know, 'The wheels on the bus go round...'"

"Yeah, yeah," Keera said, shoving past him and hurrying on to the room.

"I'm just saying," Brett called after her.

She ignored him as she pushed open the door, scooted Megan in first, then followed.

"What's this?" Reid asked.

"It's what I do in my spare time now."

"You kept her?"

"Temporarily, which I think may be coming to an end shortly. I mean, when she was sick I promised her I wouldn't let them take her to one of *those* places, and I meant it. I was there, raised in them, and there's no way they're going to do that to her. So I've been managing."

"I'm not surprised," he said, rushing over to take the food and coffee from her. "It's what I saw in you all along."

"No, you didn't. You wanted to, but it wasn't there."

"Yet look at you now."

"Someone else just said that to me," she said, pulling the bedside tray away from the wall and pushing it over to one of the chairs. "And I told him he was wrong." But not as wrong as he once might have been.

"See, there you go again."

She shrugged. "OK, so maybe I'm not as bad at this as I thought I'd be. But I'm still a darned sight further away from parent of the year than you are. Speaking of which, Emmie's being transferred right now, and they should be coming to get you in the next few minutes, once she's settled in."

"You're efficient, Keera."

"Words to turn a girl's heart."

He laughed. "What if I also told you that efficient is sexy?"

"Then I'd nominate you for man of the year." She opened the carton of yogurt and handed a plastic spoon to Megan, who dug right in. "Because most men have other standards for sexy, if you know what I mean. So it's nice to hear that something substantial like being efficient can also be sexy."

"Oh, don't get me wrong. I have the same standards as other men, as far as sexy goes. And you've got all that. But you've got more."

She laughed. "See, now the truth comes out."

A knock on the door startled them both, and a nurse poked her head in the door to tell Reid that he could see Emmie now.

"Give her a hug for me," Keera said, "and tell her I'll come by to see her later on."

"Ten minutes every hour," the nurse warned Reid, as he headed for the door. "Wish we could do better as you're a pediatrician, but I can't. Sorry."

"Then I'll see you back here in twelve minutes," Keera said, and turned her attention to breaking the banana into bite-sized pieces for Megan. Then she dialed the dreaded phone number.

"Hi, Consuela," she said, when the woman on the other end picked up. "It's Keera Murphy, and I understand you've been trying to get a hold of me."

"Hello," Reid said very quietly, as he stood over Emmie's bed and looked down. Even though it was a pediatric ward, she looked so dwarfed—by the bed, by the equipment. It was something he remembered from last time, staring at all the hugeness surrounding his little girl. In ways only a parent could understand, it intimidated him, scared him to death. But he couldn't let on—for Emmie's sake, even for his own.

"Did it come back, Daddy?" she asked weakly.

"We don't know anything yet. But soon, I promise."

"I'm so tired."

"I know you are, which is why you're in here. So you can sleep. That's the only thing you have to do now. Just sleep."

"What about your patients? Who's going to take care of them?"

"That's not for you to worry about," he said, pushing the hair from her eyes. "It's all taken care of. Brax is going to see my patients, and Beau and Deanna are watching Allie, so there's nothing to be concerned about."

"Can I see Keera? I want to tell her how all those clothes we bought got burned up. Do you think she'll take me shopping again?"

"Keera's taking care of Megan right now, but she said she'd come and see you soon. Why don't you ask her yourself if you can go shopping? I think she might…" He didn't finish his sentence. Didn't have to, as Emmie had fallen back to sleep.

"How is she?" Keera asked.

"Worried that all those clothes you bought her got burned up. She wants to go shopping again."

"And I'd love to take her again. Her and Allie, and…" She paused. Frowned.

"What's the matter?"

"I got a call from Megan's social worker," she whispered, so Megan wouldn't hear. "They've found a couple who might want to adopt her. She wants to schedule a first meeting between Megan and them."

"That's good, isn't it?"

She shrugged. "It's what I wanted, initially. No, actually, what I wanted was for you to adopt her. I told you that."

"But it didn't work out."

"And now…" Tears suddenly filled her eyes. "Now it's too late."

"But she'll have a permanent home, Keera. That's what's best for her. And I'm sure the social worker was very choosy in picking out the right parents."

"She does need parents, doesn't she?"

"Or parent. Single parenting has its rewards. If you want to keep her."

"I want to do what's best for her, and I've always known it was a home better than the one I could give her."

"Yet look at her. She's eating, perfectly contented to do it by herself. And she seems to be gaining some independence…some of your independence. That's good mothering, Keera, no matter what you want to call it. You're teaching her what she needs to know, pointing her in the direction she needs to go, and at the end of the day that's all a parent can really do besides love and protect them. So, what else did Consuela have to say?"

"I have to let her know by noon."

"That?"

"That I want to keep her myself—*if* I want to keep her."

"Are you thinking about it?"

"I don't know. Maybe. But I'm so confused. Because getting what I wanted—a home for Megan—doesn't feel as good as it should. It doesn't feel good at all."

"So, let me ask you this. Does Megan make your life better?"

"I know my life is different now, but in a good way. She gives me balance. And a purpose I didn't know I wanted, or could have."

"And you give her balance."

"But it's all a novelty right now, and that's what scares me. You know, it's like when you get a new toy and that's all you want to play with. Then eventually you get tired of it and totally ignore it."

"You think you'd get tired of Megan?" he asked.

"No, not Megan. But of the role of mothering. That's the novelty, and I'm enjoying the challenge and trying hard not to let my mother issues interfere—you know, trying to do the opposite of what my mother would do. You were right about that, Reid.

"I based a life not on what I wanted but on the opposite of what my mother would do. And I'm working hard to stop it. But I'm still at the point where it's a conscious effort."

"That will come naturally in due course, the way your feelings for Megan have come naturally."

"I do love her."

"Then adopt her. Simple as that."

Keera glanced over at the child, who'd managed to smear her strawberry yogurt from ear to ear. It was like she was wearing a pink beard. So cute, so innocent.

"I want to." She swiped at the tears beginning to roll down her cheeks. Great, fat droplets of grief that were ripping through her soul for so many things. "But is love enough?"

"Love's enough, Keera. Trust me, no matter what else happens, love is what gets you through. Loving Megan is enough. It's where it starts, and everything else builds from there. So now it's time to trust yourself. You're not the wounded little girl any more. You're the woman who has the opportunity to care for another wounded little girl. You'll make her life better, the way she'll make your life better. And I'm speaking from experience on that one."

"This isn't easy, Reid," she said, swatting at her tears and sniffling.

"The right decisions seldom are easy." He pulled her into his arms. "Weeks ago I met this stubborn, opinionated woman who didn't like kids. At least, not in the sense that she wanted to deal with them on a day-to-day basis. Now look at her, raising one, loving one, her heart breaking over one. I don't think it's a tough decision. In fact, I think it may be the easiest decision you'll ever make."

He pulled his cellphone from his pocket and handed it to her. "Make the call. You'll never forgive yourself if you don't."

Taking the phone from his hand, she nodded and swallowed hard. "I still think you'd make the better parent," she said, then dialed Consuela.

"Dr. Adams," Brett Hollingsworth said from the door, "could I speak to you privately in the hall?"

Keera reached out and squeezed his hand as she waited for her call to go through. "Want me to come with you?" she asked.

"I'm fine. And I'll feel better after I know you got through to Consuela."

"Thanks, Reid," she said, as he turned and walked away.

His response was a lackluster nod to accompany his slumped shoulders, and she wished to heaven she could make the walk with him, but she couldn't. She knew that. And her heart hurt so badly for him she could barely talk when Consuela came on the line.

"Well, the good news is it's not her appendix. Nothing in her blood work indicates she's having a recurrence of her leukemia either."

Finally, Reid let go of the breath he'd been holding. "Then what is it?"

"We think it's mesenteric adenitis." An inflammatory condition that often resulted from general weakening in cancers associated with the lymph system. "Not sure yet, because we're ruling out other things. But the lymphs in her belly are swollen. Combine that with her nausea and vomiting, her lack of appetite, the malaise, fever, and she's been complaining of a headache—all pretty classic symptoms."

"Could she have picked up a virus that caused it?"

"My best guess right now would be yes. Maybe something as simple as stomach flu. It's all interrelated with her leukemia, and not all that uncommon."

"I—I don't know what to say. I mean, that's good news. No, it's great news!"

"What's great news?" Keera said, walking up behind him.

"Mesenteric adenitis."

"Whoa, that's an offbeat kind of diagnosis." She smiled. "But a good one. And it makes sense."

"Well, I still want to do the imaging," Brett continued, "but we've ruled out appendicitis as well as leukemia."

Keera slipped her hand into Reid's. "So do the imaging. STAT," she said happily.

"Already ordered," he said. "Just wanted Dr. Adams to know what we're thinking right now."

"I'm thinking I was too involved to even consider..." Reid shut his eyes, drew in a deep breath. "Whatever consents you'll need, you know you've got them."

"What I want to do is let her sleep the next few hours then see if we can get the imaging in late afternoon, early evening. In the meantime, get her started on fluid and electrolyte replacement, and an anti-inflammatory. Then treat other symptoms as they arise and keep our fingers crossed that we caught this early enough that no other symptoms will come. Oh, and I do want to watch her overnight in the ICU, but by morning I think she'll be stable enough to transfer to the floor."

"I don't know what to say," Reid said.

"For, what, the third or fourth time today?" Keera teased.

Brett punched him on the shoulder. "Well, I say go get some sleep. You look like hell and in a few hours I think your little girl's going to feel better than you do."

"Thank you," Reid said, as Brett walked away.

"Don't thank me. Thank Keera. She's the one who dragged us all down here in the middle of the night and kept pushing us to find the problem."

"Thank you," he whispered, bending to kiss her on the lips.

"He's right, you know. You do look worse than Emmie does."

"That's what parenthood does to you sometimes."

"Guess I'm about to find out," she said.

"Really? It going to happen?"

"It's going to happen. I'm going to adopt her."

Suddenly Reid pulled her into his arms and the kiss he gave her was neither circumspect nor proper for a hospital corridor, but he didn't care because everything was right in his world. More than right. Everything was perfect.

"Well, Brax has Megan and Emmie down at the stable looking at the new foal, and Deanna and Beau took Allie, along with their kids, Lucas and Emily, to go get ice cream. So we're finally alone. At long last."

"It's a nice place. I can see why you love raising your girls here. I'm hoping Megan and I get some weekend invitations to come down every once in a while."

"See, that's the thing. I wasn't planning on weekend invitations. They're too disruptive."

She saw the twinkle in his eyes, didn't know what it meant. "So we're not invited?"

"That's the other thing. You are, but not in the way you expected."

"What are you trying to say, Reid? I'm not invited, but I am?"

"I was thinking like more in the permanent sense. And before you shoot me down, I know you vowed never to get married again, never have a serious relationship, whatever that nonsense was you kept dropping on me at camp. But that was then, and you're a mom now who needs a dad for her daughter. And I'm a dad who needs a mom for my daughters."

"What about the other part?"

"Which part?"

"Where you're a man who needs a wife for himself? Because the rest are good reasons, but that's the best one. That, and the one where I love you more than I can even tell you. For me it was love at first sight. Or else I would have shoved Megan in your arms and gotten the heck out of there. But when you opened the door..." She shook her head.

"You had me at the door, Doc Adams, and I really didn't want to be had. Although deep down I knew I did, even though I didn't think I could ever be what you needed."

"You were, Keera. I needed to make you see who you really were, though. Who you really are. Really can be. So, can you do this? Because I don't want you making all the compromises while I sit here and do nothing. You're going to get two other children in the deal, and that's a huge compromise, because they want you to be their real mommy."

"I'm not compromising a thing because I want to be their real mommy. I love those girls, Reid. Yours, mine... *ours*. But you do have to understand that I'm the one who needs to make the biggest change. For the first time in my life, though, I want to. Because I need to. There's nothing else that will ever make me complete the way you and the girls do. And it scares me how much I'll need your help in this. Maybe every day for the rest of my life. But I want to make the change. Walk away from everything I was and walk towards everything I want to be. As long as you know exactly what you're getting."

"Oh, I know. And, seriously, all your aversions to children, family and marriage scared me for a while, or else I would have proposed maybe the day after I met you. Which was when I think I fell in love with you. Or maybe it was at first sight. I'm still a little foggy on that. The thing is, I saw through you pretty quickly. Saw how much you were trying to hide, or hide behind. And always fighting to prove you were tough, and impervious to the world. Except you weren't, and I knew that."

"Your camp changed me, your girls changed me, Megan changed me. Most of all, you changed me. Made me realize I can have the things I thought I never could. The worst thing anyone could ever know about me is what you know, and it doesn't matter to you."

"Because everything you were in the past turned you into the woman I love today."

"My past isn't over, though. You've got to understand that it may rear its ugly head from time to time. And you may see that stubborn streak come back as well. That's part of who I am."

"Only a small part. And we'll face it together if it does peek in every now and then. No big deal."

"Easy for you to say."

"Easy for me to know, because I know you."

"And I know you."

"But can you be a country GP, give up your surgical practice and settle down to the kind of life we have here? Because we're a very family-centered practice, and our

families always come first, no matter what. Which might
be a little difficult for you—"

"Not difficult," she interrupted. "Although I still want
to keep my surgical practice, just limit it to maybe a couple
days a week. An easy flight to Central Valley if the man
you're married to is a pilot."

"Married sounds good, doesn't it?"

"Very good. Because for once in my life I think I'll
be able to relax, breathe, just enjoy life. And with three
daughters to raise, and take shopping!"

"About that shopping, and your choice of clothes for
them…"

"What's wrong with my choice of clothes?" she asked.

"Not traditional. Just saying."

"Just saying you think I'm not traditional? Hey, Doc!
We've got an hour to kill before anybody misses us. What
do you say to going over to your place so I can show you
exactly how untraditional the rest of your life is going to
be?"

He reached for Keera's hand, then when he had it pulled
her roughly into his embrace. "What do you say about
going over to *our* place so we can do we do just that?"

\* \* \* \* \*

# SAFE IN HIS HANDS

BY
## AMY RUTTAN

MILLS & BOON

First published in Great Britain 2013
by Mills & Boon, an imprint of Harlequin (UK) Limited.
Harlequin (UK) Limited, Eton House, 18-24 Paradise Road,
Richmond, Surrey TW9 1SR

© Amy Ruttan 2013

ISBN: 978 0 263 89915 3

Harlequin (UK) policy is to use papers that are natural, renewable and recyclable products and made from wood grown in sustainable forests. The logging and manufacturing process conform to the legal environmental regulations of the country of origin.

Printed and bound in Spain
by Blackprint CPI, Barcelona

**Dear Reader**

Thank you for picking up a copy of SAFE IN HIS HANDS, my debut book with Mills & Boon® Medical Romance™. I'm thrilled to be sharing this with you.

It's always been a dream of mine to become a writer, especially with Harlequin®, and this stems from my grandmother's hidden stash of romance novels—books we shared together when she bravely fought and then lost her battle with cancer.

SAFE IN HIS HANDS was inspired by my love of northern Canada. Even though I was raised in Toronto, my family has strong roots firmly planted in the muskeg and forests of northern Ontario. It also comes from my admiration for medical professionals who work under the toughest conditions worldwide to provide healthcare.

Also, this book is about a second chance at love, because I believe there's always a second chance—especially in light of a tragedy, like the one which separated my hero and heroine years before.

I hope you enjoy my debut Medical Romance™. I love to hear from readers, so please drop by my website: www.amyruttan.com

With the warmest wishes

*Amy Ruttan*

This book is dedicated firstly to my husband, Chris.
I couldn't do this without you.

A big thanks to my critique partner, Ann R,
who read this book in its many incarnations and never
once complained about reading it yet again, and my editor
Suzanne Clarke who whipped my hero into shape!

Also a big thanks to a certain group of ladies,
in particular Kimber, for cheering me up every day!

And lastly a big thanks to all the physicians and healthcare
professionals who do work in remote places because of
their passion to provide healthcare to everyone.

# CHAPTER ONE

*DAMN. WHAT'VE I done?*

Dr. Charlotte James had been watching the arrivals board in the Iqaluit airport for some time. She was so focused on arrivals she didn't even notice the people coming and going around her. A watched pot never boiled, or so the old saying went, but she couldn't help it. This was probably the longest she'd ever stood still. In her job there was no time to stand still. In fact, she hated it. She could be doing so many other things. Filing, for instance.

Not that she particularly *liked* filing. She preferred her organized chaos. However, there were a ton of files on her desk, and Rosie had been pestering her for a week to put them away. Instead, she was waiting here for *his* flight to arrive.

"Flight 207 from Ottawa now arriving at gate three."

The past, when it came to Dr. Quinn Devlyn, was where it needed to be: firmly locked away. She'd moved on and she had no doubt his life had, too. He was, after all, at the top in his chosen specialty, and she was right where she'd always wanted to be.

This time Quinn Devlyn wouldn't blindside her or suck her into some crazy off-kilter distracting, albeit passionate, love affair.

No, siree.

Her life was good. Not perfect but, then, whose was? Charlotte was happy.

*Courage.*

She spun around and saw the plane taxi in on the small airstrip, blending in with the stark, white landscape of Canada's High Arctic. The only color out there was the brightly painted houses that dotted the landscape. Her pulse thundered between her ears.

*He's here.*

The pit of Charlotte's stomach dropped to her knees. No. Scratch that. Make it the soles of her feet. Not since her MCATs had she felt this way, as though she was perpetually on the verge of hurling.

She was seriously beginning to doubt her sanity in bringing her ex-fiancé up to Cape Recluse. It wasn't a place where she could avoid him easily. He'd be constantly underfoot and she was dreading every moment of it. Would she be able to resist him? The only time she had resisted him had been when he'd left. When their relationship had ended, she'd never wanted to see him again, but his presence here now was a price she was willing to pay to help out her friend.

*Get a grip on yourself.*

A blast of cold air shook her from her reverie. Her gaze focused on the tinted windows, watching the passengers head across the tarmac to the warmth of the bright yellow airport building. Immediately she picked Quinn's form out of the group of passengers.

Tall and broad, even though he was huddled down under his collar against the cold. Just the sight of him made her heart beat a little bit faster, her cheeks heat and the butterflies in her stomach go crazy. Her pulse thundered between her ears like a marching band. She hadn't seen him in five years—not since he'd walked out on her—but he was making her feel like a giddy teenager again.

*Don't let him affect you like this*, Charlotte chastised herself. She'd moved on with her life. The wound he'd left in her heart had finally healed.

The double doors opened and he stepped into the airport, moving to the side to let more people in from the frigid cold. He set down his luggage and unwound his scarf.

*Damn, he still looks as good as ever.* Charlotte had been kind of hoping Quinn's fast, career-driven lifestyle would've caught up with and aged him, but he looked as sexy and charming as ever.

Even from a few feet away she could see there was a bit of gray around his sandy-brown temples, but it suited him. Made him look more dashing and debonair. Some stubble shadowed his chin, but it didn't hide the faint line of the scar that crossed his lips. A tingle of heat shot through her body as she suddenly recalled the way his lips had brushed across hers. A flush of goose bumps spread across her skin just at the thought of the way he would kiss a path down her body, his strong hands caressing her, holding her.

*What're you doing?* She was not some lovestruck goofy med student anymore. She was a physician with a thriving practice. There was no way she was going to let him in again.

Hell would have to freeze over, not that it would take much, given the current temperature outside was minus thirty.

Charlotte shut those memories away firmly, refusing to think about them any further.

Instead, she remembered how he'd brushed off the miscarriage of their child as being for the best.

As a chance to move to New York and pursue their careers.

Only New York had not been what she'd wanted. She was where she wanted to be. Not to follow him had been her decision, her right to go after her dreams.

*I can do this for Mentlana.*

This was all for her best friend. The only thing close to a family she'd had since her father had died when she was ten. Charlotte never knew her mother, who'd died when she was two. Mentlana and her family had been there with open arms when Charlotte had returned to Cape Recluse after Quinn had left and she'd lost her baby.

Correction: *their* baby.

Now Mentlana needed help and Quinn was the best when it came to neonatal medicine. For her best friend, Charlotte would face death itself. Even though, as far as she was concerned, Dr. Quinn Devlyn was far more dangerous than the Grim Reaper. She'd take him on, anyway.

Quinn would save Mentlana's baby.

Mustering her courage and holding her head high, Charlotte strode over to him. All the while her heart was racing and her knees shook like they were about to give out on her. He looked up, his chocolate gaze reeling her in as she moved toward him. His eyes were twinkling and she suddenly remembered how easy it was to get lost in those eyes.

They were hypnotizing.

The thought frightened her and she stopped a foot away from him, frozen in fear. Distance from him would be the safest.

*Remember, he left you. You can't get hurt again. You're over him.*

She couldn't let her guard down when it came to Quinn Devlyn.

Not now that she was finally whole again.

"Well, well. If it isn't the great wilderness physician," he teased, as his eyes roved over her from head to toe, a haughty smile on his lips and that damn dimple in his cheek popping up.

His mocking tone made her grind her teeth just a bit. She pressed her lips together, forcing a smile. "Dr. Devlyn. I'm glad you could come."

"It's Dr. Devlyn, now? When did we become so formal? I know we didn't part on good terms, but can we drop the formalities?" The spicy scent of his cologne—a clean scent of masculine soap and something else—teased her senses.

"Fine, but first names are as far as we go, do you understand? You're here in a professional capacity. Nothing more."

"Agreed. I would expect nothing less, Charlotte."

It was the way he said her name that triggered the memory. The two of them together for the first time, locked in a small hotel room in Niagara Falls, and the way he'd whispered her name against her neck.

*"God, Charlotte. I need you."*

I need you. Never, I love you. She should've taken that as a sign when she'd said yes to his proposal in the first place, but she'd been so blinded by love.

Charlotte nodded, but blooming warmth in her stomach spread to her cheeks. "Did you have a good flight?" she asked, trying to make small talk.

"As good as can be expected. The man next to me seemed to invade my space a lot, but overall it was as enjoyable as any other flight." He pulled up the handle to his rolling suitcase with a snap. The tone was a bit arrogant and that attitude was why she'd never brought him to Cape Recluse when they had first got engaged. Quinn had champagne tastes and was a city slicker through and through. Of course, if she'd brought him home when they had first got engaged it might've saved her some heartache.

Then she wouldn't have lost the baby, except she didn't regret carrying his baby, even for such a short time. She had known from the get-go that Quinn was not a family man. In her youthful naivety she'd thought she could change him.

How wrong she'd been.

*Let it go.*

It was no longer her job to care what Quinn Devlyn thought. "Well, we'd better get up to Cape Recluse. It's a two-hour flight there and there's talk of a storm coming in from Labrador. Also, I'd like to get up there before it's dark."

"It's two o'clock in the afternoon," he said, puzzled.

"The sun sets early up here."

"I thought this was the land of the midnight sun?"

"In summer... This is winter. We have long periods of night."

"Yikes." Quinn shook his head. "So how are we getting there?"

"I fly." Charlotte turned on her heel and strode off toward the other section of the airport where her plane was kept in a private rented hangar. Quinn kept in step beside her.

"What do you mean, you fly? As in a plane?" His tone was one of surprise and perhaps awe.

"Yes, I don't have wings." To prove her point she flapped her arms. Quinn rolled his eyes; he had never been one for foolishness in public places.

"You know what I mean. When did you learn how to fly?"

"About four years ago, after a man died in my arms from a very *mild* myocardial infarction. His death could've been prevented if we'd had regular flights from Iqaluit to Cape Recluse. By the time the air ambulance landed, Mr. Tikivik was dead. It was then I decided to learn how to fly, so I could fly my patients to Iqaluit if need be."

"So you're a physician and a paramedic, as well?" The tone was sarcastic, making her bristle with annoyance. His attitude on job specifications certainly hadn't changed one bit.

"What else are they supposed to do? Plan their medical emergencies to fit around a pilot's schedule?"

"I didn't mean to upset you. I think it's a lot to ask for limited pay."

Charlotte turned to face him. "Money doesn't mean that much to me. Lives mean more."

Quinn didn't respond but looked a bit taken aback. Guilt assailed her. She didn't want to pick a fight with him, not after he'd come all this way and on his own dime.

"Sorry," she apologized.

"For what?" he asked.

"If I insulted you."

"You didn't. You have nothing to be sorry about."

"Of course." Charlotte shook her head. Quinn never had hidden the fact that success and to be the best in his field drove him. In his eyes you were nothing without those attributes.

"I'm interested in meeting Mentlana Tikivik and ex- amining her and the baby. Still, I don't quite understand why you don't just fly her down to Toronto."

"She has a pulmonary embolus."

Quinn whistled. "Does she know about the diagnosis of the fetus?"

"Yes, I told her." Charlotte sighed. "I told her I was bringing a specialist up to determine the severity of the CCAM. She's aware of what may have to happen, and she's fine with it. She wants to do whatever it takes to save her baby."

*Just like I would've done to save mine.*

A lump formed in her throat as her mind wandered back to that horrible day when she'd spotted the mass on the baby's lungs. She'd recognized the congenital cystic adenomatoid malformation, or CCAM, for what it was, and there had been no way she could fix it. She was only a general practitioner. She wasn't qualified.

"Of course." He nodded. "Did you explain the procedure to her?"

"Oh, yes." Charlotte couldn't help but smile as she remembered having to go through each step of the procedure, like she was talking to a first-year surgical resident.

"Did she understand?" Quinn asked, confused.

"Eventually," Charlotte replied.

"Eventually?"

Charlotte laughed. "She understands, but Mentlana is very...inquisitive. I'll warn you now, she'll bombard you with questions."

"No need to warn me. I've dealt with worse, I'm sure. I've consulted on many patients before and I've a way of explaining complex medical procedures so patients understand me."

Charlotte rolled her eyes. "Your pride is healthy, I see."

Quinn smiled. "I have an excellent bedside manner."

*In your dreams, perhaps.*

"Right, I forgot about your charming persona with patients." She snapped her fingers. "You're something of a McSteamy."

"A...what?"

"Never mind, it's a *Grey's Anatomy* joke."

"Didn't that character die?"

Charlotte smirked. "I didn't know you were a *Grey's Anatomy* fan."

He sighed. "What I meant was that I have a way of getting people to open up to me. I have a winning personality."

Charlotte cocked an eyebrow. "Is that so?"

Quinn chuckled. "Okay. Look, what I meant was I'll be able to explain it to her and gain her trust. I've done this surgery before."

Trust was important, especially in the Inuk culture. Trust was important to her, too. She'd trusted Quinn. She'd never forget how deeply in love with him she'd been. Quinn had claimed her heart, body and soul. He'd taken her innocence and had then crushed all her hopes and dreams when he'd walked out on her after she'd lost their baby.

*"It's for the best, Charlotte. We're not ready. We have our careers ahead of us."*

The day he'd walked out had been the day he'd lost her trust. She'd never let him in again.

*Never is a long time.*

"Hey, are you okay? You zoned out, there, for a moment," Quinn said, waving a hand in front of her face.

Charlotte shook the painful memory away. "If you're sure you can handle Mentlana, I'll leave you to it."

"Charlotte, your friend will be totally at ease and informed during the entire procedure."

"Trust is not easily given by people in a small, close-knit and isolated community."

"Trust me." He grinned, a dimple puckering.

"I did that once before," she muttered.

"What?" he asked. He hadn't heard her, but when had he ever? When they'd been together, everything had been about him and she'd been so in love she'd been content to follow.

It had taken her a long time realize she'd been so desperate to have her own family she'd been blinded to the fact she had been engaged to a man who was already married—to his work.

"Don't worry about it." Though Charlotte wasn't entirely sure he could fit in with the residents of Cape Recluse. A man like Quinn would stick out like a sore thumb.

"Should I worry?" he asked.

"So, I was surprised to learn you're in Toronto," Charlotte said, changing the subject but also feeding her nosy side. New York had been Quinn's dream destination, his Mecca, his reason for leaving her, but when she'd called he'd been in Toronto.

"My father's health deteriorated two years ago. He offered me a position at the hospital. He wanted to groom me to become Chief of Surgery." Quinn frowned and quickened his pace. Charlotte had an inkling it was a touchy subject. At least that explained why he'd given up his practice in Manhattan and moved to Toronto. It impressed her that he'd returned home to help his father, despite his history with his parents.

"Did he retire?"

"No." His voice was stiff. "No, he died."

*Good going, dingbat.*

"I'm so sorry. I didn't know."

Quinn shrugged. "It was his fault. He didn't practice what he preached. Excessive smoker and drinker. Cancer caught up with him."

"Still. I'm sorry." Charlotte didn't know what else to say. She knew Quinn hadn't had the best relationship with his parents, but it was still hard to lose one. She was practically a pro in that department.

She led him into a warm hangar where her little Citation jet was waiting. Quinn whistled in appreciation.

"Where did you get this?" he asked.

"I bought it at an auction. It's a '93 and was in bad shape interior-wise, but I didn't care about that. I kitted it out to transport patients."

"It's a beaut."

Charlotte grinned. She was proud of her jet and it made her preen that Quinn looked up at it in admiration. When they had been choosing their specialties, he hadn't been overly impressed with her choice of general practitioner.

*You don't need his approval.*

"Well, then, we'd better get going. I'll be back in a moment. I just have to clear something with the hangar's manager."

Charlotte jogged away. Quinn's personality was the same: overconfident, arrogant and cocky. But none of that mattered right now. His self-assuredness would probably be just the thing needed to save Mentlana and her baby.

And that was all that mattered.

*What am I doing here again?* Quinn asked himself, as another round of turbulence rocked the plane. Yet he knew exactly why he'd come. Because of Charlotte.

He'd had to see for himself that she was okay. Honestly, had he expected a broken, sad woman stuck in a dead-end job in the wilds of nowhere?

Yeah, in fact, he had.

When she'd refused to come to Manhattan after her miscarriage, he'd known she was done with him. Though it had smarted, he hadn't been a stranger to rejection from someone he loved. He'd dealt with it and had thrown himself completely into his work, but some perverse part of him had needed, *wanted* to see her again. When he'd left her she'd been so ill, so fragile.

Now she was whole and healthy.

It was like the miscarriage had never happened. She was confident, happy in her job. Hell, she'd even learned how to fly a plane. When he'd seen that jet, he'd been impressed. She wasn't the same girl he'd left behind. It seemed she was stronger for their parting.

Whereas he was not.

He glanced down at his hand and flexed it. The leather of his glove creaked, his hand inside, stiff.

A year ago, he'd been in a car accident during a bad bout of fog on the highway. His hand had been crushed. Quinn flexed his hand again, curling and then releasing it. Yes, it'd been broken and he'd undergone countless surgeries to repair it, but he could still use it. His hand had mended with time. Perhaps Charlotte's heart had, too, in the five years they'd been apart.

He doubted it. When Charlotte had greeted him it'd been so formal. So forced.

"Whoa, that was a bit rough," he remarked, as they hit more disturbance. He was no stranger to flying, but that was the most jarring bit of turbulence he'd ever experienced. Of course, he was used to first-class seats instead of being crammed into a small cockpit beside the pilot, especially an alluring pilot like Charlotte.

His shoulders almost touched hers in the tight space, just a near brush of her body against his sending his blood pumping. Just being in her presence again aroused him. Charlotte was a strong aphrodisiac, like ambrosia, and she had tasted just as sweet, too.

*Blast. Get ahold of yourself. You're not some randy med student. You're going to be Chief of Surgery when you return to Toronto.*

Only he couldn't get ahold of himself. She looked exactly as she had when he'd first laid eyes on her. The slender figure and bright red curls were exactly the same. Her face, with only the barest hint of makeup, still looked as fresh and innocent. It was like time hadn't touched her.

*Perhaps the cold preserves people up here.*

Quinn shook his head. He'd never understood her desire to live on top of the world. He hated winter at the best of times. The frigid air seemed to reach down his throat and scald his lungs with ice.

"Is something wrong?" Charlotte asked casually, not looking at him.

"What makes you think something's wrong?"

The plane lurched and she adjusted her controls. "You're muttering to yourself. Not used to a small plane, eh? Prefer first class?"

"Well, at least I can get a drink in first class." He rubbed his hand. "That, and I'm not used to turbulence that seems more like bull-riding at the Calgary Stampede."

Charlotte grinned. "This is mild."

"Good God. Mild? Are you certain?"

She chuckled. He'd always liked her laughter. "Positive. There's a storm coming."

"Did we hit it?"

She shook her head. "Nope. The storm is chasing us. We'll beat it."

Quinn shuddered. *Snow. Ice.* "I don't know how you live up here."

"I like the rugged wilderness."

"I thought you were afraid of bears. Isn't this bear country?"

She laughed, her green eyes twinkling. "This is true."

"You never did tell me why you're afraid of bears."

"It's silly, really."

"Come on, humor me. There's no in-flight movie, either."

"No. I'm not telling you." She grinned and adjusted some more knobs.

"Come on. I promise I won't say anything." He waggled his eyebrows, teasing her.

She shot him a look of disbelief. "No way. And stop that eyebrow-waggling."

"What, this?" He did it again for effect. Quinn had forgotten it drove her batty and he'd forgotten what fun it was to tease her.

"Lord, you look like a demented Groucho Marx or something."

"I'll keep pestering. You know I have a bit of an annoying streak."

"A bit?" A smile quirked her lips. "Fine. It's because I'm afraid of being eaten alive."

He cocked an eyebrow. "Is that so?"

Charlotte's creamy white cheeks stained with crimson and fire flooded his veins as an image of her, naked, flashed through his mind. He could still taste her kisses on his lips, recall her silky hair and her smooth skin under his hands. Their bodies had fit so well together. It had been so right. His body reacted to her presence. So pure and so not the kind of girl his parents would want for him.

They'd never approved of Charlotte but he hadn't cared. He'd pursued her at first because she was good looking, bright and he'd known it would irk his parents to no end. She had not been like the boring girls they'd kept throwing in his path. Charlotte had not been suitable.

No, Charlotte had been exciting and taboo. Somewhere along the way he'd fallen in love with her. Only they'd wanted different things. She'd wanted a family. He hadn't. With his loveless childhood, Quinn knew he wasn't father material.

When his relationship with Charlotte had ended, his mother had reminded him frequently that Charlotte hadn't been the woman for him. His mother did like to rub salt into a wound.

And they'd been right. Charlotte hadn't been the woman for him.

They were so different, but her difference was what had excited him most.

Quinn pushed aside all those thoughts. They would do nothing but get him into trouble. He was a professional.

A surgeon.

The plane jolted and she was thrown against the dash. Quinn unbuckled and reached out, steadying her. The scent of her coconut shampoo wrapped around him, reminding him of the summer they'd spent in Yellowknife, in a cabin on the shores of Great Slave Lake. Endless nights of blistering passion under the midnight sun.

"Are you okay?" he asked, closing the small gap between them. He could see her pulse racing at the base of her throat.

"I'm fine. Fine." She cleared her throat and shrugged her shoulders. Only he didn't move his hands from her shoulders. He enjoyed holding her again and she didn't shrug out of his arms or move from his touch.

"Are you certain?" he asked again. The blush still stained her skin, her gaze locked with his and her breathing quickened. She parted her lips and he fought the urge to steal a kiss from her. But he wanted to.

So badly.

# CHAPTER TWO

*LET GO OF HER. She didn't want you.*

"Charlotte?" His voice cracked, he cleared his throat. "Are you okay?"

She broke the connection and turned away. "I'm fine. You'd better buckle up in case we hit some more turbulence." She didn't look at him but she appeared perturbed.

"Sure." He could take a hint. Quinn cursed himself inwardly for letting his guard down. When he'd decided to come up here he'd told himself to keep emotionally detached from her, but two hours in her presence and he was being swayed by her again. Just being around her and he forgot what had passed between them—for him it was like they'd never been apart.

She was like a drug that intoxicated him quickly.

Charlotte's cold brush-off brought him out of the past into the present, and keenly reminded him of how lonely his life had been without her. He didn't like to be reminded of that.

He buckled back up and looked out the window as the clouds dissipated. In the distance the white landscape became dotted with brightly colored buildings, which appeared to be raised on stilts above the snow, smoke rising steadily from the chimneys.

*So this is Cape Recluse.*

The cape was at the mercy of the elements and the Northwest Passage surrounded it on three sides. The town itself was nestled against a panorama of majestic mountains. Squinting, he faintly made out what looked like a tiny airstrip on a sheet of ice.

The whole town looked barren and very, very rustic. It was like something out of the old frontier towns of the Wild West, only snow covered. Quinn knew he was on the edge of civilization, here.

This was what Charlotte preferred over New York?

She flicked on the radio and gave out her call number. "Preparing to land."

"Roger that," came the crackling acknowledgment over the line.

Charlotte brought her plane in to land. Quinn was impressed with her piloting abilities as she brought the aircraft to a smooth landing on the slick airstrip. When the wheels of the plane touched the ice, the jet skittered slightly, but Charlotte kept control and then visibly relaxed.

As she swung the plane round towards the small hangar, Quinn saw a group of villagers milling about.

"That's quite a homecoming."

"Yes, well, there's not much winter entertainment up here," Charlotte said.

"I'll bet there isn't." Quinn regretted his muttered comment the moment it had slipped past his lips.

*Smooth move.*

Charlotte's eyes narrowed and flashed in annoyance, but all she said was, "Well, we'll get you settled."

She taxied the plane into the hangar.

"Sounds good." He could do with a long, hot shower and some sleep, but judging from the size of the town he didn't see any four-star accommodation nearby. The sooner he dealt with Mentlana Tikivik's case, the sooner he could get back to Toronto, and sanity.

Charlotte's pulse rate felt like a jackhammer at the moment and she hoped Quinn hadn't noticed how much he had affected her.

*Damn.*

One stupid little embrace during turbulence had set off all sorts of crazy hormones zinging through her body.

His stay in Cape Recluse was going to be more trying than she'd originally thought and had tried to tell herself it would be. To make matters worse, there were no hotels in town and Quinn would be staying with her. He *had* to stay with her.

When his arms had wrapped around her in the cockpit, her blood had ignited and her common sense had wrestled with the side of her that had wanted to toss aside the plane's controls and throw herself into his arms.

Totally irrational.

She was the fly to his spider, apparently.

It wasn't like she was desperate. She'd gone on other dates with good-looking, exciting men, but she hadn't lost her head around them.

And that was the point. Quinn always made her feel giddy, like a lovestruck fool. He was exciting, sexy and handsome, and made her body burn with a pleasure she hadn't felt since he'd left.

Every day she'd be forced to face Quinn, the man who had broken her heart, but she had to do this for Mentlana. She knew she'd be putting her heart at risk, and it had only recently mended since he'd left her for the greener pastures of New York. She'd rarely thought of him for the last couple years.

*Liar.*

Of course she'd thought about him, even though for the last couple years it hadn't been as constant as it had been before that. Except for one day. Every year on the anniversary of the day she'd miscarried the baby and had nearly bled out, she'd thought of him and what could've been had he not walked away.

Only, what could've been was just a fantasy. Quinn wouldn't have settled down. She realized that now.

Her throat constricted as she tried to swallow down those emotions. When she thought of what could have been, when she thought about the family she'd always dreamed of, she fought the urge to break down in tears.

*Don't think about it.*

Charlotte took a deep, calming breath, removed her headpiece and climbed out of the cockpit.

"Doc Charley!"

Charlotte glanced up to see George, her paramedic, approaching the plane. She embraced George, who was like a brother to her.

"Good to see you, Doc. Good flight?" he asked, though Charlotte knew he wasn't really *that* concerned about her flight. He was a pilot, too, and the Citation was like his baby. George moved away and stroked the side of the jet for good measure. "Any problems?"

"None. Your baby is fine and the flight was good." She glanced back to see if Quinn was disembarking okay. He appeared to be, as he climbed stiffly out of the cockpit.

"Dr. Devlyn." Charlotte waved him over, and Quinn strode over, his gaze intently focused on George. He didn't respond. Charlotte gritted her teeth. "Quinn, this is George Atavik. He's my paramedic and copilot. George, this is Dr. Devlyn, the specialist from Toronto."

George grinned, flashing brilliant white teeth. His dark

eyes lit with sincerity. "Good to meet you, Dr. Devlyn. Thanks for coming up this far north to help out."

"The pleasure is all mine and, please, just call me Quinn," he replied, shaking George's hand. He glanced at her, his dark eyes twinkling mischievously, a look that spoke volumes, like he was undressing her right there on the spot, as he whispered, "Just Quinn."

"George is Mentlana Tikivik's brother," Charlotte said, clearing her throat. Why she'd blurted that information out she didn't know. It was like she wanted Quinn to know there was nothing between George and her. She watched for any sign of reaction from Quinn, but there was none. All he did was nod politely.

"I'll take care of the plane, Doc Charley. I checked the weather satellite earlier and I was worried you were going to be delayed by that storm coming in from Labrador." George chatted away, totally unaware of the tension Charlotte keenly felt hovering over them.

"I was, too, for a moment," she answered absently.

"I'll go and collect my bag," Quinn said, walking back toward the plane, where people in the hangar were unloading his suitcase and some supplies Charlotte had brought up. So like him to be haughty.

*It's Quinn.*

Even though she knew she shouldn't follow him, Charlotte hurried after him.

"Are you still tired from the trip?" she asked.

"A bit," Quinn answered. "Don't you and George have to deal with the plane?"

"George can handle it. He'll yell if I'm needed."

"He seems like a nice fellow, I hope he makes you happy."

Charlotte did a double take. Quinn thought she was with George and, despite the fact they'd once been intimate, was wishing her happiness. So unlike the selfish man he'd been when he was younger.

"Quinn, George is like a brother to me." Again, why was she telling him that? She should've let him think George was her lover, and then she shuddered at the thought. She'd babysat George at one time and he'd been a terror. "Besides, George is too weird, too into his Westerns. I think that if given the chance, he'd trade in his paramedic bag for a saddle and six-shooter." She said the last part loudly.

"Yeah, yeah, laugh it up. Clint Eastwood is da man!" George called back.

A look of pleasure flashed momentarily across his face. "Well, that makes for a good partnership between physician and paramedic."

"Doc Charley!" The frantic call made both Charlotte and Quinn spin around. Charlotte saw Lorna, the village midwife, come running into the hangar.

Charlotte didn't need to be told. Her instinct kicked in and she grabbed her medical bag from the top of the pile of supplies. "What's happened? Is it Mentlana?"

Lorna nodded. "She started bleeding, and I don't know if it's from the fetus, the placenta or something else."

*Oh, God, no.*

Charlotte remembered the way she herself had almost bled to death when she'd lost her baby. Sweat broke out across her brow. Charlotte glanced at Quinn, who was standing close to her. His lips were pressed together in a firm line and he looked a little pale as he nodded his understanding, obviously ready to follow her lead.

"Where is she?" Charlotte asked.

"The clinic." Lorna was wringing her hands nervously.

"Thanks, Lorna." Charlotte started running, praying she wasn't too late.

* * *

"Is everything okay, Charley?" Mentlana's voice was anxious as Charlotte peeled off the rubber gloves and placed them in the toxic medical waste receptacle.

"Your cervix is irritated, that's all." Charlotte had been relieved on her arrival to see the blood loss was minimal, but enough to worry Lorna. Given all the things wrong with Mentlana and her high-risk pregnancy, Lorna had reacted quickly and done the right thing.

"Well, yours would be irritated, too, if you were carrying around an elephant."

Charlotte chuckled. "I'm going to have Dr. Devlyn, the specialist from Toronto, perform an ultrasound to make sure there's nothing wrong with the placenta or the baby. But the heartbeat is strong, and from the internal, the placenta is still in place. If it had been an abruption there would've been a lot more blood."

*And death.* Charlotte kept that thought to herself. There was no sense in worrying the pregnant woman over nothing.

Mentlana visibly relaxed as she took her feet out of the stirrups and rearranged the sheet over her lower half. Charlotte ran her hands under the tap and scrubbed them thoroughly.

"Do you want me to get Genen? He's probably climbing the walls."

"Let him wait for a moment. I want to talk to you."

Confused, Charlotte pulled her wheeled stool over to her friend's side nonetheless. Mentlana was leaning up on one elbow, a serious look on her face.

Charlotte knew that look all too well. It meant business.

"What's your question?"

"This doctor from Toronto, he's the one, isn't he?" Mentlana asked.

Charlotte's heart skipped a beat. "What do you mean?"

Mentlana's eyes narrowed, glinting as black as coal as she fixed Charlotte with the serious gaze that made Genen and George almost wet their pants. "Don't lie to me, Charley. This is the guy, right? He's the guy who broke your heart and left after you lost the baby. The one you wouldn't bring home to meet us. The one who, if I wasn't pregnant and in need of him, I'd give a stern kick to the crotch."

Charlotte stood. Letting out an exasperated sigh, she scrubbed her hand over her face. "Yes. Dr. Devlyn is the one."

Mentlana reached out and grabbed her hand. "I know how hard it is for you to trust him, to bring him here, and I know you're doing it for me and the baby. Thank you."

A sob caught in Charlotte's throat but she controlled it. She forced a wobbly smile and smoothed Mentlana's jet-black hair from her forehead. "I would do anything for you, even face the devil himself—or Devlyn, in this case."

"Witty." Lana chuckled. "Now I'm *really* interested in meeting him."

Charlotte rolled her eyes and padded towards the door. "Well, he does have the bedside manner of a bull in a china shop, most days. Stay tight. I'll bring him in to see you in a moment."

"Tight, right." Mentlana snorted as Charlotte shut the door to the exam room. Just as she'd thought, Genen was pacing, and the rest of the family was crowded into the small reception area of her clinic. Genen almost rushed her as she approached.

Charlotte held up her hands. "It's nothing, just an irritated cervix. Mother and baby are fine, but I'll have the specialist do an ultrasound to be absolutely certain."

Relief washed over Genen's face. "Can I see her now, Charley?"

"Sure. But just Genen," she said, as the entire Atavik and Tikivik clan seemed to rise. Scanning the clinic area, she couldn't see Quinn anywhere. Biting her bottom lip, she headed over to George.

"Where's Dr. Devlyn?"

"In your office. I thought he'd be most comfortable there."

The blood drained from Charlotte's face. "My office?" *Oh, God.* She hadn't had a chance to clear away her personal items, including the cherished, faded old sonogram. The ultrasound he hadn't even bothered to attend. The same sonogram he'd just grunted at when she'd shown it to him.

*"Don't you want to see? It's amazing!"*

*"It's not like you haven't seen a sonogram before."*

*"I know. But, Quinn, it's our baby."*

*He shrugged. "I have to go, Charlotte. I'm late for my rounds already."*

He hadn't wanted to see it then and even though it was childish, she didn't want to share it with him now. Not after five years. He didn't deserve to see it or share in any part of her grief.

# CHAPTER THREE

TRYING NOT TO panic, she thanked George and headed towards her office. She raised her hand to knock and then thought better of it. Why should she knock? It was her office and he was the visitor. She walked in. Quinn wasn't behind her desk, but was staring out the window at the snow swirling over the inlet. He turned when she entered, his face unreadable.

"Is Ms. Tikivik stable?" he asked.

"Yes. It was an irritation of the cervix, but I'd like you to do an ultrasound and check the status of the fetus yourself."

"I will." He glanced back out the window. "I have to say I've never seen so many houses tied down to cables and supported on metal beams. It's like they're a bunch of beach houses or something."

Charlotte couldn't help but smile. "The houses are raised because of permafrost. There are no basements in Cape Recluse. The village also has a lot of high winds. We may seem sheltered, with mountains surrounding us, but it's really very windy. We have to tie everything down."

Quinn's eyebrows arched. "I guess. With no trees to form a windbreak."

"Yeah, you could say that."

"It's quite interesting—the landscape, that is."

Now it was Charlotte's turn to be impressed. He'd never

been overly interested in anything else before, beyond the next surgery.

Well, he'd been interested in her until she'd got pregnant and decided to become a family physician.

"Yes. It is an interesting vista," she agreed.

Quinn shivered and then nodded. "This is some community. They all seem to care for one another, like family." He shook his head. "It's like the Brady Bunch up here or something."

"That's because they genuinely do care. It's a small place and everyone knows everybody. There are no secrets."

That caught his attention and he shot her a questioning look. "Really? No secrets?"

"Nope. Not a single one." Suddenly she had a bad case of butterflies. She was nervous. Perhaps it was the fact they were in an enclosed room, alone. After her reaction to him earlier, the last place she wanted to be was in a private office with him.

He strode over to her, his eyes soft, with a twinkle of devilment still dancing there. As he reached out and brushed an errant curl from her face, a zip of delight traveled down her spine. His knuckles brushed her cheek, causing her body to waken. One simple touch from him and her body responded as if it had been in a slumber for the last five years.

Maybe it had. No other man had been able to arouse her by a simple touch before. It angered her that Quinn was the only one who could.

"Don't," she whispered, her voice catching in her throat.

"What?"

"Touch me with familiarity."

Quinn moved his hand. "I'm sorry, Charlotte. It's force of habit, even after all this time."

Tears stung her eyes and she cleared her throat before taking a step back. "You shouldn't keep the Tikiviks waiting."

"Do you have some scrubs for me?"

"Of course. See Rosie at Reception and she'll get you fitted." Charlotte tucked her hair behind her ear as he stared at her, the tension in the room almost palpable. Why wasn't he leaving? "Is there anything else?"

Quinn glanced away. "No. I'll go and see Rosie now."

Quinn walked past her and Charlotte watched him go, unease and apprehension twisting her stomach. When he left the room she snatched the picture frame off her desk and stared at the sonogram, thinking about the baby she'd lost. He or she would've been five years old, now, and she couldn't help but wonder if the baby would've had the same sandy-brown hair and deep brown eyes as Quinn. Perhaps their baby would've favored her, with red curls and emerald eyes, or been a mixture of them both.

Closing her eyes, she pictured a rambunctious boy, like she always did when she thought about her lost baby. He'd have had rosy cheeks, sandy-brown hair and green eyes. She felt the sting of tears and brushed them away quickly.

Why was she letting herself feel this way again?

Why was she letting Quinn Devlyn in again?

*Because I never let him go.*

Sighing, she opened her filing cabinet and pushed the picture to the back before locking the drawer. She slipped the key into her pocket. It was really a moot point, now. There *was* no baby of theirs, not now and not ever.

Quinn peeled off the clothes he'd been wearing for the last several hours. He was bone weary and absolutely freezing, but this was the moment where he shone, being a surgical god.

34 SAFE IN HIS HANDS

His hand trembled slightly and he gripped it.

Just tired, that was all.

Besides, this was nothing big. Just an ultrasound and a consult. If this tremor continued he'd remove himself from the case. The patient's life and that of the baby were more important than proving to the world he was still a viable surgeon.

*You can do this.*

Quinn pulled on the scrubs. As he splashed some water on his face, his mind wandered to the sonogram he'd spied on Charlotte's desk.

Their baby.

The one they'd lost. It had been the scariest moment of his life. Not even the accident that had damaged his hand had been as terrifying as the moment when they'd lost their baby. Charlotte had bled badly after she'd miscarried. He'd found her collapsed on the floor of their apartment.

*"Hold on, honey. Hold on, Charlotte." He reached down and stroked her pale face.*

Quinn shuddered, sending the horrific nightmare back to where it had come from. That moment had been far worse than the accident he'd endured alone.

Seeing the sonogram on her desk, in a frame, had only reminded him of the pain when they'd parted. At the time, he hadn't been too keen on the idea of a baby in their lives. How could he be a good, loving father when he had such a role model as his own cold, detached father? A baby was not part of his plans. However, it had hurt him when she'd lost it, to see her in pain. To watch her grieve and know there was nothing he could do about it. It had made him feel powerless.

And he didn't like feeling powerless. Not in the least.

There were times in the neonatal unit, when dealing

with babies born prematurely, that his mind wandered to what might've been.

But that was in the past. Their baby hadn't survived. So he'd told himself it wasn't meant to be, and had instead focused on becoming one of the best surgeons in his field, burying his sadness over the loss in his work.

Now he was at the top of his game.

*And lonely as hell.*

Another reason why he hated these godforsaken outposts of the North. He didn't get Charlotte's fascination with staying up here.

Even though her life had been spared, the North had still cost him Charlotte.

She had refused to leave and go with him to New York. Had refused to talk to him or even look at him. All she'd done was hand back the ring, along with everything else he'd given her, because in her note she'd stated she wanted no reminders of him.

Why did she still keep the sonogram?

Of course, he had no right to pry. The baby was gone.

He jammed the clothes he'd taken off into a suitcase, stuffing the unwanted emotions to the dark recesses of his mind, as well. He didn't have time to let his personal feelings get in the way. There was a patient waiting, counting on him. He exited the bathroom, pulling his luggage behind him. The hairs on the back of his neck stood on end and he knew instinctively all eyes were glued to him. Turning, he smiled and waved awkwardly. No one returned his greeting.

*Good Lord.*

He approached Charlotte's nurse, the one who had given him the scrubs. Lavender scrubs, no less. Quinn made a mental note to see if there were any blue or green in stock. He wasn't partial to any shade of purple. Perhaps he was a bit of a pig for thinking this, but he felt a bit emasculated in such a feminine color.

"Sorry, I don't remember your name," he apologized.

"No worries. I'm Rosie, and I can take your luggage for you, Dr. Devlyn."

"Thanks. And the patient?"

"In exam room one."

"Thanks again."

The eyes, he was pretty sure, followed him all the way to the exam-room door. The tension was so thick you could slice it with a knife. Perhaps they were shocked to see a man in lavender.

Quinn knocked on the door and Charlotte answered. A smug smile tugged at the corner of her lips as she looked him up and down.

"I think that's your color," she teased.

"Think again," he snarled.

Charlotte stifled a giggle and stepped to one side. "Come in."

Quinn entered the large exam room, his gaze resting on the Inuk couple in the corner. The woman was exceptionally pretty, with black hair and eyes to match. There was a dimple in her cheek as she grinned up at her husband.

"Mentlana, Genen, this is Dr. Devlyn. He's the specialist I told you both about."

Genen stood and came over to grasp Quinn's bad hand, shaking it firmly. Quinn didn't wince, even though the man had a strong grip.

Quinn approached Mentlana and was surprised by her measured gaze. This woman was picking him apart with her eyes and he felt like a slab of meat.

"A pleasure to meet you, Mrs. Tikivik."

"And you, Dr. Devlyn. Charley wasn't wrong. You *are* cute."

He arched his brows and held back the grin threatening to erupt.

*"Ahem."* Charlotte cleared her throat from behind him and now it was his turn to stifle a laugh. Craning his neck, he looked back at her. She was conveniently staring at the ceiling, but her blush was evidence of her embarrassment. He liked the way the pink bloomed in her creamy white cheeks.

*Focus.*

"Well, thank you for the compliment. I'd like to do an ultrasound, now, if that's okay?" he asked, steering the subject back to the examination. But he planned to use Mentlana's little disclosure of information to get him a manlier color of scrubs. Right now he had a job to do. Now was not the time for frivolity or personal feelings. "Do you have a full bladder?"

"When don't I?" Mentlana replied. "Please, before I burst."

"I'll get the ultrasound machine," Charlotte said.

Charlotte wheeled the machine over and then dimmed the lights, refusing to meet his gaze.

*So, I still make her uncomfortable.*

That thought secretly pleased him.

Getting to work, he uncovered Mentlana's belly. "Sorry. This is a bit cold."

"That's not cold, Dr. Devlyn. Outside is cold."

He grinned, but didn't engage in any further pleasantries. He had a consult to complete. Quinn placed the probe against her abdomen and began to adjust the dials to get a clearer picture. Genen leaned forward, his eyes transfixed on the image on the monitor.

"Well, from what I can see, your placenta, though previa, is fully attached and not bleeding."

"That's a relief." Genen kissed his wife's hand. "And the baby?"

"The bleeding is not being caused by the baby. I have to run some more tests to determine the severity of the CCAM, but other than that, his heart is beating and he's moving well. His other organs are forming satisfactorily for a gestational age of twenty-one weeks."

"Thank you, Dr. Devlyn. I appreciate it," Mentlana said.

"I want you on bed rest, though." He turned to look at Charlotte. "I'm sure Dr. James will agree with my assessment."

"Yes," Charlotte said. "I think we've had this discussion before."

"For how long?" Mentlana's gaze traveled nervously between him and Charlotte.

"For the remainder of your pregnancy. With your pulmonary embolism and placenta previa alone, it's for the best," Charlotte said, brushing back Mentlana's hair.

Mentlana nodded. "Okay."

"We'll call you when I'm through analyzing your labs and diagnostic images." Quinn wiped the sonogram gel from her abdomen and then turned back to the machine. "Until then, take it easy."

"Sounds good, Doctors."

Quinn saved various shots of the baby's heart and other organs to determine whether or not he would have to do the surgery in utero. It would be better if he could wait until the baby was full term to deliver it via Caesarean and do the operation on the newborn.

He'd done *that* surgery several times since his hand had been damaged.

If the baby could wait until its birth, by then he might be able to figure out a way to get Mentlana to Mount Hope, where his surgical team could assist him. Even Iqaluit would be better than here.

Charlotte may be a competent physician, but she was no surgeon.

*She could've been great if she'd only come to New York with me.*

Quinn stood up and left. He knew Charlotte followed him, and so did the collective gaze of the mob huddled in the waiting room as they passed to get to Charlotte's office.

Once they were behind the closed doors he wandered over to the window and wrinkled his nose in dissatisfaction at the swirling snowstorm, which had caught up with them.

Then again, it would make a nice photograph and he was glad he'd brought his camera. Since his father's death, he had been indulging in his secret passion for photography. Something his father had always stated was a waste of time.

He was on sabbatical, as his father had just died when Charlotte had called, and he'd planned on taking a trip to India to photograph scenery. Instead, he was up in the High Arctic and not getting paid much to be there.

The money didn't matter to him.

His father would roll over in his grave if he knew, and he already knew how his mother felt about this excursion.

*"You don't have time for a charity case, Quinn. You have to prepare to take your father's place!"*

God. He hated winter. It probably stemmed from the fact he'd been forced into endless hours of hockey practice by his father, when all Quinn had wanted to do was take photography lessons. Photography hadn't been manly enough for his father, whereas hockey was the sport of champions.

"Don't they have winters in Toronto?" Charlotte asked, breaking the silence.

Quinn glanced back at her. "Pardon?"

"The way you're scowling at the snow."

Quinn shrugged. "You know I hate winter."

"How could I forget?"

"I'm not the only Canadian who does. Think about all the snowbirds that go to warmer climes every winter."

Charlotte's eyes widened. "You want me to picture you as an old man in a RV?" Her eyes twinkled with mischief.

"Ha, ha. Very funny."

"I'm sorry about the scrubs." A devilish smile played across her lips.

"You're not in the least. You enjoyed watching me give the locals a fright."

Charlotte laughed and he couldn't help but join in. "I'll see if George has any spares."

"Much appreciated."

"What do you think of Mentlana's condition?" she asked, mercifully changing the subject.

"Your assessment is correct, though I don't know the severity of the CCAM yet."

"How long will it take you to determine that?" she asked, her voice tight and her lips pursed together in a thin line. He could see she was stressed about Mentlana.

Charlotte always got over-attached to people.

"A few days. I want to be absolutely certain. I sent the scans to your computer and I'll email them to my laptop later. I have an internet stick, because I figured there's no Wi-Fi up here."

Charlotte nodded. "Wise move."

Quinn moved away from the window and took a seat on the opposite side of the desk. As soon as he sat down he noticed the little frame with the sonogram picture was gone. He didn't search the room for it as he didn't want

Charlotte to know he'd seen it. Apparently she'd hidden it. It irked him that she was hiding it from him.

Like it had never existed.

Like *they* had never existed. And that saddened him.

He shook that thought away.

"I'm glad it was just an irritated cervix." Charlotte sat across from him, her back ramrod straight, her fingers laced in front of her.

"There are no pools of blood darkening on the scans. The fetus is thriving, despite the CCAM. I take it they knew the gender beforehand. I hope I didn't make a blunder with that."

"They knew."

Quinn nodded. "I'm hoping we can get Mentlana to twenty-five weeks before I even think of doing in utero surgery to repair the lungs—that way, if we have to deliver, the baby has a better chance of survival."

*Unlike ours, who miscarried at a mere sixteen weeks.*

"In utero surgery is needed?"

"It may not be. We'll monitor her. She may go to term and then the baby's lungs can be repaired after delivery, but if there's much more fluid collection we risk hydrops. If that's the case we'll have to place a shunt in the fetus's lungs the fluid can drain into the amniotic fluid and take the pressure off the lungs. Then, when the baby is full term, we can resect the lesion on him. Really, that would be the ideal situation."

Quinn rubbed his hand, which had begun to bother him again. He needed to do his strengthening exercises. "There has to be a way to get to Iqaluit, though. You don't have the facilities here to deliver a baby by Caesarean, let alone operate on a fetus in utero."

"She has a pulmonary embolism. I can't fly her."

"What about low altitude?"

"I've thought of it, but with the sudden storms and mountains…it's risky. It would double the flight time."

"It's risky leaving her up here. When the time comes we need to get her to Iqaluit. If she makes it to twenty-four weeks, we need to consider flying her down there."

Charlotte scrubbed her hand over her face. "You're right. I know it. All right, when the time comes we'll fly her at low altitude to Iqaluit, but if her water breaks or a storm hits, we'll have to do it here. I've been stockpiling supplies."

"Supplies won't cut it. I need a *proper* surgical team to assist me. I'm sorry. You alone won't be of any use in this situation."

Charlotte's eyes flashed in annoyance. "I'm more than capable of assisting you, Dr. Devlyn."

"Have you done surgeries here before?" he asked, intrigued.

"Yes, but never this kind. It's why I need you here, Quinn." She reached across the desk and took his hand. Her small, delicate hand fit so snugly in his. Warmth spread across his chest. He wanted to pull her closer to him.

He hadn't realized how much he'd missed her.

*Don't. She didn't want you.*

Quinn pushed her hand away.

It was too little, too late. There was no going back.

She cleared her throat and her expression was serious. "Will you let me assist, Dr. Devlyn, or do I have to hire help?"

As much as he was tempted to tell her to bring up a surgical team, he knew the money would be coming out of her own pocket and he couldn't do that to her.

"If it comes down to it, I would like you to assist."

# CHAPTER FOUR

CHARLOTTE WAS TAKEN aback. She wanted to believe that Quinn trusted her abilities as a surgeon and was willing to let her help save her best friend's baby, but a niggle of self-doubt gnawed at the back of her mind.

She knew what his thoughts about general physicians and surgeons had been in medical school. Quinn had believed in the discipline, drive and focus of training for years in a specialty, which of course had been very egotistical of him. He had been obsessive when it came to his training. In med school he'd do anything to scrub in on any surgery and she knew he never gave up on a challenge. That's why he was at the top of his field so young.

Charlotte hoped he had changed, though she seriously doubted it. As her father had always said, a leopard didn't change its spots.

*Why am I worrying about this?*

Quinn was no longer her concern. She didn't care what he thought about her chosen career path and, frankly, if he was going to let her assist in a once-in-a-lifetime surgery, she was going to take it.

Even if it was because Quinn had no other option.

"I think I'm going to have a shower and peel myself out of these oh so charming scrubs." Quinn rubbed his hand, wincing momentarily, and then stood up. "Where am I staying and where can I call a cab?"

Guilt assuaged her. She wasn't heartless. He was exhausted and here she was thrusting him straight into the exam room the moment the plane had touched down. Although it hadn't been intentional, it had just happened that way.

"There are no cabs and there's no hotel." Charlotte stood and walked over to the door. She needed an escape route for what she was about to tell him. Even though she hated having to share a clinic space with him for the next twenty-and-some-odd weeks while they monitored Mentlana, it was even worse having to share accommodations with him.

Already it was proving hard to keep her attraction for him under wraps, but there was nothing to be done. Cape Recluse had no hotels, motels or anything of the kind. The people in this town opened up their homes to strangers. Quinn would be more comfortable at her home, which was connected to the clinic, than at the home of someone he didn't know.

"No hotel?" Quinn's eyes widened. "Am I supposed to crash here?" He glanced down at the old brown sofa that had once adorned their college apartment. "I think I'm too old to curl up on the 'Couch of Gibraltar,' here."

"I have a guest bedroom at my place." Heat began to crawl up her neck and she prayed the blush wouldn't reach her face.

"Are you asking me to spend the night?"

"N-no," she stammered.

Quinn grinned and crossed his arms. Even though he thought the lavender emasculated him, that was far from the truth. He was still as sexy as ever and she wanted to tear those scrubs from his body to get to what was underneath.

*Whoa, slow down.*

Where had that thought come from? True, it'd been a long time since she'd been with a man...the last time having been with Quinn. Her heart skipped a beat just thinking about it. Maybe that was the cure. To have one last night and get him out of her system. Warmth spread through her at the thought of that foolish notion.

*Get a grip on yourself.*

Sleeping with Quinn Devlyn was the last thing she needed to do.

"So let me get this straight. You're inviting me over to your place to spend the night?" He was teasing. He wasn't going to let it go. Quinn was annoying that way. He moved closer and Charlotte raised her hands and took a step back.

"It's not like it's in my bed. You'll be in the guest bedroom with its *own* bed. Same general house, two separate beds."

Quinn's brown eyes gleamed with devilment. "You're mentioning the word bed quite a lot, whereas I haven't even once."

Charlotte snapped her fingers. "Ha, you just did."

"Someone has bed on the brain," Quinn teased again.

"You're welcome to find your own lodgings, but unless you want to bunk with strangers or build an igloo you're better off staying with me. Trust me, I don't like it, either."

"Igloo? You're pulling my leg."

"No, really, and, trust me, you don't want to. The bears have been bad this year."

"Bears? You mean as in polar bears?" he asked, startled.

"Yes, what other kind of bear do you think I mean? This is the North, my friend." She chuckled at the expression of horror plastered across his face as she left the room. At least it got her out of that conversation with him.

She walked out of her office to retrieve his luggage from

Rosie. It was almost time for the clinic to close, but the residents knew she was only next door. She didn't even have to leave the clinic to go home as the door at the far side of the clinic led straight into her humble but comfortable abode.

"I'm here for Dr. Devlyn's luggage."

"Ah." Rosie got up and lifted the luggage, handing it to her. "He packs light."

"Always has."

"I find it strange he didn't bring his own scrubs," Rosie remarked, as she began to collect up her belongings.

Charlotte grinned, thinking about Quinn in his scrubs again. "Do you think we can get some blue or green ones?"

Rosie frowned over the bridge of her rhinestone-studded glasses. "What does he think this is, the local store?"

"I know. But please try for me, Rosie. He's used to the big city where everything is provided to physicians on a silver platter."

"In Canada?" Rosie asked in disbelief.

"Well, no. He had a private practice in New York for a while."

Rosie nodded. "That makes sense. I'll see what I can do." She zipped up her parka. "I'll see you tomorrow, Doc Charley."

"Good night, Rosie."

No sooner had Charlotte uttered the words than the doors of the clinic were flung open. George came rushing in with a stretcher. On it was Wavell Agluclark, a ten-year-old boy who was being taught the ways of his people in traditional hunting. George had his hand clamped over Wavell's thigh, which was bleeding heavily.

Rosie instantly peeled off her parka and quickly went about preparing a room while Charlotte jumped into action.

"What've we got here, George?"

"Deep laceration to the thigh, possibly a nick to the femoral artery," George answered.

"Exam room one is ready for you, Doc Charley," Rosie called out.

"Bring him in." Charlotte began to scrub while Wavell's dad, Sam, and George lifted him from the stretcher onto the exam bed. Wavell's face was pale with blood loss, pain and fear. A twinge of sympathy raced through her. She hated seeing a child in pain, but this wasn't Wavell's first accident. The boy seemed prone to mishaps.

"So what happened this time, Wavell?" she asked, pulling on a pair of rubber gloves, as Wavell was allergic to latex.

"I was cleaning fish after ice fishing, and the knife slipped," he said, through gritted teeth.

"Well, let's take a look."

George removed the gauze he'd been using to compress the wound. Gingerly inspecting the site, Charlotte could tell it was deep, but because the blood was being controlled and not gushing, the femoral artery was probably all right.

Rosie came back into the room.

Charlotte glanced over her shoulder. "I need ten ccs of lidocaine."

"Yes. Right away." Rosie skittered away to the locked medicine cabinet to prepare the local anesthesia.

"I don't like needles," Wavell murmured grumpily.

"I know, buddy, but this needle will numb your wound and I'll be able to stitch it up without you feeling a thing."

"Okay." Wavell pursed his lips. "I can handle it."

Charlotte smiled and ruffled his hair. "You're being very brave." She took the syringe from Rosie and injected around the laceration. "Tell me when you can't feel it and I'll stitch it up."

"Okay." Wavell nodded.

"He's okay, then?" Sam Agluclark asked warily.

"He'll be fine. He didn't cut the artery. Once we sew up his wound he'll need to rest for a couple of days."

"Can't feel it." Wavell slurred slightly.

"Good stuff." Sam was obviously relieved as he looked down at his son.

Rosie handed her a tray with everything she'd need for stitches. Charlotte thoroughly irrigated and cleaned out his cut with saline and Betadine, because she didn't think a knife for gutting fish was exactly clean.

Once she'd thoroughly inspected the site, she began to close the wound with sutures. Wavell didn't make a fuss but held perfectly still as she washed the suture site in more Betadine and packed it with gauze. In fact, Wavell was drifting off from the anesthesia.

"He's all done. I think it's best if you let him have a rest here. I'll get you some painkillers for later. He's to keep his leg elevated and come back in five days to get the sutures removed. No more fishing for a bit. He's lucky it didn't do more damage."

"Thanks, Doc Charley," Sam said.

Charlotte nodded and disposed of the syringes and gloves in the medical waste. Rosie and George cleaned up the rest of the stuff to send for sterilization.

"I'll help you take Wavell home in a couple of hours, Sam," George said. "Why don't you hit the hay, too, Doc Charley? You look beat."

"Thanks, George. I think I will." Charlotte washed up, and then headed back to her office. She was beat. It'd been a long, emotionally draining day. The office was dark and she gently rapped on the door, but there was no answer. Peeking inside, she spied Quinn slumped on the old worn couch. He didn't look comfortable, couldn't be comfortable. She'd crashed on that sofa many a time. And she was a lot smaller than him and even she couldn't fit quite right on it.

The name of the Couch of Gibraltar, as Quinn so lovingly called it, suited it. Although, if her memory served her correctly, she and Quinn had done more than just sleep on that couch when they had been in med school.

Charlotte smiled. He always looked so innocent like this. Too bad his acerbic wit didn't match the angelic impression he gave when he was asleep.

He had been a bit of a wild boy in college. Whereas she'd been quiet and studious, working her way through school on scholarships and odd jobs.

They were such opposites.

*What did I ever see in him?*

She knew exactly. He was exciting, sexy, thrilling. When he'd first walked into anatomy class with such an air of confidence, it had been like she'd been woken up from a daze. From the moment her dad had died she'd thrown herself into her work, studying, getting the best grades so she could tread in her father's footsteps. She'd ignored guys, had never gone on dates or had a hobby.

Then Quinn Devlyn had waltzed into her life and she'd found herself yearning for more. He had been talented and passionate about his work. Although animal attraction and mind-blowing sex was not what one should base a relationship on. She'd learned that the hard way. Case in point: when she'd needed him most, as she'd lain in that hospital bed after the miscarriage, he hadn't been there in the way she'd needed him to be.

He'd gone to New York to pursue a career in neonatal surgery and she had come here to take over where her father had left off, as a general practitioner in a remote community. What she'd set out to do the moment she'd had to say goodbye to her dad.

Charlotte shook her head, dispelling the painful memory, and then frowned as she looked at Quinn again. This forced cohabitation for the sake of Mentlana was going to test her to the very limits. She tiptoed over to her desk and wrote a note for him, telling him where he could find her. Then she pulled out an afghan and covered him up, but as she bent over to straighten the blanket, which had bunched up on one side, she caught sight of the scars on his right hand.

Surgical scars.

*What had happened to him?*

From the patterns of the scars it was as though his hand had been broken, severely. He'd had what appeared to be multiple orthopedic surgeries.

The blood drained from her face and she straightened, backing away from him. What if he couldn't hold a scalpel? That thought was too terrifying.

*He can operate. He has to be able to.*

If he couldn't, Mentlana's life was at risk. Was he really that arrogant about his surgical abilities?

*Yes.*

She dismissed the idea. He had to be able to, or he wouldn't have a license and he wouldn't have come. He would've told her the truth.

*Really?*

Her throat constricted, her stomach knotted with dread. Charlotte backed out of the room and shut the door behind her. She wanted to believe Quinn was still the best fetal surgeon, but her instincts told her he was hiding something, while her heart, her traitorous heart, wanted to give him the benefit of the doubt.

Surgeons have had their hands injured before and had still been able to operate, but for the life of her she couldn't recall a single name of a surgeon who had done so. Neonatal surgeons needed steady hands for their delicate work. Were Quinn's hands still steady?

Mentlana's baby was like blood to her, and Charlotte couldn't lose another child.

Instead of closing the connecting door between her home and the clinic, she left it slightly ajar, in case Quinn woke up.

Charlotte wandered over to her bookcase, where there was a picture of her father and herself. She took it down and held it, lovingly running her fingers over the glass, as if trying to reach through and touch his face once more.

Dr. Cecil James had been a brilliant surgeon in Toronto. An innovator, a lot like Quinn. But then he'd met a nurse, Amber Lees, who'd had the drive to help others. Her father had given up his practice and headed to the North with Amber, and then they'd had her.

Her father's love of the North, even after the loss of his wife, had been instilled deep into Charlotte's being.

She set the picture back on the shelf and rubbed the ache forming in the back of her neck, trying not to think about the prospect of losing someone else she loved, because if Quinn failed it would be her fault for bringing him up here.

*Dammit.*

She shouldn't trust him. She couldn't. He'd deceived and hurt her before.

And she wouldn't let him do that to her again.

# CHAPTER FIVE

*"Quinn."*

*He woke with a start at the faint whisper of his name. When he prized his eyes open he realized he was in a bed and he hadn't the foggiest idea how he'd ended up there. As he surveyed the room he realized he was in a king-size bed, and the walls were covered in rich cherrywood paneling. Like something found on a fine estate. How had he ended up here? The last thing he recalled was sitting down on the old brown couch in Charlotte's office, waiting for her to come back and take him to her home.*

*Quinn rubbed his eyes, trying to bring them into focus in the dim light of the room, but everything remained an unfocused haze.*

*"Quinn." Charlotte seemed to appear from the gloom like an apparition. Quinn gasped at the sight of her, not because she was in his room but because of how she looked. Her red curls tumbled down loose over her creamy shoulders. As he let his gaze rove further down, his breath caught in his throat and his blood ignited into flames. She was wearing a long white silk negligee, slit to the thigh, cut very low and exposing the creamy tops of her breasts.*

*"Charlotte?" he asked, stupidly because he knew it was her. Who else could it be? He'd seen her in that negligee before, when they'd gone to Niagara Falls. Just thinking*

*of that night of passion fired his blood, and it seemed like a lifetime ago when he'd experienced such a rush, such a hunger for her.*

Quinn shifted and realized he was wearing nothing but a sheet draped across his hips. What'd happened to his clothes?

Who cared?

Had Charlotte undressed him? The thought aroused him. God, he wanted her.

Badly.

"I hope you don't mind," she said, as if reading his mind. She moved closer to the bed but stayed just out of reach. "I took the liberty of undressing you."

Was she crazy?

"No, I don't mind in the least."

A devilish smile crept across her face as she moved to the end of the bed. "I'm so glad you came here, Quinn."

"And I'm glad you asked me."

Quinn got up and moved toward her, closing the distance between them. He took her tiny hand in his. It was so small and delicate. He entwined her slender fingers in his and could feel her pulse racing as he let his thumb stroke her wrist.

"Have you missed me, Quinn?" She bit her bottom lip and then smoothed back the hair from his forehead. "Please, tell me you have." Charlotte pressed her body against his, just a thin piece of fabric separating them.

So close.

Her lips brushed against his throat. Just a simple touch of softness against his neck caused his blood to burn with the fires of a thousand suns. A groan rumbled deep in his chest and he slipped his arms around her waist, holding her close.

"Quinn, have you missed me?" she asked again.

*Had he? Or was it just in this moment of lust, his need for her that made him want to drop down on his knees and pour out his heart to her.*

*Yes. He'd missed her, with every fiber of his being. "Charlotte..." But even in his dreams the words wouldn't come out.*

*"Kiss me," she whispered, her voice husky with promise.*

*Quinn leaned in.*

A draft of cold air startled him awake. Pain traveled up his neck, resulting in a pounding headache at the back of his skull. Quinn glanced down and let out a groan of dismay when he caught sight of lavender.

"God." He scrubbed his hand over his face, stubble scratching his palm. It'd been a dream. The whole thing. Of course it had been a dream. For one thing, he doubted she had a king-size bed and cherrywood paneling in her home. Also, Charlotte wouldn't have come to him, not after what had passed between them five years ago, and this wasn't the first time he'd had this dream, either.

When he first left her he'd dreamt of her over and over again. He'd tried to banish the ghost of her with nameless women, but it hadn't worked. Instead, he'd focused on work. The dreams had faded and hadn't come back so often. In fact, he hadn't had such a vivid fantasy of Charlotte in a long time. He almost wished he hadn't woken up, that he'd been allowed to savor the moment and be with her once more, even if only in a dream, because the love they'd shared once was only that, now.

A dream.

Quinn got up, his body stiff and sore from his sojourn on the sofa. Sleeping on a stone floor would've been preferable to the couch that time had forgotten. His bad hand was numb. He flexed it and the joints cracked. It was his own fault. He'd planned to do his exercises last night but had forgotten.

He shook his hand, trying to get feeling back into it, and then headed out of the office. There was a slightly open door and he headed towards it, following the rich scent of coffee in the air. Quinn paused in the doorway of a small apartment, his breath catching in his throat.

Charlotte was puttering around the kitchen. Her red hair wasn't loose but was pulled back with an elastic tie. The silky negligee had been replaced with a short, pink cotton nightie covered with garish red hearts. The nightie did have an advantage over the lingerie in his dream, for when she reached up into the cupboard he got a glimpse of her bare, round bottom.

Blood rushed straight from his head to his groin. Charlotte's bottom was like two round, ripe peaches ready for picking. He wanted to squeeze them and knead them with his bare hands.

*Calm down.*

Only, he couldn't. He remembered the first time he'd seen her, bent over her books, twirling her red curls around her finger and totally engrossed in the text. She'd seemed oblivious to the world around her. The only female who hadn't fawned over him because of his money or his looks. It had intrigued him.

It had been like a game, wooing her. He'd wanted to be the one to capture her, and he had.

As she had captured his heart.

Only he'd never let her know that because he hadn't understood love. How could he, with parents who had shown him not one iota of affection while he'd been growing up?

Charlotte had, though. He missed that.

He leaned against the door, causing it to squeak, and

Charlotte whipped around, her cheeks staining with crimson as their gazes locked.

"Quinn, you're…you're up."

"Did you forget about me?"

"No." She glanced down and her face paled. She started yanking on the hem of her nightgown as if trying to make it longer, but to no avail.

Quinn didn't mind in the least.

"I think you did," he teased.

Charlotte rolled her eyes. "Did you spend the whole night on the couch?"

"Yes." He rubbed the crick in his neck. "It's been a long time since I passed out on that thing. I remember it being a bit more comfortable."

"It was never comfortable. You're just older."

Quinn chuckled and took a seat in one of the mismatched chairs surrounding her retro vinyl kitchen table. She slid a cup of coffee in front of him. "Thanks."

"Are you hungry?"

"Starving." He took a sip of coffee, savoring the warmth spreading down his throat and chipping away at the bitter cold that crept in from outside.

"Why are you shivering?" she asked. "It's not cold in here."

"I can feel the cold seeping in."

Charlotte rolled her eyes again and shook her head. "Pansy. I'm not surprised you're hungry. You didn't eat yesterday."

"Au contraire. I had a delightful five-dollar packet of peanuts on my flight to Iqaluit." His stomach growled. "But I'll take you up on your offer of breakfast."

"Good choice. But first I think I'll change."

"Why? It makes no difference to me."

Charlotte blushed again. "All the same."

Quinn watched her head down the hall, savoring the sight of her thighs. Thighs he wished were parted for him right now. He shifted in his seat, his erection pushing against his scrubs. It was like he was some kind of hard-up adolescent again.

Charlotte returned with her nightgown covered up with a long terrycloth bathrobe. It was a shame. He'd seen her in less, but that short cotton nightie was just as appealing as the silken lingerie of his fantasies. At least the robe was much better than the scrubs he was wearing, which did nothing to hide his arousal.

"Are my bags here?" he asked.

"Just down the hall. The door to the left."

"I think I'll change." He slipped out of the seat as discreetly as he could. His room was easily found and he removed the scrubs, tossing them in the nearby hamper. There was a small basin in the bedroom and he washed his face. He'd shower later, after he'd had something to eat. The scent of bacon drifted down the hall, followed by the familiar sizzle from the stove that made his stomach growl again.

Loudly.

"Just in time." Charlotte grinned as he entered the kitchen and sat back down. She slid bacon and a fried egg onto a plate and set it down in front of him. Quinn couldn't remember the last time he'd had a good home-cooked breakfast like this.

*Probably the last time I was with her.*

When he'd moved to Manhattan he hadn't cooked at home. Even during the last two years in Toronto he hadn't spent his free time mastering the culinary arts. He'd spent his free time wining and dining, until the accident. After the accident he'd started doing photography, but even then he'd been out taking pictures, not lounging around at home where the hum of silence made him feel utterly alone.

The fork dropped out of his hand and clattered against the plate, his hand frozen and numb. He looked up at Charlotte but her back was turned as she continued frying eggs.

Quinn rubbed his fingers until he could feel them again, wiggling them slowly. He'd just picked up his fork as Charlotte sat down across from him with her plate. He would have to do his exercise later.

After breakfast.

"I could do with a shower," he said, just to break the silence. "That won't be a problem or interrupt your clinic or any appointments, will it?"

She shook her head. "No. Why should it? Anyway, it's Saturday and the clinic is officially closed, so no one should bother you."

Silence descended heavily on Quinn as they ate.

"And what will you do today?" he asked casually, because he had no idea what he was going to do to pass the time. Other than maybe venture out and take some pictures of snow.

"Oh, this and that. I'm always on duty." Charlotte finished eating and took her plate over to the sink.

"Don't you ever get a break?"

"Not really. I'm the only physician around these parts."

"Haven't you ever thought of hiring another doctor?"

Charlotte's brow furrowed in thought. "Yes, and I have tried, believe me. Mostly it's recent grads who come up, but they don't stay long. They stay long enough to get another job."

"Government incentive, then, eh?"

Charlotte nodded. "You've got it. They work the hours required to get med school paid for and then they're off to greener pastures."

"Smart kids."

Charlotte's eyes turned flinty and her spine straightened. "You think so?"

"I do."

"Is that why you came up to Yellowknife with me after residency?"

"Yes." There was no point in hiding the truth from her. His parents hadn't supported him through medical school. Even though he was their only child, they'd still felt he shouldn't have any handouts. When he'd followed Charlotte up to the wilds of the Canadian North it had been for purely selfish reasons and he'd told her why when they'd first got together. Charlotte must've forgotten. However, his presence here this time was because of her.

"I see," she said. Her lips were pressed together in a thin line. He'd seen that look before. She was not pleased with him.

"Look, it's the truth and I'm sorry, but I was always up front about that. Perhaps you forgot?"

"No, you're right. You were up front and you had no qualms about leaving when you were presented with an out."

"You could've come with me," he whispered.

"I didn't want to. I love the North. This was the path I wanted to take."

"I know. I make no apologies for the reasons I came to the North."

"Yes, to flesh out your curriculum vitae. I'm painfully aware of that and don't need the reminder." Charlotte snorted.

"It's a good solid plan and looks great on the résumé."

She shook her head. "Is that the only thing that matters to you?"

"My career, you mean?"

"Of course. What else would I be talking about?" Charlotte set down the dish towel she'd been holding. "I don't want to get into this with you. I already know how you feel about it."

"I'm sorry that my career was important, but it should be the top priority for any physician. Hell, for anyone who busted their ass studying in a tough industry. I'm sorry I thought of my career. Is that what you want to hear? You stayed up here and that was for your career, so why should I feel bad about going after what I wanted?"

He regretted the words the moment they tumbled past his lips. Charlotte bit her lip and shook her head, tossing the dish towel on the counter.

"You're right. You shouldn't. I'm going to go do some paperwork. I've fallen a bit behind. Make yourself at home."

Quinn watched her disappear through her bedroom door. It closed behind her with a thud.

*You're an idiot, Devlyn.*

He was standing stubborn on the pulpit and ideals he had preached so often. Advice he gave to fledgling surgeons in the field of obstetrics, advice that gave him nothing and no one.

He really did have the personality of a sledgehammer, most days. Pain shot up his arm and he flexed his hand.

Fleshing out his résumé wasn't the only reason he'd come to the North. Charlotte had been the reason. The true reason, and he'd blown it.

He shook the morbid memories away, suddenly craving a drink. Only he knew Nunavut was a dry territory. Not a drop could be brought in. He'd watched the Mounties confiscate liquor from some guys who had been on their way up for some ice fishing in Iqaluit.

Quinn wandered over to the fridge and opened it. Orange juice beckoned him. He pulled it out and resisted taking a swig straight from the carton. Instead, after opening several cupboards, he found a glass. He poured himself some and drank the tangy juice down in one gulp. It burned his esophagus. Since his accident he was a little bit more sensitive to acidic things, but the burn felt good.

The burn helped him forget.

*"You've already made up your mind. You don't need my approval." She was lying in the bed, so pale against the crisp white hospital bedding. The IV was still embedded in her vein, giving a transfusion. She was pallid as she stared at the far wall, not responding to his announcement about going to Manhattan to a lucrative job.*

*Didn't she understand? Life would be better for both of them.*

*"Charlotte..."*

*"No." She turned and looked at him, her face devoid of expression. "No."*

The sound of shattering glass shook away the ghosts of his past and he stared in disbelief at the shards on her linoleum floor. His bad hand had frozen in a crab-like vise.

Quinn cursed wearily. He cleaned up the shards of glass and then headed over to the computer in the corner and wiggled the mouse. The monitor came on with a faint hum and he went directly to the folder on the desktop. Tikivik, Mentlana. He clicked on the pictures and brought up the multiple sonograms of Mentlana's baby.

Although the baby was thriving, the lesions in the paracheynma were quite visible.

*Dammit.*

If the lesions continued to grow then fluid would begin to collect in the lungs and he would be forced to perform in utero surgery.

Quinn rubbed his eyes, trying to shake the sleep out of them. He wasn't sure if he was up to this in these conditions, but he'd promised Charlotte. It was the least he could to do make up for the hurt he'd caused her five years ago.

*Perhaps I won't have to perform the surgery.*

Perhaps he could get Mentlana down to Toronto where he *could* perform the surgery, and if not him, someone just as good as him.

He'd see to it personally.

When Charlotte came out of her bedroom, Quinn was nowhere to be seen and even though she was frustrated with him, she wondered where he'd got to. She snuck off to her office, intending to spend the day doing some administrative stuff.

For an hour Charlotte stared at the paperwork. She'd been holding the same manila folder for what seemed like forever.

"This is ridiculous." She dropped the folder back onto the large amount of files teetering on her desk.

*Get a grip.*

She'd known when she'd called Quinn up here that it would be hard to deal with him. She'd known that, but she'd been willing to ignore her own hurt feelings, her attraction to him for the sake of Mentlana and her baby.

Why was she mad that he'd followed his dreams, just like she'd chosen to stay in the North?

*Because it broke your heart that he left you.*

Yet here she was, hiding away in her office instead of doing what she always did on a lazy Saturday morning, which was slumming around her house and enjoying the solitude. But she didn't want to appear like a bum in front of him.

So, what? She shouldn't give two hoots that he was in

her house. She was the reason he'd come up here, so why was she allowing Quinn Devlyn to dictate her schedule? *I'm not going to let him.*

Charlotte stood up and marched purposefully, head held high, to her house. She opened the door with a "look at me, here I am" attitude and was stunned that Quinn was nowhere in the vicinity of her living area. His plate was still on the table, her carton of orange juice was sitting on the counter and her computer's tropical-fish screensaver bubbled with activity.

"Quinn?" she called out cautiously, but there was no answer.

*Great.* She mustered up the courage to face him, to show him that she didn't care he was here. To prove to him that he didn't affect her anymore. And he wasn't even here to see it.

*Blast.*

Charlotte ran her fingers through her tangle of curls and proceeded into the kitchen.

Just like him, leaving a mess behind.

His residence, before they'd roomed together, had been known as the sty for very good reason. The man was a meticulous surgeon but a veritable pig, though Rosie would say the same about her filing habits.

She picked up the orange-juice carton and shook it slightly. There was a bit of juice in it, but when she peered inside there was barely any worth keeping. Except orange juice was damn expensive up here. She'd treated herself to this carton. Charlotte chugged the remainder of the juice so she wouldn't waste a single drop.

A smile tugged the corners of her lips briefly as she recalled the numerous arguments they'd had over his propensity to leave barely a dribble in the bottom of a carton. The last time, they'd fought over a carton of eggnog during Christmas and they'd ended up making love under the Christmas tree.

Her pulse raced as that memory replayed in her head like a cozy movie. It'd been so long since she had thought about it. Her heart began to beat faster and butterflies began to swirl around in her stomach.

*Damn.*

Charlotte crumpled the carton in her hand before tossing it out under the sink. She slammed the cupboard shut, angry at herself for letting herself *feel* this way about Quinn again.

"Domestic duties prevail over paperwork?"

Charlotte startled and spun around. He was inches from her, half-naked. The scent of his body wash was masculine and spicy as she inhaled deeply.

"Uh—uh," she stuttered, and backed up to the counter. She gripped the cheap melamine as if her life depended on it.

"What?" he asked, cocking an eyebrow. "I thought I'd shower and wash off that certain smell that seems to permeate most planes."

Charlotte couldn't think straight as her gaze trailed hungrily down his body, abruptly ending at the tropical beach towel tied around his waist.

His hair curled and glistened with drops of moisture. She ran her tongue over her lips. Oh, how she wanted to run her tongue over his chest, particularly around his nipples, which she knew were particularly sensitive.

"Charlotte, you're starting to scare me."

She shook her head. "Sorry." She turned back to the sink and turned on the faucet, hoping the rushing water would drown out the erratic beat of her pulse and make him move away. "Yeah, going to do some dishes."

Only he didn't move away. He moved closer, and the

heat of his body permeated her back, through the thick sweater and turtleneck she was wearing. Gooseflesh broke across her skin and she held her breath.

"Is there anything I can help you with, Charlotte?" he asked, his breath branding her flesh at the base of her neck.

Charlotte turned around again, staring deep into his deep brown eyes. *Oh, God.* She was falling again. She had no strength when it came to him. He still made her weak at the knees.

"I..."

"What do you need, Charlotte?" He reached out and ran his knuckles against her cheek. "Tell me what you need. I'd do anything for you. You know that."

# CHAPTER SIX

He was so close to her that her heart was racing. Her traitorous body was reacting to him.

"Charlotte," he whispered, and reached out to touch her.

"Hey, Doc… Whoa…sorry!"

Quinn jumped back and Charlotte saw George, a shocked look on his face, standing dumbstruck between her clinic and her home. In his hand was a plastic bag bulging with what looked like blue-and-green scrubs.

"George, come in. Dr. Devlyn and I were just talking about…" She trailed off, her brain totally blank, and Quinn just cleared his throat. He was absolutely no help.

George blushed and looked away, staring at the ceiling. "Sorry, Doc Charley. I should've knocked."

"No, it's okay, George. I was just doing dishes." She pushed past Quinn, feeling humiliated that George had walked in on them in such a compromising position. George would definitely blab about this to Mentlana and she'd never be able to live it down. Ignoring what had happened, she feigned nonchalance. "Is something wrong, George?"

"Nothing. I just brought some scrubs and came to remind you about a certain appointment today." He pointed at his watch. "You didn't forget, right?"

"Shoot," she cursed. She had. Today was her scheduled checkup on Anernerk Kamuk, Cape Recluse's oldest woman and George's grandmother. The woman who had taken in Charlotte when her father had died. Anernerk would certainly have something to say if she was late for the checkup. "I'll be ready in a few, George."

George nodded, a funny smile plastered across his face. "Okay, Doc Charley." His dark gaze landed on Quinn. "Dr. Devlyn, pleasure to see you again."

Charlotte could hear his chuckles as he closed the door to her clinic.

*Dammit.*

"What did you forget?" Quinn asked.

"Today is my bi-weekly check on Cape Recluse's oldest resident. She's one hundred and one, and an artist."

Quinn's eyes flew open in surprise. "One hundred and one?"

"Hard of hearing, Devlyn?" She grabbed her parka off the coat rack, but a smile tweaked at the corners of her lips.

"I'm sorry. I'm amazed, frankly. In my line of work I don't meet many people who've passed the century mark."

"It's the fresh air up here." She fished around in her pocket for the keys to her snowmobile.

"You said she's an artist. Would I know her work?" Quinn asked.

"Doubtful. Unless you're an expert in traditional Inuktitut artwork."

"Ah, no." Quinn rubbed the back of his neck. "Don't get me wrong, though. I've seen some really intriguing native art in New York."

"Her name is Anernerk Kamuk. Does that name ring a bell in the 'it' crowd of Manhattan?"

"Not in the art scene, no, but didn't you live with her after your father died?"

Charlotte was impressed. "Oh, so you actually did listen to me when I spoke."

Quinn rolled his eyes. "Give me some credit."

Charlotte blushed. "Sorry. Yes. She's George and Mentlana's grandmother and she took me in when my dad died. Look, I have to get going or she'll raise a stink."

"Can I come?"

Charlotte paused in the middle of rummaging through her bag and stared at Quinn. "You...you want to come?"

Quinn ran a hand through his damp hair. "Yeah. If that's okay?"

She blinked in disbelief. "Sure. Can you be ready in ten minutes? I have to collect a few things from the clinic. Dress warmly and I'll meet you outside."

"Excellent. See you in ten."

Charlotte watched him pad off towards her guest bedroom. When the door shut she shook herself out of her daze and headed into her clinic to collect her bag and instruments. Actually, she was quite looking forward to seeing how Quinn dealt with Anernerk. He'd never had the best people skills when dealing with non-medical professionals, and Anernerk was a bit of a handful at the best of times.

She was going to eat Quinn alive and that thought gave Charlotte a secret thrill. It would be an entertaining appointment, that was for sure.

As she shoved Anernerk's file in her rucksack, Quinn entered her office. He was, surprisingly, kitted out in appropriate cold-weather gear and she was impressed he'd done his homework before coming up here.

"Ready?" she asked with a bit of trepidation.

"Whenever you are."

Charlotte nodded and led him outside. George was waiting on his snowmobile, ready to lead the way through the snowdrifts to the cabin on the outskirts of Cape Recluse, where Anernerk lived and still worked as an important Inuk artist.

"Hey, Dr. Devlyn. Good to see you're going with us. Grandma sure likes to get her hands on fresh meat." George chuckled again and, despite the bitter cold, Charlotte felt her face heat with a blush.

She sent a silent warning of *shut up* to George as she pulled her rucksack on. Charlotte mounted her snowmobile and glanced over her shoulder at Quinn, who was still standing by the door, shifting from foot to foot.

"Nervous?" she asked, pointedly staring at his shuffling feet.

"No. I'm freezing out here. I'm trying to keep the circulation going in my lower extremities."

Charlotte bit back her smile. "Well, let's get going. It's freaking cold out here."

Quinn chuckled and climbed on behind her. His body nestled against her back, his arms wrapped around her waist. Even though many layers of thick clothing and snowsuits separated them, she squirmed in her seat. She was suddenly very warm and it wasn't her winter clothing that was causing it.

"Are you sure you're not nervous, Devlyn?" she teased, trying to dispel her own nervousness at having him so close to her.

"Not in the least," he said. Although something in his voice told her she wasn't the only one feeling a bit edgy about being so close together again. She smiled and revved the engine. It felt so good to have his arms wrapped around her.

"Hold on to your hat."

"Wagons, ho," George shouted above the roar of the Bombardier machines, pumping his fist into the air. They took off across the snow, northeast toward the sea and Anernerk's home.

Charlotte had tried time and time again to get Anernerk to move closer to the clinic, into the main town with one of her children. Anernerk refused on the grounds that the spirits had told her that in order to paint, she needed to see where the sea met the sky without the clutter of town in the way.

A thin column of smoke rose in the air as they crested a bank of snow. Charlotte let out an inward sigh of relief, glad to know Anernerk was still alive. Anernerk also refused most modern technologies and didn't have a phone.

Anernerk's little red house on high stilts looked warm and inviting. This was where Charlotte had lived when her father had died. This was home. Charlotte parked her snowmobile beside George's. George was humming and grinned at Quinn as he stumbled off the back of her snowmobile.

"Your first time, Dr. Devlyn?"

"On a snowmobile? Yes." Quinn chuckled. "I guess you could say I am a virgin in that respect."

George let out a large guffaw. "Well, you're a virgin no more, Dr. Devlyn. You're officially deflowered."

Charlotte rolled her eyes at the men's childish banter. The door to Anernerk's door swung open quickly to reveal a little wrinkled face peering outside. Dark eyes flashed under a mass of wrinkles.

"Are you just going to stand out there all day? I'm not going getting any younger, you know," she called down from her porch high above them.

"Oh, hush, Anernerk. We're coming, we're coming."

Quinn was stunned by the Inuk woman. Though she was a mass of wrinkles and weathered skin, he wouldn't have guessed from her fluid movements that she was over a century.

Anernerk's beetle-black gaze rested on him. There was a twinkle to them and a smile tugged at the corners of her lips. The intensity of her perusal unnerved Quinn slightly. It was as if the old woman was peering deep into his soul.

"Who've you brought to visit, Doc Charley?" Anernerk asked.

"A friend of mine from med school. He's come here to take care of Mentlana."

The woman's eyes widened. "Mentlana? Well, this is good news indeed." Anernerk stepped aside as George and Charlotte crossed the threshold into her home.

Quinn followed up the steps, seeking the warmth that emanated from the wood stove in the center of the large room of Anernerk's clapboard shanty, which, like most of the other homes, was tethered down and on stilts. He peeled off his coat and hung it on a peg near the wood stove.

He rubbed his hands together, fast. Even though he had been wearing thick mittens, which the man at the wilderness store had assured him would keep out the cold, the bitter temperature of the top of the world still clung to his skin, sending its frosty tendrils deep into his body. His hands ached and he couldn't get the feeling back into them, no matter how hard he rubbed.

The hairs on the back of his neck stood on end and he had the sense that someone was staring at him. Quinn craned his neck and caught Anernerk's gaze. She was watching him, a strange look on her face. His face heated and he slid his hands into his pockets.

"Anernerk, how are you feeling today?" Charlotte asked.

Anernerk snorted. "How do you think I feel, Doc Charley? Cranky. I'm cranky today."

George, who Quinn had lost sight of, came in through another door on the far side of the room with a load of firewood in his arms.

"She's always cranky, Doc. You should know that by now."

Charlotte smiled patiently as she rolled up the woman's sleeve and pulled out a blood-pressure monitor. The rip of Velcro echoed in Anernerk's sparse cabin, but it was then that Quinn glanced at the walls and realized what he was actually looking at.

"Oh, my God," he whispered.

He moved closer to the nearest wall, enraptured by the thick, bold lines and swirl of primeval colors.

"Pretty cool, eh, Doc Dev?" George said.

"It's...it's like nothing I've ever seen."

Anernerk chuckled over the top of the steady pumping of the blood-pressure cuff. "I think your friend fancies my art, Charlotte."

Quinn spun round. "You've done all of this? This is your art?"

Anernerk nodded slowly, grinning, obviously pleased with his awe. "I was taught by my grandfather. A shaman. Way back when Nunavut was just a lowly outpost on the far reaches of the Northwest Territories and Iqaluit was known as Frobisher Bay."

"I've seen some of these in The Met."

Charlotte grinned. "Yes, Anernerk's art is world renowned. I told you she was an artist."

"Yes, but I had no idea she was this prolific. I can't believe I'm standing here in front of the originals."

"Of course." Anernerk rubbed her hand as Charlotte removed the cuff. "Not so hard next time, Charlotte. There's no meat left on these bones."

"Hush," Charlotte chastised gently.

Quinn found himself drawn immediately to one particular painting, one that featured a man and a woman. The man was harpooning a walrus and the woman was sewing and casting the man evil looks. He felt a bit dizzy and sick staring at it and he didn't know why.

"Hold tight, Anernerk. I have to sterilize this," Quinn heard Charlotte say, and he glanced at her briefly to see her head towards the kitchen, which was tucked off in the corner behind some swing doors.

Quinn tore his gaze away and came face-to-face with Anernerk. She was staring at him.

"I see you're particularly drawn to the depiction of the obstinate man. Do you know the story?"

"No, I don't."

"Come sit by the fire, Dr. Devlyn. I have some liniment for your hands."

"What are you talking about?"

"You may be able to fool other people with your walls, Dr. Devlyn, but you don't fool me."

"I don't?"

Anernerk shook her head. "Come, and I'll tell you all about the obstinate man."

Quinn didn't move and Anernerk rolled her eyes.

"Dr. Devlyn, I may be older than time itself but I don't bite…much." She grinned, displaying her missing teeth. She looked like those typical old witches he used to be terrified of as a child, but there was no malice about Anernerk Kamuk. He nodded and allowed her to lead him to two rockers that sat near the wood stove.

Quinn sat across from her.

"I think this tale will hit you personally, Dr. Devlyn. I

think you'll find similarities between your destiny and the destiny of my dear Charlotte." Anernerk reached down in a big basket, which was overflowing with various yarns and knitting needles. She pulled out a dark innocuous bottle with no label.

"How do you know about me and Charlotte?" Quinn asked, intrigued.

Anernerk's black eyes twinkled. "There are no secrets in Cape Recluse, Dr. Devlyn."

"Are you some kind of mind-reader or shaman yourself, Anernerk?"

She raised a thick gray eyebrow. "Are you crazy? Of course not. Just because I'm Inuk doesn't mean I can converse with Nanook of the North or anything." She laughed. "Besides, I talk to Mentlana."

"Mentlana is on bed rest. She's not supposed to leave Cape Recluse. Is she coming out here, Anernerk? I need to know."

"No, of course not!" Anernerk chuckled conspiratorially and pulled out a small phone from her trouser pocket. "Shh. Don't tell. It'll ruin the whole illusion for George and Charlotte." She hid the phone back in her pocket. "Besides, I like their visits."

Quinn couldn't help but laugh. "You have a smartphone?"

"How else do I keep in touch with my agent? The laptop is in my underwear drawer. Ain't nobody going in there. Now, where was I?"

"You were going to tell me about the obstinate man and the significance it plays in respect to me and Charlotte."

"Give me your hands," Anernerk ordered.

Quinn held them out. Her hands were rough but strong. She undid the bottle and poured the thick corn-syrupy-looking liquid into his hand. It instantly warmed as it touched him. Anernerk began to rub his shattered hand vigorously and the aches and pains began to fade as the old woman's liniment began to work some kind of magic on him. It was better than the exercise regime his physiotherapist forced on him.

"There once was a very stubborn man. Not unlike yourself, Dr. Devlyn. His wife lost their child, but instead of letting her mourn he made her work for him. As she worked, the Moon Man's dog came out and attacked this obstinate man for making his wife work before her mourning time was done.

"The man overcame the dog, killing him. The Moon Man came and fought the obstinate man, but again he was no match for such stubbornness. The obstinate man won. The Moon Man invited him to join him at his home, but told him to take the dark side of the rock and not come around the easier sunny side, or he would lose his heart."

"Lose his heart?"

Anernerk smiled and continued rubbing his hand. "The easiest path is not always the wisest, Dr. Devlyn."

"Is that so?" Quinn wanted to change the subject, but he had the feeling he wouldn't be able to.

"So the obstinate man came around the sunny side and saw an old woman sitting there, sharpening a blade. He thought he could overcome the old woman. She was weak and feeble, whereas he was strong, but he overestimated his ability and lost consciousness. When he came to, his heart had been torn from him.

"The Moon Man saved him, returning to him his broken, tattered heart. It was then that the stubborn man saw the evil, dark thoughts coming from his wife and what he had done to her, how he had hurt her by forcing her to work before her mourning time was done."

Quinn's throat constricted and he glanced towards the

kitchen. He could hear water boiling and in his mind's eye he could envision Charlotte cleaning the instruments thoroughly. Did she have dark thoughts about him?

He was pretty certain she did.

*"No. You're being stubborn, Quinn. Why do I have to give up my life here?"*

*"What kind of life is this?"*

*"A good life."*

*"We can have a good life in Manhattan."*

*Tears ran down her face and she turned her head away. "No."*

"How do your hands feel now, Dr. Devlyn?"

Quinn shook himself out of his stupor and flexed his hands. They were warm, pliable.

"Ahem."

He looked up to see Charlotte leaning against a post, expressions of confusion and intrigue playing across her face.

"Thank you, Mrs. Kamuk."

He stood up and jammed his hands quickly in his pockets.

Anernerk chuckled and then whispered under her breath, "Stubborn, Dr. Devlyn. So stubborn." She looked back at Charlotte. "So, are you ready for your quart of blood, Doc Charlotte?"

Charlotte *tsked* and Quinn moved away so Charlotte could do her work. Quinn watched in admiration. She was so sure of herself now, and though he hadn't seen it at the time, this had been the right path for her.

The path away from him.

# CHAPTER SEVEN

CHARLOTTE WAS CLEANING up the rest of her instruments and tucking away the specimens from Anernerk. The resident old coot was back in her rocking chair, knitting and telling stories as her needles clicked together. George was sitting beside her, listening to her and laughing.

Sometimes Charlotte wondered if it was George, the overly concerned grandson, who insisted on these visits out here. Everyone in Cape Recluse loved Anernerk.

Charlotte smiled as she watched the woman who had raised her for over a decade, warmth flooding her veins as she recalled all the good times she and Anernerk had shared. How Anernerk's entire family had welcomed her.

When her father had died she'd had no one. Her father had had no other family except distant cousins. It'd been the same on her mother's side. Charlotte often wondered if it was why her parents had been drawn to each other. Her parents had both been orphans.

As their daughter had become.

The only difference was that Charlotte had had people to love and take care of her. Her parents hadn't had someone like Anernerk to take them in.

She felt blessed.

Anernerk was as healthy as could be for someone over a century old. There was nothing to worry about in regard to the old woman's physical well-being. Charlotte was more worried about what she'd seen between Anernerk and Quinn. Anernerk had a way with people. She could win them over, charm them, and they ate up everything she said.

Even Quinn, who had never believed in all these old hokey remedies and anything even mildly spiritual in nature, especially when it came to medicine, had been mesmerized.

Charlotte had watched Anernerk rub his hands and she had also seen how quickly Quinn had hidden them and brushed off Anernerk when he'd realized she was standing there.

Why was he hiding it from her? What had happened to him?

It wasn't rocket science for Charlotte to figure out in ten seconds that he'd been injured, but he didn't seem bothered by it. Still, she needed to have a frank talk with him about the surgery.

Mentlana was not going to be used as a guinea pig to see if Quinn Devlyn's masterful surgical skills were still intact. There was a reason people donated their bodies to science.

Hell, there were dummies now that could be used to mimic surgery. He could practice on one of them, but not Mentlana.

Charlotte snapped her bag shut and wandered over to him. He was still standing in front of Anernerk's paintings. Staring at them in awe.

"I didn't think you were so interested in Inuktitut art, Quinn."

"I wasn't until I saw an auction at Christie's in Manhattan about four years ago. It was to raise money for a charity and Anernerk Kamuk's art was prominently featured. I didn't recognize the name when you said it. They raised over a million dollars that night and Anernerk's lithograph of Kagssagussuk accounted for a quarter of that million."

"Ah, so you became interested in it because of its worth."

Quinn looked at her, his gaze so intent it sent a shiver of delight down her back. He leaned in closer and she closed her eyes, reveling in the feel of his hot breath against her neck. "It was a beautiful piece. I was ignorant and had no idea."

Charlotte shrugged. "I'm impressed. But you don't know the stories related to them."

Quinn chuckled and moved away. "No, those I didn't know. That information is not readily available in Manhattan and I didn't have the time to really go searching. My practice was flourishing by then." His self-satisfied grin made her grind her teeth just a little.

She spun round. "Well, George, I think we've outstayed our welcome."

"You going?" Anernerk put down her knitting. "You just got here."

Charlotte grinned at her elderly patient. "Anernerk, we got here three hours ago."

Anernerk stood up. "I'll make you something to eat." She turned round and fixed her impenetrable gaze on Quinn. "How about muktuk, Dr. Devlyn? I can make you a nice meal of muktuk."

Quinn's eyes widened and he looked at Charlotte. Even though she was tempted to let him eat some blubber, which was what muktuk was, she wasn't that heartless. Charlotte shook her head subtly.

"Ah, thank you, Mrs. Kamuk, but I think just this time I am going to forgo your delicacy of muktuk," Quinn replied with grace.

Anernerk's eyes narrowed as she stared at Charlotte,

then she crossed her arms and snorted. "All right. But at least it puts meat on your bones. Dr. Devlyn is too skinny for my liking."

"Hah!" George chuckled, jamming on his cap. "Meat on your bones, eh, Aanak? Hasn't seemed to do you any good."

Anernerk directed her wrath at George by slapping him across the back of the head.

"I thought her name was Anernerk?" Quinn whispered out of the side of his mouth.

"Aanak is the Inuk word for grandmother," Charlotte explained.

"Ah." Quinn nodded.

Charlotte stifled another laugh and Quinn looked a bit awestruck by it all. Then again, he didn't really have much interaction with others. Even when they had been together she wasn't absolutely sure if Quinn had had any *real* friends.

When they had been in medical school and interning, his whole life had been the hospital, and she'd never met his family. In fact, for a long time she hadn't thought he had any family as he rarely mentioned them. Then one day, after they had settled in Yellowknife, he'd shown up with two air tickets for Toronto. She had been going to fly out to Toronto to meet his mother and father, but two weeks before the flight she'd miscarried.

*His father died. Was his mother still alive?*

It made her pity him. She had lost the only parent she had known before she'd gone into med school, but she'd had the Tikiviks, she'd had Mentlana, she'd had a home.

Cape Recluse.

She had lived here for ten years before med school. It was why she'd wanted to become a physician and work in the northern communities. If her father had had access to a physician, he might not have died from the aneurysm that had claimed his life.

"Sorry, Aanak," George grumbled, rubbing the back of his head where Anernerk had cuffed him. He bent down and laid a kiss on Anernerk's cheek. Although Anernerk still looked a bit put out, Charlotte could tell she was mollified by George's apology. George snuck out the front door into the cold.

"It was a pleasure to meet you, Mrs. Kamuk."

"And you, Dr. Devlyn. I do hope I get to see you again before you leave us."

Quinn grinned and followed George outside. Anernerk turned her focused black gaze on Charlotte.

"I'll come out and see you again soon, Anernerk." Charlotte embraced the old woman.

"Find it somewhere in your heart to forgive him, Charlotte." Anernerk tucked Charlotte's red curls behind her ear. "He's a good man, just obstinate."

Charlotte's throat tightened and she fought back the tears that threatened to spill. "I'll see you in a couple of weeks."

Anernerk nodded. "You take my advice." She held out a bottle. Charlotte looked at the brown bottle in confusion. "Give it to Dr. Devlyn. He needs it. It will help him heal on the outside, anyway."

Charlotte nodded and stuffed the bottle in her pocket. "See you later."

Anernerk nodded, her eyes glistening as she hugged Charlotte tightly again.

George and Quinn were waiting for her, George on his snowmobile and Quinn shuffling back and forth in the cold, waiting for her.

She made sure her backpack was secure and climbed onto her snowmobile.

Anernerk poked her head out the door. "Next time you come I'm making Dr. Devlyn a nice big meal of muktuk, and there will be no refusal."

Quinn waved and Anernerk shut the door. "What the hell is muktuk?"

"Blubber," Charlotte replied, as she slid on her goggles. She glanced over her shoulder and saw Quinn's eyes widen.

"You're joking...right?"

Charlotte chuckled. "Nope."

"Good God!" Quinn made a choking sound, like he was going to retch.

George, sitting on the snowmobile beside them, grinned. "Aw, c'mon, Dr. Dev. It's not as bad as some of that stuff you hoity-toity physicians eat down there in Manhattan."

"Like what?" Quinn asked.

"Foie gras, caviar, tentacles." George made a wiggly motion with his hand and stuck out his tongue. "Gross."

Quinn laughed. "I'll have you know—"

"Enough!" Charlotte interrupted. "If you two have forgotten, it's below freezing out here. You can talk about strange gastronomical treats at the clinic, in the warmth. Right now, I'd really like to head back to Cape Recluse before the lab samples freeze." She turned and glared at George. "And if they do freeze, guess who's coming back to take them again?"

"Right you are, Doc Charley." George revved his snowmobile. "Let's go." He shot off west back towards town and Charlotte followed, trying to ignore Quinn's arms around her, his body pressed against hers as she raced to get back to the warmth of her home and clinic.

Honestly. Men.

Quinn did take his debate about cuisine inside with George. He quite liked George, which was odd. Especially as he'd considered George competition when he'd first arrived, but Charlotte had quickly quelled any thoughts on that score. Now, George was like a buddy. Quinn knew he didn't make friends easily and didn't have many people he really considered friends. His parents hadn't encouraged any camaraderie in his childhood. Only competition.

The only real friend he'd made had been Charlotte, and look how that had turned out. He'd hurt her. Terribly.

The hum of the centrifuge echoed in the quiet clinic and he followed the noise to her little lab at the far corner of the building.

He paused in the doorway; she was hunched over the counter, her head down on her arms, watching the whirling of the machine.

He wished he had his camera on hand so he could capture this moment. She was so beautiful. Her red curls were tied back, except for one errant strand, which every so often she would blow out of her face. Quinn could remember lying in bed with her on their days off, when they'd had hours and no one to disturb them, and he would take that one curl and wrap it around his finger, as she had done that first time he'd seen her. It had been so soft and he'd felt so relaxed, so at home with her.

He'd never felt that way before meeting her.

His father had been a workaholic and the best damn cardiothoracic surgeon in Toronto. It was ironic it had been a myocardial infarction that had killed him. Quinn's mother had set her son on a pedestal when he'd got into medical school at Harvard. She'd expected the same results as his father had achieved in his chosen field, not ever accepting any failure from him.

Quinn remembered how angry his mother had been when he had started dating Charlotte.

It had made him wonder, later, when he'd realized how

foolish he had been to lose Charlotte, if his parents had ever truly loved each other.

Quinn hadn't realized it at the time, but Charlotte had made life worth living and he'd thrown it all away.

As if sensing his presence, she turned her head, her eyes widening when she saw him. She sat up and tucked the lock of hair behind her ear.

"Is something wrong, Quinn?"

"No… Yes."

"Is it something I can help you with?" There was a look of anticipation on her face, and she bit her lip, almost as if she was silently urging him to talk.

He clenched his fist, biting back the pain.

*No.*

"Just wanted to know what you wanted for dinner."

Charlotte chuckled. "Since when do you cook? Never, if I recall."

Quinn laughed and glanced down at the pristine tiled floor. "I don't suppose there is any takeout in Cape Recluse, is there?"

Charlotte shook her head. "No takeout, but there is a diner. Would you like to go get some there?"

"As long as I'm not forced to eat that blubber stuff, sure."

Charlotte smiled, her grin lighting up the dimness of the lab. "Let me just put Anernerk's specimens away and we can grab something to eat."

Quinn tracked her movements. God, she was beautiful. Even though he knew the reasons why he had gone to Manhattan and that they'd made sense to him at the time, he now wondered why he'd left her behind.

*You're an idiot.*

"Come on." She took his hand and led him out of the lab. They slipped on their winter jackets and Charlotte

jammed a furry toque down far on her head and wound
her scarf around her face.

"It's not far, is it?" Quinn asked. "No dog sleds are
needed?"

"No," Charlotte replied, despite being muffled under
her thick scarf. "Just a short jog."

He hoped so. He wasn't enjoying the frigid temperatures of the Arctic. She opened the door and he was hit by
a blast of icy air. He should've been used to it by now, but
the low temperatures still surprised him.

They said nothing to each other as they shuffled through
town to a little shack near the hangar. A steady stream of
exhaust fumes floated up from the chimney—the aroma
of old-fashioned cooking.

He could smell fries and his stomach growled at the
thought of poutine. He was so hungry he might just take
Mrs. Kamuk up on her offer to eat muktuk.

Chimes over the door jingled and they stomped their
feet on the mat to shake off the snow. When he looked up,
the patrons of the restaurant were all staring in wide-eyed
wonder and Quinn felt like a specimen under examination at that moment.

"I should've mentioned that this diner is run by the
Tikivik family," Charlotte whispered as she hung up her
coat.

"Ah, so these are the hordes that were waiting in your
clinic when I arrived yesterday?"

Charlotte nodded. "Yep, that would be them." She
turned and waved and the group waved back then returned
to their regular restaurant chatter.

"Do we wait for someone to seat us?" Quinn asked,
looking around.

"It's not that kind of place, Devlyn." She took his hand
again and his blood heated at her gentle touch. She led him

to a corner booth and they slid into it. He sat down across from her. Charlotte handed him a vinyl-covered menu.

It was one sided and a bit smeared. She laughed as he held it with disdain. "The food is safe, Devlyn. You're hungry, I'm tired and you can't cook."

"Right. This stuff has to be better." Only his mind began to wander to the disgusting conversation with George earlier. If he continued thinking like that he wouldn't be able to eat anything.

Charlotte nodded and glanced at the menu.

"Ah, so the two doctors are gracing us with their presence tonight."

Quinn looked up at the pretty young waitress, who was the spitting image of Mentlana.

"Hey, Lucy. You haven't met Dr. Quinn Devlyn. Dr. Devlyn, this is Mentlana's twin, Lucy."

"Pleasure." He nodded.

"So, what'll it be tonight, Charley? Usual?"

"Yep."

Lucy nodded and looked expectantly at him. "What can I get for you, Dr. Devlyn?"

"What is a usual?"

Lucy chuckled. "A BLT, a salad and a diet cola."

"Sounds good, but make mine with fries. Oh, do you do poutines here?"

Lucy grinned. "Of course."

"Then that's what I'll have."

She nodded and headed back to the kitchen.

"I forgot about your affinity for poutines, Quinn. I guess you don't get many of those in Manhattan."

"Only on lunch breaks. Dinner out was more…a bit more top of the line."

"Escargots and the like?"

"Dammit." Quinn banged the table.

"What?" Charlotte asked, stunned.

"I forgot to tell George about escargots. I bet he'd be seriously squicked out."

Charlotte laughed. "He knows. He's been to Toronto many a time. He's just having some fun with you."

"That little…" Quinn laughed.

"He likes you." Charlotte smiled. "I think it's nice."

Lucy placed their drinks in front of them, grinning before leaving discreetly again.

"So, what is your obsession with food today?" Charlotte asked, playing with the straw in her glass of diet soda. "Have you suddenly miraculously learned how to cook?" There was a sparkle of devilment in her eyes.

He leaned closer to her across the table. "Do you remember the time I tried to make hamburger and cheese out of the packet and used lard instead of butter?"

Charlotte choked on her water. "Yes. It was horrific. Epically horrific, in fact." She shuddered. "I think I repressed that memory."

Quinn laughed and reached for her hand. Charlotte's eyes widened in shock at his touch, but she didn't try to pull away. Her hand was so slender and gave off the illusion it was delicate, but really it was strong. She'd had such potential to become a brilliant surgeon. Only Charlotte hadn't wanted that. She'd wanted to be a general practitioner. Her hand felt so snug in his. So warm. So right.

"Remember the time I tried to make brownies and they only baked around the edges."

There was a twinkle in her eye. "I remember. Hard as a rock around the edges."

"But soft and gooey in the unbaked center. I must have tried to cook those brownies for three hours."

"I remember," Charlotte whispered. "I remember the smell. I was going through such bad…" She trailed off.

The mirth disappeared. She straightened her spine and pulled her hand away.

He knew why she'd retreated emotionally. Quinn had known when he'd been making those brownies that she had been going through horrid morning sickness. She had been on Diclectin because she hadn't been able to keep anything down. It had killed him to see her suffer like that. So sick.

He'd tried to bake the brownies to cheer her up and butter her up to go to Manhattan. That day, the day of the miscarriage, the day Charlotte had lost the baby, had been the day he had been offered the private practice and fellowship in Manhattan. The offer had come from Dr. Robert Bryce, one of the leading neonatal surgeons on the Eastern Seaboard, and Dr. Bryce had wanted him, but Charlotte had refused to leave the godforsaken North.

That's how he'd felt about it.

Godforsaken.

Now he wasn't so sure. Charlotte was happy, and a successful physician.

And he was lonely.

"Anyway, I remember."

"Here are your meals, Doctors. By the way, Jake said they're on the house."

"No," Charlotte said, shaking her head vehemently. "We can pay, Lucy. You tell him we'll pay."

Lucy smiled, that cute dimple like her sister's appearing in her cheek. "You know Jake. He won't take no for an answer." Lucy looked at him then, her black eyes shining with warmth. "You are saving his nephew and my nephew. Jake is Genen's brother."

Charlotte sighed. "Lucy."

"It's done, Doc Charley. Deal with it." Lucy left them.

"That's awfully generous of them." Quinn turned and

waved to the man behind the counter, the man he presumed was Jake.

"It's his way of saying 'thank you.' Everyone up here is family. Mentlana and Genen's baby means so much to this community."

Quinn's stomach rumbled and he looked down at his poutine. The meaty smell of the gravy made his mouth water in anticipation. The fries were fresh cut and thick and it had been a long time since he had real, home-cooked poutine.

"Lucy is actually going to be leaving us after Mentlana has her baby," Charlotte said, spearing a piece of lettuce.

"Really? Where's she going?"

"To Hamilton, Ontario. She's training to become a midwife and a registered nurse. I'm hoping she returns to Cape Recluse. I could use her."

"Doesn't Cape Recluse have a midwife? You mentioned her."

Charlotte nodded, chewing. "Lorna is getting old and ready to retire. Besides, if Lucy becomes a nurse she'll have much more training and knowledge than Lorna did. Lorna was trained by her mother...Anernerk."

"Anernerk is an impressive woman. So, midwifery is a generational thing. Well, I don't mean to interfere, but what you really need is another physician up here."

Charlotte nodded. "I know, but we've had this conversation before."

"I know." Quinn took a bite of his poutine and it was absolute heaven. God, he loved cheese curd. So bad for the arteries, but he was enjoying every bite.

"What do you think of Jake's cooking?" Charlotte asked. There was a smug smile plastered across her face.

"My compliments to the chef, for sure."

"Does it beat out all those fancy Manhattan restaurants?"

"Some. I won't lie to you, Charlotte. New York is a gourmand's paradise."

She smiled. "Really? I suppose your favorite restaurant is some crazy-ass posh spot where all the 'it' crowd goes."

"Nope. But it does serve the best fettuccine in the world."

"Mmm. I do love fettuccine."

"I know." Quinn took her hand again. "Perhaps you'll go there someday."

Charlotte put her head to one side, staring at him. "Perhaps."

Then he heard it, the distant rumble of something, something that was stirring at the back of his mind. A sound he should have recognized instantly. Charlotte heard it, too, and pulled her hand away. She stood and looked out the windows of the diner, like the rest of the patrons. Her phone started buzzing and she cursed under her breath when she pulled it out.

Far off on the horizon he could make out the flashing lights of a chopper, and the closer it got the louder the spinning of its blades became.

"What in the world...?" Quinn asked, puzzled.

"I'll wrap up the rest of your food and bring it over to the clinic, Doc Charley," Lucy called.

"Wrap up our food?" Quinn asked.

"Medical. There's an emergency. That was the text I received," Charlotte said quickly, before dashing off to get her coat. Quinn got up and tried to get his coat on before Charlotte disappeared out the door into the bitter cold towards the landing strip.

He zipped up his parka and went after her as she ran to meet the helicopter, which was making a quick landing.

Quinn's heart beat in time with each revolution of the helicopter's blade. George appeared by Charlotte's side, a gurney ready as they ducked to avoid decapitation.

Quinn hovered to the side, wanting to do something but not quite sure how trauma scenes played out up here. He watched the transfer and watched the paramedics climb into the helicopter again. Charlotte and George carried the gurney through the snow towards the clinic with a man dogging their heels.

He ran to head them off, opening the doors to the clinic and flicking on the lights.

Charlotte paid him no attention and he heard the patient's moans of pain as they came closer. His throat constricted when he got a good look at the patient on the stretcher and the obvious swelling under her thick blankets.

He could tell what was happening just by the woman's grimace and her husband's pained expression. An expression he had seen far too often, in countless men and women in waiting rooms.

The woman on the gurney was in labor and about to give birth.

He was the only qualified obstetrician currently in Cape Recluse.

Now was his time to shine.

# CHAPTER EIGHT

"How far apart are the contractions?" Quinn asked.

"The medic said every fifteen minutes," Charlotte responded.

Quinn helped her wheel the gurney into exam room one. It was the largest room she had, but still a bit of a tight squeeze. Charlotte had delivered babies on her own before, but usually at the patient's home with Lorna in attendance. And there hadn't been that many births up here in recent years. This baby, for better or for worse, was on its way. The eyes of the patient, Mrs. Grise, were wide with fright, her mouth a thin line and her face white with pain.

"I tried to get her to Iqaluit," the patient's husband said nervously. "I thought we had time. It's our first and the baby is three weeks early."

Quinn shook his head and let out a *tsk* of frustration at what he saw as the man's stupidity. Charlotte could tell by the look on his face what Quinn thought of the husband's assumptions.

"You should've taken her down weeks ago." Quinn snapped as they wheeled the patient over to the far side of the exam room and transferred her to the bed.

"I wouldn't let him," Mrs. Grise panted. "I didn't want to be alone."

"It's all right, Mrs. Grise—" Charlotte started.

"Rebecca," the woman interjected through her deep breathing. "Please, just Rebecca."

"Rebecca," Charlotte said soothingly. "I'm Dr. James and I'm going to do everything I can to ease your discomfort."

"If you wanted an epidural, I'm afraid there's no time. I'm sorry," Quinn said gently to the panicked woman. The patient was terrified, and he was being very gentle with her as they continued to prep.

She was amazed. When they had been doing their residency he had never been this calm and soothing with patients before.

"It's okay. No drugs. I'm ready," Rebecca said.

"You're sure?" Charlotte asked.

Rebecca nodded. "I want a natural birth."

"Dr. James, may I speak with you?"

Charlotte was stunned by Quinn's formality. This wasn't some big city hospital. This was a small clinic, her small clinic at the top of the world.

"What?" Charlotte asked, never taking her eyes off of the patient.

"Do you have the supplies in case of an emergency C-section?" Quinn whispered.

"Do you think her case warrants it?"

Quinn shrugged. "I don't know. I'm just being prepared."

"Yes. I have everything."

Quinn gave her a half smile. "Keep her comfortable and I'll handle the rest." He turned to walk away, but Charlotte gripped his arm.

"You know you won't get paid for this. I've delivered babies before."

"And I've delivered probably ten times the amount you have. As for payment, I don't care. This is an emergency."

She should fight it, throw him out of her clinic, only he was the specialist and she knew nothing about this patient. He was right and she was stunned he was willing to do this delivery with no compensation, something the Quinn Devlyn of five years ago wouldn't have been happy about.

Still, there was his hand to consider.

"Dr. James?" Mr. Grise said, his voice panicked.

"Everything is going to be fine. Dr. Devlyn is one of the best." Charlotte turned away from Quinn, silently handing him the reins of her clinic and praying to God she had made the right decision.

"Thank you," Rebecca whispered, as her husband squeezed her hand.

Charlotte stood back with George, feeling utterly useless.

"Is Lorna on her way?" Charlotte asked.

"Her contractions are coming close together," Quinn said. "Doesn't look like Lorna's going to get here in time. Are you allergic to latex, Rebecca?"

"No," she said. "Not allergic to anything."

"Good." Quinn turned to the sink and scrubbed his hands. Charlotte helped him by drying his hands and putting on a pair of gloves. Their eyes locked for a moment as he slipped his scarred hand into the glove. Charlotte couldn't help but wonder if he'd be able to deliver the baby. She'd watched him do exercises yesterday, had watched Anernerk massage his bad hand. Would his hand be strong enough to hold such a fragile life?

*Step in.*

Only she didn't. Charlotte didn't want to frighten Rebecca and she didn't want George to blab to anyone that she had doubts about Quinn, the man who was going to save Mentlana's baby's life.

Quinn sat on the rolling stool and Charlotte adjusted the lamp. There was no time for modesty.

Quinn preformed the internal. "Ten centimeters and fully effaced." He looked up at Rebecca and smiled encouragingly. "Time to start pushing. Bear down. Now."

Rebecca nodded and began to push, as George counted with Mr. Grise.

Charlotte stayed by Quinn's side, watching a new life enter the world.

*Please, God. Please let it be an easy birth.*

She'd never seen Quinn deliver a child before. He hadn't liked her to watch him during his residency and she'd been very busy with her own. But he was gentle as he urged Rebecca on. He guided the frightened woman through the birth with so much care and concern that Charlotte's heart fluttered, and in this moment she felt very connected to him. For all his talk about power and position it was evident he was just as passionate about health care and his profession as she was.

"Good. Take a deep breath and push. Hard, Rebecca. Hard." He was easing the baby's head out. "You're doing great, Rebecca. Again."

Charlotte smiled behind her mask as the top of the head began to appear. Doctoring in a remote community was never so rewarding as at this moment. And Quinn had always questioned her about why she hadn't specialized. Here, she had a taste of it all.

Rebecca screamed, a gut-wrenching cry of agony, and Charlotte didn't blame her. This moment was known as the "ring of fire" for a good reason.

"Scalpel," Quinn said. Charlotte handed him the blade and he made a small incision to control the tearing. His hand was strong and steady as he made the cut.

"Come on, Rebecca. One more good push and your baby will be here," Charlotte urged.

Rebecca grunted as the head passed easily and the rest of the baby slipped into Quinn's waiting hands.

"A girl," Charlotte announced as she stared in awe at the tiny little life so delicately cradled in Quinn's hands. His gaze locked on her. She saw a glimmer of envy and longing mirrored there. Hope flared somewhere deep inside her. The baby took her first lusty cry of life and Quinn looked away.

"Take the baby," he said, his hands shaking a bit. Charlotte grabbed a blanket and reached down to hold the squawking infant.

As she stared down at the baby, tears stung her eyes as she thought of her own lost child. Rebecca had been so brave having a baby up here, away from what most people considered civilization. Braver than she was, even for having a baby, something Charlotte was terrified to even entertain the notion of again because she couldn't bear the thought of losing another child.

*Get a grip on yourself, Charlotte.*

She carefully placed the baby on Rebecca's chest, and Quinn cut the cord once it had stopped pulsating. The proud father cuddled his new daughter while Quinn delivered the afterbirth and stitched Rebecca up.

"Good job, Dr. Devlyn and Mom." George grinned at the happy parents, but Charlotte could see they were oblivious to everything. Rebecca's gaze was focused on her crying, thriving baby.

She recorded the APGAR and rubbed ointment on the baby's eyes to reduce infection. After that she gingerly placed the baby on the scale.

"She's seven pounds eight ounces."

Charlotte then took measurements of the baby. When

five minutes had passed she recorded the APGAR again and gave the baby a vitamin K injection. The hospital in Iqaluit could do the heel stick tomorrow.

Charlotte swaddled the baby and took her over to the proud parents. Rebecca's arms were outstretched, tears streaming down her red cheeks. The new mother nuzzled her baby eagerly. A pang of longing rocked Charlotte to her core.

Charlotte wanted that. More than anything. More than any fear of what might happen.

"Thank you, Dr. James."

"It's Charlotte. Everyone up here calls me Charley, though."

Rebecca grinned. "Charlotte. I like that name."

"I think it's a perfect name for her," Quinn smiled. "I've always loved that name."

Charlotte blushed and smiled at Quinn. His eyes were twinkling and for a moment it was like the years had never separated them, that the hurt was forgotten. He returned her smile before turning away with the tray of instruments and medical waste.

"You can rest the night here, Mr. and Mrs. Grise. We'll take care of you, and tomorrow George or I will fly you down to Iqaluit. We'll need to notify the hospital that you've given birth here."

Rebecca nodded. "Thank you, Doctor... Thank you, Doc Charley."

"My pleasure." Charlotte peeled off her gloves and began to scrub. "George, make sure you set up a recovery room for them. I think there's a bassinet here. I always have stuff on hand. There's also some diapers and formula, if needed, in the supply room."

"I'm on it." George seemed to hesitate as he began to

place instruments on a tray to be sterilized. "What happened to Dr. Devlyn?" he asked in whispered undertone.

"He's right…" Charlotte trailed off as her eyes scanned the room. He'd disappeared. "Probably went to clean up. He's done his job."

"Of course. He was fantastic. It gives me hope he'll help Mentlana." George's voice shook at the mention of his sister.

A lump formed in Charlotte's throat. "You okay to fly to Iqaluit tomorrow?" she asked, changing the subject.

"Yep. My schedule is free."

"Good."

She left the room and shut the door. Taking a deep breath, she slid down to the floor. Her knees were knocking and exhaustion hit her in waves. Emotions and adrenaline were still rushing through her. It had been watching Quinn hold the baby that had brought back a flood of emotions she'd thought long gone. He had been so tender, for a man who had always insisted he didn't want or particularly like kids, which had never made sense to her, given his chosen specialty.

The door to the clinic opened and Lorna shuffled in. Her face was haggard and she looked worn out.

"Am I too late?"

Charlotte stood, her body protesting. "Healthy baby girl. Sorry for dragging you out of bed."

Lorna shook her head. "No problem. I'll be glad when Lucy leaves soon to study midwifery. I'm getting too…"

"Tired. You're ready to retire." Charlotte offered.

Lorna smiled. "You're just too polite to say old, Charlotte."

"You're not old. Your mother, Anernerk, is old."

"I'll be sixty-eight soon, well past retirement age."

Lorna slumped down in the waiting-room chair and Charlotte sat across from her.

"You can crash here for the night instead of trudging back home."

Lorna smiled weakly. "I just might take you up on that offer, help the new parents out and give you some rest."

"Thanks. Even though I was nothing more than a glorified nurse, it was an amazing experience."

"Does it make you change your mind?"

Charlotte dragged her hand through her hair. Lorna knew about her miscarriage and how Charlotte felt about becoming pregnant again. Charlotte blamed herself for losing the child. She had been an intern and had taxed her body way beyond its limits.

That's why she'd lost her baby.

"No," she answered uncertainly.

As the only doctor for kilometers around she was just as stressed, and she wouldn't lose another baby. She couldn't. It would kill her.

On the other hand, holding that baby tonight and watching Quinn cradling that tiny little life with all the care in the world had made her rethink the decision she'd made five years ago.

If she was given the chance to carry and have another baby, she'd do so in a heartbeat.

Lorna arched an eyebrow. "There is uncertainty there."

Charlotte shook her head and stood. "I'll make you up a bed in the other recovery room."

Lorna shook her head. "Avoiding a touchy subject. Obstinate."

"You know, you sounded just like your mother, then." Charlotte chuckled and walked down the hall.

"Low, blow, Doc Charley. Really low blow. I'm old enough to be your mother."

"Keep talking...Anernerk."

Lorna let out a guffaw as Charlotte disappeared round the corner to the recovery room. She made up Lorna's room and could hear George making up the other one. Charlotte helped him settle the happy parents and the baby in the larger recovery room, the one usually used to house two patients, and got Lorna settled in the room opposite.

It was quite handy because Lorna was well versed in postpartum needs and she said she would keep watch on the new mother and baby during the night.

George collapsed on the waiting-room couch and was snoring by the time Charlotte finished sterilizing the instruments and cleaning the exam room, not wanting Rosie to have a heart attack when she came in on Monday.

As Charlotte closed down and turned off the lights, she stared at the door that connected to her home. It was slightly ajar and she could see the flicker of a television. Quinn was still awake.

She wanted to see him, to wrap her arms around him and kiss him. To finish what had almost started earlier today, but fear froze her in her tracks.

No. She couldn't deal with him tonight.

Instead, she grabbed her dinner, which had been parceled up from the diner, and wandered to her office, staring bleakly at the old couch that had adorned their apartment. Her eyes were heavy and the couch was surprisingly inviting. She locked the door to her office, peeled off her clothes and settled down on the couch, covering herself with the afghan she'd draped over Quinn only a day ago.

She was absolutely exhausted and tried to drift off to sleep, but the damn blanket smelled like him.

# CHAPTER NINE

SHOUTING ROUSED CHARLOTTE from her slumber. She stumbled to her feet and the container from dinner last night fell onto the floor, scattering a few fries onto the carpet. One squished under her foot when she stepped forward and it stuck to her sock in a cold, mushy clump, making her curse under her breath.

Charlotte hopped on one foot to peer out the window. She gasped, not because it was snowing, which it was. It was the sight of Quinn outside in the snow that made her voice catch in her throat.

*Quinn's outside? Voluntarily?*

He was kneeling down and in his hand appeared to be a very expensive camera with a large telescopic lens. The shouting was from some of the village kids, who were rocketing past him from the slope just outside her office.

The clinic was on the far edge of town, nestled up against a slope, and because there were no houses on the one side, the village kids loved to come over and toboggan on nice days. When it was snowing big fat fluffy flakes, it was not as bitterly cold out as it would usually be.

As a kid zoomed past Quinn, the camera would follow. He was photographing the children.

*I never knew he liked photography.*

Or children, for that matter.

A smile quirked her lips as he moved the camera and urged a large sled of five kids down the hill. The children were laughing and he was making funny faces as the child at the back pushed off.

Quinn cheered and disappeared behind the camera, getting ready to take his picture. Charlotte was extremely attracted to this side of him, a side she'd never been privileged to see before. Watching him out there now with the village kids warmed her heart.

She left her office, changed her mushy sock, and freshened up quickly. She had her winter gear on in no time flat and was out the door to join him. There was no way she was going to miss this opportunity.

There was no wind and it wasn't bitterly cold when she stepped outside. It was just a nice winter day, with soft flakes floating down.

"Watch out, Doc!" Charlotte jumped back as a sled full of laughing kids whizzed past her. Quinn stood and grinned at her, his cheeks rosy from the cold.

"Good morning, or should I say, afternoon?"

"What time is it?" She'd been in such a rush to get outside she hadn't checked the time.

"It's one. Hey, hold up, guys. Doctor coming through." Quinn held up his hands and the eager tobogganers paused, but with a few "Awwws" as Charlotte jogged across the path of danger to stand beside Quinn. "All right, go, guys!"

With a shriek from one of the kids, the next sled set off and Quinn snapped a few shots as it whizzed by.

"I'm impressed," Charlotte said.

"By what?"

"You, out here in the *dreaded* ice and snow."

Quinn chuckled and he capped his camera lens. "I couldn't resist it."

"I didn't know you did photography."

Quinn shrugged. "It's no big deal. I dabble a bit." He shielded the glare of the sun from the screen on the back and flicked through the images. They were beautiful photographs of the kids and other scenery. He'd also managed to take a shot of the northern lights. It was a stunning photograph that captured the green-and-purples hues of the aurora borealis dancing over the village.

"These are beautiful. When did you take that?" she asked, pointing to the image.

"Last night. You know, I've never seen the aurora borealis. I never bothered when we lived in Yellowknife, and when I was in Manhattan I kicked myself constantly for not making the time." Quinn switched off his camera. "Light pollution in the big city sucks."

"What time did you get up?" she asked, changing the subject from the city, which was a point of contention between them.

"About nine. George was taking the Grises down to Iqaluit. He was going to wake you, but you looked so darned cute huddled up on that old couch, food scattered all over the place."

Charlotte groaned, embarrassed he'd caught her flaked out and vulnerable instead of poised and sophisticated. "Thanks for doing that."

"No problem." His eyes glinted as he watched the kids haul their sleds back up the hill. "You know, I've never tried that."

"What, tobogganing?"

Quinn shook his head. "Nope, never. My parents wouldn't take me or even buy me a sled."

"I thought your dad was very much into sports. At least, that's what you told me."

"Hockey, yes, sledding, no. You can't win a gold medal for sledding."

"You can for bobsledding," she teased.

Quinn shrugged. "He wasn't much for being a team player. I just had to be the best."

A pang of sympathy hit her. Quinn may have had two parents but he hadn't had a fun childhood. Some of Charlotte's best memories of her and her father had been out on the snow, sledding and snowshoeing. Charlotte grabbed his hand and tugged him towards the hill. "We're going."

"What?" He chuckled. "You're nuts. What about my camera?"

"Jenny!" Charlotte called out to Wavell's younger sister. She came bounding up, out of breath.

"Yeah, Doc Charley?"

"Can you hold Dr. Devlyn's camera while I take him on your sled down the hill?"

Jenny's face broke into a huge smile. "Yeah, I can do that!"

"Charlotte…" Quinn started as she took the camera from him and handed it to Jenny. "I don't know."

"Come on, you big wimp!"

He raised his eyebrows. "Wimp, eh?"

She screeched as he lunged for her. She grabbed Jenny's small sled and ran up the hill, Quinn following her. When they reached the top she sat down. "Sit behind me and hold on."

"How do we push off?" he asked as he sat down, his arms wrapping around her.

"With your feet. But once we're going, tuck them up so your feet don't slow us down."

"Gotcha."

"Ready?" she asked.

"Yep. Let's get this over with."

Charlotte could hear the kids shrieking and laughing as she dug her feet in and pushed off. The sled picked up speed fast from their combined weight and they rocketed down the hill, past Jenny and the clinic. Charlotte screamed with pure joy as the wind whipped at her face and the cold air sucked the breath from her lungs.

Quinn yelled and stuck his feet out as they headed towards the only road in Cape Recluse. The sled careened to the side and they were tossed out. Charlotte did a small roll and landed on her back. Quinn rolled and landed on top of her, pinning her to the snow.

"Are you all right?" he asked breathlessly. "And my apologies for the excessive bad language."

Charlotte couldn't stop laughing. "I'm fine."

"I think I like this sledding business." He grinned down at her, his dark eyes twinkling. "You've popped my cherry twice since I've been here."

Heat spread through her like wildfire, while her body zinged with arousal. His body was heavy, pressed against hers, but it was the kind of weight she was longing for. If only all these layers of clothing weren't separating them. If only they were in her bed, naked.

She sobered instantly when she realized Quinn was still lying on top of her, in front of her clinic, in front of the village children. She could hear them laughing.

"Hey, you're too heavy. Get off me, already!"

Quinn shifted and rolled over. She scrambled to her feet and brushed the snow from her. "I'd better go change. I'm not wearing any snow pants and my jeans will be soaked in a few minutes."

She spun round and ran for the clinic, not looking back. She'd forgotten for a moment that he was not her fiancé. He wasn't anything to her anymore. Just a colleague, up here for a consult.

Quinn retrieved his camera from Jenny and bid his new fan club farewell. The sun would be setting soon and the kids had to head for home. Besides, his hand was numb from the cold, but, like he'd told Charlotte, he hadn't been able to resist the photographic opportunity.

When he was back in his bedroom he scrolled through the pictures and saw one of him and Charlotte, racing down the hill. It seemed that Jenny was a bit of a photo aficionado, as well. He didn't mind in the least. It was something to remember that moment by.

He thought Charlotte's cold reserve was melting a bit. She was playful and laughing again, but when they had been lying in the snow, something had clicked. He'd seen it in her eyes and her barriers had gone up again. He turned off the camera and set it down.

A zing of pins and needles shot up his arm. Quinn stared down at his scarred hand and flexed it. It wasn't as stiff as it had been. His hand had been steady and sure when he'd made the episiotomy. He'd seen the look on Charlotte's face when she'd helped him put the gloves on, the moment of uncertainty. He wasn't a fool. Quinn knew she'd seen the scars. He wanted to tell her about the accident and reassure her there was nothing to be worried about, though his mother would beg to differ.

Quinn scrubbed his hand over his face and picked up his hand exerciser, clenching his hand into a tight fist and then slowly allowing it to flex again.

*"You'll never regain full use of your hand. I would suggest you open up a consultation practice or move into a general practice instead of surgery, Dr. Devlyn,"* the orthopedic surgeon said.

*"I don't accept that."*

*"Quinn, see sense. Even Dr. Szarsky thinks you won't be able to continue to be a surgeon. When will you listen to reason?"* his mother lamented. *"You had such potential, too."*

*"I still have potential. I'm still a surgeon."*

*"Perhaps,"* his father said. *"But it'll take about a year at the minimum to recuperate. By then you'll have lost your professional edge."*

*"Like I lost mine having you!"*

His mother's tone had been so hard and cold when she had uttered those words, *I lost mine having you.* Quinn shook those horrible memories away. His parents had never been supportive except when he'd excelled.

Mediocrity had never been an option.

Except with Charlotte.

Charlotte had never judged him when he'd had a minor setback. She'd always cared for and loved him, no matter what he'd done, and had cheered him on to do better next time, without any hint of malice or remorse.

A slow-paced life in a rural clinic or a small-town hospital was what he'd secretly craved since his accident, but he'd never admitted to it because he could've had that with Charlotte, and Quinn never admitted his mistakes.

He cursed under his breath and set the hand exerciser on the nightstand. He got up and splashed some water on his face at the basin. When he glanced in the mirror he saw a thick growth of stubble and dark circles under his eyes. He hadn't slept well. Every time he'd closed his eyes, all he'd seen had been Charlotte.

In that moment when he'd passed the baby to her it had been like their painful past and their separation had been washed away. Back then, all he'd wanted had been his parents' approval. Once he'd achieved what they'd wanted from him, it still hadn't been good enough, and when his father had died he'd realized it never would be.

Just like he'd realized as soon as he'd left Charlotte that there would be no going back. He'd lost her trust.

Yet that look they shared... That moment of connection had seemed so genuine, so real, and he'd felt like he'd never been away, that they were right back to where they'd started. Of course, he could've just been seeing things. Charlotte had made it pretty clear when he'd arrived that their association was going to remain purely professional.

If he had the chance to start all over again with Charlotte, would he?

Damn straight, he would.

His phone chimed with the familiar sound of a text message coming through. Quinn groaned and picked his phone up from the nightstand. Only two people would be texting him. It would be either the hospital or his mother, and Quinn had a gut-wrenching feeling it wasn't the hospital.

As he glanced at the screen he recognized the area code of Toronto. Two words were on the screen.

Call me.

Quinn rolled his eyes. He knew why she was doing this. She knew where he was and she didn't approve. Not one bit. His mother wasn't impressed in the least that he was giving a pro bono consult, especially for a patient of Charlotte's.

His phone vibrated in his hand.

What could possibly be so important you can't call your mother to discuss an urgent matter? I bet you would've called if it was your father.

Quinn rolled his eyes. His mother was laying on the guilt trip pretty thick—another aspect of his childhood he hadn't particularly enjoyed, being the pawn between his parents. His mother had been a master of guilt. "Had" being the operative word.

He really couldn't care less. Instead, he called his physiotherapist. He wanted reassurance.

"Ted Jones speaking."

"Hey, Ted. It's Devlyn."

There was a pause. "Devlyn! How's it up there?" Ted asked pleasantly.

"Cold."

"I bet." Ted chuckled. "How's the hand?"

"Stiff, sore. The usual." Quinn scrubbed his hand over his face, preparing himself mentally for what he wanted to ask, dreading the answer. "My hand, do you think...? Will I regain full use of it?"

*You can't avoid him for the rest of the day.*

Charlotte groaned. Her conscience pricking her, she'd spent a most uncomfortable night on the couch in her office because of her conflicted emotions about Quinn. She was still wearing the same clothes as yesterday and now her jeans were soaked.

As much as she wanted to go and talk to Quinn about what had happened out in the snow, she couldn't will herself to do it. It was like her body was frozen to the spot, some sort of primeval defense mechanism to prevent her from facing Quinn and appearing like a schmuck in front of him, thus protecting her heart from further injury.

At least, that's what she kept trying to tell herself she was doing.

Really, she knew deep down she was being a coward.

"That's it." She quickly changed out of her wet clothes. She couldn't hide out in her bedroom. She was going to face Quinn and see where the chips fell.

When she opened her bedroom door she heard his raised voice filter through from the guest bedroom.

"Honestly, tell me the truth, Ted."

Quinn sounded agitated and worried.

Charlotte tiptoed down the hall. The door to his bedroom was slightly ajar. She could just catch a glimpse of Quinn sitting at the desk, holding his head in his hands and staring down at the phone, which was on speaker.

"I really can't say, Quinn. I'm only stating the facts from what I've seen in other cases."

Her heart skipped a beat. *Cases? What cases?*

"I need some kind of a ballpark idea, Ted. Just give me that. It'll put my mind at ease."

There was a loud audible sigh over the phone. "No, you probably won't regain full function of your hand again. Your hand was crushed. You're lucky you still have it and have some range of motion."

This time her heart didn't skip a beat. It almost stopped completely. The blood was draining away from her face and the room began to spin.

*Couldn't. Operate?* The implications were too horrific to fathom.

She wanted to move away. Her stomach was knotting, her throat was constricted as she fought the urge to be sick. All she could think about was Mentlana and the baby. He was risking her reputation, as well. If Mentlana or the baby died because he failed to mention he was no longer fit for duty, her reputation would be on the line. The people of Cape Recluse wouldn't trust her as freely as they did now.

His ineptitude could cost her the only home she'd ever known, and that thought was too frightening.

There was no way she was going to risk her family, the people she loved, because Quinn's pride might be hurt. If he couldn't operate then there was no way he was going near Mentlana Tikivik, or anyone else, for that matter. But she also felt sorry for Quinn. His whole focus in med school had been about becoming the best, the top of his field, and now he couldn't operate. How must he feel about that?

"Can I operate?" Quinn asked.

"I don't see why not, but you'll most likely need assistance."

"I don't have access to other surgeons."

"Look, I could say you'd be fine, but without assessing your hand I can't give you a definite answer. Just keep up with the exercises.

"Thanks, Ted."

"Call me if you need some more help. Sorry I couldn't ease your mind."

Charlotte heard Quinn end the call and shut off his phone. She tried to move away from where she was standing, but once again she was frozen to the spot.

Quinn whipped open the door and his eyes widened as he saw her, standing still in the hallway, shaking with anger and betrayal. It was her own fault. She'd allowed him into her life again. At least this time she hadn't lost a baby. At least this time her heart hadn't been blown to smithereens.

"Charlotte." His tone was weary and he rubbed the back of his neck. "I didn't know you were here."

"No," she said quickly. "No. I don't suppose you did."

# CHAPTER TEN

"CHARLOTTE..." QUINN'S HEART stuttered at the sight of her. She was dressed casually in a soft-looking lavender sweater and blue jeans, her red curls hanging loose over her shoulders. Her posture, however, was anything but casual, and her face was like thunder. She stood like she was on the edge of a precipice, and that one wrong move by him and she'd jump.

"Well?" she asked.

"Charlotte, I wanted to tell you. It's been something I've been trying to tell you since I arrived."

Her gaze dropped to his hand and the scars that marred the surface of his skin. He was sure she was looking past the physical ones he carried to the ones deep inside him and the haunted past that had scarred them both, and he watched as the anger in her face ebbed away.

"Tell me," she urged gently, at last.

*Do not be the obstinate man.*

He met Charlotte's gaze. Though her face was now unreadable and passive, her eyes were full of concern. He longed to pull her into his arms once more, to tell her everything would be okay.

Only he didn't know how to say the words, or if it would all be okay.

"Quinn, please."

"I'm still a surgeon, if that's what you're wondering. I have a medical license." It was all he could say. He was having a hard time trying to tell her that his hand had been broken. It would be like admitting his own defeat, admitting to her that he was the shadow of his former self.

"Okay," she said, confused. "I assumed so. Tell me about the scars, Quinn. What happened?"

"A car accident."

She nodded. "Go on."

"Fog caused a massive pileup on the highway. My car flipped, my hand became lodged in the door. For a while I didn't think it could be saved. Hell, when I was trapped, waiting for the paramedics, I thought I was going to die."

Charlotte's face paled and she moved into his bedroom. "Why didn't you tell me this before?"

"You brought me up here to operate on your friend. I couldn't tell you what had happened to me."

"So putting Mentlana's life at risk is not as important as saving face?"

"Of course not!" he snapped, and then took a deep breath as he sat down on the edge of his bed. "I'd never put a patient at risk. It's why I was calling my physiotherapist."

Charlotte closed the distance between them and sat next to him, taking his shattered hand in hers.

"If your physiotherapist or orthopedic surgeon cleared you for surgery and you still have your license, you can operate." It was if she was stating it because she couldn't quite believe it, and he didn't blame her one bit.

"Yes" was all he said.

"You know you can, or else you wouldn't have boarded that plane and come up here."

*What if I came up here for purely selfish reasons?* Which was what he wanted to say, but didn't. Instead, he pulled his hand out of hers and stood.

"I won't put your friend's life at risk. I hope you can trust me on this. Do you trust me, Charlotte?"

Charlotte didn't know what to say. The room began to spin and she was still trying to take in everything. She knew something had happened to him, but didn't know the extent. She stood and turned her back to him, unable to process what he'd just asked. Did she trust him? She didn't even know that answer herself, so how could she tell him otherwise?

"I don't...I don't know what to say."

"You don't have to say anything. You have no reason to trust me. I deceived you. I didn't tell you about my accident, but I want you to know I'd never do anything to harm a patient."

Charlotte heard his footfalls as he closed the space between them, the heat of his body against her back as he stood behind her. She moved away, stunned and not sure she could believe him. If she did and he was wrong and something happened to Mentlana... The thought was too horrifying to comprehend.

She glanced over her shoulder and her heart skipped a beat, her stomach fluttering just looking at him. Charlotte nodded slowly. "I trust you."

"Thank you." Quinn moved past her to leave, but she reached out and took his hand again. He paused and she traced the faint scars with her thumb. She could only begin to imagine the hours of pain he'd endured as they'd put the pieces of him back together.

"I'm sorry I wasn't there to help you," she whispered.

He tilted her chin so she was forced to look at him. "You have nothing to apologize for."

Charlotte's knees began to knock just a bit as she stared

into his eyes, getting lost in them. His eyes were like melted chocolate and she *so* loved chocolate.

It'd been so long since his strong arms had wrapped around her. His absence in her life was akin to physical pain. A pain that had been numbed by throwing herself into her work and reminding herself of the pain he'd caused her.

Quinn's hand slipped around her neck, his fingers tangling in her hair at the nape, bringing her closer to him. His hot breath fanned her cheek. She closed her eyes, waiting for the kiss that she didn't know she longed for, but which she did, all the same.

*What am I doing?*

Yeah, she trusted him in his surgical abilities, but she wasn't ready to let him into her heart again. She placed a hand on his chest, keeping him at bay. "I can't. The day you left was the worst day of my life. I lost you and I lost..." She trailed off, not wanting to share the pain of losing their child. She'd borne it alone for so long.

He nodded. "I understand. I'm just grateful you trust me to do right by your friend. Thank you."

Charlotte turned on her heel and left his room. He'd gotten to her again and she'd almost let down her guard.

She hated how he affected her so.

Charlotte avoided Quinn as much as possible. She was angry at herself for momentarily allowing him to break through to her and she was angry that her hormones seemed to be overruling her common sense.

Of course, it was hard to block Quinn out of her life when they only had two thousand square feet of combined clinic and house space. Add that to a blinding blizzard that lasted three days, keeping them housebound.

At least she had her regular work to keep her busy,

when patients desperate enough were able to slog through the snow to keep their appointments. Most of her day was dealing with her job, locked in her office with only the roar of the storm outside to accompany her and her jangled thoughts.

Alone in her office, she kept reliving their doomed relationship over and over again. After it had ended, when she'd first looked back on it, she'd chastised herself for not noticing that things would never have worked out between them.

And it hadn't only been about their very different career paths. Quinn wasn't a family man. That was one thing that hadn't changed about him. Charlotte wanted a family, more than anything, and Quinn was a workaholic.

When and if she ever did meet Mr. Right, she wanted to provide two parents for her children. Charlotte wanted to give them what she'd never had.

"Doc Charley?" Charlotte looked up to see George standing in the doorway.

"Yeah, what can I do for you?"

"Closing time." A smile spread across George's face.

Charlotte glanced at the clock on her computer monitor and balked. The afternoon had flown by. She had still been working on Wavell's file, although she had pulled out the boy's sutures earlier that day.

"Have a good night," she said absently.

"It's bingo night at the community center. You up for some B.I.N.G.O?" George asked, enunciating every letter in an annoying way.

Charlotte shook her head. "I don't relish going out in that storm."

"Storm ended hours ago, Charley," George said, confused. "You must've been really engrossed in filing if you didn't even notice the silence."

Charlotte shook her head. No, she hadn't noticed the howling wind had stopped. She'd grown so accustomed to the deafening sound that she hadn't even noticed that it had ended. Apparently she truly had zoned out, because the coffee in her cup from that morning was stone cold and the cup was still full. She dropped the file and scrubbed a hand over her face.

"Are you all right, Charley?" George asked, concerned.

"Fine. Just a bit tired." She bit her lip, hoping George wouldn't see through her lie. If he did, he didn't say anything.

"Come out to the community center. Everyone is coming tonight for bingo, a way to celebrate the storm being over. I'm even going to fetch Aanak and drag her in."

A smile tugged at the corners of her lips. "No, thanks. I think I'll keep up with my filing. Besides, I hate bingo."

George shook his head. "Suit yourself. I guess it's just me and Doc Devlyn, then."

"Quinn's going?" Charlotte was stunned. Absolutely and utterly flabbergasted. Quinn was not the community-center, bingo-card-stamping type. Except for formal mixers, Quinn had never gone out with the other students, unless it had been with her.

"Yep." There was a twinkle to George's eye. "He said he's really looking forward to it."

Now she *had* to go. She wouldn't miss seeing this for the world. "Well, I guess I can come out, seeing that Anernerk will be there and everything."

George grinned. "Ri-i-ight. You're going because Aanak will be there."

Charlotte frowned. "What exactly are you implying? And tread carefully."

"Nothing. Nothing." George held up his hands and backed out of the room. Charlotte chuckled to herself when he'd disappeared. He knew not to mess with her. He might be taller than her, but she could still give him a good noogie if she was so inclined.

She wasn't lying about wanting to see Anernerk, but the real show would be watching Quinn interacting with the townsfolk. He was not a natural people person. In fact, she knew he was only in the medical profession because it'd been forced on him by his parents, and she couldn't help but wonder what his chosen profession would've been if he'd had the choice.

He'd never had hobbies when they'd been together, other than traveling. He'd liked to see new places and had often talked about the trips he wanted to take. Perhaps he would've taken up photography.

Was that why he was taking it up now, as a fallback because of his hand injury? Charlotte groaned, annoyed with herself for expending so much thought on Quinn Devlyn. His life, his choices were not her concern anymore. Once he did his job up here she was over 100 percent positive he'd be on the next flight to Toronto.

Back to his job at the hospital in the big city and working as much as he could to stay at the top of his game.

And that was a bet she could take to the bank.

# CHAPTER ELEVEN

THE COMMUNITY CENTER was packed and blaring out music. Charlotte handed her coat to the young girl behind the coat check.

"You'd better hurry up, Doc Charley. They've already started the first round," the young girl said.

"Thanks, Lizzie."

Charlotte hadn't gone over with George and Quinn as she'd had to make a house call on a sick patient, the only resident in Cape Recluse, besides Mentlana and Genen, who wasn't in attendance at bingo tonight. Besides, Charlotte was in no rush. She wanted to watch Quinn from afar to see how he interacted with the residents.

She'd been so shocked when George had told her Quinn had agreed to go. This was one bingo night she wasn't going to miss for the world. She lingered in the doorway of the main auditorium and easily picked out Quinn, near the back and by himself.

His brow was furrowed as he was bent over the cards. A smile touched her lips. They'd suckered him out of at least twenty bucks because he had about four cards sprawled out in front of him and he couldn't keep up with marking his tickets with the chips.

"He sucks. Big time."

Charlotte turned to see Anernerk at the table beside the

door. Anernerk was a pro at bingo. She could carry on any kind of conversation without missing a beat.

"What do you mean?"

Anernerk snorted. "He sucks. What more is there to say?"

"B seven."

"Boo!" Anernerk shouted. "Call something good for a change."

Charlotte stifled a laugh. Poor George was the caller and sent his dear, sweet Aanak a withering look, but only because Anernerk was engrossed in her bingo cards.

"You think I should go help him?" Charlotte asked.

"Yeah, but if you win…" Anernerk sent her a brief but silent warning.

Charlotte just grinned and made her way round to where Quinn was seated. "Having fun?"

Quinn glanced up and then laughed. "No. I think George should've been an auctioneer instead of a bingo caller."

Charlotte took the empty seat next to him and aided Quinn in catching up. "He's neither. He's a paramedic. They're trained to move quickly."

"Well, his training in this situation is not needed," Quinn grumbled.

"You wish he was slower in this case?" she teased.

"Of course," Quinn said, as he placed another chip. "I'm a novice. I was promised a night of cheap fun."

"Cheap fun? You're in the wrong town for *cheap* fun."

Quinn grinned and then chuckled. "Well, I'm used to attending soirees where plates go for at least fifty dollars and up."

"It's all relative, I guess." Charlotte placed another chip. "There, you've caught up now."

"For now." Quinn cursed under his breath as George

called out three more numbers in rapid succession. "Drat. I'm literally all thumbs tonight."

"Slow it down, you!" Charlotte called out, trying not to laugh.

George raised his eyebrows in question and then spied Charlotte. He shook his head and continued in his normal tempo of firing off numbers.

"Hey, you heard the doctor. Slow it down or else." This time the demand came from Anernerk and this time George dared not ignore the request.

Quinn was stifling his laughter. "She's a bit intense about this game."

"She's competitive."

"I see where you got it from," Quinn said.

"What do you mean?"

Quinn rolled his eyes. "Oh, come on. You were out for blood at medical school. Always had to be top in the class, win every competition and every scholarship. It was damn annoying."

Charlotte glared at him, but saw the mirth in his eyes and retracted her claws a bit. "All right, I'll give you that. So, if I was *so* annoying, why did you pursue me?"

She regretted the question the moment it had left her lips when she saw the dark, hungry glint in his eyes, a look that caused warmth to spread through her body. She almost forgot where she was. Charlotte felt like that giddy med student in anatomy class, shyly watching Quinn on the other side of the classroom.

"G fifty-eight."

Quinn tore his gaze from her and set down a chip. "Damn, I think I won. Did I?"

Charlotte leaned over. "You did. You'd better call it."

"Bingo!" Quinn yelled out, standing up waving his card, letting the chips scatter everywhere. "Damn."

"Forfeit! He dropped his chips!" Anernerk said loudly, with a hint of triumph in her voice.

Charlotte couldn't control her laughter, then. She got down on her knees and began to retrieve the bingo chips from the floor. Quinn got down and helped her.

"Anernerk is right."

"How's that?" Charlotte asked, setting a fistful of chips on the table.

"I do suck."

Quinn took a swig of his soda and leaned against the bar in the community center. He used the word "bar" loosely as it only served sodas, coffee and tea. He had excused himself from this round of bingo and had left Charlotte to hold down the fort.

In spite of Anernerk's protests, he had still won because they could track the previous numbers called.

It surprised him how much he enjoyed the game and socializing with the people in the community. That snowstorm had lasted for what had felt like an eternity. He was Canadian and used to blizzards, but nothing of this magnitude and ferocity. But then again, he'd grown up in a city, and tall buildings did serve a good use as windbreaks against whiteouts and squalls.

There was nothing here, no trees, just water on all sides and a mountain of rock, ice and snow behind the town. They were certainly at the mercy of the elements here. It was raw and powerful and for the first time he actually understood the reason why Charlotte loved it up here.

Quinn shook his head and ran his fingers through his hair. Perhaps the deafening roar of that snowstorm had addled his brain.

One thing not confusing him was how much he was enjoying his time with Charlotte. After he'd told her what had happened to him, she'd kept her distance from him. A tense silence had fallen between them and it saddened him. She ate her meals in her office and their only conversations were just cursory politenesses or talking about Mentlana's case.

He was used to silence, but he'd been alone for far too long. When he'd arrived in Cape Recluse he hadn't realized how hungry for company he'd been, especially for Charlotte's.

He'd missed her, but he'd never really let it sink in how much. Being back in her presence reminded him of it, keenly.

Quinn didn't know what had changed and why the tense barrier that had fallen between them these last few days was gone, but he was thrilled. She seemed to be enjoying herself immensely, even though George told him she never usually came to bingo as she didn't particularly enjoy it.

Charlotte was beaming from ear to ear and she was very at ease with the people, and they with her. It was like they were family—for all intents and purposes, they were. He envied Charlotte that she really loved what she was doing.

Here she shone like the bright star she was.

Quinn had never seen her like this. Five years ago, in Yellowknife, he hadn't seen any job prospects, any chance for advancement. He'd thought of Canada's North as a dead-end career, but it wasn't.

He'd been so wrong.

He'd been too hasty when he'd left.

Watching Charlotte now, he was regretting the decisions he'd made.

"Are you going to play the next round, Devlyn?"

Quinn turned to see Anernerk beside him. She looked a bit frailer then when he'd first laid eyes on her a few days earlier. He hoped, for Charlotte's sake, that nothing was seriously wrong with her, but then, the old gal *was* over a hundred.

"Well, are you?" Anernerk winked at him.

"I may," Quinn conceded.

"I like competition. Especially, fresh meat."

"I believe your grandson remarked on that the first time I met you."

"He knows me well." Anernerk smiled and then picked up his bad hand. "Has it been troubling you much?"

"No, not too much. The blizzard caused a bit of an ache."

Anernerk nodded. "Your hand is steady enough. I wouldn't worry."

Quinn cocked an eyebrow. "I'm not. Not in the least." *Liar.*

"I see," she said carefully. She released his hand and then shook her finger at him. "I'm going to get you next round. You had beginner's luck, but I think that's run out. I shall have victory."

Anernerk hobbled off and Quinn trailed after her, sitting next to Charlotte and sliding a can of ginger ale across to her.

"Milady," he said, giving a little flourish with his hand.

"Thanks." Charlotte popped the top and stuck a straw in the can.

"How are we doing?" he asked.

"Not well, I'm afraid."

"O sixty-seven."

"Boo!" Quinn called out. "This game is rigged."

Charlotte snorted and several people laughed. George was shocked, but grinned and continued with the game.

"I'm shocked, Dr. Devlyn, by such a display," Charlotte teased.

"Are you thoroughly scandalized?"

"Of course."

Quinn chuckled. "Perhaps we should call it quits. Besides, Anernerk warned me that she'd have victory, or else."

"Well, in that case, we'd better leave while the going's good." Charlotte finished her soda and Quinn collected up the game paraphernalia and handed it back to the ladies who had persuaded him in the first place to buy four cards.

They retrieved their coats and headed out into the freezing night. The moment they stepped outside, a brilliant display of vibrant green aurora borealis erupted across the sky.

"I can't believe how I missed this during my year in Yellowknife." Quinn wasn't watching where he was going and lost his footing. Charlotte reached out and steadied him.

"I think you've had a bit too much pop tonight," she teased.

"Perhaps. Or my eardrums were shattered by that raging blizzard." He gazed at Charlotte, bundled up in her parka. All he could see was the twinkle in her eyes and the tip of her nose, and he fought the urge to lean forward and press a kiss there. Charlotte let go of her hold on him, though. The light-hearted jesting they shared at the community center had vanished, replaced once more by the uneasy tension.

"It's freezing out here." Charlotte laughed nervously and stepped back, jogging the rest of the short way back to her clinic.

Quinn followed, because it was freezing, but he didn't know what had changed again and he was sad that it had.

# CHAPTER TWELVE

CHARLOTTE SPENT THE night tossing and turning, just like she'd spent the last several. Quinn had changed. When he'd first arrived, she hadn't been sure that he had. He'd still seemed like the same old workaholic who'd left her.

The Quinn who had shown himself to her now was a completely different man, a man she only caught glimpses of when they were alone together away from prying eyes. A man he never allowed out in public. There were still shadows of his former self, but she was learning more about him. More than she'd ever thought possible.

Last night at bingo she'd thoroughly enjoyed herself.

Charlotte gave up any pretense of trying to sleep. She got up and dragged herself to the shower, using the last bit of hot water in her heater for the morning. She got dressed in warm layers as today she had to make a visit to Mentlana.

Quinn was nowhere in sight when she left her bedroom. She couldn't help but wonder where he was. He wasn't in the guest bedroom, because the door was wide open.

There was a pot of coffee waiting and a note from Quinn that stated he was out with George, ice fishing.

*Ice fishing?*

Charlotte pinched the bridge of her nose. Quinn had willingly gone out on the ice? With George?

She shook her head, filled her travel mug with some coffee and collected the items she'd need for Mentlana's checkup.

When she headed outside she could see a few brightly colored huts out on the water and she couldn't help but wonder which one Quinn was in. She could picture him bundled up, cursing at the stupidity of sitting out in the bitter cold, watching a hole for a bite on his pole.

Actually, what would be even better would be if a seal ended up popping up through Quinn and George's hole. That would certainly give him a fright. She'd be willing to endure a few hours of ice fishing just to see that.

"Quick lollygagging and get in here!" Anernerk was hanging out the doorway.

"What the heck are you doing here?" Charlotte asked. "More importantly, how the heck did you get here?"

"Genen picked me up last night from bingo. I just decided to stay here for a few days. I didn't think I was confined to my home." Anernerk pointed at her cheek.

Charlotte leaned over and gave her a kiss. "Well, since you're here, maybe I'll give you a checkup, too."

"Don't you dare!" Anernerk grinned and took Charlotte's coat. "Where's Dr. Devlyn today?"

"Ice fishing with George."

"Really? I'm impressed."

"What's going on out there?" Mentlana called out.

"You better go see her," Anernerk said. "She's going a bit squirrely, being on bed rest."

Charlotte walked down the hallway to Mentlana's bedroom. The television had been moved into the room. Actually, it looked like most of Mentlana's living room had been crammed into her small bedroom.

"How are you feeling today?" Charlotte asked.

"Don't patronize me." A smile quirked on Mentlana's lips. "Fill me in on all the gossip."

Charlotte set her bag down on the table and pulled out a blood-pressure monitor. "Gossip? There's no gossip."

Mentlana snorted. "Please."

Charlotte strapped the cuff on Mentlana's arm. "Please, what?"

"How has it been, working with Quinn?"

Charlotte groaned. Of course Mentlana had to ask that. How *had* it been, working with Quinn? Awkward at first, annoying at times and maddening as she had to constantly wrestle with her emotions, emotions she'd thought were long since buried.

"That good, huh?" Mentlana said, as Charlotte took her blood pressure.

Charlotte tapped her nose. The last thing she wanted to do was talk about it. "Your blood pressure is a little high. We'll keep an eye on it." She pulled out her portable Doppler to listen to the baby's heartbeat. She listened and didn't like the sound she heard. "Is Genen here?" she asked.

"What's wrong?"

Charlotte squeezed Mentlana's hand. "I'd like Genen to go out and get Dr. Devlyn for me. I just want him to listen to the baby's heartbeat, that's all."

"He's on the ice." Mentlana picked up her phone and texted him. "He's with George and Dr. Devlyn."

"Good." Charlotte wrote down the baby's irregular heartbeat. She'd have to get Mentlana in to the clinic for another ultrasound to check on the progress of the CCAM.

"Okay, you owe me gossip now that I'm all stressed until Dr. Devlyn gets here. Now, spill."

"There's nothing to spill."

Mentlana's gaze narrowed. "You can't fool me. You've

been scarce, quiet and very unlike yourself. You've been locked away in your clinic for days."

"There was a snowstorm."

"I'm not talking just about the blizzard, Charlotte."

Charlotte sighed. "It's hard."

"Being around him?"

Charlotte nodded. "He left me."

Mentlana bit her lip. "You left him too, though."

"What do you mean? He went to New York. He picked his career over me."

"I know. His timing sucked when he left, but you didn't go with him, either. This is going to sound harsh, and I should really be careful, considering you're my doctor, but did you ever think about how he felt when you didn't go with him?"

Tears stung Charlotte's eyes. No. She never had considered his feelings, just like she'd never even considered following him to New York.

Both of them had been so stubborn, so pigheaded and set in their ways.

There had been no compromise. There never had been.

"I think you still care for him, Charlotte, even if you don't want to admit it, and I think you should give him another chance."

Charlotte wasn't sure she could. She was terrified to put her heart at risk again.

The door opened and she heard stamping by the door.

"Charlotte?" Quinn called out.

She cleared her throat, to knock the nervousness out. "In the bedroom."

Quinn opened the door, his face rosy from the cold, his hair tousled by the wind, and there was stubble on his chin. The dark green of his fisherman's sweater really brought out the dark brown of his eyes. He looked like he should be gracing the cover of some outdoor magazine. His appearance was rugged and it made the butterflies in her stomach flutter.

"Is everything okay?" he asked, a little out of breath.

"I need you to listen to the baby's heartbeat. Also, Mentlana's blood pressure is slightly elevated."

Quinn nodded. "Sure."

Charlotte stood up and let him sit down beside Mentlana. He used the Doppler, his brow furrowed in concentration as he listened to the heartbeat. After a couple of minutes he switched it off.

"Well?" Mentlana asked nervously.

"Your baby is fine. However, I'd like to do an ultrasound to check on him." Quinn stood. "Genen is on his way back. Have him bring you over to the clinic as soon as he can."

Mentlana nodded. "Okay."

Quinn gave Mentlana's shoulder a squeeze, the scars on his hand vivid against his skin because of the cold.

"It'll be all right, Mentlana. You'll see." Quinn turned and gave Charlotte a serious look, which conveyed his concern, and her heart sank.

"Walk with me back to the clinic, Charlotte." Quinn left Mentlana's bedroom.

"Of course." Charlotte packed up her things and bent down, giving Mentlana a quick kiss.

"Give him a chance, Charlotte. He didn't come up here because of me," Mentlana whispered.

Charlotte didn't answer. Instead, she left the room in silence and then slipped on her coat, following Quinn outside. The crunching of the snow under their boots was the only sound that penetrated the uneasy tension between them.

"What's your assessment?" she asked finally.

"I think it's progressed, but I won't know how much

until I do an ultrasound." He opened the clinic door, holding it open for her.

"And her blood pressure... Do you think that's cause for concern?"

"We'll run a urinalysis on her when she's here." He slipped out of his coat and then helped her with hers. "Like I said to Mentlana, it'll be okay."

"How do you know that?"

"Faith?" Quinn smiled. "You said you trusted me. That meant a lot, so I hope you trust me when I say it'll be okay."

"I do," Charlotte said, and touched his arm. She did trust him, but as for everything else she wasn't sure. She moved it away from him. "I'll go get the ultrasound ready."

"Sounds good. I'll wait here to help Genen and Mentlana."

"Okay." Charlotte turned and walked down the hall away from Quinn. She was taking the coward's way out, running away from the reality that she'd played a large part in the demise in their relationship, that she may have left him long before he'd left her.

# CHAPTER THIRTEEN

JUST WHEN QUINN thought he was making some headway with Charlotte she pulled away from him again. Something else had transpired at Mentlana's, but he wasn't sure what. The ultrasound had been tense, but the baby's CCAM hadn't progressed much. It wouldn't be too much longer before they'd have to fly Mentlana to Iqaluit.

Quinn helped Genen take Mentlana home and get her settled. When he returned to the clinic, Charlotte was locked away in her office, working on files, and he didn't want to disturb her, though he should. He wanted to know what was bothering her, but he also didn't want to push her away.

Instead, he pulled out his camera. First he uploaded all the pictures on his memory card to his computer and then backed up the photographs on his USB stick. Once his memory card was free of the camera, he sat down at Charlotte's kitchen table and took apart the telephoto lens to clean it out. When he'd been out ice fishing, some salt water had got into the lens so the camera's automatic zoom was not working right. The last thing he wanted was his expensive photographic equipment to get ruined.

It was the first thing he'd bought when the bandages had come off and he'd gained a bit of strength back in his hand. He loved photography, but had never able to indulge in it.

When he'd been a kid he'd wanted to be a photographer for *National Geographic*, but when he'd announced that to his father his subscription to that magazine had ended, to be replaced by a medical journal.

*Great magazine subscription for a kid of fourteen.*

Quinn snorted and shook the thought of his father out of his head. There was no place for him there. Instead, he focused on the task at hand. It was delicate work, but he didn't mind it in the least. His hand hadn't been bothering him and he was able to keep a steady grip on his tools as he took apart the lens and began to clean it.

"I hope that won't void the warranty."

Quinn glanced up to see Charlotte hovering in the connecting door between her clinic and her home. She leaned against the doorjamb, watching him in fascination. The invisible wall she had put up only a couple of hours ago seemed to be down once more.

"The warranty was voided long ago." Quinn continued with his work. This time she'd have to come to him. He held his breath, waiting, and then he heard her soft footfalls as she crossed the distance between the door and the kitchen table.

"That looks like pretty intricate work. You sure you know what you're doing?"

"You doubt my mad skills?" Quinn wiped the dried salt from around the rim. "There. That should do it."

"How did you get salt into your lens?"

"I was snapping some pictures out on the ice today."

Charlotte smiled and tucked her hair behind her ear. "You weren't fishing."

"No. I hate fishing. I was there for the scenery." Quinn put his telephoto lens back together. "That was actually something my father enjoyed. He liked fishing and made me go all the time. I never caught anything, much to his chagrin."

"What do you think of the scenery up here? I mean, you weren't too interested in seeing the sights in Yellowknife."

Quinn met her gaze. "That was a different time. I was a different person."

She didn't say anything for a few moments. "I want to show you something, as you're so interested in scenery."

"I'm intrigued."

"It's outside, in the cold." Charlotte stood up.

"I'm game, but we better hurry before the sun sets."

"That's the point." She hurried into the clinic and returned with their parkas. She tossed him his and Quinn caught it.

"If it's just a sunset, I've seen many."

Charlotte grinned. "Not like this." She zipped up her parka.

"If you say so." Quinn pulled on his parka. "Lead the way."

They headed outside, towards the water. The sun was setting, and it was so low that it seemed to be touching the horizon. Being so far north, the sun looked larger in the sky. As it set behind a cloud bank, it seemed like two other small suns peeked through the clouds, giving the illusion that three suns were setting on the water.

"Wow." Quinn raised his camera and took a shot. "That *is* amazing."

Charlotte nodded. "It is. They're called sun dogs."

Quinn glanced at her. The last rays of light touched her red hair, making it seem like it was aflame. He snapped a quick picture of her, looking out over the water.

"Hey, I didn't say you could take one of me," Charlotte protested.

"I was just admiring the view."

A pink blush tinged Charlotte's skin. He slung his camera over his shoulder and moved towards her, running his hand against her cold cheek.

"Quinn, please... I'm not sure."

"You trust me, Charlotte?"

"I said I did."

"Then tell me what's wrong."

Charlotte bit her lip. "It's nothing about you. It's me this time."

Quinn was confused. "I don't understand."

"I don't, either." Charlotte sighed. The wall was up once more and he knew he couldn't press her. "It's getting dark. We need to get back to the clinic."

"Sure."

They walked in silence back to the clinic, but as they clambered over a snow bank Charlotte let out a cry of horror at what was on the other side.

Anernerk was huddled in the snow, unmoving and with no jacket.

"Oh, my God." Charlotte scrambled down quickly. "Anernerk. Oh, God. No."

Quinn was by their side in a moment. He whipped off his parka and wrapped it around the old woman. "She's breathing, but barely." He picked her up in his arms. The cold was biting at his skin, but he didn't care. This was Charlotte's family, and he cared about Anernerk, too.

Charlotte ran ahead and held open the clinic door. Quinn rushed her inside, following in the wake of Charlotte, who was preparing a nearby exam room.

Anernerk's breathing was harsh. There was a rattle in her chest.

"Set her down here," Charlotte said, placing his camera on the counter. Quinn hadn't even known he'd dropped it or that Charlotte had picked it up. The moment he'd heard

Charlotte cry out, he hadn't thought about anything else except helping Anernerk.

Quinn laid the old lady down on the bed. "She can't breathe well. I'm going to have to intubate her."

"I'll get an intubation kit." Charlotte disappeared from the room.

"It'll be okay," Quinn whispered, brushing back hair from Anernerk's forehead. Anernerk reached out and grabbed his arms, gripping him tightly with a surprising surge of strength.

"No," she said in a barely audible whisper. "No."

Quinn moved closer to her. "Anernerk, we have to."

A small smile tugged at the corner of her lips. "Don't be obstinate, Quinn Devlyn. Let me go."

Anernerk's breathing became shallower, her skin was waxy and the rattle in her chest became louder. The same sound many patients took when they were taking their final breaths.

"I have the intubation kit!" Charlotte rushed back into the room.

"She wants to go. She doesn't want intubation. It's her time."

"She can't breathe," Charlotte said, flustered and annoyed. "Goddammit, Quinn. We have to intubate her."

"No," Anernerk said. "I told him not to."

Charlotte paled. "What? Anernerk, I don't—"

"It's my time to go, Charlotte. You're a wonderful doctor, as is Dr. Devlyn, but it's my time to pass. The spirits have spoken to me."

Tears welled up in Charlotte's eyes as she leaned over Anernerk. "I can't let you go. You're all I have. You took care of me when my father died. I can't lose you."

"You have Dr. Devlyn." Anernerk reached out and stroked Charlotte's face. "I shall miss you, daughter."

"No," Charlotte cried as she gripped Anernerk's shoulders. "No, I won't let you go."

"Don't be the obstinate man's wife with dark thoughts, my child. You have to let those fears go."

Quinn held on to Charlotte's shoulders, trying to pull her away, but she shrugged him off roughly and laid out the intubation instruments.

"No," Charlotte shouted, to no one in particular. "We have to intubate."

Anernerk stretched her body and took one last breath. Her chest stopped moving. A breeze entered the exam room and Quinn swore he could feel the old woman's soul pass through him, if he believed in that sort of thing. Which he didn't. But in this moment of Anernerk's death, he wasn't so sure.

"Time of death—sixteen-forty." Charlotte slammed the intubation tray and pushed past him, leaving the room. He heard the distant slam of her office door.

Quinn scrubbed his hand over his face and then closed Anernerk's eyes and covered her body with a sheet. He cleaned up and washed his hands, giving Charlotte her privacy as she grieved.

Twenty minutes later the door to the clinic opened and George entered the exam room. His face was broken and pale when his gaze landed on Anernerk's body.

"Charley called me. I've come to take her to the special building we have. We store the bodies out there until we can bury them."

"Of course. By all means." Quinn stepped to one side. "Do you need help?"

George shook his head. "Thanks, but no. It's Charley I'm worried about, Doc. Even though they bickered, like when you saw them, it was Grandma who reached out and healed Charlotte when she came back from Yellow-

knife, her and my sister. Just like when Charley's dad died,
Grandma was there because Charley didn't have anyone
else."

There was a bitter taste in Quinn's mouth.

He'd been the cause of her need to heal on her return
from Yellowknife. He'd left her alone. It'd been his fault.

"I'll take care of Charlotte." Quinn left the exam room
and headed straight for Charlotte's office, but she wasn't
there.

The door to her apartment was slightly ajar and he
peeked inside. She was curled up on the couch, staring
blankly at the wall. She'd changed out of her heavy sweater
into a T-shirt and yoga pants, her hair loose over her shoulders and a blanket lying over her hips.

When she looked at him a shudder ran down his spine.
It was the same expression she'd given him when she'd
been in the hospital in Yellowknife. All that was missing
from the scene was the antiseptic smell of the hospital and
an IV pumping blood into her veins.

Why had he walked away from her then? He'd been
such a fool, but after he'd told her about New York she'd
told him to go and had refused to see him. Even though
they'd been engaged, they hadn't been legally family and
the hospital had had to respect her wishes. He'd remained
at a distance, making sure her discharge from the hospital had gone well, although she hadn't known he'd been
there. And then he'd left.

It pained him that she'd shut him out of her life.

"Charlotte, I'm so sorry for your loss."

"I should've intubated her."

"She didn't want it."

Charlotte's gaze narrowed. "It doesn't matter. If I'd intubated her she'd still be alive."

Quinn moved toward her. "Be reasonable. Anernerk was a hundred and one. It was her time to go."

"No," Charlotte shouted, jumping up to face him. "They're my family. Mine. They're all I have…"

Charlotte's anger dissipated and she sat back down on the couch in defeat. She was taking out her grief on him. He didn't deserve it. He'd only been listening to the patient's wishes, whereas she had only been thinking about herself. She had let her emotions rule her. Quinn was right.

She had a tendency to be over-emotional at times. She was so used to bottling up her feelings that after a time they would erupt out of her like putting a mint in diet soda.

She was being unreasonable.

The cushion next to her dipped as Quinn sat beside her. He took her hand in his broken one. It was strong and didn't tremble.

"I'm so sorry for snapping at you, Quinn."

She leaned over and buried her face in his neck, drinking in his scent, his warmth and his strength. Strength she needed now more than ever.

Right now she needed to feel something besides pain. What she needed was physical contact with him. Even though she'd promised herself she wouldn't let him in, at this moment she wanted to drown her sorrows in him. For so long she'd been anesthetized to life and she hadn't even realized it until this moment.

Making love with Quinn would remind her she was still alive.

"Charlotte," Quinn whispered, causing goose bumps to spread across her skin. Her nipples tightened under her shirt. She pressed her body to his, trying to close off any space that remained between them.

Charlotte wanted nothing to separate them. Not at this moment.

"What can I do for you, Charlotte?" He kissed the top of her head gently as he cradled her. "I'll do anything."

"Make love to me, Quinn."

A moan escaped past his lips and his hot breath fanned her neck. "Are you sure?"

Her answer was to simply wrap her arms around his neck and run her fingers through his hair, bringing his lips to her mouth. "Yes. Make the hurt go away. Please. I need you."

No more words were needed in that moment. Her plea was silenced by a searing kiss that made her melt into him. Charlotte didn't want to let him go. As the kiss deepened he pressed her against the cushions of the couch.

"Not here," she said, reluctantly breaking off the kiss.

Quinn scooped her up in his arms, without breaking the connection of their lips as he kissed her again. He carried her the short distance down the hall to her bedroom. Her blood thundered in her ears as she thought about what was going to happen and about how much she wanted it.

He set her down and she gripped the collar of his shirt while his hands roved over her back. Quinn's pulse raced under her fingertips as she undid the buttons at the base of his throat. "I want you, Quinn."

*I've never stopped wanting you.*

The air seemed to crackle with almost tangible tension. It was like her first time all over again and it was only fitting. Quinn had been her first and only.

"I want you, Charlotte, but only if you're sure. You've been through so much today."

"I want this. Please."

He seemed to hesitate, but only for a moment. "I can't resist you. I've never been able to." His lips captured hers in a kiss, his tongue twining with hers. Charlotte pulled him down onto the bed, until she was kneeling in front of him. His eyes sparkled in the dim room. "I've missed you, Charlotte. God, how I've missed you."

"Me, too," she whispered. She slipped off her shoes and they clattered to the floor. Reaching for him, she dragged him into another kiss. His hands slipped down her back, the heat of his skin searing her flesh through her thin cotton shirt, making her body ache with desire. Quinn removed her shirt and then his hands moved to her back to undo the clips of her bra. He undid each one painstakingly slowly, before he slipped the straps off her shoulders.

The sharp intake of breath from Quinn when his gaze alighted on her state of half undress sent a zing of desire racing through her veins. He kissed her again, his hands moving to cup her breasts and knead them. Charlotte closed her eyes and a moan escaped at the feel of his rough caresses on her sensitized skin.

She untucked his shirt from his pants then attacked the buttons and peeled it off, tossing it over her shoulder. She ran her hands over his smooth, bare chest, before letting her fingers trail down to the waist of his trousers. He grabbed her wrists and held her there, then pushed her down roughly on the bed, pinning her as he leaned over her. He released her hands and pressed his body against hers, kissing her fervently, as though he were a condemned man, yet there was tenderness there, too.

Charlotte had missed this.

She kissed him again, snaking her arms around his neck, letting his tongue plunder her mouth, her body coming alive as if it had been in a deep sleep.

He broke the kiss and removed her yoga pants, his fingers running over her calves. Each time his fingers skimmed her flesh her body ignited, and when his thumbs slid under the side of her panties to tug them down she went up in flames. Now she was totally naked and vulnerable to him.

Quinn stood and she watched him remove his pants. Moonlight filtered through the slatted blinds. He was glorious as he bared his well-honed body to her. She remembered every exquisite inch of him. She helped him roll on a condom.

When he returned to the bed he trailed his hand over her body, lingering on her breasts. Pleasure coursed through her at his touch. He pressed his lips against one of her breasts, laving her nipple with his hot tongue. She arched her back, wanting more.

"I love making you feel this way," he said huskily.

*I love it when you make me feel this way.* Only she didn't say the words out loud. His hand moved down her body, between her legs. He began to stroke her, making her wet with need.

All she could think about was him replacing his hand with his mouth. The thought of where he was, what he was going to do, made her moan.

As if reading her mind, Quinn ran his tongue over her body, kissing and nipping over her stomach and hips to where he'd just been caressing. His breath against her inner thighs made her smolder and when his tongue licked between the folds of her sex, she cried out.

Instinctively she began to grind her hips upwards, her fingers slipping into his hair, holding him in place. She didn't want him to stop. Warmth spread through her body like she'd imbibed too much wine, her body taut as ecstasy enveloped her in a warm cocoon.

She was so close to the edge, but she didn't want to topple over. When she came she wanted him to be buried inside her.

Quinn shifted position and the tip of his shaft pressed against her folds. She wanted him to take her, to be his and his alone.

Even if only for this stolen time.

He thrust quickly, filling her completely. There was a small sputtering of pain, just like their first time. She clutched his shoulders as he held still, stretching her. He was buried so deep inside her.

"I'm sorry, darling," he moaned, his eyes closed. "God, you're tight. It's been far too long." He surged forward, bracing his weight on his good arm while his bad hand held her hip. She met every one of his sure thrusts.

"So tight," he murmured again.

Quinn moved harder, faster. A coil of heat unfurled deep within her. She arched her back as pleasure overtook her, the muscles of her sheath tightening around him as she came. Quinn stiffened, and spilled his seed.

He slipped out of her, falling beside her on the bed and collecting her up against him. She let him and laid her head against his damp chest, listening to his rapid breathing.

*What am I doing? What have I done?*

She knew exactly what she'd done. She was angry at herself for being weak and for possibly hurting them both again.

# CHAPTER FOURTEEN

SHE WAS BEING watched.

Charlotte could feel Quinn's gaze boring into her back. It made her feel uneasy. Why had she slept with him again? What had she been thinking?

That was a foolish question. She knew exactly what she'd been thinking and she was now regretting it whole-heartedly in the pale light of morning. Though she had to admit she'd liked being in his arms again. Every touch, every kiss had been like a dream come true, one she hadn't woken up from when the best part had come.

Grief had pushed her carefully guarded emotions over the edge and her walls had come tumbling down.

*I'm an idiot.*

Charlotte glanced over her shoulder. Quinn smiled lazily at her.

"What're you looking at?" she asked.

"I just like watching you." He propped himself on his elbow. "Where are you going?"

Her stomach twisted as she thought of that little building on the edge of town and she turned her back to him again. "To see Anernerk." She stared down at her knees and tried to keep back the tears threatening to spill.

The mattress dipped and Quinn scooted towards her. "Do you think that's wise?"

"Wise or not, I thought of her as a mother. She raised me as her own and it's my duty to be there." Besides, she had to put some distance between her and Quinn. Last night had been wonderful, but it needed to end there.

"A tradition?"

"Yes." A sigh escaped. She was not relishing her duty because she didn't want to face the reality that Anernerk was gone. Someone else she loved who'd left her.

*You have Quinn. All you have to do is reach out and grab him.*

Did she have Quinn? He hadn't said anything to the contrary. She might trust him for his surgical abilities, but she didn't trust handing her heart over to him again. Charlotte didn't want to pin all her hope on the notion that he *might* stay. She wasn't sure if he truly understood why it meant so much for her to stay up here and devote her life of medicine to these far-flung communities.

And she couldn't ask him to stay with her, giving up the life he wanted. Neither would she hold it against him this time when he left.

"I understand. I'm just worried about your emotional state."

Charlotte stood, but wouldn't look at him. She wasn't brave enough to meet his gaze, to let him have all of her.

"My emotional state is fine." Then she met his gaze and saw tenderness, concern and perhaps something more in his eyes.

*Walk away, Charlotte.*

"I have to go."

"Will you be back soon?" he asked.

"Does it matter?"

"It does. I want to talk about going to Iqaluit."

Charlotte took a step back, shocked. Did he want to work in Iqaluit? She hoped she hadn't led him on. "Why?"

"Unless you have laparoscopic equipment up here, I need to get to a facility that does. We're going to do a dry run of Mentlana's procedure in a skills lab."

Her heart sank in disappointment. *What were you expecting? Really.* "Yes, well, I don't… I mean, I'll have to file a flight plan."

"Then file one. We need to get down there as soon as we can."

"You want me to come with you?"

Quinn raised an eyebrow. "How else are you going to assist me?"

"Assist you? I thought you were joking before."

"I don't joke about surgery."

"I'm flattered, but I can't go to Iqaluit with you."

Quinn frowned. "I thought you still had a surgical license."

"I do. I can still perform some surgery, but I can't leave Cape Recluse."

"Why not?"

"I'm the only physician here."

"And your only current high-risk patient is Mentlana?"

"Yes."

"Then what choice do you have? You need to go through a dry run with me in a skills lab. You fly, George flies and it's a two-hour flight, so you won't be separated from your patients up here. You can spend a few days in Iqaluit with me, practicing. This is for your best friend, Charlotte."

*Damn.* Quinn was right.

"I'll talk to George. We'll arrange something, but after Anernerk's funeral."

"Deal."

She turned to leave then spun back round. "You're serious? You want me to assist?"

"Positive." He lay back against the pillows. "Only you."

*Only me?*

It gave her pleasure to know that he did trust her, that he had faith in her abilities to assist him, a renowned neonatal surgeon.

Of course she'd be an idiot to pass up this opportunity.

She'd file the flight plan with the airfield as soon as she was able to. Right now she had to focus on Anernerk and it was going to be hard. Even thinking about Anernerk laid out, waiting until they could dig through the permafrost, made her throat constrict. They'd have a memorial in a day or so and then bury her when the ground was softer.

Charlotte slipped on her parka at the door and headed out into the cold, but winter's bite didn't have any effect on her. Her mind was whirring with several things, Anernerk, Mentlana, the baby and, of course, Quinn.

Charlotte paused in front of the little cabin and took a deep, steadying breath.

*I can do this. Anernerk wanted me here. She wanted me to be a part of this moment.*

The handle to the door shook in her gloved hands as she opened it and stepped inside. The local ladies, including Lucy and Lorna, had placed Anernerk's body on one of the hides Anernerk's father had cured—a caribou which had been special to the old woman.

Charlotte stepped forward without saying anything. She'd seen this ritual performed before and she'd taken part in it as well. This time, however, it was much more personal. She took the wet rag Lorna handed her and gingerly picked up Anernerk's arm. She began to wash Anernerk's paper-thin skin.

A draft rushed at her back. Charlotte turned as Mentlana lumbered into the room. Two steps and Charlotte was by her side.

"Is everything okay?"

"I'm all right," Mentlana chided.

"You shouldn't be out of bed." Charlotte gripped her shoulder. "Don't you understand what bed rest is?"

Mentlana snorted. "Please. Genen already gave me that lecture. He brought me over on the dogsled, tied to the back of his snowmobile."

"What?" Charlotte was going to have a stern talking to Genen.

"He went like five kilometers an hour. Besides, it was my idea."

"Apparently, pregnancy has rendered you into a lunatic."

Mentlana sighed. "I wanted to be here. Let me braid her hair. I'll just do that and go back home."

"Okay. But then Genen's taking you home."

Mentlana nodded. "Thanks, Charley." She moved slowly to Anernerk's head and began to brush out the snowy white hair.

They finished preparing Anernerk's body. Mentlana braided the hair beautifully and was taken back home by Genen. The elders dressed Anernerk in traditional clothing and then wrapped her body in the caribou hide on which she'd been laid out.

Charlotte stood back, tears blurring her vision, but they didn't escape. She watched the final rituals. Later there would be requiems for Anernerk and her life.

There was nothing more she could do here. It was at times like this Charlotte felt helpless, useless. She was a healer and death was a blow to her. She'd lost and death had won.

"Can I have a moment alone with her?"

The other women nodded and exited the cabin. The sound of the door shutting behind her thundered in her head like a deafening blow of finality. She was alone with

Anernerk, the outside world closed out so she could say her private farewells.

Charlotte would have to be quick. It was too cold outside for the other women to be out there long. She took a step toward Anernerk, the woman who had kept her from being lost in the system as an orphan. The woman who'd encouraged and nourished her dreams. The only mother Charlotte had known. She brushed her fingers across Anernerk's cold cheek.

"Aanak," she whispered. "I love you. You saved my life. I don't know how I'll go on without you, but I know you would want me to and I will. I hope you have the peace you were looking for." Tears rolled down Charlotte's face and she brushed them away.

"May the spirits guide you home." Charlotte opened the door and the elders returned to finish the preparations. She nodded to one of the elders and slipped out of the cabin. The sun was beginning to set and the stiffness in her shoulder alerted her to the fact she'd been tending to Anernerk's body for some time.

The lights from her house flooded out on the snow and a warm sensation built in the pit of her stomach. Quinn was there, waiting for her. She didn't have to be alone tonight if she was willing to take the risk and be with him again.

That was not a risk she was willing to take. She wouldn't lead him on.

Too much water had passed under the bridge and Charlotte couldn't see a way back to reclaim what they'd had. She wouldn't lose her heart to him again.

When she entered her home the scent of garlic hung heavily in the air and her stomach rumbled in response. Her home smelled like an Italian eatery, which was odd. Nothing in town was open. Today was a day of mourning for Anernerk. When someone died, communities became ghost towns for a couple of days.

Charlotte hung her jacket on the hook by the door and peered into the kitchen. The windows were steamed up and Quinn was moving back and forth between the stove and the table.

She suppressed a chuckle when she spied the old frilly apron, which had been her mother's, wrapped around his waist. She'd kept it for purely sentimental reasons, but seeing Quinn in it, tearing around the kitchen, amused her.

On the table was a clean white lace tablecloth, and two emergency candles were alight in a couple of old pickle jars. Two glass tumblers were filled with grape juice. It was the most romantic thing he'd ever done for her.

*Damn. What is he doing?*

Quinn cursed as he lifted the lid on a steaming pot. He shook his hand and stuck his finger in his mouth.

"There's some aloe vera in the living room. That's best for burns."

He spun round. "You're back. I wasn't sure when you were going to come back."

"Neither was I." She took a cautious step into the kitchen. "What're you doing? I didn't think you could cook."

"I can cook one thing. Garlic bread. But I felt I needed to feed you more than that." He gestured to the bubbling pots on the stovetop. "I found some spaghetti and sauce in the cupboards. Not much fresh stuff."

"Fresh stuff is hard to come by and very expensive."

Quinn sighed. "It's pretty bad when the town's doctor can't even afford some button mushrooms."

Charlotte chuckled and picked up a spoon, stirring the clumps of spaghetti before it was too late to be saved. "There's some canned mushrooms in the cupboard."

"Sacrilegious," he teased, but he pulled out the can and opened it, draining the juice into the sink before rinsing the mushrooms off. "Oh, look at that, they're even sliced."

"Extra fancy," she teased.

"But essential for this dinner."

"Oh?" Charlotte was intrigued. "Why essential?"

"I'm trying to replicate the meal we had in Niagara Falls on our first spring break away from medical school." Quinn dumped the mushrooms in the sauce.

*The first time they'd made love.* She remembered. They'd stayed in a cheap motel on the Canadian side of the falls and had got two coupons for dinner at an Italian restaurant.

The last thing she needed tonight was to be reminded of that moment.

"Quinn, this isn't necessary."

"Let me do this for you, Charlotte. You're tired and grieving."

Charlotte sighed in resignation. There was no harm in letting him make dinner. They'd been sharing meals since he'd arrived and they had been innocent enough.

"Hey, bring that pasta here. The sauce is ready."

"Sure." Charlotte dumped the spaghetti back into the pot and placed it on a cool range.

"Go sit down. I'll be serving you tonight." Quinn pushed her towards the table and she didn't fight him. She sat down and waited for him to serve dinner. The garlic bread smelled heavenly and she couldn't remember the last time someone had made her a spaghetti dinner. Hell, she couldn't even recall the last time she'd eaten spaghetti. When she cooked for herself, when she allowed herself time to eat, it was fast and quick. She worried, briefly, how long the ingredients had been in her pantry.

It wouldn't matter. Quinn had tried and she was going

to eat the meal, though she might regret it later. The way she was feeling now, she could eat a whole plate of muktuk if given half the chance.

"Voilà." Quinn set the plate down in front of her. A huge mound of spaghetti with Bolognese sauce and a crispy side of cheesy garlic bread made her stomach growl loudly in appreciation.

"The first taste is with the eyes."

"Is that your subtle way of telling me it won't taste good?" she asked.

He winked. "Taste is all in the mind."

"Oh, dear." She grinned.

Quinn picked up his tumbler of juice. "To Anernerk and the wonderful century she graced this earth."

"To Anernerk." The words were hard to get out and it was even harder to swallow the juice. She set down the tumbler and Quinn's hand slid across the table, his fingers twining with hers. She pulled her hand away.

"I'm sorry. I can't." She couldn't let him touch her. She was too weak.

"It's okay. You're mourning. You have every right to mourn her. You loved her."

"Thank you for understanding. I need my space."

"I went through my own situation not that long ago."

"Your father. Of course. I'm sorry."

Quinn shrugged. "Don't be. He wasn't the most loving of fathers."

"You never really told me how your parents felt about me."

"I know." Quinn didn't meet her gaze.

"That bad, huh?"

He grinned. "He wanted me to marry a socialite, or whatever Toronto's equivalent is to that. Marrying the daughter of some 'hippy'—even if she was a physician—wasn't good enough."

"My father was a doctor. He was far from being a hippy."

"You weren't my father's ideal idea of a wife for me."

"Apparently not for you, either." She regretted the words instantly.

Quinn's smiled faded and he took a bite of his spaghetti. "I could say the same in reverse."

Guilt washed over her. "You could."

They ate in silence, but it was hard to chew. The food was like sawdust in her mouth.

"My cooking is that bad, then?" Quinn asked, breaking the tension.

She glanced up and the earlier twinkle was back in Quinn's eyes. "It's great—better than those brownies."

He groaned. "Let's not bring that up again. Please tell me I'm improving."

Charlotte picked up a piece of garlic bread and took a bite. It was like pure heaven, compared to the clumpy mess that was the spaghetti. The garlic bread melted in her mouth like cheesy goodness. She could marry the garlic bread and she would if it asked her.

"I take it from your orgasmic expression that I did quite well with the bread."

"You did," she said between bites. "You're right."

"About what?"

"You can cook garlic bread. It's divine." She took another bite. "Of course, it could be because I haven't had *real* garlic bread in about three years and I'm desperate for it."

They ate the rest of the meal. She'd forgotten how delicious someone else's cooking was, even if it was Quinn's.

"What do you think?" he asked, as he poured another glass of juice.

"Could be better." She grinned and then winked.

"Better? I ought to take you over my knee and spank you for that remark."

Quinn's jest instantly sobered her up. She set down her fork and then picked up her plate, taking it to the sink.

"Did I say something wrong, Charlotte?" he asked.

"No. Nothing." It was all becoming too easy with Quinn again. He was charismatic and broke through her defenses so easily. "I'm really tired. I need to go to bed."

"Okay. I'll clean up," he said.

Charlotte nodded and without so much as a look she retreated to the safety of her bedroom, locking the door behind her. The bed was still messy and Quinn's scent still lingered in the air, causing heat to creep up her neck. The memory of last night's kisses were suddenly fresh in her brain once more.

She wanted him still, but she wouldn't give in.

Instead, she stripped her bed of the sheets and shoved them in the laundry hamper, shutting the lid firmly.

For her own sanity, she had to stick to her original plan and keep her heart on ice.

# CHAPTER FIFTEEN

AFTER ANERNERK'S MEMORIAL, Quinn and Charlotte moved down to Iqaluit. Quinn's reputation as a surgeon had preceded him and the hospital was willing to bend over backwards to accommodate them. He knew the hospital was trying to woo him into staying permanently.

For a month Charlotte traveled between Cape Recluse and Iqaluit as they prepared for Mentlana's eventual surgery.

Charlotte was polite to Quinn and willing to learn, but the barriers were back up and it smarted. Although what could he expect? The night they'd made love, Charlotte had been looking for comfort, not to renew their relationship.

And he had to respect her wishes, even though he wished the reverse. Once Mentlana successfully delivered he would return to Toronto and she'd remain here.

*You could stay.*

Only what would be the use of staying if Charlotte didn't want him?

There were times Quinn thought she was pulling away, distancing herself from him, building those walls back up. Then at other times it was like the years hadn't passed them and their separation had never happened.

"That's it, keep the needle steady." Quinn watched the monitor as Charlotte manipulated the laparoscope in the lab. She was doing quite well. They'd done a couple of dry runs for placing a thoracoamniotic shunt, the most minimally invasive treatment for Mentlana's baby.

Quinn began to teach Charlotte everything he knew. Charlotte kept in close contact with George, who flew in once a week to take Charlotte back to check up on Mentlana and her other patients. No one else was seriously ill or needed the kind of care Mentlana did.

The residents of Cape Recluse understood what Doc Charley was doing and they didn't mind. The community was still shaken by Anernerk's death and everyone was rooting for this baby. Cape Recluse needed a happy event. This baby represented the hope of a small community.

When he'd last checked on Mentlana, her baby's CCAM was still within the safe range and wasn't pressing on the heart yet. "Yet" was the operative word. At any moment the CCAM could worsen. He was holding off operating, hoping to get her further along in her pregnancy.

The pressure to succeed was keenly felt. Mentlana was thirty weeks, now, but if he could get her to thirty-five then the baby had a better chance of survival should he have to deliver him early.

Quinn wasn't a praying man, but he was wishing for that right now with all his heart. He didn't want to have to perform an in utero procedure. The pediatric specialist in Iqaluit would be quite capable of handling Mentlana's baby and the CCAM if delivered after thirty-five weeks.

It was the surgery that had the young specialist apprehensive. Dr. Richards, the pediatrician there, hadn't done many. Indeed she spent as much time in the skills lab as Charlotte.

Plans were being put in place with the obstetrician, as well. Everything seemed to be running smoothly. However, when Charlotte had returned from her last stint in Cape Recluse three days ago, she'd seemed out of sorts.

She'd been aloof since the dinner he'd made her, but now she looked drawn, tired and ill. He hoped she wasn't catching a cold. If she got sick, she couldn't be allowed near the O.R.

"Dr. Devlyn?" Charlotte said, disturbing his silent rumination. She'd taken to addressing him in a professional manner in front of the other surgeons.

"Good. Now place the shunt. Do you remember how?"

"I do."

Even though they weren't practicing on living tissue, there was a certain finesse about placing such a small shunt inside something so tiny and fragile.

"Then let's see."

Charlotte bit her lip, her brow furrowing as she concentrated and placed it.

"Good." Quinn let out an inward sigh of relief, his shoulders relaxing. Charlotte hadn't managed it yesterday, but each day, she was improving. His hope was that she could perform the surgery with Dr. Richards, should his hand fail. He rubbed the appendage in question. It'd been paining him after too many hours in the lab, and the thought of it not being strong enough to operate worried him.

"Excellent job, Dr. James," praised Dr. Richards, who was taking copious notes in a flipbook.

Charlotte took a deep breath and smiled. "Thank you, Dr. Richards. Now, I'd better head back to the hotel and pack. George should be here soon for my trip back to Cape Recluse."

"Of course," Quinn said. He would miss her. He always did when she returned to Cape Recluse.

"I'll call you about Mentlana's status when I examine her later today."

"Thank you, Dr. James. I look forward to your assessment."

Charlotte left the skills lab while Quinn cursed inwardly.

*You're being selfish, Quinn Devlyn. Tell her you miss her.* But he couldn't. Even though he didn't want to be parted from her and wanted to heal the rift between them, he wasn't sure if he wanted to spend the rest of his life in Nunavut in the cold and ice.

The selfish side of him wondered if she'd come to Toronto to be with him, but he doubted that very much. She hadn't left the North five years ago when they'd been engaged, so why would she now?

This was where Charlotte belonged. But he wasn't sure if he did.

He turned to Dr. Richards. "I'd better be off. I have some sonograms to review." Quinn excused himself from the lab, relieved he didn't have to talk shop with Dr. Richards, who usually talked his ear off. Right now his head was pounding behind his eyes.

When he was in the locker room he pulled off his scrubs and deposited them in the laundry receptacle before washing his hands. As soon as the water hit his skin the muscles in his palm tensed, forcing his fingers to curl upwards, freezing in a clawlike position.

"Dammit," he cursed as he gripped his bad hand with his good one. He massaged the palm, willing the spasms to cease before someone walked in on him. His whole arm was tense, the muscles rigid up past the elbow. It'd been a long time since he'd had a spasm like this, where it locked his entire arm into a useless tangle of sinew and flesh.

How the hell could he even contemplate operating on

Mentlana? This just proved all his fears. There was no way he could risk doing a delicate surgery such as a thoracoamniotic shunt or fetal resection when his muscle spasms were so unpredictable.

Bile rose in his throat as he thought about holding such a delicate, fragile life in his hands and having a spasm like this. He would crush the fetus.

His muscles began to relax under his ministrations. Once his arm ceased tensing up he was able to relax his fingers. Quinn's other hand ached from massaging his damaged one so long and so hard.

*Dammit.*

His phone buzzed and he pulled it out of his trouser pocket. It was a text from Charlotte, who needed to speak to him before she left for Cape Recluse. He didn't want her to see him like this. He texted back that he had been held up at the hospital and then jammed his phone back in his pocket.

Quinn pulled his arm close to his side, cradling it as pins and needles coursed up and down from his elbow to the tips of his fingers. The aftermath of the spasm always felt like he'd fallen asleep on his hand. He had to leave the hospital before anyone saw his hand all clenched and tense, before anyone suspected anything. He quickly dressed in his street clothes, his hand impeding the process slightly.

How the hell was he going to tell Charlotte he couldn't do the surgery?

Right now he needed some liquid courage, but he didn't know where he was going to find it in Iqaluit and he didn't relish the idea of wandering through bitterly cold streets in an attempt to do so.

"Ah, Dr. Devlyn. Just the man I was looking for."

Quinn groaned inwardly as the chief surgeon approached him, followed by members of the board of directors. He'd nothing against Dr. Spicer or the board—in fact, he was grateful they were willing to open up their hospital and allow him to be here when their hospital was full of surgeons—but he didn't want to be stopped at the moment.

He didn't want them to see him this way.

Dr. Spicer stopped in front of Quinn and the board members closed in around him. He was trapped, his escape route cut off.

*Deep breath.*

"Dr. Devlyn, may I introduce you to our board—Mr. Leonard Saltzman, Mrs. Jennifer Chenery and Mr. Harry Westman."

Quinn shook each member's hand, forcing out pleasantries through gritted teeth, keeping his bad hand behind his back.

"Dr. Devlyn is a renowned neonatal surgeon. He's up here preparing for surgery on a possible congenital cystic adenomatoid malformation on an Inuk woman's fetus."

"Impressive," Jennifer Chenery said, looking him up and down with an appreciative eye. "Are you carrying out the entire procedure as well as the birth?"

"No," Quinn replied. "No. Your head of obstetrics is more than capable of assisting me. He will be delivering the infant at term."

There were a few murmurs, and Quinn knew without a doubt they were impressed. He knew Mrs. Chenery was, from the way she was eyeing him like he was piece of chocolate cake or something.

"You worked at Manhattan Mercy for a time, is that correct, Dr. Devlyn?" Leonard Saltzman asked.

"Yes, I did, and then I returned to Canada. I worked at Mount Sinai for a couple of years before taking a sabbatical after my father's death."

"Dr. Devlyn is highly praised by Manhattan Mercy's chief of surgery," Dr. Spicer told the board members.

Quinn's stomach twisted and he had a feeling about where this conversation was going, but he wasn't sure if he was in a position to listen to it. Dr. Spicer was still talking him up to the board members and Quinn supposed he was talking to him as well, but Quinn couldn't hear anything but muffled words.

"Dr. Devlyn?" Dr. Spicer said.

"Sorry, Dr. Spicer. I was thinking about... I was contemplating something about a patient's procedure. Please forgive me." Quinn tried to extricate himself from the conversation, but it didn't work.

"No problem, Dr. Devlyn. I know you're a busy man. The board members were just leaving."

Quinn nodded and shook their hands as they left, until it was only he and Dr. Spicer standing in the surprisingly quiet corridor.

"I'd best be on my way, as well," Quinn said, but Dr. Spicer reached out and grabbed his shoulder.

"A moment of your time, Dr. Devlyn."

"Yes, of course. Lead the way." Dr. Spicer opened the door to a small consult room they'd been standing in front of.

Dr. Spicer shut the door and motioned for Quinn to sit. "I think you know why I've asked you in here."

"I have an inkling."

Dr. Spicer grinned. "We want to offer you a position here in Iqaluit. We want you to head up a world-class neonatal unit. Right now we're currently flying cases like Mrs. Tikivik to Ottawa or Toronto because se don't have the facilities or surgical capabilities, but our board of directors is planning to change that. We want to provide a service like that for our community."

Quinn scrubbed his hand over his face. "Do you think the territory will fund an endeavor like this?"

Dr. nodded. "I think so and I know the communities will rally for federal support, too. We need physicians with the know-how up here. We need to provide a more extensive neonatal facility for our patients and we want you to spearhead it."

"I don't know, Dr. Spicer." Quinn, for some unknown reason, couldn't come flat out and turn Dr. Spicer down and he couldn't think of an excuse.

So what was holding him back from accepting?

The position his father had left for him in Toronto? No. He didn't care about becoming Chief of Surgery. Not really.

Dr. Spicer looked crestfallen, but smiled nonetheless. "Understandable, but the board is willing to do whatever it takes to get you, Dr. Devlyn."

"Let me think on it."

"Of course, take all the time you need, Quinn. The offer doesn't have a termination date."

"Very generous of you."

Dr. Spicer opened the consult-room door and Quinn exited, Dr. Spicer shaking his hand as he was leaving.

*Why didn't I just say no? Why didn't I say yes?*

Quinn couldn't figure it out. He couldn't think straight and his mind was a bit too full at the moment. All the expectations were weighing heavily on his shoulders. And then there was Charlotte.

Beautiful, wonderful, loving Charlotte, who'd let him back inside her protective walls, or so he'd thought.

"Hey, Quinn!"

Quinn glanced over his shoulder to see Dr. Patterson, the OB/GYN on Mentlana's case, approaching. He was dressed in street clothes, with a duffel bag slung over his shoulder.

"Carlisle." Quinn greeted him, as Dr. Patterson approached. "I thought you'd gone home."

"I'm on my way." Dr. Patterson looked him over from head to toe. "You look like roadkill."

"I feel like it."

Carlisle clapped him on the back. "You need a stiff drink."

"I do, but didn't know where I'd be able to find one."

"I know just the place if you care to join me."

"I would." Quinn relaxed. "Lead the way."

# CHAPTER SIXTEEN

THREE DAYS AGO, when she had last been in Cape Recluse, her life had changed because a month ago she'd lost her head and had made love with Quinn. She hadn't believed the over-the-counter pregnancy test she'd used and had Rosie draw some blood.

The blood test confirmed it as well.

She was pregnant. And shocked because they'd used protection. The condom must've failed, because there was no denying it. She was already a month gone.

It thrilled and terrified her to her very core.

She wanted a family. She wanted to be a mother, but being pregnant scared her witless. What if she lost this one? It would be too much to bear.

Charlotte stuffed some clothes in her duffel bag, trying not to think about having to leave again, especially leaving Quinn again. She tried to distance herself from Quinn, to keep her walls secure, but to no avail.

She thought about him constantly. Her heart once more belonged to him, but she wasn't sure how she could tell him that. As well as tell him that she was pregnant again. The last time she'd told him they were expecting it hadn't gone well at all.

An hour ago a text had come in and she'd picked up her

phone. Quinn had got her text about needing to speak with him, but he had been held up at the hospital.

She was tempted to text him and tell him why she needed to speak to him, but a text wasn't going to cut it. She needed to tell him face-to-face, even though she was afraid to risk her heart again.

Charlotte wondered if he suspected her condition. He'd been so distracted and aloof in the skills lab today and she'd been having extreme morning sickness. She could barely keep anything down and it was beginning to show in her pallor.

No, he couldn't know. She'd only just found out herself and he hadn't noticed last time she'd been pregnant.

Perhaps he was regretting his decision to allow her to assist.

Yesterday, when she had messed up and inserted that test shunt too roughly, causing the laparoscope to go deeper, thus killing the fetus, he'd come up behind her and placed his hands over hers, guiding her through another run. His gentle, firm touch was so sure and steady.

*Don't be a coward.*

Charlotte had to see him, couldn't go to Cape Recluse without telling him. She left her packing and was about to go track Quinn down when there was a knock at her door. Charlotte opened it and there he was, leaning against the doorjamb.

"Quinn?" Charlotte was surprised to see him. He looked a bit disheveled and there was a strong odor of beer. "Are you drunk? Where did you find alcohol?"

"Dr. Patterson is a member of the local legion."

Charlotte stepped to the side and allowed him into the room before shutting the door. "You shouldn't be drinking. Mentlana might go into distress any time now."

Quinn shook his head. "First of all, I'm not drunk. I only had pop. Someone spilled their beer on me."

"Well, that's a relief. The last thing a surgeon of your caliber needs to be doing is drinking."

Quinn snorted. "My caliber indeed," he mumbled, as he sat down on the edge of the bed.

"What's wrong? You were acting very strangely in the lab today."

He ignored her question. "Secondly, you don't need me. You're perfectly capable of doing the surgery on your own."

Charlotte paled. "What're you talking about? I'm just a GP—you're the surgeon. You've done this countless times. You know the call to make and when to make it. I'm just here to assist."

"You're not just an assistant, Charlotte. You're going to take point on Mentlana's baby."

"You are drunk." Charlotte snorted.

"Not at all."

"Then why am I suddenly taking point?"

"My hand spasmed. I don't want to risk that happening during surgery. You have to take over. I know you can do it."

The room spun. She felt dizzy. She sat down next to him on the bed. *Take point?* She was a general surgeon, not a specialist.

"I can't take point, Quinn."

"I've already talked to Dr. Patterson. He'll vouch for your ability and be overseeing you every step of the way."

Dread coursed down her spine. "And where will you be?" she asked cautiously.

"I don't know, Charlotte. Where will I be?"

The blood drained from her face. "What do you mean?" Though she knew.

"You know what I mean." He raked his fingers through his hair. "Damn it, Charlotte, I can't stay here."

Charlotte's heart skipped a beat and it felt like a great weight was pressing on her chest, stopping her from breathing. He was doing it again. He was finding some excuse and running away.

"What about Mentlana?"

Quinn cursed under his breath. "I just told you, you and Carlisle Patterson can handle it. I can't."

"I think you can."

He looked up at her, angry. "Dammit, Charlotte, my hand spasmed. If you let me near Mentlana and her baby, I might kill them."

She was opening her mouth to say something when her phone began to ring. She answered it. "Dr. James speaking."

"Doc Charley, it's George. I'm at the airport and we're transporting Mentlana to the hospital. She's gone into preterm labor."

"I'll be right there." Charlotte snapped her phone shut. Her stomach lurched and she came precariously close to losing her lunch. There was so much more she wanted to say to Quinn, but she didn't have time to deal with him and his brooding.

Mentlana needed her.

"What's wrong?" he asked.

"What does it matter to you? You're heading back to Toronto to wallow." She tried to push past him but he grabbed her arm and spun her round.

"Charlotte, I won't risk her baby. If I do the surgery on Mentlana and she or her baby dies, you'll loathe me."

"You care how I would feel about you?"

Quinn's face relaxed. "Of course, I do. I don't want to

kill the baby. I'm afraid. My hand...it clenched so hard today."

Charlotte touched his face. "You won't. I'll be with you every step of the way."

"If I'm handling the fetus... Oh, God, I don't even want to think about it." He tried to move away, but she gripped him by the shoulders.

"You can do this. I'll help you."

She held her breath, waiting for his response. Quinn nodded. "All right. And you're right. I can."

"Good. Now, we have to head to the hospital. That was George on the phone and Mentlana has gone into preterm labor."

Quinn nodded again. "I'll grab a coffee in the cafeteria. Hopefully the on-call obstetrician is smart enough to try and stop the contractions. Let's go."

Charlotte grabbed her purse, ready to face whatever fate had to throw at them.

Charlotte was reading Mentlana's chart while Mentlana was napping. The obstetrician on call had been able to stop the contractions, so they had that going for them: the less stress on the baby the better, and a contracting uterus wasn't particularly helpful to a fetus with a CCAM.

Genen had been absolutely frantic until they'd got everything under control, then he'd crashed and was sleeping on a nearby cot while Lorna knitted in the corner. The clicking of Lorna's knitting needles mixing with the beeps and hums of the monitors in the dim room was oddly soothing to Charlotte.

She'd been on her feet for almost twenty-four hours since Mentlana had arrived. George had gone back up to Cape Recluse as they needed someone with some medical experience there.

"How's it looking, Doc?" Lorna whispered.

"She's stable. Dr. Devlyn is going to do a portable sonogram soon. He's just gone to get the machine. And then we'll assess what needs to be done."

Lorna nodded slowly. "How about you take a rest? You're in your first trimester and with your history of the previous miscarriage you need to take it easy."

Charlotte's mouth dropped open. "How did you know?"

Lorna shrugged but didn't look up from her knitting. "I've been a midwife longer than you've been alive, Charlotte James. I know when a woman is expecting." Lorna glanced up at her. "I'm thrilled for you, by the way."

"Thank you. I have to admit I'm nervous."

"You have every right to be, but I'm sure everything will be okay."

"No one can be certain of that." Charlotte sighed. "I mean, there are so many variables, so many things that could go wrong."

*Like car accidents.* Look at Quinn—he'd had a terrible one that had damaged his surgical hand and only his hand. What were the odds on that?

"Yes, that's true," Lorna admitted. "But if you worry about the what-ifs, you'll make yourself sick. You're a physician. You're looking at statistics of what can go wrong all the time. But look at the number of births that go right. What happened to you was a tragedy, Charlotte, but it wasn't anything you did that caused you to lose your baby."

Charlotte nodded. "You're right."

"I know it." Lorna went back to knitting, a smug smile plastered across her face. "Your baby will be healthy, as will you, Doc Charley."

"What?" Mentlana asked groggily. "Who's pregnant?"

Charlotte pulled a rolling stool up beside Mentlana. "How are you feeling?"

"Like a beached whale, of course." Mentlana winced. "Now, who's pregnant? Dish the dirt. I may be drugged up with who knows what, but I know I heard Lorna and you talking about a pregnancy." Mentlana's eyes widened and Charlotte didn't need to tell her anything. Her friend had figured it out. "You're pregnant."

"Yes. It's me."

"Oh, my God, that's wonderful, Charley." Mentlana paused. "It's Devlyn's, right?"

Charlotte rolled her eyes. "Who else's would it be?"

"Does he know?"

"No." Charlotte's cheeks flushed. "I want to tell him but…"

"You're afraid," Mentlana offered.

Charlotte nodded. "Terrified. The last time didn't end well. He wasn't thrilled about the prospect, either."

"You need to tell him. He has the right to know." Mentlana reached out and took her hand, giving it a squeeze. "And if he wants no part of it, you'll have a baby. You'd make an excellent mother."

Charlotte smiled. "Thank you."

Mentlana grinned. "I'm so happy for you." She rubbed her belly. "You know, I always wonder about that phrase about God only giving you what you can handle. I wondered about the purpose of making me and my child so sick and putting us through this torment, but I think I know why, now."

"Mentlana, I wouldn't wish that kind of fate on anyone."

Her friend smiled. "'Oh, ye of little faith.'"

"How are we this morning?" Quinn asked as he pushed a portable sonogram into the room. Genen roused from his slumber with a groan. "Sorry, Genen," Quinn apologized, realizing he'd woken him up.

"It's okay, Doc." Genen yawned.

Quinn set up the machine but he squeezed Charlotte's shoulder as he passed. "You okay? You need your rest. You look beat."

"I'll rest after I know how Mentlana's baby is doing." Charlotte saw Mentlana's pointed look, but Charlotte kept her mouth shut as Dr. Richards walked into the room, followed by Dr. Patterson.

"Genen, Mentlana, this is Dr. Richards, a pediatric specialist, and Dr. Patterson, the head of obstetrics. They'll be helping us with your baby."

"Nice to meet you," Genen said quietly, taking a seat beside his wife.

"I'll just do a quick sonogram to see how the baby's CCAM is progressing."

"Sure thing," Mentlana agreed, but Charlotte could tell by the waver in her voice that she was nervous. It was the first sign of apprehension Mentlana had expressed in a long time. Even when they'd wheeled her into the hospital yesterday she had been pretty upbeat. Nothing seemed to faze Mentlana Tikivik.

Charlotte admired Mentlana's bravery. She reached out and brushed Mentlana's hair back from her forehead, but when she looked up she saw a strange expression—a cold, calculating look—pass over Dr. Richards's face, like she was trying to find some fault with her.

The sound of the baby's heartbeat filled the darkened room and Charlotte forgot about Dr. Richards and watched the baby on the screen. The lesion was growing and soon hydrops would start. Mentlana could develop mirror syndrome. If that happened, the baby's chance of survival greatly diminished.

Charlotte's stomach twisted and she resisted the urge to give in to the morning sickness. *Please, don't let me throw up now.* The last thing she needed was Dr. Richards poking her nose into why she was vomiting during a routine sonogram.

"There we go," Quinn announced. "All done." He wiped off Mentlana's swollen belly and then sent Charlotte a quick look which conveyed his concern, one she understood all too well.

"Well, Doc Devlyn?" Genen asked, his voice tight with barely contained worry.

"We're going to discuss the next steps, but I'm pleased your contractions have stopped now, Mentlana. That's very good."

Mentlana nodded and gripped Genen's hand. "Thank you, Doctors."

Quinn escorted Dr. Patterson and Dr. Richards out of the room. Charlotte kissed Mentlana's forehead. "I'll be back as soon as I can with some news. Just relax, take it easy, bug the nurses for anything you want...."

Mentlana chuckled. "Okay."

Charlotte left the room and pulled a cracker out of her pocket. She had a sleeve of them in her lab coat. Her morning sickness was turning into all-day sickness. She had to get a consult with Dr. Patterson soon and get some Diclectin to keep her vomiting at bay.

When she approached the meeting room she could hear raised voices. It was never a good sign when surgeons disagreed.

"Dr. James shouldn't be allowed to do the surgery."

Charlotte paused, hearing Dr. Richards's voice over the din. Her heart skipped a beat and then sank to the soles of her feet. Her first instinct was to back away, but Mentlana was her patient and Quinn needed her. She wasn't going to be bullied by the other surgeons. With a deep breath she pushed open the door. The arguing stopped immediately

Dr. Richards's lips were pursed in a tight thin line as their gazes locked.

"Dr. Richards." Charlotte nodded curtly. "I understand you have some problem about my involvement in this case."

"Dr. James, it's nothing," Quinn said, trying to soothe the tension in the room.

"I would love to hear everyone's opinions, Dr. Devlyn." Charlotte took a seat across from Dr. Richards. "Every surgeon's input is invaluable, especially when it involves Mentlana Tikivik."

It was a good move to pump up a young surgeon's ego. Surgeons could be silly and petty creatures that way. It was like her mother's old saying about catching more flies with honey than vinegar. Or Anernerk's saying of always treating your children with respect because they'll replace you one day, and from the way it sounded, Dr. Richards was trying to replace her in the surgical suite.

Dr. Richards was shocked. A small smile even cracked her usually serious facade. "It's not that I question your skill and value as a physician, Dr. James. I have spent a lot of time with you in the lab and am vastly impressed with your handling of instruments. You have the skills of a surgeon, but I'm concerned about your familiarity with the patient."

"What do you mean?" Charlotte asked.

"There's a reason physicians don't operate on family members, whether blood or a close bond."

"And your point?"

Dr. Richards's eyes narrowed. "I don't think you will act rationally in there. With myself, Dr. Devlyn and Dr. Patterson, I think Mrs. Tikivik will do just fine."

Charlotte gripped the edge of the conference table, her stomach lurching with a wave of nausea. "I understand your concern, Dr. Richards. Yes, I will admit I have a close relationship with my patient, but I can assure you I will not be irrational. Are you from Nunavut originally, Dr. Richards?"

"I don't understand the point of the question. What does that have to do with this situation?"

"A lot, in fact," Dr. Patterson interjected. He sent Charlotte an encouraging look. "I think I understand what Dr. James is getting at."

"Well, I don't."

"Just answer it," Quinn said.

"No. I'm not from here. I'm from Vancouver."

"People in remote communities can be very untrusting of strangers. This territory is very close-knit, given its vastness. I've know the Tikiviks for a long time and they trust me. If you try to remove me from the O.R., it will only upset Mrs. Tikivik, possibly putting her into distress."

"Dr. James is correct. And Mrs. Tikivik is very...strong-willed," Quinn said delicately, though a hint of a smile played on his lips. "I need Dr. James to assist me. I've known her for a long time, too, and I value her skills. Dr. Richards, you are needed to monitor the fetus and take care of the child if an EXIT procedure is required. Dr. Patterson's main concern is the health of the mother."

Dr. Richards assessed Charlotte. "Your points are valid. You've swayed me and I concur."

Quinn sent a glance that conveyed his relief. Charlotte nodded and pulled out another cracker, shoving it into her mouth as Dr. Richards flipped open her notebook.

"Now, can we discuss the real reason we're here?" Quinn clicked on his slide show and the large screen in the boardroom lit up with sonograms of the fetus. "The fetus is at a gestational age of thirty weeks and, as you can tell, the lesion has grown." Quinn used a pointer to indicate the lesion. "The fetus will develop hydrops soon."

"And given Mrs. Tikivik is already a high-risk candidate, I have no doubt she'll develop mirror syndrome, which will quickly escalate into fatal pre-eclampsia," Dr. Patterson added.

"What're you suggesting, Dr. Devlyn?" Dr. Richards asked.

"We need to perform a fetal resection today."

"And that is the best course of action?" Charlotte asked. "It won't tax Mentlana, having two C-sections so close together?"

"It's the best option, Dr. James," Quinn said seriously. "The fetus will feel nothing and will have the benefit of his mother's blood supply from the placenta, a chance to heal in the womb and to let the lungs develop more. Mentlana will have to remain in Iqaluit and be monitored for preterm labor."

Charlotte nodded. "I'll inform my patient."

Quinn turned to Dr. Patterson. "We need an O.R. prepped."

"We'll have one ready within the hour. The longer we wait, the greater the risk her blood pressure will climb." Dr. Patterson stood.

Charlotte got up and left the boardroom. Her heart was pounding and it felt like it was going to burst out of her chest.

*You can do this. I know you can.*

She could, and she would for Mentlana. She paused at the door to Mentlana's room and saw she was alone, staring at the wall. The room was still dark, but Genen and Lorna were no longer there.

When Charlotte entered the room, Mentlana looked at

her, her face drawn and all the apprehension her friend had been trying to hide finally bubbling to the surface.

"Hey, Charley." Mentlana's voice wavered. "What's the verdict?"

"Where's Genen?" Charlotte asked, sitting on the edge of the bed.

"I sent him to get breakfast. Someone had to eat something around here."

Charlotte nodded. "You'll be able to eat soon."

Mentlana inhaled, her hand shaking in Charlotte's. "Tell me."

"Do you want to wait for Genen?"

"No. Tell me."

"The lesion has grown quite a bit since the last sonogram. The baby is at risk of developing heart failure and you are at risk of developing pre-eclampsia, which is fatal."

Two big fat tears rolled down Mentlana's cheeks. "Oh, God."

"We're going to do a fetal resection of the CCAM."

"What does that mean?"

"We're going to do something similar to a C-section but not deliver the baby. We'll partially delivery him, repair the lesion and place him back in your womb."

"Why don't you deliver him?"

"The idea is to try and keep him in there for as long as possible, until he's full term and we deliver him via C-section."

Mentlana's face paled. "That's the best course?"

Charlotte nodded. "Yes."

"Will the baby feel pain?"

"No." Charlotte squeezed Mentlana's hand. "This is the best course of action. Trust me."

"I do. You'll be there, right?"

"Yes. I will." Charlotte stood. "I know this is a lot to

take in. Two C-sections are not ideal close together, but your baby has a better chance of survival this way."

Mentlana sighed and closed her eyes. "I'll face whatever I have to, to have my child."

"I know. I admire you for that."

Mentlana opened her eyes. "You will, too, when the time comes."

Charlotte nodded. She was beginning to believe it, but Mentlana was still something amazing and special to her. "I know physicians aren't supposed to say this to their patients, but I love you."

Mentlana grinned. "I love you, too. I'm glad you're here."

Charlotte hugged her, tears flowing. "Oh, dammit, stupid pregnancy hormones."

Mentlana laughed and brushed away her own tears. "I like seeing this side of you, Charley."

"What side?"

"The non-obstinate one."

Charlotte just shook her head. "I'll find Genen for you."

"Thanks, Charley."

Charlotte nodded and left the room. She didn't care who saw her tears, even Dr. Richards. She was done hiding her emotions.

She was done being obstinate.

# CHAPTER SEVENTEEN

CHARLOTTE WATCHED QUINN scrubbing up. They were alone for the first time since she'd decided to tell him she was pregnant. She prayed she was doing the right thing, telling him before the surgery, but she couldn't keep it in any longer. She had to tell him.

"How are you feeling?" she asked, cautiously.

"Nervous, but I'm confident."

"The only fear is fear itself." She was quoting something her father had always said to her when she'd been hesitant to try new things as a child.

"Easy for you to say." He gave her a half smile, teasing her.

"I'm afraid of other things, but I'm willing to face the thing that terrifies me the most."

"What?"

"I'm afraid of carrying another child, Quinn." Tears stung her eyes. "I'd never thought of becoming a mother again, but I watched Mentlana and her trials and tribulations to have one. She was brave, but for me the idea hurt too much. I'm still terrified, but I'll face the fear of losing it again because it's what I want."

Quinn's eyes widened, and he paused in scrubbing. "You're pregnant?"

Charlotte nodded and her knees began to knock. "I'm

not telling you this to force something from you. I can do this on my own. I want this. I just... You have the right to know."

Quinn remained frozen. "I don't know what to say."

"There's nothing to say, Quinn. You don't have to be a part of it."

"Thank you for letting me know. It's a lot to process."

"I know you're not thrilled—"

"Who says I'm not?" Quinn interrupted.

Charlotte sighed. "You weren't exactly over the moon last time. You were relieved when I lost it."

Quinn shook his head. "No, not at all. I was just as hurt as you were. I was trying to ease your pain my stupid foot-in-mouth way by hiding it. I thought by telling you about a great medical opportunity you would follow me, but I thought you were blaming me for the loss of our baby and that you hated me."

Charlotte felt the blood drain from her face. "I...I don't know what to say."

"Charlotte, you want to know my fear?"

"Of course."

"I was afraid of being a father. I didn't have the best role model to base any experience on. I was afraid of screwing up our child's life."

"Excuse me, Dr. Devlyn?" A nurse from the O.R. appeared. "We're ready for you to go over the instruments with the scrub nurse."

Quinn nodded. "Thank you."

The nurse disappeared and Quinn shook the water off his hands. "We'll talk about this later, Charlotte."

Charlotte nodded. "Of course."

He disappeared into the O.R. and she felt like she was going to faint. She felt relieved and over-the-moon happy.

He'd mourned the loss of their first child just as keenly as she had.

Yes, she'd carry this child, no matter what the outcome. She wanted this baby.

Badly.

Quinn stood by the surgical table in the operating room. He was scrubbed in and ready to go. Mentlana hadn't been brought in yet, but he knew they were prepping her.

It'd been a long time since he'd been in this position. He stared at the surgical tools on the tray in front of him. Tools he was all too familiar with. He knew every nuance of them, how they functioned and at what step in the procedure he would need them, but still replayed it over and over again in his mind.

It was a way to calm and reassure himself he was capable of doing the surgery.

*Steady. Just count.*

He focused on the instruments—the scalpel, the sutures, the small, delicate tools he'd need to operate on such a fragile being. He flexed his fingers in the glove. There was no pain, just a bit of numbness.

*Steady.*

He took a deep breath. The room was chilly and the antiseptic smell calmed him. The nurses were shuffling around the room, doing their own counting as they set up the instruments, and that was reassuring.

*Everything is going to be okay. I can do this.*

Quinn closed his eyes and replayed in his mind the last fetal resection he'd done. The one he'd done before his accident. The baby was a healthy, thriving toddler now. Just like Mentlana's would be in a year's time.

When he thought of babies, though, his mind went to the one Charlotte was carrying. He smiled, though no one could see it behind the surgical mask. What if Charlotte was going to be on this table and it was their child's life in another surgeon's hands or his own? How would he deal with it? He had to be at the top of his game. He wouldn't let Genen down.

This baby was going to survive. His hand wasn't going to spasm.

*I will succeed.*

"Are you all right, Dr. Devlyn?" the scrub nurse asked cautiously, as she began to lay out the instruments in order.

"I am, thank you…"

"Bernice."

"Bernice. Good. I do like to know the name of my scrub nurse. Have you attended a surgery like this before?"

The nurse nodded. "At SickKids in Toronto."

Quinn's eyes widened. "This isn't where you work?"

Bernice shook her head. "No. I'm from Toronto and came as a favor to Dr. James. She said you needed a scrub nurse who'd assisted surgeons in this procedure before."

Quinn exhaled, relief oozing out of his very pores as the tension in his shoulders dissipated and he loosened up. Charlotte had done this for him? Any lingering concern he had vanished in that moment. With a good scrub nurse he'd be able to focus on the task at hand and not worry about instructing some other nurse on what he needed and when. Bernice would instinctively know what to hand him at each stage.

"I could kiss Dr. James right about now. I'd kiss you, too."

"You can't tamper with the sterilized field, Dr. Devlyn." Bernice chuckled, her eyes twinkling above her surgical mask. "I really don't fancy scrubbing in again, but I do appreciate your enthusiasm for my presence." Bernice moved off to continue her preparations.

*I can do this.*

The doors to the operating room slid open and Dr. Patterson entered the room. The nurses slipped on his gloves and Quinn nodded in greeting to the obstetrician.

Ready to do this again.

"It's time." Charlotte stepped aside as the orderlies wheeled the gurney in the room. Genen looked nauseous and worried. It broke Charlotte's heart, but she couldn't let her emotions take hold of her right now. At least her own nausea had subsided, thanks to some Diclectin that Dr. Patterson had given her a few hours ago when she'd approached him about morning sickness. Each pregnancy was *supposed* to be different, but again she was being plagued with horrible morning sickness. You'd think the odds would be in her favor.

Of course, she didn't want to think about the odds right now. If she did she'd only dwell on the statistics, which weren't in Mentlana's favor right now. Charlotte took a deep breath, trying to take Lorna's advice to heart. She was trying not to worry about a bad outcome, and to think on a good one. Though it was hard to break a habit of a lifetime when you kept getting dealt a rotten hand most of the time, and had to work for every little thing.

Mentlana and her baby would survive.

She had to believe it. For the first time in her life she had to believe in more than medical science. She had to put her trust and her hope in faith.

Mentlana and Genen kissed, which tugged at her heart-strings. The orderlies lifted Mentlana onto the gurney while her nurses began to hang the IV bags and catheter.

"Genen, you can walk us down the hall," Charlotte offered. "But because she's going under general anaesthesia, you can't come into the theater."

"I want to be with her," Genen protested.

"I know you do, but you can't. When we deliver the baby at the end of her pregnancy, you can. She'll have a spinal then and be wide awake. Trust me. It's for the best you wait out here, Genen."

Genen nodded and held tightly to Mentlana's hand as the orderlies wheeled the gurney out of the room. Charlotte followed beside them as they whisked Mentlana off to the operating suites. They stopped at the double doors and Charlotte moved away, pulling Genen to the side as Mentlana disappeared.

"You can't go any farther, Genen. I'm sorry."

Genen was visibly shaking, his dark eyes moist with tears. "Please, take care of her, Doc."

"Of course I will…I promise." Although she never promised any patient, the words just slipped past her lips and she prayed that she'd be able to honor that promise.

Genen nodded and Charlotte went through the double doors into the surgical suites. Her stomach twisted in a knot as she tied back her hair and scrubbed her hands. Through the window she could see Mentlana was already laid out on the table, the lights dimmed save for the bright surgical light.

Mentlana's face was pale as she stared at the ceiling, terrified. Charlotte glanced at Quinn, who appeared calm as he chatted to the scrub nurse from SickKids.

Bernice was an old friend and a bit of a present from Dr. Harriet Preston, who'd suggested Charlotte call Quinn when she'd first discovered the lesions on Mentlana's fetus.

*"You know who the best in that field is, Charley. I don't have to tell you."*

She hadn't wanted to call Quinn, but Harriet had been right. He *was* the best and now she was so glad she'd screwed up her courage and called him.

Once she'd finished scrubbing, she entered the O.R. and was gloved. She headed over to Mentlana's side.

"It's going to be okay, Lana."

"Charley?" There was relief in her voice. "Is Genen okay?"

"He's fine."

"Good." Dr. Patterson began to wash Mentlana's swollen abdomen with Betadine. "Ugh, what's he doing down there, painting a fence or something?"

Dr. Patterson chuckled. "I'm quite adept at fence-painting, too, Mrs. Tikivik, though don't tell my wife."

"I like you, Dr. Patterson." Mentlana grinned, but her lips quivered. "I'm scared, Charley, so scared."

"It'll be okay, Lana. I promise."

"What if...?" Mentlana trailed off and then shook her head.

"No what-ifs. It'll be okay. Trust me."

Mentlana nodded. "I do. I trust you with every fiber of my being and I trust Dr. Devlyn because you do. You do trust him, don't you, Charley?"

"I do. He's the best."

Mentlana sighed. "I'm ready."

"Are you ready, Dr. Devlyn, Dr. Patterson?" the anesthesiologist asked.

"Yes," Quinn replied, his voice steady and calm, which reassured Charlotte. "Ready when you are, Dr. Horne."

Dr. Horne stepped forward. "We're going to put you under now, Mrs. Tikivik." A nurse placed an oxygen mask over Mentlana's face while Dr. Horne injected something into her IV line. "Just breathe deeply, Mrs. Tikivik. Good. Now start to count back from one hundred, please."

Charlotte left Mentlana's side as she counted, each number sounding more and more slurred. She stood beside Quinn.

"How are you feeling?" Quinn whispered.

"Fine. Dr. Patterson gave me something for nausea, but I'm ready to assist. How are you?"

"Excellent. This will be a success, Charlotte."

"Do you promise?"

"I never promise."

Charlotte bit her lip. "I know you can't."

He leaned over and whispered, "Off the record, I do. I promise."

"The patient is sedated," Dr. Horne said.

"All right, ladies and gentleman, let's proceed." Dr. Patterson stepped forward to perform the incision. "Ten blade."

Charlotte watched in wonder and amazement as Dr. Patterson skillfully operated on Mentlana, exposing her uterus and cutting into it. It'd been a long time since she'd assisted in surgery and she'd forgotten what a thrill it was, but she wouldn't trade this thrill for the high she got by dealing with her patients every day.

Often she wondered if she'd done the right thing by turning down a residency as a surgeon and entering general practice, but standing here and knowing every aspect of Mentlana's medical history, whereas these specialized surgeons only knew snippets, made Charlotte realize she'd made the right choice. Charlotte knew everything about her patients. She knew and understood the whole picture, and for that she was thankful.

"We're ready now, Dr. Devlyn." Dr. Patterson stepped back.

Charlotte looked at Quinn and nodded. *You can do this, Quinn.* She hoped she conveyed everything she wanted to say to him in a single look as he moved into position and began the fetal resection.

She stood by his side, waiting to see if she'd be needed,

but he didn't ask her for help. His hands were fluid and gentle as he carefully lifted the baby out of Mentlana's abdomen and began the surgery to remove the lesion.

"Amazing," Dr. Richards whispered behind Charlotte. She glanced over her shoulder to see the pediatric specialist watching Quinn with total hero-worship.

Charlotte grinned in admiration at the man she loved, handling the baby so gently. The procedure flew by. He'd been so terrified that he'd need her, that he'd hurt or kill the baby, but he'd had nothing to worry about. All Charlotte did was hold the retractor and Bernice handed him the instruments he required.

"Damn," Quinn cursed.

The blood drained out of Charlotte's face as he paused, the baby resting in his hand.

"Dr. Devlyn?" Bernice questioned.

Quinn shot Charlotte a look.

"Cramp?" she asked.

"Yes." There was tension in his voice.

"Are you okay, Dr. Devlyn?" Patterson asked.

"Perfectly. My stamina is the worse for wear, but if Dr. James assists me, I should be fine. I'm almost finished."

Charlotte nodded. "Dr. Richards, please hold the retractor for me."

Dr. Richards stepped forward and she slipped her hand over Charlotte's, taking the retractor without moving it and applying the same pressure Charlotte had been using.

Charlotte gently gripped Quinn's hand. The muscles were taut, and she began to palpate the palm, easing the muscles.

"You can do it," she said under her breath, encouraging him.

Quinn nodded and finished the resection. Charlotte stared down at the almost-full-term baby. Though he had ten weeks to go, he was beautiful, with the start of a full crop of thick black hair and some baby fat was beginning to flesh out his limbs. The baby's body was still covered in protective lanugo. Tears stung her eyes as she looked into that tiny, precious face. Mentlana and Genen's whole world, being held in Quinn's healing hands.

*Live.*

"There," Quinn announced, relief and joy in his voice. "Help me place the fetus back in the womb, Dr. James."

"Of course." She cupped her hands underneath Quinn's and they gently placed the baby back in his mother's uterus.

"Amazing," Dr. Richards whispered again in awe.

"It is." Quinn's gaze locked with Charlotte's just for a brief moment. As they placed the baby back in utero the baby's arm shot out of the incision and latched onto Quinn's finger, squeezing it.

A sob caught in Charlotte's throat as she watched the baby in amazement. The tiny infant was reaching out for human contact and comfort.

"Will you...?" Quinn's voice shook. "Help me, Charlotte."

She brushed the little hand off Quinn's finger, despite its firm grip, and set it back in place.

"She's all yours, Dr. Patterson," Quinn said, stepping back.

"Thank you, Dr. Devlyn. Okay, let's get Mrs. Tikivik closed. Zero Vicryl, please, Bernice."

Quinn walked away from Mentlana towards the scrub room. His job was done. Charlotte didn't follow but remained by Mentlana's side. She was confident Dr. Patterson and Dr. Richards would be able to handle the rest of the surgery expertly, but she'd promised her friend that she wouldn't leave.

Charlotte glanced over towards the scrub room. She

wanted to follow Quinn, wanted to hold him in her arms
and thank him for saving her friend's life, but that would
come later. She moved around to Mentlana's head. The
anesthesiologist was monitoring the machines and Charlotte pulled over a rolling stool and sat by her friend. Ignoring the tube that helped Mentlana breathe and her taped
eyes, she stroked her friend's hair, hoping Mentlana could
sense her presence.

"Everything's all right, Lana," she whispered. "The
baby is fine."

*And I'll be fine, too.*

# CHAPTER EIGHTEEN

QUINN KNEW CHARLOTTE couldn't follow him out. He knew she'd be faithful and remain by Mentlana's side, but right now he could use her. He needed to see her friendly face and share in the joy that was surging through him.

*I did it.*

His hands shook as he leaned against the cold tiled wall of the scrub room. He peeled the rubber gloves from his hands, disposed of them and then removed the surgical gown and stuffed it into the laundry bin, followed by his scrub cap.

His knees were wobbly as he pressed his foot against the bar, allowing the water in the scrub sink to rush over his skin without having to touch anything. Quinn glanced down at his hands, his broken one and the scars that crisscrossed his skin, scars he'd been ashamed of. They no longer bothered him.

They represented a point in his life he'd rather forget and wished had never happened. The memory of the accident that had almost cost him his life would remain with him, but the crash would no longer haunt him. Anything life could throw at him was not insurmountable, not with Charlotte by his side.

In that moment when the baby had reached out and

curled his hand around his finger, squeezing him to let him know he was there and alive, had been a miracle.

Never in his years as a fetal surgeon had he ever experienced such a moment, such an affirmation of life.

A life he'd saved.

He'd survived the accident that had damaged his hand, when so many hadn't. He was lucky he had been given a second chance, at surgery and at a future with Charlotte.

Quinn scrubbed his hands. He'd been terrified at the prospect of this moment, but had kept it to himself.

Now there was one more life he had to save.

His own.

There was no way he was going to allow Charlotte to walk out of his life again because they couldn't agree to practice medicine in the same place. Quinn was not going to make the same mistake twice.

He was lucky she hadn't moved on, that she was still single and wanted him. He wasn't going to tempt fate. This time the odds were in his favor. The fates were smiling on him and he was going to make everything right.

Quinn left the O.R. suites. First he'd find Genen and update him on his wife and child and then he was going to make some changes.

It was time to stop being so selfish.

It was time to live.

"Where am I?"

Charlotte straightened and leaned over Mentlana's bed in the recovery room. She took her friend's hand and rubbed it gently. Mentlana was still groggy. They'd woken her in the O.R. after the surgery was complete, but she hadn't been quite awake after several general nudges.

Charlotte remained by her bedside in Recovery, wanting to tell Mentlana herself that her son would be fine.

"Where am I?" Mentlana asked again.

"Recovery."

"Charley?"

"I'm here." Charlotte smiled as Mentlana's eyes fluttered open.

"Thank you for staying with me." Mentlana's eyes closed again.

"Don't fall asleep again. You need to stay awake." Charlotte stood and gestured to one of the nurses. "They're going to check on you, okay?"

"Don't go, Charley. Please."

"I promise I won't."

Charlotte stepped back so the recovery-room nurses could check Mentlana's vitals, the baby's vitals and the incision, but she stayed where Mentlana could see her. The effects of the anesthesia were wearing off. Charlotte watched as Mentlana came out of her haze of medication.

"I'll be back again in ten minutes, Dr. James," the nurse said as she drew the curtain around Mentlana. Charlotte sat back down.

"How's the pain?" she asked, rubbing Mentlana's leg.

She winced, her face pale. "Not pleasant, but the nurse shot some morphine into my butt."

Charlotte grinned. "You should be feeling good in a few minutes."

Mentlana nodded. "So tell me. I'm ready to hear whatever you have to say, good or bad."

"All good," Charlotte whispered, barely containing her glee.

Mentlana perked up, more alert. "What?"

"Dr. Devlyn corrected the baby's CCAM. If we can keep him inside you for a bit longer and get him closer to term, everything should be okay."

Tears began to roll down Mentlana's face, and her shoulders shook as she reached out and grasped Charlotte's arm. "It hurts to cry."

Charlotte tried to swallow the lump in her throat but couldn't, and soon she was weeping in joy along with her friend.

"Thank you," Mentlana said, wiping away the tears with the back of her hand.

"You're welcome."

"You thank Quinn, too." Mentlana closed her eyes, tears still streaming. "I don't even know how to begin to thank him."

"You'll find a way." Charlotte's voice was still wobbly and she cleared her throat to regain her composure. "Why don't you make him a great big honking plate of muktuk?"

Mentlana grinned. "Perhaps I should, but I think he'd rather receive my thanks through you. He didn't come up here because he's a humanitarian, Charley. If you were just any old physician he wouldn't have come. He would've found another one or I would've had to fly to Toronto and break the bank to do it. The reason he came up here, at his own expense, was you."

Warmth crept up Charlotte's neck. Mentlana spoke the truth. Quinn loved her and she loved him. "Still, I think he has a certain fondness for you, Mentlana."

"Good. Or I'd have to kick him in that soft spot I spoke of before." Mentlana winked. "Don't let him get away, Charley. Don't let him walk away from you and that precious bundle you carry. Even if it means you have to leave us in Cape Recluse and head to the bright lights of the city."

"I won't." Charlotte stood. "I know I'll have to leave here to live in Toronto. I'll miss you."

"And I you, but you can always visit. You do know how to fly."

Charlotte laughed and stroked Mentlana's face affectionately. "The nurses are going to give me heck for getting you all emotionally riled up."

A devilish grin spread across Mentlana's face. "I'll tell them where to go. You helped save my baby. You and Dr. Devlyn have given me everything I've ever wanted."

Charlotte kissed her forehead. "Rest. I'll see you later."

"Tell him, Charley. Tell him and don't let him go."

Charlotte nodded and left the recovery room. Her heart was singing with joy as she walked down the corridor of the hospital with a spring in her step.

*Tell him, Charley. Tell him and don't let him go.* Mentlana's words were weighing on her. Her friend had never been so right. For five years she'd waited and mourned the loss of their baby and the loss of Quinn.

Now he was back in her life and she was pregnant again. She'd do anything to keep Quinn in her life, even if it meant leaving the North and moving to the city, be it Toronto, Manhattan or Abu Dhabi. Charlotte didn't care. She just wanted Quinn.

She had to be flexible and not so stubborn.

Charlotte's hand drifted down over her abdomen and she thought about the little life just starting out in her womb. She meant to go and find Quinn, tell him how she felt and how she was willing to go anywhere, risk everything to be with him.

This was for the best. Her baby needed a father. She'd finally have the family she'd always dreamed of since she'd lost her parents.

She also needed Quinn. Charlotte was aware of that now. She couldn't live without him.

Her phone buzzed and she pulled it out. Quinn had texted her, asking her to meet him in the on-call room on the fourth floor.

A heavy weight had been lifted from her shoulders and

right now she was going to make everything right. She wasn't going to let Quinn Devlyn get away. She was going to show him exactly what he meant to her and she hoped he'd feel the same.

The on-call door was open and she slipped inside the room. When she entered, Quinn was seated on a cot, his elbows resting on his knees as he stared at a small box in his hands. He looked down at it, seeming sad and puzzled. What did he have to be sad about? He should be rejoicing. Two lives had been saved. A miracle had been performed, thanks to him. Charlotte crossed the room and sat down next to him, placing her hand on his knee.

"Quinn, are you all right?"

He gazed at her and smiled. "Of course."

Charlotte let out a sigh of relief. "I thought you were upset."

He shook his head. "Fine. I'm fine. How's Mentlana?"

"Sore, but very grateful." Charlotte kissed his cheek. "You did it. You kept your promise to me."

"My hands cramped, but I did it. With your help."

"They're healed. I hope this outcome gives you more confidence."

"It gives me a bit." He grinned.

"It should give you more than a bit, Quinn. You're a surgeon, a surgical god again. Unfortunately, our outcomes are not always what we want or expect, but if we don't try…if we don't try to save a life, that's the real crime."

Quinn leaned over and kissed her, a tender kiss that brought tears to her eyes. He stroked her face. "I'm ready to come back from my sabbatical."

Charlotte's heart skipped a beat, her stomach churned. He was going to return to surgery, but *where* was the big question. Wherever it was, she'd follow him. She was ready, as much as she hated living in the city.

"What's wrong?" he asked, confused. "Look, I know you don't want to live in the city…"

"No. I'm certain of what I want, too."

"Certain of what?"

"That I can leave here to follow you." She ran her fingers along his jaw, the stubble tickling her fingertips. "I'll go wherever you need to. Wherever you want to."

"You don't have to leave. You belong up here. This is your home."

"Quinn, you're my life now. Wherever you are, I'm home. I won't lose you."

"You won't. I was made an offer by this hospital to be the head of the neonatal unit. They want a state-of-the-art facility here and I'm the surgeon they want to lead that project. I accepted, Charlotte."

Charlotte was floored. Her mouth dropped open. She knew she must look like a gaping fish by the way Quinn started to laugh. "You…you what?"

"I'm head of the up-and-coming new neonatal unit. Honestly, Charlotte, how hard can that be to understand?" He was teasing her.

"What about your chief of surgery position in Toronto? The one your father groomed you for?"

He shrugged his shoulders. "My life is with you and your life is here. You wouldn't be happy in Toronto, in close proximity to my mother."

"I thought you hated the North. The cold? The ice?"

"I did, but that was the old me. I'll grow used to the cold, and there are other aspects I love, but the most important draw is you, Charlotte. Besides, there are always vacations." Quinn stood and pulled her into his arms. "I love you, Charlotte. If it wasn't for you, I wouldn't be so damn happy again."

"And I love you."

"I do have one condition, though, and it does involve a city."

Charlotte cocked an eyebrow. "Oh?"

"You need to find another physician for Cape Recluse. I need my wife in Iqaluit with me."

"Deal." Charlotte kissed him, lightly brushing her lips against his.

Charlotte knew there was no way she was going to be able to hold back her tears. She was getting everything she wanted. Cape Recluse wasn't too far away that she couldn't keep an eye on it from Iqaluit—she could easily open a practice in the city. All she wanted was Quinn. She wouldn't be obstinate. He was sacrificing big money and the metropolitan way of life for her.

"If it wasn't for you, Dr. Devlyn, I wouldn't have a chance at motherhood again. I love you."

Quinn stepped back and held out the box. "I know I couldn't afford one before, being in med school and all."

Charlotte took the box and opened it. The sparkle of a diamond took her breath away. "Oh, my God."

"It's a diamond from a mine up here. I was assured of that. I wanted you to have a stone that came from the land you love."

"Quinn, it's beautiful."

He took her hand and slipped the ring on her finger. "Marry me, right away. Tomorrow even. We've waited long enough and I can't wait even a second longer. I don't want to waste any more time."

Charlotte wrapped her arms around him. "Yes, I'll marry you as soon as possible. I've waited a long time for this moment."

Quinn grinned and slipped his hand into her hair, dragging her into another toe-curling kiss.

"Shall we go visit Mentlana and Genen and bask in their happiness?" he asked breathlessly a few moments later.

"I'd like that."

They kissed one more time and walked out of the on-call suite hand in hand, with the future ahead of them.

There was no place in their world for obstinate people. Charlotte knew beyond a shadow of a doubt she'd always fight for Quinn, their family and the love they'd been given again.

Always.

\* \* \* \* \*

# *A sneaky peek at next month...*

## CAPTIVATING MEDICAL DRAMA—WITH HEART

### *My wish list for next month's titles...*

In stores from 4th October 2013:

❏ Gold Coast Angels: A Doctor's Redemption – Marion Lennox & Gold Coast Angels: Two Tiny Heartbeats – Fiona McArthur

❏ Christmas Magic in Heatherdale – Abigail Gordon

& The Motherhood Mix-Up – Jennifer Taylor

❏ The Secret Between Them – Lucy Clark

& Craving Her Rough Diamond Doc – Amalie Berlin

Available at WHSmith, Tesco, Asda, Eason, Amazon and Apple

### *Just can't wait?*

# *Wrap up warm this winter with Sarah Morgan…*

## *Sleigh Bells in the Snow*

Kayla Green loves business and hates Christmas.

So when Jackson O'Neil invites her to Snow Crystal Resort to discuss their business proposal… the last thing she's expecting is to stay for Christmas dinner. As the snowflakes continue to fall, will the woman who doesn't believe in the magic of Christmas finally fall under its spell…?

**4th October**

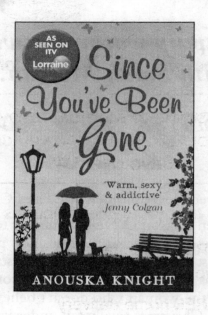

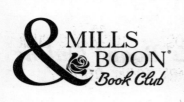